LEO FLOWER

Also by Norman Isaacson, Ph.D.

Hablando En Publico (Public Speaking) A Dual Language Text
Oracle Press, Baton Rouge, LA.70808

Library of Congress Catalog Number 82-06-2534
ISBN Number 0-88127-011-3

NORMAN ISAACSON

iUniverse, Inc.
New York   Bloomington

Leo Flower

iUniverse books may be ordered through booksellers or by contacting:

iUniverse
1663 Liberty Drive
Bloomington, IN 47403
www.iuniverse.com
1-800-Authors (1-800-288-4677)

Because of the dynamic nature of the Internet, any Web addresses or links contained in this book may have changed since publication and may no longer be valid. The views expressed in this work are solely those of the author and do not necessarily reflect the views of the publisher, and the publisher hereby disclaims any responsibility for them.

ISBN: 978-1-4502-4568-5 (sc)
ISBN: 978-1-4502-4567-8 (dj)
ISBN: 978-1-4502-4566-1 (ebook)

Library of Congress Control Number: 2010932916

Printed in the United States of America

iUniverse rev. date: 08/3/2010

For SuHaRu

It is an illusion to think that comfort means happiness.
Happiness comes of the capacity to feel deeply.
To enjoy simply, to think freely,
To be needed.

Storm Jameson
1891-1986

CHAPTER 1

AS LEO FLOWER WALKED west on Fourteenth, he tried to keep the definition in mind. At one time, whatever he wanted to remember would just be there, available. Now, at 60, he was forgetting things. Was it old age? He wondered. Was it Alzheimer's? Whatever it was—it was. Lately, he had been doing a linguistic shuffle. Like a stutterer fleeing a potentially disruptive word to a friendlier one, he had been doing the same thing by filling voids with bullshit when he forgot what he was talking about.

Details about cases, names, and locations seemed to melt away when his mind sought them. But of all the anguish the muddling caused, the most painful was the all too frequent inability to name a vocalist after hearing a few bars. Voice qualities, chord patterns, even instruments—those facilities were also drifting away. Was it all the same package?

Last week in the Riviera Bar, Ella was on the jukebox and it had taken him time to figure out who was singing. That's when it hit him. He was losing his ears. Not instantly recognizing Ella was like falling over a table but thinking you tripped on a cow. It was unbelievable, but it was happening. Hell, it had happened! Now he had to remember he forgot things.

That brought back a dumb memory. Miss Parvey, the seventh grade English teacher, pointing a bony finger and saying prissily, "Do not forget, Leo Flower, you have been forgetting things. You must remember you are forgetting."

He smiled as he walked, but it was no joke. Earlier in the day, Sullivan had asked about one of the cases waiting for a check with the FBI's AFIS files. He didn't know what he was talking about.

"You mean the Hotel Westover's intrusion?"

Sullivan had stared at him. "No, Leo, that one's in. I mean the one we sent out Monday- the Libyan thing." He had forgotten about that. Two days!

Maybe the Department's policy is not dumb or mean spirited. Retirement is possible at 55. But how could I do that, he asked himself. I have nothing else.

He cut left on Fifth, right on Thirteenth and it was a different world. The traffic noise almost vanished. One block and you can hear yourself think. Walking slowly, he retraced his thoughts, recalling he wanted to keep a definition straight in his mind. He frowned when he realized he couldn't remember what definition he wanted to retain.

Standing in the middle of the sidewalk, he reviewed his biography. Here you are, 60, never married, no women friends, no close men friends, no pets, no family—alone! Well, almost alone. Ilene and Father John are almost my family. Thank God for them and the Department. What would I do without them? I haven't traveled to any place I would want to see again. I'm an inside person and an apartment is an apartment. As long as the central air and the heat work, I could live in Milwaukee, Alaska or New York. What the hell difference would it make? What difference does it make?

He started to walk again and crossed Sixth Avenue passing the bar on the corner. The last time he was low, he had stopped in there and got a super surprise. He never knew the place was strictly for the lesbian trade and as soon as he got to the bar, a "lady" in leather who was bigger than he was growled at him.

"Hey Bruno, I think you're in the wrong place."

Leo looked at her, then looked at the others sitting at the bar and at the various tables—he was the only guy. Looking her straight in the eye, he said, "Yes Ma'am, I guess I am." and walked out.

He stopped once again, but this time to stare at his reflection in the bar's plate glass window. He looked okay—six two, trim and muscular, dark hair, sleek in a suit and attractive enough for the ladies.

He resumed walking, heading for his building at the end of the block. It had 23 floors and was almost new. Well built, soundproof. The only other building on the block about the same height was the Salvation Army's Single Women's Residence. The Department had an arrangement with the Army to keep extra patrols on the block. The result was a safe street. It wouldn't be good Department PR to have the young ladies from Iowa and Utah raped and murdered with any regularity—at least not where they slept.

Most of the block was two and three story townhouses as was most of the West Village. Years ago they were cheap, but no more. The one next to his building just went for a million two. From his window he watched workmen build a patio in the rear garden. It was a great idea as long as the lazies in his building didn't toss stuff from their windows and create an evening rain of beer bottles and butts.

He saw Roberto through the lobby's glass doors just as Roberto saw him and opened the front door with a flourish.

"Good evening, Lieutenant Flower...the day's work is done?"

"It's finished until they call."

"And they always do. I wish my agent would call me as often." He said wistfully.

"Still trying for the acting bit?"

"Absolutely, and if things turn out for me, I will be the next Latino actor most closely associated with New York City."

"Let me know if you're going to be in something. I'd love to see you act in a different costume."

Roberto grinned broadly. "I'm glad someone has finally realized this doorman's job is just another role. However...1 am a little sad my acting was not good enough to have you believe this job was my real and only love."

"I thought about that, but you have too much on the ball for this."

"Lieutenant Flower, that is a compliment I will not forget."

Leo smiled, saluted, and walked through the small lobby to the elevators. The local car was waiting and as usual, it took eight seconds to get to the third floor. His apartment, just to the left of the elevator, was his haven, his private place. It was all he had.

He recalled the nutty phone conversation he had with the rental agent before he moved in. It still made him laugh.

"Sir, the apartment is an executive suite."

"A what?"

"An executive suite."

"Great. How many rooms is that?"

"Well...you can call it a junior three."

"What is a junior three?"

"Well sir, it is not quite three rooms, but it has more space than a one room apartment."

"Does that mean a junior three has two rooms or three rooms and what about the executive suite...weren't we talking about the executive suite?"

"Well, sir, a junior three does not have three rooms, but it is larger than a typical two room apartment which is essentially the executive suite."

"So a junior three has two rooms, right?"

"Well, sir, not exactly."

"Miss, this is turning into Abbot and Costello...if the apartment doesn't have three rooms and it doesn't have two rooms, then it must be only one room, right?"

"Oh no, sir, it is much more than a one room apartment."

"Now wait a minute."

"Sir, forgive me, but may I ask if you are from New York City?"

"Yes, I am, but what does that have to do with anything?"

"Well, sir, I often speak with out-of-towners who do not know New York buildings."

"Okay...now you know I'm a native... so what?"

"Well, sir, now I can tell you an executive suite is one big room with a bend at either end."

The next day he signed a three-year lease and after endless renewals, never needed more than the apartment offered. He liked its size, no matter what it was called. You could see every part of it from any other part and that compelled him to keep it orderly. Attending to details had enabled him to progress in the Department. He was neat and extremely competent no matter the chore.

For the past three years, he had worked in the Scientific Research Division as head of the Ballistics unit. Now, a new Commissioner was reorganizing the Department and Leo had been reassigned. In a short time, he would be working in the Inspection Services Bureau's Intelligence Division as part of the Public Security Section's Dignitary Protection Unit. His transfer was the work of Deputy Chief Reynolds, who had always liked him, and said he would really enjoy working in Dignitary Protection or 'Dig Pro' as it was known

Ballistics was an area involved with specifics. There were bullets or weapons to analyze or a case report to complete. Every job had a conclusion even if some were dead ends. Now things would be different. Now he would have to start thinking the way others thought. To protect public officials and visiting dignitaries, it was essential to understand the mind-set of those who wanted to do them harm. The new job, he realized, was not after-the-fact like Ballistics. Now, crimes had to be stopped beforehand. A smoothly functioning unit could eliminate disorder before it bloomed. With total success, there never would be a crime.

He could still hear Chief Reynolds. "Leo, your new assignment does not come with a dust pan and a broom. You can't be sweepin' up the folks you're supposed to protect. The Department doesn't shine if we send the Ambassador from Gitchee-Goomee home in a coffee can. You're a smart man, Leo... this will be an opportunity to use your brains. You ran Ballistics with real efficiency so we know you're a competent administrator. Now, you can use some of your other talents for the Department."

Well," Leo had said, "we'll see about that."

He hung his jacket in the hall closet and started the nightly ritual—stereo on, bath water running, coffee pot on, phone call to Ilene and John. Since he called them every night, he had the timing down pat. He would finish his conversation and turn off the bath. There was never much to say since the three of them led relatively unchanging lives...almost the same from day to day... the tub had never overflowed. As he waited for the connection, he wondered if this was it... the daily ritual that would go on forever.

Every so often he would get in a mood and pity himself for allowing his life to become what it had. What had brought it on this time? Young couples walking hand-in-hand in the street was the usual igniter. They found each other, he would think, why couldn't I find someone? Am I such an emotional cripple? Leo wasn't good enough at introspection to know the reasons, but he did recognize the miserable mood coming on...a drifting and floating in thick sadness. He dreaded the next few hours.

The busy signal was a surprise. Ilene knew he called at this time every night and she was always eager to speak to him. It must be my suspicious nature, he thought, and went to bathe.

Twenty minutes later he called a second time. The line was still busy. That was unusual. He called the operator, identified himself by badge number and asked for a supervisor's line check. Within two minutes he was told the line was open, but no one was speaking. Alarm bells rang.

Both of them were so old, he thought. They could easily have a problem. Possibilities flashed through his mind... Maybe John had a heart attack or Ilene fainted, fell and hit her head or broke a hip. He dressed and headed uptown.

CHAPTER 2

MUCH EARLIER THAT SAME morning, Angel Martinez squatted behind filthy garbage cans staring at the entrances to the brownstones across the street. Like a malevolent sniper, he waited for someone to come out into the gray, early morning cold. The sour stink of the cans was making him sick, but it was a good place to hide. Almost invisible in his filthy little fortress, he waited to rob anyone exiting one of the buildings.

He knew it wasn't smart to walk the West Side streets at that time of the morning so he figured a push-in would work. Though he knew the police were cold weather lazy, they would not be blind to him. Angel was a New York street kid—small, gaunt, and unmistakably Hispanic. Even sluggish cops would instantly figure him an intruder in an old-line Irish neighborhood like West 48th Street.

Aside from needing money to live, Angel wanted a new knife. He ruined the one he carried by trying to carve his initials on the handle. Since he could not read or write, his friend Carlos wrote 'A' and 'M' on paper for Angel to copy, but when Angel tried to scratch those shapes onto the handle, he messed it up and now he wanted a new knife. The one he craved was in a Jewelry store on 43rd and would cost one forty. The owner said he would engrave his name on the blade, so Carlos wrote 'Angel Martinez' on another piece of paper. Carlos told Angel he was dumb to put his name on the knife since he couldn't read and also, the store-man could write 'fuck you' on the blade and Angel would never know.

Staring at the entrances, he remembered his answer when Carlos asked, "Why don't you get a gun? Why are you still carryin' that pig sticker in your boot?" He told Carlos that he once had a gun and used it for a while, but didn't know where to get bullets or even what kind to get, so he dumped the piece on a guy in a bar for fifty bucks.

Angel preferred a knife because it was quiet and scared old people more than a gun. He understood a gun to be abstract when compared to the immediate and primitive threat established by a large knife. A gun could be empty or a bullet could miss, a knife was messy, but it always worked.

Alerted to movement like a wolf spotting a rabbit, he tensed when a white haired woman came out of a building, scurried down the steps to the sidewalk and turned right at the corner onto Ninth Avenue. She wore a heavy looking black coat and clutched her purse in front of her with both hands. That's where the money is, he thought. If she had it in a pocket, she'd have a hand in there to keep it company.

He had quick choices to make. If he let her get as far as a store, she might spend what she had. If she was going to eat, she might do that and then continue to a job, He wondered if she could be going to a job right now, He hoped she would buy food and then go back to make breakfast. It was a choice between running over and grabbing the purse now or waiting.

He decided to wait and follow her and he smiled when she walked into the Ninth Avenue bakery in the middle of the block. He waited at the corner and when she came out and headed back, he turned and ran to the building from which she had come.

Running up the steps, he opened the unlocked outer door and looked around. It was typical—stairs to the right and two apartments to the left. If she came from the downstairs back, it would be simple. He would hide under the stirs, wait for her to pass, grab her and shove her to the door. If she had come from upstairs, it would be complicated. Waiting under the steps, he watched the outer door. A few minutes later, she entered the building looking behind her. She was worried about people on the street who might follow her into the building. She had no idea of the surprise under the stairs.

Moving quickly, she headed for the back apartment and he grabbed her when she passed. Placing a hand over her mouth, he held the knife high. She froze when she saw it and he became aware of how thin she was. Slowly, he moved the knife to her throat and gently poked her. Then with one hand over her mouth and the other holding the knife to her neck, he pushed her to the apartment door.

In a macabre ballet, the two of them, locked together, shuffled and lurched forward. Whispering in her ear, he told her he was going to remove his hand and that if she made any noise, he would kill her. The trembling woman nodded, When he released her, she placed the bakery bag on the floor, took a key from a pocket and opened the door. He turned the knob, grabbed the bag and pushed her inside.

They were in a small foyer about four feet square with doorways leading to other rooms. Glancing quickly, he made out a kitchen, a bathroom, a sitting room and two closed doors. Staring at each other, neither spoke until the woman noticed the gold cross Angel wore. She told him her brother was a priest and good Christians shouldn't steal. Mystified, Angel looked at her and then following her eyes to the cross, laughed.

"Lady, I took this cross from a fuckin' guy 'cause that's all he had. Now gimmee the money or I'm gonna cut you."

"You don't have to do this. You can work." She protested. "You can get a job. My brother can help. He's a priest at St. Ignatius and knows everybody in the neighborhood. He's asleep right in there." She motioned to one of the closed doors.

Angel thought for a moment. "Lady, I been in that church and I seen them guys getting' money from people. They get plenty from everybody. Gimmee that money. I want that money."

"That money is for the church, not for my brother. It doesn't belong to him."

"Lady, don't bullshit me. You get that fuckin' money or I'm gonna stick you."

He moved closer and pressed the blade's tip to her throat. She gasped, opened her purse and pulled out a crumpled wad of bills, which she pushed at him. He grabbed the bills with his free hand. "Where's the rest? Get the rest of the money."

"My brother is sleeping in there." She said, pointing to the closed door. "Let me wake him. He'll tell you the money is the church's... it's not his."

"Hey," He said, drawing out the word. "You think I'm stupid? Get me the money!" Angry now, he pressed the knife into her meager flesh until a bubble of blood popped from her pale skin. She moaned as the door to the bedroom opened. Framed in the doorway was an old man. Angel figured him to be the brother the lady was talking about... the priest.

Seeing what was happening, the old man raised his arm and quickly moved towards Angel. Reacting automatically, Angel slashed at the extended arm, and then plunged the knife into the man's chest. As the man groaned and fell backwards, Angel pulled back on the knife.

The amount of force he needed to free the blade once again surprised him. It had happened before. Street talk said that the dead person's soul became part of the knife that had killed them. Why else would it be so hard to pull a knife out of someone? Maybe, he thought, maybe he had used this knife too often. Maybe there were too many souls attached to it. That was another reason to get a new knife.

The priest's sister, seeing her brother stabbed, thrust herself to him hoping to cradle his body as it slumped downwards. Angel, aware of nothing but another shape moving towards him, slashed out. The large blade caught the woman on the side of her neck and effortlessly sliced through skin and flesh. Silently, she collapsed on top of her brother.

Slightly bewildered, Angel stared at the bodies. He felt no remorse, for his actions were like those of a trained fighter——come at him and he will react. Minutes later, as his heart slowed, he became aware of gurgling sounds from the bodies and of the blood covering his hands, arms and feet. A recollection of a TV program he had seen at Carlos' flashed through his mind. It showed lions eating a water buffalo they had killed. Their faces, covered with blood, did not match their usual tan color. Angel liked that bloody look and felt he looked that way now——dirty and covered with the blood of those he killed.

Immediately, he began seeking his prizes. The woman's purse was turned inside out. The priest's pockets were searched. The bedrooms were next. Every drawer, every closet was thoroughly examined. Nothing escaped his practiced eye. What ever could be turned into a dollar was put into a small suitcase he found under a bed. A half hour later he had nothing more than three gold crosses on chains, some ten-dollar bills, and a book.

He had taken the book because he had never seen one like it. It had a zipper that went around three sides, a gold cross on thick leather covers and white pages filled with handwriting. He guessed it was the priest's. Wishing he could write in such a book, he struggled to imagine the important things that could be put into it. Cursing his illiteracy, he slammed the suitcase shut and went into the kitchen.

Seeing there were sufficient things to eat, he went to the bathroom, slipped out of his clothes and showered. Afterwards, he ate a breakfast of eggs and still warm bakery rolls. When he had eaten all he could, he stepped over the bodies in the foyer and suitcase in hand, slipped out of the apartment into the morning's gray, dismal cold. He went first to the jewelry store on 43rd to give additional money toward the new knife and then to Carlos' to show him the gold and the book.

CHAPTER 3

RACING FROM THE BUILDING to the corner of 7th Avenue, Leo scanned the traffic—saw no empty cabs so he crossed 7th and went to 8th. At 14th he got a cab and in nine minutes was at Ilene's and John on 48th. As he doubled-timed up the outside steps, he wondered if he was overreacting. A few strides later he was inside the building at their door. He rang the bell. There was no response and no sounds from inside. He called out. "Ilene- John- it's me, Leo. Open the door."

Silence. His eyes followed his hand as he turned the knob. The door was locked. Maybe they went out. A movie. Maybe a visit to some parishioners. But he could not dismiss the telephone. It was off the hook. He took out his key ring, found theirs, unlocked the door and slowly pushed it open.

"John. Ilene. Are you here?" The same silence.

He stepped in, found the light switch and flipped it on. Another step and he would have fallen over their bodies. Jumping when he saw them, his mind sought alternatives. First, he thought it was a pile of clothes or a blanket. He closed his eyes and refused to look.

Backing out, he stood in front of the door and listened to himself breathe. Moments went by. Minutes passed. He was frozen, unable to move. He couldn't go back inside. Then suddenly, he heard the metallic noise of a doorknob to his left. The door to the front apartment was opening and someone was coming out. Instantly, Leo crouched and pulled the automatic from his belt holster.

"Don't move." he said. The man in the doorway froze. Leo straightened as the man turned to face him.

"Leo, what the fuck? It's me, Vince. Put the goddamned gun down." It took Leo a moment to realize who he was looking at—who was talking to him. Vince? Vince—he lived in that apartment. It was John's neighbor. Leo lowered the gun.

"Vince. Something happened. Call 911 now."

"Sure, Leo, sure." Vince jumped back inside and Leo heard him make the call through the still open door. He hung up and came out to the hallway. "Stay inside, Vince." Leo said.

Without a word, the door was closed and Leo was alone in the hallway. Time passed and then the street door opened and two uniforms stepped in. Leo recognized them and they recognized him—it was Charley Davis and Joe Sullivan.

"Leo. What's goin' on? Did you call?" Charley asked.

Leo motioned to the door behind him. "Something's wrong in there."

The two cops looked at each other and then Joe asked if Leo had been inside. Leo said he looked in but went no further. Charley brushed past and pushed open the door. Leo saw him look down and then he saw his jaw muscles tense.

"Oh, shit, Charley," Leo cried out. "They're dead. I can tell from your face. They're both dead, aren't they?"

Saying nothing, Davis knelt out of sight behind the door. A minute later he came back into view, looked at Leo and slowly nodded. Reeling like he took a punch, Leo lurched to the wall behind him and after a moment, slid down to a sitting position. Then he looked up at Joe Sullivan and started to cry. "They're all I have, Joe. They're all I have." he muttered between sobs.

"What's that, Leo? Joe asked.

"They're my family. I'm lost without them. I'm alone again without them..."

Joe started to say something but stopped when his partner came out. "Call it in, Joe. Tell 'em we got the works here—two victims and a ransacked place. We need the CSU and we need their best people. The perp cleaned up." Without a word, Sullivan went out to the car.

"What the fuck, Charley?" Leo asked, standing up. "What do you mean 'cleaned up'?"

"Can't tell for sure, but it looks like the fucker took a shower."

"A shower... the bastard took a shower?" As he spoke, Leo hunched to the apartment door and was about to enter when Charley said, "Wait a minute, Leo, wait...you don't want to see them like that."

"I gotta see 'em, Charley. I want this in my memory so when I find the fuck who did this I can remember what he did."

Davis grabbed Leo by the shoulder and slowed him down enough to hand him a pair of latex gloves he took from his pocket. "Better put these on. It's second nature for you to be in there and you might touch something. Put the gloves on, Leo."

Leo looked at him and realized the sadness in the man. Charley had been in this precinct for years and always did what he could for Ilene and John. He had known them for a long time. Leo realized his pain was not private when he saw deep grief in the other man's face. Does having company make it better? Easier? He reached out for the gloves.

Putting them on took some of his anger away, since it's impossible to do quickly. As he struggled with the second one, Charley said, "Leo, this is really hard right now, but you've got to stay in control. You'll be good for nothing if you lose it."

Calmer, Leo adjusted the gloves and went into the apartment. He knelt beside the bodies and noticed an incredible amount of congealed blood—more than he had ever seen. Not being able to look at them any longer, he walked from room to room, checking everything, touching nothing. Torn between his feelings and training, he tried to tell himself it wasn't Ilene's and John's apartment, but a crime scene and he had to treat it as such. Shuffling through the darkened rooms, he realized it was better they were both dead. What if one had survived?

Every drawer was out and emptied. Clothes were everywhere. He recognized shirts, pajamas, things he had given as Christmas presents. He recollected walking through other crime scenes when he was a rookie and realized the apartments always looked the same. It was the same mess repeated a thousand times. An endless search for what... What could the stupid perp expect to find in a place like this... the crown jewels?

It may look the same, he thought, but this time I know the people, Ilene Murphy and Father John Murphy... the couple that pulled him out of that Catholic orphanage when he was a kid. They had been his parents. Now a cretin, a lunatic who thought there'd be money here, murdered them. What a laugh. A run-down place a step away from being a slum. What dumb-shit would think there was money here? What trash could do this? He began to sob.

His last visit flooded into his mind. He saw himself in the outside hall ringing the bell and then hearing her footsteps coming to the door. She was coming from the linoleumed kitchen—four steps to the front door then one hand on the knob, the other at the peephole.

"Who's there?"

"It's me, Leo."

"Leo, how wonderful." The heavy metal door swung open quickly and silently. He hugged her as she said, "It's good of you to come. He's been asking for you. He's always asking for you."

"Ilene, you and John are special and I'm always available. Call and I'll be right over."

"Go on with you, Leo. Don't try to charm me with that big city blarney."

He was endlessly amused at her attempts to play the Irish lass. True, she had been born in Ireland, but had come to America as a baby. The only green and open country she'd ever seen was in the Catskills. All her time had been on Manhattan's West Side, but she liked to perpetuate her image as an Irish country girl—a typical maiden devoted to the Church.

He remembered smiling and confirming her 'act' and then recalled his scolding. "Ilene," he had asked sternly, "was that door open? I don't remember hearing you undo the locks."

"Oh, Leo, don't be mad at me if I forget to lock the door. You know I like the idea of a door open to the world."

"Look, dear, in this city you can't have an unlocked door. What good are the locks I put on if you don't use them?"

She looked at him and then at the heavy brass hardware. "Oh, Leo, I'm sorry... but don't think we don't appreciate them. I know they were expensive."

"Ilene, they aren't worth a penny if you don't use them. You must lock that door and never open it unless you know who's outside."

Twisting her body coquettishly and smiling up at him, she said, "You're right, Leo. You're absolutely right and I promise. I really do." She closed the door and reached out for his jacket. He looked at her. Puzzled, she stared back and then put her hand to her mouth to suppress a giggle. "Okay, okay." she said, as she reached behind him to turn the knob of the big deadbolt.

"That's better," he said, taking off his jacket and handing it to her.

"Come," she said. "He's in the sitting room. You go in. I'll make tea."

He walked the few steps past the kitchen to the living room—the 'sitting room' to Ilene. John was in his favorite chair making notes in a book. Hearing Leo's footsteps, he looked up and then down at the book. He tried to smile, but his face wasn't smiling, only his mouth. He looked grave, serious. Quickly closing the book, he very deliberately pulled the zipper closed around the sides and then stuffed it into the space between his thigh and the arm of the chair.

"Leo, my boy. How good to see you." He started to raise himself, but Leo rushed the few feet.

"You know what the Doc said—keep the weight off that knee or it will never heal."

"I know... I know, but I always forget."

"What's in the book? You writing your memoirs?"

"Church business, Leo. Serious stuff. The Cardinal himself has me workin' for him."

"What kind of business?"

"Nothin' for you to get concerned about, my boy." Leo recognized that unmistakable note of finality in his voice. The subject was closed. So many conversations had ended with that flat, finished tone. When John decided a conversation was over... it was.

"You take care of that knee and we'll have a game of handball."

"Leo, I think I could beat you from a wheel chair. You're a strong player, but not quite devious enough to beat me... gimpy leg or not." Leo laughed.

"Don't fret my boy. Some of us are born to greatness and some are just born."

As both men laughed, Ilene brought the tea. Setting the tray on a small table, she poured as they watched. This was her life, serving her brother and Leo. Marrying had been a possibility many years ago, but it hadn't worked out. John always needed her. The Church had always needed her. She was a nun without habit, self-ordained and totally devoted. She once told Leo she would have married if God had wanted her to marry. He wondered how could he or anyone question a belief like that. She was solid, loyal and fully accepted the Church and her unofficial role.

Like any mother would be, Leo knew she was proud of him. He was the child she never had. She was the mother he knew. She had been to all his graduations, to all his Departmental promotions. She had shown the same concern and love a real mother could show, and like a real mother, she was sad he never married. She would have treated his children as if they were real grandchildren. If Leo had married, both their lives would have taken on another dimension. But that would not be. At his age, Leo could marry, but children were not in the cards.

Ilene knew Leo would soon retire and maybe move out of the City. She secretly hoped he would and buy a small house upstate where they could all live out their years in quiet and peace. That was her dream.

"You know, Leo, I've been thinking about your retirement... have you?"

"Yes, I have Ilene, but that's all. I don't even know if I want to retire. I don't know what else I want to do. I don't know what else I could do."

"Leo." John said. "You're not an old man. You're only sixty. That's more than middle age for sure, but you're not an old man. Look at me. I'm almost seventy-five and I can still take care of myself."

"John, I really like my work... it's been my entire life. If I retired I'd be like a bird that could no longer fly."

"Oh, don't be silly. You'd find something else in no time."

They sipped the tea silently. Leo looked at the floor, his attention caught by the daylight reflecting from the linoleum. "Leo," John asked, "Are you sad about how your life turned out?"

"Oh no, John, not at all. If anything, quite the opposite. You two are my family. I like my work and it has given me more than most. I would be an idiot to complain about anything."

"Are you still going out with that nice lady we met at the ball game?"

"No, Ilene. She was ready for ocean liner trips around the world. She wasn't ready for a guy like me. I don't think I'm considered a hot item."

"Exactly what, if I may ask... is a hot item?"

"Well, John, a hot item is about my height and weight, in fact, physically, I think I'm pretty much okay, but when the ladies get around to listing what they want to do and where they want to go... well, I turn out to be not quite what they want."

"Why not?"

"John, you know how I am. I don't have to go here or there. I don't like to travel much. I hate sightseeing. If anything... I like to go. I don't like to get there."

"You just need someone to go with. You've been alone too long."

"Maybe... maybe you're right."

After a short silence, John leaned over to Leo and asked, "Leo, you know Jim Mulrooney?"

"The guy from 23rd street?"

"Right."

"Why do you ask?"

"No idea?"

"Oh, I see." Then after a moment, Leo added, "No. It may seem like a good idea, but I don't want to do that."

Ilene thought she hadn't heard a conversation like that since Mantan Moreland and Willie Best did it in the old *Charley Chan* movies. "Will you two please tell me what that was all about!" she demanded.

The men looked at each other, then at Ilene and laughed.

"Ilene," said John. "I'm sorry for laughing, but your expression was priceless."

"Priceless was it! You two sounded like an old movie. You remember how Mantan Moreland and that other fellah would get into those conversations where each knew what the other was going to say and cut him off before he said it?"

"Leo, Ilene must mean those movies with..."

"Sidney Toller, when he played..."

"*Charley Chan,* but not when the part was played by..."

"Warner Oland." finished Leo.

"I suppose you think you're Martin & Lewis. It's too bad Ed Sullivan is dead..." she crossed herself while muttering, "God rest his soul"... you two could be on that show."

"Ilene... don't get upset."

"Oh, John, don't be silly. I'm not upset. I just want to know what you were talking about."

"I was just reminding Leo that Jim Mulrooney owns a sporting goods store and sells a lot of guns. Leo understood me to be saying that when he retires, he could take his years of expertise to that store and put it to good use."

Leo smiled. "I thought about something like that, but I don't think a retail operation makes sense. If I'm going to retire I don't want to work more... Mulrooney is open six days... that's more than I work now."

He paused, sipped some tea and stared though the window into the darkening sky. "John, you have to understand my position. I want to keep my technical involvement. I enjoy my work. The problem is there are no jobs like mine in the civilian world."

"Well, Leo that's true and then again, it's not." Leo stared at him. "Look, you started out in the lab with actual guns and actual bullets, but now, being in charge, you're more an executive, an administrator than a bench worker."

"You're right about that. All I do is schedule, write reports, get others to write reports and make sure all the work that comes in gets back out. I am forever locked in my office... You know something... I don't think I can remember the last time I fired a gun in the lab."

"Leo, you're far more a manager than a policeman and I do think there'd be plenty of work for a skilled administrator with a police background."

"You know, when I hear you say that, I realize I think about myself in old terms. I see me as I used to be. I bet I could find something with a security outfit."

"Now you're talking. Just you start looking around. I bet something will pop up."

"There's no rush, John. Everyone I know who's retired has had a rough time."

"Leo... the cops are like the Church... you're in for life. I never think of retiring. The Church is not a job you leave."

Ilene broke into the conversation by reminding them it was close to dinner and that she intended to broil the gigantic steak Leo brought the other day.

"Is it mashed or baked?" she asked.

"Which ever is easier for you, my dear." said John.

"Makes no difference to me," said Leo.

Nodding, she left them and went to start the dinner.

When the Crime Scene Unit arrived a short time later, they found him in the kitchen. He was crying while holding the frying pan Angel had used to make the eggs.

CHAPTER 4

AFTER ANGEL PAID THE additional money for his knife, he walked to 50th to see if Carlos was home. He wasn't there. The other place Angel knew to look was at Marty's store on 8th between 46th and 47th. If Carlos wasn't home, he was at Marty's.

As Angel walked down 8th Avenue, he showed no concern for the bloodstains on his clothes, for he knew people didn't really see him. But if he was noticed, it was easy to see they hoped he'd disappear. That bothered him a lot, but what annoyed him most was their look of fear mixed with disgust. People he didn't know; people who didn't know him, looked at him like he was trash. Like he would dirty them if he talked to them or touched them. He hated them for that. People didn't have to look at him like that.

Marty's store windows mimicked the look of a pawnshop, but his place wasn't a pawnshop. What he sold was bought from people off the street and at pawn auctions. Actually, Marty's was a licensed second-hand store even though more than half of the merchandise he sold was new. Going into Marty's with something decent to sell usually meant you came out with a few bucks. But since all sales were final, once you handed it over, you were out of the picture.

Angel loved Marty's windows and could stare at the merchandise for hours. There were hundreds of things. Watches, tools, guitars, trumpets, rings, cameras- everything you could ever want. Angel brought everything he stole to Marty who gave him a meager percentage of the item's worth. It angered Angel when he got only a few dollars for a watch, which he'd later see in the window going for two or three hundred, but there was nothing he could do. Marty was the only guy willing to buy what Angel had to sell.

He walked in and watched Carlos wrap up a sale for an electric guitar.

Carlos could play a little and was good at selling the instruments. After taking the money for the guitar, Carlos saw Angel.

"Angel, my man. How you doin'?"

"I'm cool. I got some stuff."

"Great. Take it in back, Marty's there."

Angel shuffled into the merchandise filled back room past showcases filled with kitchen knives, harmonicas, video cameras, and handcuffs. Marty was seated at a desk staring at an intricate looking balance scale. "Hey, Marty, how ya doin'?" Angel called out.

Marty's head and hand moved simultaneously. His hand went for the gun in his belt, but when he saw who it was, he smiled and relaxed. "Angel, my man, good to see you, good to see you." As he spoke, he looked at the small valise Angel carried and knew there was something worth his time inside. Angel had never come in with a package that didn't hold good merchandise. Marty could smell the profit.

"What's in the case, man?"

"Some stuff, man. You want to see?"

"Of course I do. Waddaya think?"

Angel knelt and opened the case keeping the cover between him and Marty. He closed the case and held out the gold crosses and meager jewels he had taken from the Murphy's.

"Gold." said Marty. "Gold is cool. I love the stuff, man. Come over closer."

Angel walked to the desk and Marty pointed to the balance scale. "You see this scale, man? This scale is what I use to weigh out the gold I get." He pointed to a plastic tube on the desk. "You see that there? Pick that up."

Angel reached out for the tube and hefted it. It was very small, but very heavy. "Wow, man, what's in this. It's really a load."

"That's gold, man. Gold dust."

"Where do you get gold dust, man?"

Marty leaned back in his chair. "Look, you know people got plenty gold in their teeth, right? Well, the dentist's get that gold stuff made in dental laboratories and I get all the sweepings. I melt down what I get and wind up with pure gold. There's always a market for that." Marty loved to boast about his dealings. He liked to brag and knew Angel was just smart enough to understand what he was telling him, but not smart enough to be a threat.

Angel put down the tube of gold dust and handed Marty the crosses and neck chains. He hefted the handful and then placed it on the scale. "This is good stuff, man… heavy and big. It's worth money."

"How much money?" Angel asked

"I'll give you a hundred and a half for it all."

Angel smiled. That would be enough for the new knife and some other stuff. "Cool. Give me the money." Marty took a roll of bills from his pocket and gave Angel three fifties. "Thanks man." Angel said, as he turned to go.

"Hey man, wait a minute. What else you got in the case? Anything else for me?"

"No man, just some clothes and other shit I took. There's nothing you can sell." Angel backed away and then walked to the front of the store where he saw Carlos putting a guitar in the spot of the one he sold.

When the store was empty, Carlos asked Angel what was in the case and Angel told him about the book. Carlos wanted to see it, but both knew Marty's was not the place for a look at anything that might be worth money.

"Angel," Carlos said, "go to my place, change and come back. I'll be free at one when Armando comes in. We can get something to eat."

"That's cool, man. Gimmee your key. First, I'm gonna go get my new knife, then I'll go to your place change clothes and come back." Carlos gave him his keys and Angel left.

On the street Angel disappeared into the crowds. He went first to the jewelers, got the knife with his name on the blade, then bought a new pair of jeans. When he met Carlos outside Marty's he had the new knife in his right boot and was wearing the new jeans. The book was in a paper bag.

They went to Hector's on Broadway to eat. After they ordered, Carlos took a look at the book and Angel could see he was immediately interested. He, too, had never seen one like it. The pages had dividers between them creating about twenty separate sections. Each section had a name of a church. There was St. Patrick's, St. Thomas Aquinas, St. Theresa, and others. The St. Patrick's section had names and comments after each name.

Carlos thumbed through the pages. "Where'd you get this?"

"I got it this morning."

"But where?"

"I got it at this apartment where I knocked off two people. The lady said her brother was a priest. I guess the book was his 'cause it got a cross on the cover there."

Carlos stared at the book. "Man, I don't know what all the shit in here means, but I'm gonna figure it out and we're gonna make some money out of it. You'll see."

"Why do you think anybody'd pay money for a fuckin' book? What's it say?"

"My guess is that it's a list of churches in Manhattan and a list of priests at those churches."

"Who the fuck cares about a list of churches?"

"But wait, my man, don't be so quick to jump. Look here..." He spread the book open, but when Angel stared at him instead of the book, he remembered Angel couldn't read. Picking it up, he read from a page. "Right here it says Father Lionel and Father Dimitri were seen goin' into a movie, holdin' hands and then jerkin' each other off. And here it says that Father Hector spent the night with Father Amos at the rectory."

"I can't read that shit, man, but if I could, I still don't see why anybody'd pay for that news. So what if one priest saw other priests jerkin' each other off on the movies... so what?"

"Don't you understand, man, if you and me see priests screwin' around in the movies, we don't give a shit. But if the people who don't like the idea of priests doin' each other sees that stuff or hears about it, they get pissed off. They don't want their priests fuckin' around. They want them priests to be like perfect people. This book says they ain't so perfect."

Angel stared at Carlos as he spoke. He was impressed that Carlos was able to get so much from reading pages in the book. "Do you really think we can make money with this book?"

"I bet there are some newspaper guys or other priests who would pay a lot to get this book to disappear. The problem is we can't go around advertisin' we got it since you snuffed the guy who probably owned it."

"Do you want to tell Marty? Do you want to cut him in?"

"I don't know. I trust him and I don't trust him. Why don't we wait a while and see what's in the newspapers about what you did. Maybe we can get some info about the priest and what he was doin'."

"That sounds okay to me." Angel said, as he bit into his tuna fish sandwich.

CHAPTER 5

TWO DAYS AFTER ANGEL and Carlos had tuna for lunch, Seymour and Ida Aptin plodded the vinyl tiled aisles of the Key Market on 9th and 43rd. Seymour Aptin hated to shop, but he hated it most when he was in that particular store.

"Ida, this place is a pain in the ass. What do we buy here; a can of soup, some frozen stuff, bread, some fruit? Why don't we go to the Italian on 47th?"

"Seymour, don't you be a pain in the ass. The Italian charges a fortune for the same stuff. Why would you want to go there?"

He glanced to the front of the store. "I don't like the spics looking at us through the window. They watch what we buy and they watch how much change we get. If they see enough money, they'll follow us home to rob and kill us. The Italian guy got crap all over his windows... you can't see inside."

She followed his eyes to the front. The store windows were floor to ceiling and the entire street beyond was visible. Three of them were sprawled on the front of a car. Three young men. She would never call them 'spics' and she did not think them murderers or thieves. She knew he had never had any trouble with the Colored or the Spanish, but he insisted on calling them names and being wary of them. He was becoming more and more afraid as he got older.

Turning to him, she said, "Seymour, I don't think those boys outside are going to rob us or kill us or do anything to us. Let's just shop and go home. We can watch the afternoon movie on Channel 9."

He grunted and they continued walking the aisles. Watching her shop had always given him pleasure—with her it was serious business. With him— shopping was a pain and even eating was becoming less important. As long as he got his vitamins and minerals, he didn't care what he ate. She, however, dealt with their meager diet as if he was training for the Olympics with her cooking being the difference between a loss and heaps of gold medals.

"What do you want for dinner?" she asked.

"I don't care. Maybe some dairy."

"You shouldn't eat eggs, you know that."

"I'll have some yogurt and some fruit. I like that yogurt." He said, starting towards the dairy section. "Wait!" she ordered, stopping him in his tracks. "What kind of dinner is that? Yogurt is for breakfast or lunch."

"Do you think my stomach has a clock in it? I like yogurt. After that, I'll have some coffee and cake... that'll be enough."

"That will not be enough. You're a big man and you need more food than that."

"Did you forget my vitamins? You know I take "C" and the "B's", and the "E" pills increase my strength as well as my sex drive."

Smirking, she said, "I'm glad you told me. How else would I know?"

Nodding and smiling back, he said, "Cute, very cute."

"So... what do you want for dinner?" she asked, once again.

He realized his first answer overlooked the obvious. Like a good lawyer, Ida knew the answer to every question she asked. "Let me ask..." he said. "What would you like to make for dinner?" A small smile played at the corners of her mouth as she looked up at him and said, "I think I'd like to make a chicken."

With decisive finality, he said, "Chicken will be fine. I would love some chicken." She nodded and he smiled, happy he had put the right amount of sincerity into his reply.

Now, on a mission, Ida led the way to the poultry section where she set about the task of selecting the right chicken. Watching her sort through the packages, he thought they had been too long in this neighborhood. He recalled going to a butcher shop where you pointed to what you wanted and watched the guy weigh it and wrap it in brown paper. Nothing was in plastic. Now, everything was in plastic. Everything now was noise, bad manners, pushing and shoving. Now, nobody gave a shit.

Dropping a yellow chicken wrapped in yellow plastic into the cart, she said, "Come."

This was the worst part of it for him since paying exposed them to the loiterers outside. He thought of writing a check, but remembered he didn't have his checkbook.

"Twelve twenty-four." said the bored teenager. He took out a twenty and as she put the change in his hand, he watched them outside. They were watching everything. They were watching the way a falcon watches a pigeon. It was like being naked.

He hoisted the plastic bags off the counter and followed his wife outside. The three boys seemed preoccupied as they passed. Maybe eight dollars was not worth their time, nevertheless, he watched for them over his shoulder and their reflections in store windows they passed.

Ida strolled as if it was Easter Sunday and he was Fred Astaire. To her, getting out of their apartment was the equivalent of a Paris promenade and she always dressed for the occasion. Today, it was a short fur jacket and jewelry. He argued against the jewelry because he felt the neighborhood unsafe, but to her it was Manhattan. It was New York City. It wasn't Iowa or Nebraska. It was New York City and she was a native New Yorker.

Their brownstone on 44th was neat and clean as was their ground floor apartment and tiny backyard. She loved the yard since it permitted spring and summer entertaining. He didn't like it because he had to continually paint, trim, clean and lately, pick up the cigarette butts, and the cans and bottles thrown into the yard by the side neighbors. That morning he had to clean up the regular crap plus something new- bottles thrown over the fence from the backyard facing theirs. It was all becoming a shithole.

As they walked, the traffic loaded streets, he thought of the many times he had carried groceries home and then decided it was a waste of time to think about it, since it was more important to check if they were being followed. He wanted to move and to convince her to leave the City. It had to be done. She was not as nervous as he, but he knew she was afraid. It was impossible not to be afraid. The police were no help. Black and Spanish kids ran wild in the streets doing whatever they pleased. It made no difference there were decent Black and Spanish people, they weren't the problem. He thought of the people with whom he had worked in the Garment Center. Fifty years with the Blacks and the Puerto Ricans. The old ones were okay, but the young ones in the streets, they did what they pleased.

He figured it was time for them to join the 'white flight' and get out. Go someplace where it was safe to walk. As he saw it, the courts hindered the police and the politicians afraid to act because they might lose their soft jobs, screwed up everything. He thought them all corrupt and incompetent.

Without incident, they got to their building and to their apartment. Inside, he double locked the door and breathed a long audible sigh. "You know, I feel like we passed through enemy lines and all we did was go to the store."

"Seymour...stop being so negative. You make me feel guilty for just wanting to go shopping. Nothing has happened to us and nothing will." As they were emptying the bags, he stopped, reached out and took her hand, "Ida," he said, with real seriousness, "let's make plans to get out of here. I can't take it anymore. I'm nervous all the time. This isn't the way people should live. Especially since we don't have to live this way. We can afford to get out. I got my pension and I can always make some extra like I am now, doing that work for the priest."

She knew he was right- they would have to leave. It had been clear for longer than she would admit. At her age, she was not afraid of a sexual attack, though it was not unheard of, but she could not accept the idea of a man wanting sex with a woman almost seventy years old. She was more afraid of being attacked for the few dollars that might be in her purse. The crazies would never know she didn't carry money. But what did that matter? They would grab her bag if they thought there was money in it.

"I think you're right." She said. "We probably should move, but where?" Silently, he was overjoyed, but answered with sincere seriousness. "I don't have an answer to that, but as long as we're agreed, we'll find a place. Your sister in North Carolina is always telling us how wonderful it is. Let's visit and see. Okay?"

"Okay." she said, and started to nod, but froze when there was a knock on the door.

"Who is it?" he yelled. There was no answer. He moved to the door and looked through the peephole. He turned to her and shrugged... nothing. As he was about to say something, there was another knock. It was low, down by the bottom of the door. He looked through the peephole again, standing on his toes trying to look downwards. He turned back to her.

"I don't see anything... nobody's there."

"Pay no attention, it's probably those nasty upstairs kids playing a little game." A moment later there was another knock. "Go away." he yelled. "This is not a fun house. Go away and don't bother us."

There was silence, then a faint voice from outside. "I'm hurt. I need help... please."

He looked through the peephole again. Nothing. "Help me. Please help me." The soft voice pleaded. After a moment, his wife went to the door and put the chain in place. Then backing away, she said, "Open it a little, you'll be able to see better."

"I don't know about this... I don't trust this." He said.

"Seymour, what if someone is hurt? We have to help them if they're hurt."

"But what if it's some smart ass kids who just want to rob us?"

"Please," she insisted. "Open it an inch. See what's there."

He unlocked the first of the deadbolts and waited. Nothing. He unlocked the second and was turning the knob to open the door when it burst inward pushing him back. As he stumbled, he saw pieces of wood from the splintered doorjamb fly across the room along with the screws that had held the chain in place.

Three kids came rushing in. "Ida!" he yelled. "The police. Call the police." He ran at them and tried to push them out through the open door, but one of them swung at him with something and his head exploded. Slowly flowing to the floor, he saw the kid had a piece of lead pipe. He was surprised he wasn't unconscious. There was blood on the rug next to him and when he looked up, he saw two of them grappling with his wife. They were trying to pull off her rings. She was screaming and hitting at them. They laughed and pulled at her fingers. There was a sound like a baseball hitting a bat. He had been hit again. Everything disappeared.

As the room slowly came into focus he wondered how long he was out or how badly he was hurt. Books and papers covered the floor around him. The bastards had been into everything. The book closest to him had a gold cross on its leather cover. It was the book the priest had given him. No wonder the little shits threw it down. They couldn't read his code. They probably couldn't even read English. His head hurt and it was wet. He was bleeding. Slowly, his eyes focused and he saw his wife across the room on the floor. She was staring at him.

"Ida," he called out, "Ida, are you okay?" She was motionless. He struggled to move closer. He had no idea how long it took him to crawl to her, but throughout his struggling, she never moved.

With great effort he pushed up from the floor and touched her face. Her skin was cold and stiff. He cried out, "Ida, my Ida. They killed you—the bastards killed you." He stared, hoping for her to move, waiting for her to take a breath and then smile as she did every morning when he opened his eyes from sleep. But there was nothing, no smile, nothing, just blank empty eyes.

He started to cry and in the middle of a wrenching sob, grabbed at his chest.

CHAPTER 6

LEO KNEW MEMORIES NEVER fade...his early days should be as available as yesterday, but he couldn't remember the last time he'd been in St. Ignatius. It probably had looked better. Now he could see it was shabby and worn and everything in it was ready for repair or replacement. John always said the Mother Church would tend to St. Ignatius and match its physical presence to the spiritual glow he said he saw. Leo never said so, but he had doubts, for he knew the Church was not about to spend hundreds of thousands of dollars repairing a church few saw and even fewer attended.

The congregation was small as was the building. It was truly a neighborhood church—a side street building with side street worshippers. Nevertheless, John had ceaselessly sought to bring to his parishioners the joy the church brought to him. Throughout the years, he had never stopped trying to increase Leo's participation and involvement, but Leo had kept his distance. He had once been too much a part of it, but now lacked the willing surrender the faithful possessed. The skepticism that grew in the Army and flourished in the cops was layered on top of the doubts that began in the orphanage. The orphanage was the key. There was no way to bypass the years of deprivation, the unfulfilled longing, the unhappy days and weeks.

As was natural for a kid, he had blamed everything on those immediately available, those who ordered his life. He never outgrew the anger directed at the nuns and priests, though he rationally understood they were guilty of nothing more than trying to help. As he grew wiser, the anger dissipated, but he couldn't shake the feeling that somehow they had cheated him, had abused him and robbed him of what he was promised.

His confusion had crowded his love for John in a way that forced him to seek a separation between John the man and John the Priest. Growing older had made everything easier, for when the furious passion of youth melted away, Leo was able to recognize John's innocence. Now, as he sat on the pew's thin cushion, he wondered if its inability to ease the pressure from the hard wood beneath was deliberate. It seemed wise to prevent the mourners from getting so comfortable they might miss the point of the mass. As he wondered about it, he looked at the prayer card he had pocketed at Ilene's funeral. Reading it, he hoped the message would be borne out and she would be granted eternal life in the village of her dreams. "...O merciful Savior," it said, "send thy angels to conduct Thy departed servant to a place of refreshment, light and peace." She was truly that, he thought, a 'departed servant' and so was John. Both of them connected to a world they saw in their day and night dreams. He was not that lucky. His day and night dreams didn't resemble what he believed John's and Ilene's to be. He did not dream of an eternally peaceful life or of being a captive soul in Purgatory. He dreamt of parents he never knew, of a family he never saw, of a partnership that would tear away the tethers of loneliness. Most of all, he dreamt of finding someone who would become part of his life. He dreamt of not being alone.

Sitting in St. Ignatius for John's funeral was difficult for he found himself feeling more sorrow for himself. Am I so self-absorbed, he wondered, that I'm unable to feel for them, unable to understand my debt, unable to understand that they're really gone... that they will never again see a sunrise or anything else... that I will never again see them and they will never again see me? As his mind churned, he grew so disgusted with himself; he let his thoughts turn to imaginings of their killer's capture. Though attractive, those thoughts were no haven for he recognized their absolute and complete futility. There was as much chance of finding that monster, as there would be of concrete evidence of an afterlife. So either in defeat or punishment, his thoughts turned to his own death and he tried to understand what it would be like. Was it merely going to sleep, like he did every night, but that one time, you don't waken? Was that it? Going to sleep? He liked the idea of sleep and he vowed to hang onto it. John and Ilene were sleeping. They had gone away and were sleeping somewhere. Like the billions who had once been alive... who were now also sleeping somewhere and one day, Leo knew, he would join them. He would go to sleep and not waken. That might not be so bad.

That evening and for the first time since he moved in, Leo was pleased the apartment faced the rear. There would be too much light if it faced the street and he wasn't in the mood for light. He was sitting on one of the two small chairs that faced the sofa. Neither was very comfortable. Earlier, he had been sitting on the sofa, but when he realized his ease, he switched to a chair. The decorator had insisted on the pair of them.

A Shiva call he once made came back to him and he realized the Jews knew how to handle this. Visiting that grieving family, he had inadvertently sat on a small wooden stool. Quite politely, he was told the stools were for the immediate family, who sat on them to ensure their general lack of comfort. In their sorrow, they were to suffer, symbolically suffer. He thought of that when he moved from the sofa to the chair. Being alone made mourning hard. No one was available to speak of the past. All his memories were his alone—there was no one else.

He wondered if he was normal since he didn't think he had expressed sufficient grief at either funeral. He thought maybe the enormity will hit later, but then he suspected there would never be grief like he had seen others display when they lost family.

Living alone had pushed him into books and he had read about his situation. Being raised without a real home, without parents, without home lessons, he didn't know how to act. He didn't know how to show what he felt—he didn't even know what he felt. He had never learned how to feel. The psychologists said a child raised as he was would never be able to display normal feelings. Worse than that, some insisted he would never develop normal emotions. He would forever remain an unfeeling cripple unable to suitably react to death. Since he had lost his parents before he knew them, they said it was inappropriate for him to mourn them and it would be equally difficult to mourn a second, artificial set. He had been too old, they said. If he had been adopted when he was a baby, there would no difference between adoptive parents and real parents. But he had been adopted, if you would call it that, when he was twelve... and twelve years in a Catholic orphanage is no substitute for parents.

He sensed truth in what the experts said. His real parents were gone— forever a mystery, but these others who tried to fill the void were close and now they were dead. He knew he had lost two who had said they loved him, but he also knew he was unable to truly involve his heart. He thought that maybe he didn't know what love was. He felt like a stone, like a worthless, humiliated lump.

Ilene and John were closer to him than anyone, yet he didn't know if he felt sad enough. What was appropriate? How do you judge if you are sufficiently wounded? TV and movies provided a gauge, but that was acting. He grew up without the joy and sorrow other kids experience. Rarely, did he display normal emotion. Right now, he felt more anger than grief.

Maybe it wasn't so strange he couldn't hit it off with women. Every relationship seemed to reach a point of meaninglessness, never getting past a certain level of regard. He was always more comfortable alone—as he was now—sitting in his not so very comfortable chair trying to cry as he had when he found them. His crying that day surprised him. When his first partner was killed in a shoot-out, he almost cried. Never again had anything like that ever happened. But the other day, real tears were on his face. Were they tears of rage and frustration? Or was he really sad? The telephone interrupted his thoughts.

"Lieutenant Flower?" a man asked.

"Yes. Who is this?"

"Lieutenant Flower, this is Monsignor Healy. We have never met, but John told me much about you." He paused, waiting for a response, but Leo remained mute. "Lieutenant... Lieutenant, are you there?"

Coldness swept over Leo. He didn't want to talk to this man. There was something... "Lieutenant?"

"I'm here," he finally said.

"Is something wrong? Oh, I didn't mean that. I mean am I calling at a bad moment?" There was another pause. "Lieutenant, I know this is a bad time, it's been only a few days, but I must talk to you about something very important. If you don't want to talk now, may I call tomorrow?"

"No," said Leo. "It's okay. It's just... I don't know. Your voice. It reminded me of someone. I'm sorry." Pausing, he started over. "Monsignor, how can I help?"

"It has to do with a project Father John was working on for us, but if this is a bad time..."

"It's as good a time as any." Listening, Leo tried to place the voice.

"Okay, but I can't talk about it over the phone. Can we meet?"

"Of course. Where are you?"

"I'm here at St. Patrick's, but I can come to your place."

"You know where I live?" Leo asked with surprise.

"John's papers have you listed as next of kin." Healy said.

Leo was never concerned with John's relationship to the Church; beyond knowing he was a devoted worker. As a ward of the Church for years, Leo was familiar with all of it. He heard many conversations about diminishing contributions, losses to atheism, attacks by the "tent people"—now TV preachers, too much talk about the stock market and not enough about God and piety. There was too much complacency; too much political involvement; too little talk about injustice; too much fear of rocking the nourishing boat. Even though Leo knew he owed almost all he had achieved to the Church, he nevertheless resented the grip they had on people like Ilene. She was too much the servant.

"Lieutenant Flower?" asked the Monsignor.

"I'm here... just surprised at being next of kin. I never thought I'd ever be that."

"John had great affection for you. He saw you as the son he never had."

Leo got up, stretched and carried the phone to the other side of the bookcase divider that sat between his "living room" and his "bedroom". He sat on the edge of the bed. "Now," he said, as to where we can meet. I don't mind coming over during the week."

"I don't want to talk here. I would much rather come to you."

"Fine with me. When?"

"I'll be there in 10 minutes."

"In ten minutes?" Leo asked incredulously.

"Yes, I have a driver waiting."

"You have a driver waiting? Did the parish come into money?"

"My assignment is very important and I am being helped to achieve my goal."

"I'll be here. The apartment is 3A."

"Ten minutes," he said and hung up.

Leo lay back on the bed and looked out the window at its foot. The rear wall of the building on 14th faced him. Some sort of factory. He had never gone over there to find out what kind of factory. Most times he saw lots of women, Hispanic women sitting at sewing machines, most likely a sweatshop. Sitting up he looked out the side window and admired the brick patio of the brownstone next door. It was nice, but as he watched, a cigarette, still lit, came floating down from above and landed smack in the middle.

"I knew it," he said aloud. "Everything nice gets fucked up. No way out of that."

After some minutes of face washing, hair combing, and tie tying, he got out the scotch and put away his belt gun. He carried two. The hammerless .38 Colt was on his hip. That was regulation. The ankle gun was far from regulation. A gunsmith friend took a standard .38 auto and re-chambered it to .357 Magnum, turning it into a great weapon. Hit like a freight train and rose only a half inch at 50 yards. Just point, squeeze and hold on. He had killed three people with it.

As he was filling glasses with ice, the lobby intercom rang. He pressed the button. "Lieutenant, this is Roberto. There is a man here who will not give his name. He says he has an appointment."

"Ask him when he made that appointment." There was silence. "He said, '10 minutes ago'."

"That's fine Roberto, ask him to come up and I thank you for your diligence."

"You are most kind, Lieutenant."

Leo heard the elevator stopping and its door sliding open. Then the moment's hesitation for Healy to read the wall-mounted directions- A, B, C to the left, D in the center, E, F, G to the right- then the ring of his bell. Leo opened the door. The monsignor's voice had seemed familiar and now, seeing him, Leo knew that somewhere in the past their paths had crossed.

"Lieutenant Flower," he said extending his hand. Leo shook it and ushered him from the short hallway to the central living room. Gesturing to the sofa, Leo asked, "Some scotch?"

The Monsignor nodded and sat down as Leo poured the drinks. Sitting down in the uncomfortable chair, Leo asked, "How can I help you?"

"I'm going to get right to the point, Lieutenant, because the issue is important. Did John ever leave any notes or writings with you?"

"Notes... Writing? What kind of writings?"

"Not a story or anything like that, but lists, names and addresses."

"No, he never gave me anything he had written." After a pause, Leo added, "What is it you're after?"

Monsignor Healy looked around the apartment like an auctioneer making an appraisal. When he had made his decision, he asked, "Lieutenant, may I call you Leo?"

"Certainly." Leo said, taking a long sip.

Healy stood and walked to an opposite wall to look at a painting Leo had purchased at the Washington Square Art Show. It was a farm scene, something like a Wyeth. Gesturing to it, Healy said, "It would be nice if everything was as peaceful as this, but I'm afraid it isn't."

"Why don't you tell me what's going on?" Leo said.

Healy came back to the sofa, sat and took a long drink. "Leo, you must know the Church is in a constant battle. We continually seek to create a picture in the public's mind and we are ever alert to anything that might soil that picture. The institutions of this country do not fare well. Politicians are incompetent at best, the military and the police are not loved, and the Church is seen as well meaning, but of little consequence. Everyone is battling for a ray of sunshine. For us, good regard from the public means contributions and we need that money to do the work of the Church. The work for which we are here."

Leo was more surprised by the candor than by the conclusion. "I agree," he said. "But I feel the Church should be more concerned with its primary mission than with public relations?" He took another drink and asked. "So what is it that can blacken the Church's reputation to such a degree it will lose face with the public?"

"John once told me you had a quick grasp. I see he was right." Taking the glass from the small marble coffee table, he leaned back and continued. "John was working on a sensitive project for the Archdiocese." He took a drink. "You must understand how hard this is for me. I trust you, but I don't find it easy."

"If you'd rather not. It's okay with me."

"No. It's important and maybe you can help." He took another drink. "You see... John was compiling lists of those in the Church engaged in homosexual activities."

"Why?" Leo asked, his voice emotionless.

"Leo, these days the media rule. They provide people with perceptions and it doesn't matter if truth is involved. If the masses think you're a hero- you are. If the evening news says the Church is evil- we are."

"But that's almost always true. The public has no way to verify anything. If we don't take the media's word, we're lost. Either you accept what they say or swear off current events." Anyway, what was John doing?"

"We assigned him the task of coordinating an undercover look at several churches here in Manhattan. We wanted to know who were the homosexuals and what they were doing. It wasn't a witch-hunt. We just wanted to know who they were and then, when we knew, we could advise them to modify their behavior or be ready for a transfer to a less conspicuous diocese."

"What did he find out?"

"We don't know. We don't know where he recorded what he did uncover—if he did uncover anything. We're in the dark."

"And what is it you want from me?"

"We thought he might have taken you into his confidence or given you some material to hold."

"No. He never mentioned any of this to me and he never gave me anything relating to it." Healy got up and walked around to the back the sofa. The floor to ceiling bookcases Leo prized caught his attention. "This is an impressive array of books. Have you read them all?"

"Books" flashed a memory in Leo's mind and he remembered John in his chair writing in a zippered leather-bound book. Was that what Healey was after?

"Yes, I have. The ones in over there are 'in progress'," said Leo, motioning to the two cases which separated the "end" of his living room from the "beginning" of his bedroom. Monsignor Healy nodded and slowly walked back to the sofa and sat.

"You understand, Lieutenant, what would happen if the papers or TV got hold of the information John uncovered? It would be a nightmare. The Cardinal would have to call in many favors to get it suppressed—if it could be suppressed."

"The Cardinal as whitewasher." said Leo.

"Lieutenant, its more a matter of protecting the Church. If the press gets this stuff, they make us look like crap...even if it is a case of the pot calling the kettle black."

"I know what you mean. TV news does more to create violence than the movies and they're the first to scream about inadequate law enforcement. The Department has a liaison team to help the media. You know...better we control what they get than let them dig around, but I don't think it works out."

Leo refilled the glasses and then asked. "You said John was leading an undercover operation? Was someone working with him?"

"We know he had two young priests helping. What they found we have. But John did a lot on his own and, I'm sorry to say, we think he had some civilians helping."

"Why do you think that?"

"The priests overheard him give instructions to someone on the phone. They asked him about it and he told them he thought it wise to have an outsider snoop around as well. We thought he meant you." Leo shook his head.

"I was hoping it was."

"Tell me, Leo asked, "do you have any idea where he kept what he found?"

"No, a blank wall. Your people and ours searched everything. There could be a bank box and if there is one, you can get everything as next of kin."

"You know it's possible the killer has what you're after."

"We realize that, but that's too monstrous to think about. But... if it's true, we could be blackmailed and, let me tell you, we would pay."

"So what is the next move?"

"The Cardinal would appreciate you checking any papers you can find, since as next of kin you're the legal heir. The diocese lawyers can help if you would want."

"I'll be glad to help anyway I can. John and his sister meant a lot to me."

"Good. That's all we can ask, I guess." Healy placed the glass on the table and got to his feet. "Whatever you can do through the Department or as a private citizen will be helpful."

Leo rose, shook his hand and walked with him to the door. "Before you leave, Monsignor, would you answer a question?"

"Certainly, Leo what is it?"

"Did you ever have a connection with the orphanage here in the Village?"

"Leo, at one time I was in charge."

"When was that?"

"Oh, years ago. More than fifty. A long time ago. Why do you ask?"

"I was raised at that orphanage. I think I was there when you were there."

"Well, that's interesting. We'll have to talk about old times, one day."

"Yes." said Leo. "We certainly will."

They shook hands once again and the monsignor left, leaving Leo to finish the scotch. After a short time, he switched on the TV for the news.

A pretty reader said no leads had surfaced in the priest killing and then they flashed a phone number and mentioned a puny reward. A new murder was next... another senior couple killed by robbers. Leo watched the usual shots of a reporter outside the building, a patrol car with flashing lights and some of the apartment interior. That was it. The report was no more than twenty seconds, but something caught his eye. What the hell was it? He wondered. How can I see it again? As he headed out for a session at the gym, he figured he'd deal with it in the morning.

CHAPTER 7

SATURDAY MORNING WAS OKAY. Sun flooded in as Leo opened his eyes. He turned on his side and realized his elbow and right forearm hurt. Every time he went to the gym and used the free weights, he had next day pains. Probably lifting too much.

Getting old was getting interesting. After years of instant response with no consequences he now considered almost every move. He wondered if one day he'd have to think about how fast he should zip his fly. A quick piss could lead to a broken wrist... wonderful, just wonderful. But the gym had benefits. He remembered seeing himself on a Department recruitment video. At first, he thought the image was a younger man, but when he recognized himself, he felt good. He looked nimble, physically fit, with a full head of wavy hair and a swarthy, handsome look... almost a movie version of a detective.

As he admired himself, he heard the Times bounce off the front door. With juice, toast and coffee, he knocked off the puzzle and covered the world news. Then he called the Manhattan South Crimes Against Seniors Unit to check on the TV report from the night before. To his surprise, he learned that Mallory of the Precinct Detective Squad was handling the Aptin's case. The Department's reorganization had the Crimes Against Seniors Unit merged with Manhattan Robbery except when a homicide was involved, then, the CAS people were back in it. It all made sense on paper they told him, but he knew it made the street guys nuts, since so many longstanding allegiances were now being altered.

This was another reason pushing the idea of retirement. The force he joined and understood was changing right under his nose. Maybe for the better, but that didn't matter. At one time, he knew who would answer the phone at almost every office he called. But now, that guy might not be there and the guy who answered might not know Leo Flower from a hole in the wall.

That made everything tough. With open communication lines, information flowed. Now it might be okay or it might be your ass on sandpaper.

He couldn't get Mallory, but he did get Berkowitz who filled him in on the Aptins. "Best as we can piece it out, the perps got them to open the door and then pushed in. It's crazy, 'cause it ain't like they pushed in as them old folks came in from outside. The Aptins were already inside and the door was locked."

"Hold on Berky, how do you know the door was locked?"

"We found pieces of the door jamb where the safety chain was attached on the inside. The chain would have to be on for the jamb to get busted up like that. I figure the door was locked, but they put the chain on and then for some stupid reason, opened the door."

"They must have had a good reason. The TV said they were old-timers who probably knew the ropes. Why would they open the door?"

"Who the fuck knows. People get old they get friendly. They get nice. It takes a lot of energy to be all the time paranoid."

"Berky, you're gonna wind up a shrink yet. That's a clever observation."

"Why thank you, Lieutenant Flower. Please buy my latest book."

"Put me down for two, but in the meantime, how do I get into the Aptin's apartment? I need to check something."

His voice took a different tone. "Did you know them?"

"No. It was something I saw on the news last night. Something in that apartment got my attention, but I don't know what it was. Just when I wanted an instant replay, the bit was finished."

"As far as I know, the CSU got tapes up and a uniform at the door."

"Okay, what's the address?" Leo could hear him flipping pages. "Three nine nine West Forty-Four, ground floor."

"I'll be there if you want me. Take it easy and thanks, Berky."

"Anytime, Leo. By the way, before you go, let me ask, are you gonna put in your papers?"

"I've been thinking about it, but I don't have anything else and the street might not be a good idea."

"Yeah, I know what you mean. I'm almost where you are and I swing yes and no. My wife is buggin' me to go... she wants Florida. Me, I hate goddamn sand, sun and ocean, so I figure if I keep on workin' the decision is off."

"Berky, get yourself a bunch of articles about skin cancer from the sun and leave them around. Don't say anything, just leave them on a table by your bed."

"Leo, you are one smart and devious sonofabitch. What a lovely idea." He laughed, and then said, "Take it easy, and pal. I'll be seein' ya."

"You too Berky. Take it easy."

Leo hung up and dressed. Twenty minutes later he was outside deciding whether to walk to 44th rather than cab it. Figuring thirty blocks would do no harm; he cut over to 14th and 8th and started walking. There was no rush... the weather was decent... if he got paged he could find a phone.

Walking up 8th always made him feel romantic. The Spanish women had something that rang his bells. If there was a connection though, it escaped him. He thought genetic, although he looked more Italian than Spanish. Clear skin that tanned perfectly, dark brown hair, and hazel eyes. At six two and 185 pounds, he may not have been a travel poster Mediterranean but nonetheless, Latin ladies flipped his switches.

Whenever he pondered this, he flashed back to Army time at Fort Bliss in El Paso. Walking past the 8th Avenue bars and young Spanish girls was like walking in that part of Juarez the soldiers called 'pig alley,' not a very good play on Place Pigale, but the name mattered little. The young Mexican girls were outstanding. Other guys in his squad had lived far more adventurously than he had, so they never thought of Pig Alley as anything more than what it was —dirty bars filled with Mexican hookers. But for Leo, those joints and those girls represented a look at life he had never seen. His time in the orphanage was exactly what anyone would think—deprived and dull. The Army, Juarez, new places and people- it was a miracle. Five years in the Military Police and then back to New York and into the cops.

The Mambo craze of the fifties had also left a mark. He never danced much, but loved the music. The Palladium Ballroom on Broadway was the place for Tito Rodriguez, Tito Puente, and the Mambo Aces—what great music. He would go often, especially for the shows on Wednesday nights, but never dance. He didn't know the steps and there was no one to teach him. He was never brave enough to ask a girl to dance and have to confess his lack of ability. So he watched from the sidelines.

Walking at an even pace, he matched the cars creeping along in the street. A stand out was a white convertible with the top down. Two great-looking young girls dressed in white were sprawled in the front. He stared at them as shafts of heavy-looking, oily, blue-tinted sunlight lit them like yellow tipped flares. He was sorry they had to breathe the fumes that enveloped their car as it inched along. But it was a great morning for walking.

As he got into the high Thirties, he remembered it was matinee day and the suburban hordes would be all over the place. With so many thousands coming in for shows, he always thought the suburbs would be empty, but several trips to Long Island changed his mind. There were too many people in the City and there were too many people out there in the 'country'. There were just too many people. He wished they would all stay home, but he knew that wouldn't happen. As long as they poured in, the Department would be busy toning down the locals.

He looked into the shop windows as he passed. Not much in the way of merchandise. He felt the same about the girls in the local bars- not much worth buying. When he crossed the broken pavement of 43rd, he promised himself he would stop at Marty's after the Aptins' apartment. Marty might have some news, since he had a hand in so many dirty deals.

Not seeing a uniform at the Aptin's place was no great surprise. Manpower was stretched too thin to have a guy watch a door where only ordinary folks got done in. The celebs always did better. It took fifteen minutes to find the super, who let him into the apartment after studying his badge long enough to memorize it.

The Aptin's place was familiar. It looked like all the places he had seen growing up on the West Side. The furniture was old and soft. The tables had a sheen that was the end product of a thousand and one waxings. A decent looking rug was marred by chalk body outlines and wood chips. Aside from the rug, the apartment was like a friendly antique shop.

Books and papers he expected to find on the floor had been picked up and stacked on the coffee table. The apartment was not the mess he thought it would be. He went into the bedroom and poked around, looking for nothing special, but hoping he might see that something that caught his eye. The newscast had featured a shot of the living room with the bodies still on the floor, so he went in there to focus his search. He recalled the angle of the picture and realized the cameraman must have been outside sticking his lens into the room. The stuff from the floor was what he had noticed on TV and now it was on the coffee table. He sat on the sofa and went through the pile.

The fourth book from the top was it. It was the same kind of book he had seen John write in—black leather, zippered on three sides with a gold cross on the cover. In the TV report it had been on the floor next to the man's body. That was what he had seen. Leo unzipped the covers and looked at the neat writing. It was in code.

The look of the first page suggested English because the words had familiar form, but that was it. There were three words on the first page. The second page and all the rest looked like a list, but made no sense. Leo wondered if this old guy worked for John. The books looked alike, but what did that mean? Was this murdered old guy one of the independents Healy talked about? He would have to figure out what was written to know that. After a brief look for anything else that made sense, he left. The super, lounging outside, paid no attention to the paper bag Leo carried as he headed to 8th, on his way to Marty's.

As he walked, he remembered the first word on the book's first page: IDWKHU. He figured a cipher; the conversion of individual letters, not words. If it is a code then the first word would have been converted into another word. Six letters. Could be a word, but he figured it to be a cipher based on nothing more than a hunch. It was probably a simple alphabet substitution. He would figure it out tonight, he told himself.

Marty's place was a throwback. The idea of putting hundreds of pieces of merchandise in the windows came from a time when window shopping and strolling were what people did. Now, with shoppers scurrying from safe harbor to safe harbor, few strolled and peered into shop windows. He remembered a watch he bought from Marty for John. It was a good buy. A gold Omega for a hundred and a half. As he pictured the watch, he recalled the smile and satisfied look on John's face when he gave it to him. I'll remember him that way, thought Leo. I don't want to remember him as he was in that apartment, covered in blood and staring into space.

Less than two weeks it was. What's an appropriate mourning period? Is getting up at 3 AM every night enough? He still was pained by thinking he didn't feel, as he should. They have been dead for so little time and here I am, he thought, playing detective.

He wondered when he was going to start looking for their killer? That thought brought a smirk. How could he find their killer? In this City there are hundreds who kill exactly that way. The Aptins were good evidence of that. They were killed without a knife, but it still could have been the same guys. They might not even be guys. Maybe it was a group of cute little gang girls who would charm you and then knock you over. I'll find the bastards, he swore to himself. I'll feed them to the fish.

There were three guys staring at the golf clubs in one window and four others looking at the stuff in the other. He could see some of them looked doubtful- probably wondering if the goods were legit. Leo bought quite a bit second hand and felt if you knew what you were buying, there was little reason to insist on things being new, but you had too know what you were buying.

Walking in, Leo spotted Marty behind the front-facing rear counter. To his right stood Carlos, his chief clerk. Glancing left, Leo noticed a new face; a dignified, white-haired old guy whose dress and bearing looked much too majestic for 8th Avenue.

As Marty looked up, his blondish hair fell across his forehead forcing him to sweep it back in place with his hand. Marty was short, stocky and wearing his usual 'uniform'... dark pants, white dress shirt, but no tie.

"Well, well. Look who's here." He said, extending his hand and adding, "Leo, it's been a while."

Leo shook his hand. "And from what I can see, nothing much has changed."

"Hey...what do you expect? Do you think my select clientele is going to insist upon tuxedos and a merchandise change to Hummel birds?" Marty said, faking defensiveness.

Carlos called out, "Hey Marty, don't you mean hummingbirds? Both Leo and Marty looked at him and laughed.

"I see you're not paying his tuition at NYU." said Leo.

Still laughing, Marty said, "No Leo, I pay them just enough to have them show up." He moved the cigar to the other side of his mouth. "Now, tell me, what are you doin' here?

"I was in the neighborhood and thought you might be able to give me a hand on some goods you might have seen or might yet see."

Marty's expression changed. Now he was talking to a cop and he had to watch what he said and did. No mistakes in general and in particular, no mistakes with Leo Flower. He knew Leo and never wanted a problem with him.

"What exactly are you talkin' about?"

"Some gold. A heavy cross, the kind a priest might wear. Bigger than we might have on." Leo looked around the store and particularly at Carlos who immediately started rearranging harmonicas in the showcase.

"Leo, give me a break. You know how I operate. When I buy gold I melt it down. A cross is a cross is a Star of David. I don't pay attention to a damn thing except the weight. My buyers want gold. They don't give a shit what it was and neither do I."

"Yeah," said Leo. "I know how you operate. An inch this side of legal, but that's okay. What rubs me is that you're buyin' swag and you know it. That gets me upset. It always got the boys in robbery upset... you remember?"

"Leo...those days are over."

"Sure," Leo said sarcastically. "They're over like the Dodgers are gonna leave LA and rebuild Ebbets Field." Marty stared at him in silence. Breathing out, Leo said, "Look. Marty. I didn't come here to break your balls. I just want you to keep an eye out. If any heavy and religious gold comes in, remember the seller, okay?"

"You got it, Leo. You can count on me." There was a sigh of relief in Marty's words.

Leo turned, took two steps toward the door and then stopped to look up at the guitars hanging from metal pipes attached to the ceiling. He noticed some nice instruments. The white haired guy following his eye, asked, "Any one in particular?" Leo stared at him trying to place the face, but nothing came. "Nope, just looking."

"You a cop?"

Leo walked over to the side showcase and looked at the man. "Yes." he said. "I'm a cop. Why do you ask?"

"No special reason. You can call me Abe." Returning Leo's stare, he took a fat cigar from his shirt pocket and after he lit it, he asked. "What's your name?"

"Leo, Leo Flower."

"Never heard of you." he said, exhaling a cloud of thick, blue smoke. "You shouldn't smoke that thing. It'll kill you for sure."

"Hey, be serious. I do as I please."

"Am I supposed to be impressed?"

"I should think you'd be more impressed by my looks than what I say. What do you think? Handsome or distinguished? Take your pick." Leo laughed, but said nothing.

"Come on... make up your mind. Let me help." Abe turned to the side offering his profile. Still chuckling, Leo said, "You're more the distinguished type... too old to be handsome."

"Too old? Are you blind or dumb? What kind of cop are you anyway? Do they have you in charge of the horses?"

Surprised by Abe's wit, Leo asked, "What are you doing here? Marty's usually hires only barely literate minimum wage murderers?"

"He needs me. He'd be lost without me." After another long, slow drag on the thick cigar, he asked, "Did you ever hear of Georgie Tuchman?"

Leo thought, Tuchman... Tuchman. The name was familiar. Georgie Tuchman. Suddenly it came to him. "Torchman, Georgie Torchman."

"Well, well," said Abe, "you're not as dumb as you look."

Laughing, Leo asked, "Okay...Georgie Torchman. So what?"

"Hey... if you go to any precinct and ask an old timer about Georgie's right hand, you know who'd they'd finger?"

"I'm beginning to get an idea."

"Right you are, pal. Georgie and me was a pair. We burned down half this city and half of Chicago. Georgie Tuchman and Abe Rosenberg."

"Okay... so what are you doing here?"

"Marty the schmuck needs me." Hearing his name, Marty scuttled across the store to stand alongside Abe. "What did he say to you, Leo? What did this crazy son-of-a-bitch say to you?"

"He quite plainly said he's here because you need him."

"That's right. That's what I said. I'm here in this den because I know diamonds and this schmuck knows zero."

Without real rancor, Marty said, "Bullshit. I know gold and I really know instruments."

Abe looked at Marty the same way an umpire squints at a .150 hitter arguing a called strike. "I give you gold, but the instruments—hell—you think a trumpet is good because it's shiny."

"Give me a break," pleaded Marty, as he puffed a cloud of cigar smoke that matched the clouds from Abe's cigar. Leo watched them and thought of Borscht Belt comics. "Hey, you two are almost Jessel and Burns... You guys got an act."

"Yeah, some act." said Abe. "Ventriloquism maybe...Rosenberg and the Dummy." Leo laughed while Abe blew smoke in Marty's face.

"Leo... Leo, look what I have to put up with. I give an old geezer a break and hire him when nobody else will give him the time and look what I get. He blows smoke in my face."

"You should consider yourself lucky. The smoke I am blowing at you is from a three-dollar cigar. It ain't like the ten cent rolled horseshit you smoke."

With sorrow-filled eyes, Marty looked at Leo. "You see, you see what I mean. This old fucker has been smoking Cuban cigars for how long... what... fifty years?"

Smiling, Abe looked at Marty and then at Leo. "I started smoking Cubans after I knocked off a local importer. That was more than fifty-five years ago when I was twenty-five and..."

"Wait a minute... wait a minute." Leo interrupted. "Are you saying, you're eighty and you killed someone?"

"Your hearing's still pretty good."

"I don't care about your age, but I do usually notice confessions, particularly when a murder's involved."

Abe looked at Marty. "Marty, did you hear anybody confess to a murder?"

"I am officially deaf, dumb, and blind." Marty said, covering his eyes.

"Cute, you two are really cute." said Leo, and then pointed his finger at the old man. "You don't want to make jokes like that."

"Why would I tell a lie? I'm too old for that and too old to care about it anyway. I'm fearless- eighty and not afraid of a fucking thing."

Leo stared at Abe and figured the old guy was not lying and really was an old-time hood. He told himself to check out this Rosenberg back at the precinct. "Well, guys, it's been fun, but I have business. Marty, remember what I want you to look for- heavy religious gold and anything that says Church. Anything- even a book that looks like it's from the Church. Okay?"

"You got it Leo. I'm on the phone if anything turns."

"And you," Leo said, looking at Abe. "I don't want any trouble from you.

Being funny is one thing, but old gangsters aren't funny. They're just old gangsters. So keep it under control, right?"

Abe stared at him and blew thick smoke in the air. "Screw you."

"Right," said Leo, turning and heading for the door.

CHAPTER 8

LEO WAS BACK AT his place by four. Made an omelet, ate it, then cleared the table so he could work on Aptin's book. He felt he had a couple of good solid facts- that Aptin was hopefully not a cipher genius and used a system John provided and John, himself an amateur, would not choose a difficult process.

The easiest system would be a straight alphabet substitution. The hard part was figuring the letter shift. One to the right makes an "A" into a "B", twice and "A" is "C" and so on. No way but trial and error. He cut several blank pages into strips and wrote the first word, IDWKHU, on one. Then he wrote several complete alphabets on other strips and set to work.

He aligned each strip vertically to view the substitutions. First, he shifted to the right:

ABCDEFGHIJKLMNOPQRSTUVWXYZ
BCDEFGHIJKLMNOPQRSTUVWXYZA

With B under C, IDWKHU equaled HCVJGT. Shifting again produced GBUIFS. The next shift produced FATHER. Hoping they had not used a different set-up for each word, he started work on the rest of the first page.

The second and third words MRKQ PXUSKB translated to JOHN MURPHY. The next line spelled out ST IGNATIUS. The third line, PU VHBPRXU DSWLQ was MR SEYMOUR APTIN. The fourth was XQGHUFRYHU MHZLVK ZRUNHU IRU WKH FDWKROLF FKXUFK, which turned out to be UNDERCOVER JEWISH WORKER FOR THE CATHOLIC CHURCH. Leo got a kick out of that and felt sorry he never met Aptin. If John had trusted him, he must have been an okay guy.

Now knowing how to proceed, he put Mozart on the stereo and a bowl of salted sunflower seeds by his elbow. After four hours he had all of the writing translated. It was a series of sightings Aptin had made following one specific priest. A typical entry read: August third, Fr. Williams and another man. Prst? entered Greenwich Theatre- hand holding, hands inside pants, some kissing.

It went on like that for pages. Knowing John, he probably assigned one watcher for every suspect. Aptin had followed Father Williams; others were probably assigned similarly- one watcher for each subject. That arrangement kept everything neat and it also prevented anyone from dealing with more than a small piece of the entire affair. Smart. At that point, Leo realized his luck at getting his hands on Aptin's book. There was no way to know how many other books John had out, but the vital one would be John's, since it probably held specific information about who was working with him. He wondered if John's book was also in code. Why Aptin's book was coded was a mystery, not that it mattered now, but how could Leo get John's book? He was sure the killer had it.

By ten, Leo had Aptin's book decoded. It was as he expected- page after page of the doings of Father Williams. Leo didn't condemn the priest or the Church, since both were caught in a grief-filled struggle. He wondered if homosexuality was typically an element of single-sex organizations. Maybe it was always like that. But now, with twenty-four-seven scrutiny by a holier than thou media, the Church had to present a different picture. The 'face' the public saw had to be presentable. Everything had to look right. Even if everyone knew the 'face' to be a lie, the appearance had to be there. It was perfected hypocrisy. Nonetheless, the more he thought about all of it, the more sorry he felt for Father Williams. What could the poor bastard do? He was trapped in a system that sowed its own destructive seed.

So, he thought, the Church is shot through with homosexuals and perverts and who knows what else. So what. There was nothing Leo could do. Nothing Father Williams could do and nothing Healy could do. It was what is. The subject disgusted him so, he tossed the book across the room for want of some expressive action. Afterwards, he sat staring at it. Then, almost leaping from the chair, he grabbed the phone and called Healy. The angry need to vent was squelched when he was told the Monsignor was not available. Not fully understanding why he was feeling so strongly about it, Leo knew he had to shed himself of the book and the subject of Church perversion. He had to get it out of his sight so he told the priest who answered the phone, he would be sending an important package that night. It would be delivered to the Church by a private messenger service and the package should be held for Monsignor Healy. The priest gave Leo some instructions about entrances and then hung up.

It took Leo about fifteen minutes to write a note to Healy explaining how he got the book and that the translation of Aptin's material, which he included, would remain secret. The messenger service arrived about thirty minutes later and soon after that, the book was on its way. Eventually, Leo managed to drag himself to bed and get to sleep.

About thirty blocks north of Leo's apartment, Angel Martinez stalked a victim near the parking lot at 10th and 44th. The man, carrying a small case, stopped for a moment at the booth looking for the attendant before he walked into the lot. Angel knew the attendant bugged out on Saturday nights, since the cars were locked and the owners had the keys. Lighting in the lot was poor and it took the guy fifteen minutes to find his car. As he started to unlock the door, Angel came up from behind.

"Hey man, give me your money. You hear, give me your money."

The man turned and started to say something, but swallowed it when he saw the large knife in Angel's hand. The smooth blade flashed in the dim light and looked like a sword.

"Hey, are you deaf? The money. I want your money. Gimmee the money."

The man stood silent and unmoving.

"Hey, what the fuck. Are you crazy? Don't fuck with me, man, I'll cut you up."

The man remained motionless except for a slight shifting of his balance, which caused the case in his hand to sway slightly.

Increasingly tense, Angel cried out, "Hey mothafucka, you deaf? I said I want your fuckin' money. Now get it out or I'll cut your throat."

The man continued to stare at Angel who was growing very nervous and wishing he had never started. I should stick to old people, he thought. I don't need this shit. Then suddenly, the man moved and caught Angel by surprise.

While they were facing each other, the man had held the case in his right hand and Angel watched it because once before, a guy had walloped him with one like it and knocked him cold. When Angel stopped this guy, he brought the case in front of him, as if for protection, and throughout the confrontation, the guy had not moved his arm. He had held the case motionless, but now, he dropped it. As if in slow motion, he opened his fingers and let it fall. Angel watched it falling and realized as he did, he should be watching the man, not the case, but by then it was too late.

The man's right foot swung in a graceful arc ripping into Angel's wrist with sufficient force to send the large knife flying into the air. Angel felt tremendous pain in his wrist and yelled. A second later, the man's hand was more than halfway to a strike on the side of Angel's throat. There was a thud and like a sack of sand, Angel slumped to the ground.

When he opened his eyes about twenty minutes later, he was on his back staring up into the night sky. He couldn't move his right hand because of the pain. His left, down at his side was resting in a puddle. The man and his car were gone. Consciousness brought such agony, he wondered if the guy had run him over when he drove out. Raising his head, he tried to look down at his right hand, but hearing the bones in his neck make a noise, he froze, terrified. After a minute, he slowly moved his head enough to see his wrist bent at a strange angle. "Sonofabitch!" he cried out. "That mothafucka broke my wrist."

Staring up at the stars, he tried to sort out his pain. His wrist hurt as did his neck, but that was not it. There was a pain in his belly- in his gut. His middle hurt. He tried to sit up, but couldn't. He focused along his left side and looking past his hand, saw his knife on the ground close by his knee. Next to it was a shiny lump. He thought it was dog shit. Slowly, Angel moved his left hand to his middle and felt the wetness. He was dripping wet. Thinking he had pissed his pants, he cried out, "I'll kill you mothafucka! I'll kill you."

As his left hand searched, he realized his clothes were torn and his shirt was out of his pants. He hand moved lower and when he felt his dick, he breathed a sigh. He thought the guy might have cut it off. His fingers continued their search and found torn flesh. Probing further, he touched more damp cloth and wet, torn meat. As his fingers touched the torn flesh, they felt blood pulsing from an open wound, and it all became clear. "My balls." he screamed. "The guy cut my balls off. Oh, nooooo!" He cried.

Screaming into the night for untold minutes eventually brought help. A precinct patrol car with open windows and a silent radio had been slowly cruising the area. The car stopped as the two cops tried to pinpoint the yelling.

When they located him, they positioned the vehicle so its headlights could light the scene. Moving slowly, they approached, with guns drawn, one from each side of the car. When they were about four feet away, they saw him. The driver, nodding at Angel, said, "Better call an ambulance. We can't let this little fucker bleed out. If he dies here, they'll charge him weekend rates." The other cop laughed as he walked back to the car.

When he returned, they surveyed the scene. Neither cop needed much time to figure what happened. The giveaway was the knife. If Angel had been attacked, the weapon would still be with the attacker. Since the knife was left behind, they knew it was Angel's knife and after using it on him, the perp left it to show the world.

Looking down, one cop asked, "Never figured this would happen, did you wise guy?"

His eyes wide with pain and pleading, Angel cried out. "Oh man, help me. Help me. Some guy grabbed me and cut off my balls. You gotta help me! I don't wanna die!"

"Hey you little scum bag, stop the bullshit. It's clear what happened. You tried to stick somebody and they got you instead. Busted your wrist and cut off your balls. I'd give that fucker a medal if he was here. It's sure as shit you ain't no model citizen and I don't give a fuck if you do bleed to death... right here, right now."

"Oh man...oh man...I'm dyin'!" Angel moaned.

"Well... maybe you will and maybe you won't," said the driver, "but that don't matter." He looked down at Angel. "What does matter is that no fucked up kid of yours is gonna suck dough from this city. Your days as a daddy are over. One less scumbag on welfare."

Neither cop made any move to ease Angel's suffering. They stood, side by side looking down at him. "You know, I was thinking," said the driver, "is it possible they can sew this fucker's balls back on and get them workin'?"

"Damn... what a thought. I sure as hell hope they can't. I really don't want to see that."

"Well... neither do I, so why don't you go back to the car, check for the ambulance, get this dickhead a blanket, while I solve that problem."

As the cop walked back to the radio unit, the driver kicked the glistening lump that was Angel's balls about ten or twelve feet deeper into the lot. The fleshy mass came to a rolling stop under a new Buick.

Moments later, the other was back with a blanket. Helping to get it under Angel's head, he noticed the lump that had been near the knife was no longer there. Looking up at his smiling partner, he said, "Well... I guess that solves the microsurgery question."

"Nothing like a little street initiative." said his partner.

The ambulance came floating around the corner, stopping at the lot's entrance. Almost immediately, two attendants burst from it clutching bags of equipment. With no display of emotion, they bandaged what they could, immobilized what they could, and had Angel on his way to the hospital in less than four minutes.

The cops bagged the knife and listlessly looked for anything else that might clarify what happened. Finding nothing, they followed the ambulance to Roosevelt Hospital.

The only apt description for Saturday night in Roosevelt Hospital's ER was a direct comparison to a front-line combat surgery. Every place that could hold a body had one on it or in it: bed, gurney, wheel chair, waiting room bench and side chair.

The EMS people brought Angel into the wailing midst, first filled out paperwork, then gave verbal details to an unmoved senior nurse as stiff as her starched, blood spattered uniform. She listened to their story with hands on hips and an indifferent look on her face. When she heard enough, she waved them away as if they were responsible for the on-going bedlam. Her fingers flicked at them, as if to say, if not for you two, this place would be clean, empty and above all, quiet.

Her detached look matched the wave of her hand. The surrounding craziness was not what she envisioned when she had prepared for nursing. Stranded in the eye of this storm, she wanted justification for the mayhem. Vietnam had made sense. As sick and wasteful as that was, at least it was war and you expected those close enough to it to be blown up or shot to pieces. But this was absolute insanity. Here were people slicing each other, smashing each other, burning each other, or shooting each other for no reason. Talking to them 15 minutes after their 'event', she heard the standard response..."I don't know what happened. I guess I sort of lost it."

She thought these victims society's trash- New York's misfit brigade. In India's slums there were no emergency rooms. She admired that arrangement. Since street scum will never be more than that, let them do as they please and collect the bodies in the morning. Though admittedly beyond her understanding, she thought about the amounts of money, energy, time, and education wasted on these people. Doctors, nurses... every imaginable specialty working like mad to help mend trash that would not help themselves. Stitch them, bandage them, and see them next week for new stitching and new bandaging. It was all a waste- an incomprehensible waste.

The EMS attendants stared back with guilty kid faces- hands in the cookie jar faces, until she absolved them with a smile.

"I'm sorry," she said. "I shouldn't take it out on you. You're as innocent as I am." Looking around, she said, "Shit...we're the victims." Then she gestured to the coffee machine, "C'mon, I'll buy you a cup." As they walked the fifteen feet, they passed Terry Sullivan and Barry Stern, the cops who found Angel. They were telephoning facts and their suspicions to their sergeant. They wanted to fingerprint Angel, but the sergeant refused permission. He saw Angel as a victim and disagreed with Sullivan, who insisted Angel was a perp who had to have outstanding warrants.

"No way," Insisted their sergeant. "Get the guy medical attention; find out who he is; locate relatives and write it up. Later, get the knife to the precinct clerk so it can be checked for latent prints... when you're done there, get your asses back on patrol."

While Sullivan was on the phone, Stern tried to question Angel. A nurse had jammed a towel against Angel's groin and told him to hold it tight to his body. All the while, Angel continued to moan and scream for vengeance. The bleary-eyed nurse told him, "Look pal, you can scream all you want, but right now we've got to stop the bleeding. Hold the towel tight and shut your mouth." Then she turned to focus on another patient who was holding his upper left arm with his right hand. Blood bubbled through his fingers, falling into a growing puddle on the floor. Stern paid no attention to any of it except to cover his gun butt with his hand whenever anyone came near.

"Hey, pal, you're gonna be fine. Don't worry. The doc'll stitch you up fine. Don't sweat it." He paused and asked in a softer voice, "Now, why don't you tell me who you are. Give me the name of a relative we can all."

"Fuck you," cried Angel. "I ain't tellin' you shit and I got nobody to call. I jus' wanna get the fuck outa here."

"Hey, Johnny, take it easy. We're on your side. We want you to get better and get out of here. Just tell me who you are and who did this to you."

"Go fuck yourself, cop. I don't know nothing. Get me a doc, man. I need a fuckin' doctor." As Angel yelled, Sullivan came over to ask Stern what he learned. When Stern told him Angel wouldn't cooperate, Sullivan said, "Look, Barry, I don't give a fuck about this guy. If he don't want to talk, he don't have to. The Sarge says we are to get what we can and bring in the knife. If this little fucker don't want to talk, fuck him."

Not quite ready to bounce back on patrol, they watched the EMS guys calmly check the condition of each patient. Just as Sullivan was going to congratulate them for their care and concern, the two guys lifted a body from a gurney, sheet and all, and laid it on the floor. Then they grabbed a clean sheet from a pile, tossed it on the gurney and wheeled it out the door.

"Well don't that beat shit." Said Sullivan.

Seeking help, they advised the head nurse of their predicament with Angel and she told them a doctor was on his way to suture Angel's wound and also, a patient in an ER does not have to give any information in order to be treated. They don't have to cooperate at all.

"You know, Officers," she added in a soothing and resonant voice, "It isn't against the law for a patient to be uncooperative. In fact, he may be in shock, but anyway, I'll try and get some information for you."

Sullivan moved closer to her. "Look, I think that guy is dangerous, so you be careful. Don't be in no room alone with him and don't tell him anything about yourself. Treat him like he got leprosy and call for help if you need it. Don't try to be a hero... okay?"

"I think I am more the heroine type, don't you, Officer?" Sullivan blushed then smiled. They stood silent for a moment and then Stern walked towards the exit. "My name is Wilson," said the nurse, "...and I'm here all the time."

"I'm Sullivan and that's Stern, my partner," he said, lifting his chin toward Stern, who was headed for the exit. After a beat, he added, "We gotta get back out there. You take care and remember what I said about Pancho Villa."

"You take care, also, Officer Sullivan." She said, as he turned to go.

In a few steps he caught up with Stern. "Been introducing yourself?"

"Yeah. We exchanged names."

"Seems kind of stupid, doesn't it? She's got a name tag and you got a name tag and I got a name tag."

"It's different if you tell someone your name. Sure they can read it off the tag, but me tellin' her and her tellin' me- well, that's a whole different thing. Sayin' it out loud is what makes the difference."

Stern smiled at him as they reached the patrol car. "Are you fallin' in love?"

"It can happen." Sullivan said. "It can happen."

Nurse Wilson watched them walk out. That Sullivan is one hunk of a man, she thought. With that in mind, she turned to look at the bloody mess in her ER. Fortunately, the guy with the sliced arm was gone and an orderly was mopping up the blood puddle. Walking towards Angel, she confronted an intern coming through the double doors who asked, "I understand we have a castration?"

She nodded and gestured toward Angel. "What happened?" the intern asked.

"From what we've been able to determine, it was a conversion ceremony... this guy wanted to become Jewish and the guy doing the circumcision slipped and cut off his balls instead of the foreskin." The intern smirked.

"You're Jewish, aren't you?" she asked. "Yes." he answered. "Why?"

"I was wondering about his status. Being circumcised is one thing, but being castrated seems beyond the call of duty. Is castration as good as circumcision?"

"Only if he's married." The intern replied dryly.

Now she smirked and said, "Seriously, we don't know anything. The cops found him in a parking lot and EMS brought him in."

They walked to Angel who was moaning and cursing as he pressed the towel to his groin. Reluctantly, he let the intern inspect the wound. After his examination, he told Angel they would get him an operating room, clean him up, sew him up and that he'd be fine. Angel stared at him incredulously. "Fine? I'll be fine? Ya fuck. Are you crazy? I ain't got no balls."

"Don't be upset. The damage is done and cannot be undone. We have treatments now that will make it far less a problem than you think. Are you married?"

"Fuck you, mothafucka. I ain't tellin' nobody nothing." He grabbed another towel and pressed it to his groin. "You say you can fix me up, then do it and stop askin' me questions I ain't gonna answer."

The doctor looked at him, sighed, and then gestured to Nurse Wilson. "Call OR 5... tell them what we got. I'll do the work."

In less than thirty minutes, Angel was in the OR slipping into dreamland. Two hours later he was still sleeping peacefully. The bloody flesh had been trimmed, sewn, and bandaged and his wrist was set and plastered.

CHAPTER 9

AT 7:30, LEO WOKE when the Times bounced off his apartment door. Sunday was his favorite day, for he would be able to read for the entire day with no excuses. He liked the Sunday New York Times for it was immense, with more information than a medieval man would confront in his entire life.

The all-news radio and television stations were like police radios, spewing out endless streams of who, what, where, when and how. No one managed to spend time with- why. Was information worth anything without a clue to the why? Leo didn't think so. Ten homicides on the subway in November. Why? The newspaper tried to tell why. Reading a reporter's facts slowly and carefully, then reading a columnists' view of those facts might makes things a little easier to understand. Reading was the key to it all.

Television was a great hoax. People saw event after event and felt informed, but what did it mean? No one had any idea. The pompous and the arrogant spewed out answers, but it was easy to see they were full of it and of themselves. There were no answers on television. There was no why on television. By watching it, you learned a little about the people on television. That was it.

Ever since he was a kid, reading was his escape. The grimy walls of the orphanage had vanished as he opened a book and let its words fill his mind. Almost 50 years ago, Father John had given him his first book, *Kipling's Stories for Boys*. Now it was in a special place in one of the two bookcases in his 'living room.' That one book got him through the dismal and lonely years. Near the bookcases was a painting of a regal sailing ship under a heavy wind. Depending on his mood, that painting was his space and time machine as the ship sliced the sea, fleeing danger or sailing to adventure. Coming home to the apartment was always a gift.

His last visit to the Department psychologist focused on why he could never bring himself to marry or live with a woman. He was not sure if he had adequately explained why he needed this apartment to be his space and that sharing it with someone, even someone he cared for, would have been an intrusion. The doc didn't fully get it. No one really got it. Some people, he figured, were meant to be alone.

He thought the evidence abundantly available. If parents were psychos the odds were not good for their kids to live a normal life. Children of alcoholics, children of abusers, carried those scars around- and the opposite was true. If you came out of a loving and caring home, you probably would create a similar one. That would be a normal occurrence. You reproduced what you lived through. Leo never thought he could be a good parent.

He showered, shaved, made breakfast and started to read the paper, discarding only the job offerings- no point.

Angel opened his eyes to see a nurse looking at him through some sort of a window. He shut his eyes. Let me rest... let me get strength, he thought. He had never felt so weak. Looking around, he saw he was alone in a tiny room. One bed. Nothing else. There wasn't even a door. What kind of shitty hospital is this, he wondered. No doors. There was a pain in his right arm. Attached to his arm was a plastic tube that ran to an upside-down bottle hanging from a pole. He had seen that in a movie. What was in the bottle? It couldn't be blood- blood was red. This stuff looked like water, but it couldn't be water. He could just drink water. He knew it must be medicine.

The nurse came in and touched his forehead. "I know you're awake. Are you trying to hide?" He opened his eyes to look at her. She looked like a nurse.

"What kind of a dumb room is this? Why ain't there no door?"

"This is a recovery room. They brought you here after the operation. You don't go to a regular room until they know the surgery was okay." He wondered how long he would have to stay here. He wanted to leave. The nurse, sensing his unease, tried to reassure him.

"Please don't worry, everything went well. You've been patched up by the best."

"Hey, are you crazy?" he said. "Patched up? Man, that sonofabitch cut my balls off. You talk like I got a splinter taken out. Tellin' me I shouldn't worry... are you fuckin' nuts?"

"Are you in pain?"

He hadn't focused on the pain until she asked. He hadn't thought about it. The more he sought to answer her question, the more he felt it. He felt like an elephant stepped on him. "Are you in pain, Mr.- what do I call you? I don't know your name."

"Never mind my name. Yeah, it hurts a lot."

"Let me get you something." She walked to a little desk and took some pills from a jar. He took the two she offered and in less than ten minutes they hit. He smiled when he realized he was high. Drugs are the best, he thought. How else can you get such a great feeling? As the drugs took full effect, he drifted off to a semi-sleep.

Eventually, the doctor came to examine him. He told Angel about the 'procedure'- what he had done. He had trimmed flesh to even up the edges and then it was only a matter of closing everything off. The stitches would soon dissolve. Everything went fine. He said Angel was strong and young and he would be fine. Angel heard him, but did not respond. He didn't give a shit. He was flying. Question after question came at him. Where do you live? What is your name? What is the name of your closest relative? What is your religion? He just looked up and smiled a crooked smile. Fuck you all, he thought. Those pills were great.

They told him his clothes had to be disposed of because they were bloody and torn. His relative or a friend could bring new clothes. What is the name of your friend? What clothes do you want your friend to bring? Fuck you! They said his possessions were safe. They had his money and keys. The attacker probably took his wallet. Angel thought of the guy with the case. Someday, someday maybe they would meet again. He smiled at that thought.

Angel told them nothing. All he wanted to do was stay high. When he came down he would get some clothes and go to Carlos'. He had to get some clothes.

Three hours later he was fully awake and felt pretty good. The nurse checked him and made arrangements for him to be transferred to a room. He was moved within an hour. The room had three other beds in it. There were old people everywhere, crowding around and talking to the people in the beds. Where am I? He wondered. Is this an old people's hospital? He considered what would happen if a person he had mugged was in this room. Would they know him? He had attacked so many old people- one of them could still be recovering.

Fuck that shit, he thought. I ain't goin' to worry about that. It never could happen- they can't tell one Puerto Rican from another.

When Angel was settled in, he managed to ask a nurse what was going on. She told him these were people brought in from the streets. Each had been either mugged, hit by a car or hurt in some way. She said every day and every night people were brought here. The old people were always the victims. They were beaten, robbed, and left like dogs in the gutter. Old people took crap from everyone and nobody gave a damn.

She said he was special since very few young men are brought in and what had been done to him was terrible. She told him the Detectives would soon come to get his statement. That was how it worked. The victims were brought in and when they recovered enough, the police would come to get the details. Angel listened, but paid no attention. Getting clothes and getting out of there were his only thoughts. His keys and money were in the drawer of the table by the bed. He put them under his pillow.

The nurse told him it would be okay if he wanted to go to the bathroom and that he should expect some pain and some blood in his urine, but that would be normal. In a few days, he would feel fine. He was young and strong, she said. In a few days he would be in great shape. His wrist would be fine and the cast would be ready to come off in a couple of weeks.

Hours later, he had no idea how many, he managed to get out of bed and wander into the hall. The place was a madhouse. Cops, detectives, nurses, doctors, visitors- people were everywhere. It hurt to walk, but he had to get out of there. He didn't want to talk to any cops. He walked the corridors until he saw a guy with a mop and pail come out of a room. He went in. It was a maintenance closet. On a shelf he found some clothes, a jump suit with words on the back. He put it on. There was a lumpy bandage under his cock, but he managed to get the suit on and zipped. He came out of the closet with a mop and wandered around until he found his room. He got his money and keys. When he walked in to get his stuff, he laughed to himself, because no one even looked at him. To them, he was just another scumbag, just another nobody not to see. He wondered if they would see him if he burst into flames. "What's that?" They would ask. "Oh, nothing," another would answer. "Just another spic on fire. Don't pay attention. Someone will put him out."

Holding the mop, he strolled the corridors, walked in and out of rooms filled with people. He opened closets and looked under beds until he found a pair of sneakers and socks. He went back to the closet to put them on. It was easy to get a coat from the racks in the hall by the elevators.

He kept opening corridor doors until he found a staircase. He slowly walked down the many flights until he saw daylight. A few minutes later, he was in a taxi heading to Carlos' apartment. Better to go there than his place, he thought. Carlos would get him stuff at the drug store. He wished he had more of the pills the nurse gave him, but that didn't really matter. He would get high on something else.

Unconsciously, Leo reached up to turn on the copper lamp near the sofa. It had a large shade- black on the outside; coppery metallic on the inside. Its soft red/yellow light brought out the red and maroon of the chairs and sofa. Leo thought the light dark and warm, the opposite of bright... but it wasn't dull. He laughed softly at his inadequate description of the lamplight. An appropriate moment to realize words can be a problem, he thought.

He was trying to finish the crossword and was stuck. Though stymied, he enjoyed this puzzle because of its theme. Too often the puzzle was stupid. Hard or easy was never the point. Clever was the point. Anyone could create an impossible crossword. The art was to make it hard enough so when finished, the puzzler felt something had been accomplished- something beyond the average. A little smug is okay.

This one was about ships and he was ready to fill in a word when the lobby intercom rang. Getting up from the sofa, he walked the few steps and pressed the button. "What?"

"Lieutenant Flower, this is Roberto. Is it possible for me to come up and speak to you?

I can't say no, Leo thought. It wouldn't be right, but he really didn't want to talk to anyone about anything. He so enjoyed the solitude, but guilt won out. "Sure, Roberto, c'mon up."

Seconds later, his doorbell buzzed. Opening the door, he saw Roberto out of uniform. For a moment, Leo didn't recognize him. Flashing through his mind was the scene from Murnau's *Last Laugh,* when the doorman's neighbors humiliate him because without his uniform he deserves none of their respect. Clothes make the man? Absolutely!

"I look different without the fancy coat, don't I?"

"Yes you do. Come in."

Leo stepped aside leaving Roberto just enough room in the narrow hallway to get by. "Please sit down." Leo said, gesturing to the sofa. "What is it? No trouble I hope?"

"On the contrary, it is a fine piece of news. Tonight I will be acting in a new play at the St. Marks Playhouse and I have a ticket for you if you are not busy."

"Well, that's a pleasant surprise and very nice of you to think of me."

"I auditioned a few weeks ago and got the part. Tonight's performance is the last preview prior to the grand opening and I thought you might like to see me do my other stuff."

"Absolutely, I'd love to come. What is the play about? Is it a drama... a comedy?"

"I think it is best if I do not tell you. Better you see it and figure for yourself if it is a comedy or drama?"

"Oh..." Leo moaned. "It's one of those, huh?"

"I am certain you will find it interesting. You will come?"

"Sure. What time?"

"We will start at seven. I will leave a ticket in your name at the box office. You know where the theater is?"

"Yes, Roberto. I know the Village. I was brought up here."

"Lieutenant, you have made me a happy man. I will be pleased knowing you are in the audience. It is my hope you have a satisfying theatrical experience."

"Believe me, Roberto, that is also my profound wish."

With that, they rose and Leo escorted Roberto to the door and into the corridor to wait for the elevator. A moment or two later, it arrived and Leo bade him good-bye. Back inside, Leo realized that to be at the Playhouse at seven left him time for a quick bite and rather than eat in, he decided to go out. Ten minutes later he crossed Seventh and walked to the Cafe Brigitte on Greenwich. Since the place held only eleven people there was always the chance there'd be no room, but there was and Leo marched in and sat at the counter.

He ordered pea soup and a dish Brigitte called Boeuf Ragout- deep reddish brown gravy, lumps of beef over broad egg noodles. Good simple food. He picked up pie and coffee at the Deli to take back to his place. While he had eaten and while he walked, he kept his eye on the locals. Throughout the last years, the Village had changed. At one time, the perps stayed in the Alphabets. Now they poured out of the East Village, so the West Village was not as safe as many thought. Because the buildings were fancier and store prices higher, residents rhapsodized about security. Leo knew better; he was never without his guns and he had envisioned a possible shooting situation many times. He had hard and fast rules- no hesitations- no delays.

As he changed his clothes, he wondered how many times he had walked to St. Marks Place. The more he thought about walking through the Village, the more he knew he would start to think about being alone. On a Sunday night, the streets were filled with couples. Young guys with young girls, old guys with old girls, and every other imaginable combination. There were very few men like him walking alone.

He never tried to pick up women on the street. It was something he avoided even when he had a yen for a woman he noticed. Not looking his age and being a cop attracted some women, but the whole idea seemed laughable so he avoided it.

Leaving his place at six, he headed east in an easy stroll and he was outside the theater at a quarter to seven. The box office was open and he gave his name, got his ticket and walked into the small lobby area. To his surprise, he was alone. There was no one else in the lobby and for a moment he thought he had misunderstood Roberto, but when he saw him, he knew he hadn't.

"Lieutenant Flower, you will have to forgive me," Roberto said.

"Why? What happened?"

"Well, this was supposed to be the last preview performance, but the writer, who is also the director, has not yet decided if we need it. I think he is saying the actors have reached their peak and additional rehearsal might be harmful."

"Why aren't you sure about what he says?"

"Lieutenant, he is a bit unusual." As Roberto said that, a short blond man dressed in black came into the lobby and strode to where they were standing.

"Halooo. I yam Mikhail Yuziden. I weeel assyume yew are Rowberto's fraynd. He toll me yew woooould be here. Iz that right?" Leo stared at him trying to figure the birth of his dialect—middle-Europe or deep Mississippi. He sounded like a Slav who had spent years in a Confederate school system. Leo told him he was correct and that he was eager to see the play.

"Whale..." Yuziden said, "Ahm not syurr whather eet ees wahs to pyut eet ohn." He stopped and gave Leo the once over. His almond shaped eyes slowly taking in everything- from Leo's shoes to his hair. Then he asked, "Dew yew wont tooo see eet?"

"Certainly." Leo responded.

After several moments of silence, Yuziden said, "Whale ...den wee weell do eet fuh yew. Okeh?"

"I think that would be great." Leo answered. With that, Yuziden swirled and led Leo into the theater. "Yew seeet hyar. Eeeet eees a goood seeeet. I weeel seee yew whain eet iz ovah."

Leo looked around and saw he was still totally alone. That produced a strange feeling since he had never before been the entire audience for anything. He thought it funny until he realized his responsibility. If I go to the John to take a leak, will they stop and wait for me? What about a laugh line? If they are expecting an audience reaction and I don't react, will they get upset? Will it throw the actor's off? He decided to laugh at whatever even appeared funny since it was better to be an enthusiastic audience than a reticent one. As he was wondering about his role, the curtain opened and he saw Roberto alone on the stage.

Listening intently, he decided Roberto was playing the role of one brother who was insanely jealous of his younger sibling. All sorts of angry screaming about dates and screwing and losing lovers to one other. That went on for almost thirty minutes. For the entire time, Roberto was alone on stage screaming at his yet to appear younger brother. Then, as suddenly as it had begun, everything stopped. All the lights went out and there was silence. A minute later, the lights flashed on, but now there was a different actor alone on stage. He began shouting out his hatred for the way Roberto's character had treated him. This went on for about twenty minutes and Leo assumed he was seeing the other brother.

Then, everything stopped once again. Lights out- total silence. When they came on there was a new character on stage. Leo couldn't tell if the new actor was a man or a woman. He/she had a on a costume that was half male clothing and half female- split down the middle- right side male- left side female. This character screamed that she/he loved men and women and that the brothers were his/her true love. After twenty or so minutes of that, the other two actors came on stage and all three yelled at each other until the lights went out. When they came on, the stage was empty. Nothing happened for a moment and then the curtain slowly closed.

Leo was amazed. It was like being hit in the face with a surprise pie. He had no idea what was going on, but he slowly applauded to show that he was still awake. The house lights went on and rather quickly Roberto and Yuziden were by his side.

"Telll meee, deeed yew understan mah play?"

Suppressing a laugh, Leo said, "No. I'm afraid I didn't. At least I'm not sure right now. Maybe if I think about it, it will become clear."

Cocking his head to one side, Yuziden looked at him. "Telll meee... arugh yew a homo sexyouwall?"

Leo stared, wondering if it all was a practical joke. He played it straight and said, "No. Mr. Yuziden. I am not a homosexual. Why do you ask?"

"Whale... I wrote it whain I wuz twenteee and I yam a homosexyouwall. Maybee yew got to beee twenteee and a homosexyouwall to understahn eet."

"That's a very deep insight." Said Leo. "You're probably absolutely right."

"Whale.... I hop duh criteeeks lak eeet."

"I wish you great success and I do appreciate your letting me see it."

"Yahs. Gut naht." He twirled and was gone. Roberto, grinning strangely, stood alongside Leo. "I find the theme a bit confusing myself. Every time we do it, the meaning gets a little more elusive. Eventually, it will be meaningless."

"You mean it isn't meaningless now?"

Roberto hesitated, looked at the stage and then at Leo. "As an actor, I do not want to involve myself in directing or critiquing. It is better I act as I am told and keep my thoughts to myself."

"You know something, Roberto... for all I know the critics will love it and understand every bit, but as far as I'm concerned... well, let's say I don't think it's going to win a Pulitzer."

Extending his hand, he said, "Lieutenant, you are a generous man." Leo shook it.

"See you during the week. Thanks for the chance to see you work."

"It was my pleasure to know you were here." Said Roberto, as he turned and walked down the aisle toward the stage. Leo headed to the lobby and then the street.

It was close to nine and the crowds were moving downtown. Leo walked up Second and turned west on ninth. He was heading for the Cedar Street Cafe- once a hangout for some odd and sometimes funny people. Kerouac, Franz Kline, and many painters had made the place famous years before. Now it was just a bar with a noisy crowd trying to recreate the atmosphere of the sixties. That was tough since almost all of the patrons were under thirty. Another thing he liked about the Cedar was that it really wasn't a date place. He was always able to get a drink without having to stare at meshed couples working themselves up to the rut.

As Leo got to the corner of Stuyvesant and Third, a fight erupted from a bar across the street. Two guys swinging like crazy burst through the front door onto the sidewalk. Cheering patrons waving beer bottles followed. Figuring the last thing he would do was cross the street and try to establish order, Leo stopped to watch. One of the lugs looked like he had some training because he circled and tried to jab. The other guy was big and wanted to get in one good punch, but now, he was faced with someone who could box and the chance to get in a KO was remote. The jabber hit the big guy with a left hook and probably broke his nose for bright red blood poured out. That made the big guy angrier and even wilder. He was charging in, arms flailing and doing nothing but getting smacked. The less control he showed, the greater the likelihood he was going to get his head knocked off. The boxer was getting in more shots because the big guy was growing tired and slowing down.

The crowd loved it, but after a bit, their yelling died and they settled in like they were watching television. The big guy was probably the bar-bully and a great many locals were not unhappy to see him get his ass kicked in public. No one was going to stop this fight.

Engrossed, Leo crossed and watched from the street side of the parked cars. He smiled when he saw some of he crowd go back in the bar to bring out fresh beers. It really was the Friday Night Fights. Amidst the mayhem, though, one particular guy caught Leo's eye, a short, dark character wearing a suit. He had been one of the early cheerleaders for the big guy, but now he separated himself from the inner circle and moved to the edge. Leo watched him. Everyone else was moving with the circle- to the left- this guy was moving to the right, but he wasn't going home, instead, he very slowly pulled out a gun from inside his jacket. Leo couldn't believe it. It was like watching a movie.

Staying on the street side of the cars, Leo moved to his right and came parallel to the gunman. Crouching, he pulled the .357 from his ankle holster, leveled it and yelled loud enough to be heard over the fight.

"This is the Police. Drop that gun."

The crowd froze. Even the fighters stopped. The guy with the gun also froze as his eyes darted left to see who yelled out. He spotted Leo from the corner of his eye.

"I'm not going to fool with you. Drop that gun and don't move." Leo shouted.

It is impossible to know what people think until they behave, until they do something. Everyone is a mystery until they illustrate their position. A person's attitudes, beliefs, or values are invisible until by an action, they are demonstrated. The gunman probably figured he would have no trouble with someone fifteen feet away. Like in a bad Western movie, the guy swung to face Leo, raising his gun as he moved. What a schmuck, Leo thought. I got him covered. All I have to do is squeeze the trigger. He has to move his body, locate me for sure, aim and fire. What an asshole.

Leo shot him through the right shoulder. The bullet's impact was so great the guy spun a full circle and hurtled backwards to bounce off the building behind him. The gun he had held flew about ten feet straight up, coming to rest about where he had been standing. In the confined street, Leo's gun sounded like an exploding bomb. Nonetheless, no one moved.

Viewing the scene, Leo thought the tableau should be a competitive art form. If it were, he would have entered the scene now before his eyes. The fighters were in the middle of the sidewalk, hands up, but frozen. The blood pouring from the big guy's left nostril was the only movement. The crowd, in a circle around them, stared with mouths and eyes wide open. The only sounds were music from the bar and beer gurgling from a bottle someone had dropped.

For maybe a full minute nothing happened, then the tableau exploded. People ran in every direction. Some ran back into the bar, a few ran past Leo, while others charged up the street away from the bar. Leo had not moved. He was still in a crouch, showing little of himself. As a patrol car, all light and noise, came screaming around the corner, he straightened, holstered the gun and placed his badge in his outside top pocket. As the car screeched to a stop, he turned to face it, giving the patrol cops a good look at him and the gold badge.

The first officer out was a short Hispanic female who looked tough and capable. With gun drawn, she came up to him and asked if he was hurt. He said he was okay, but they better get EMS for the perp. The guy was sitting against the building with his left hand holding his right shoulder. The front of his suit was blood covered, as was a good hunk of sidewalk. The pistol he had been holding was about five feet away. Leo was relieved since he was sure there'd be no trouble with the shooting. There were witnesses galore and the gun was available for all to see.

Other officers arrived and took statements from the people who had gone back into the bar. After the ambulance took the wounded guy away, things quieted down. The policewoman searched the street and managed to find the shell casing from Leo's automatic. Appreciating her conscientious work, Leo invited both patrol cops into the bar and ordered cokes. They drank in silence letting the tension slip away.

After a while, the bartender leaned to Leo and said, "You better go back to the range and practice."

Surprised, Leo asked, "What do you mean. I shot him perfectly. He'll probably have nothing but a scar, unless the bone is broken."

"That's what I mean." said the bartender. "If you could shoot you would have put that bullet in his eye. What is this shoot them in the shoulder shit? Are you in the cops or the Salvation Army?" As he mouthed off, he refilled the glasses and winked at Leo and the policewoman before moving to serve other customers.

Leo rode to the precinct in the patrol car and spent an hour filling out the shooting forms and reports. Some time later, he was back in his apartment and after a shower and coffee, he went to bed. Before he fell asleep, he wondered why he hadn't shot the guy in the eye. He could have killed him and wasn't sure why he hadn't. Word would get around that he did not shoot to kill and there would be talk. There was an unwritten policy for dealing with those who attacked police and it was clear- kill them so they never got another chance.

CHAPTER 10

ANGEL SAT WATCHING TELEVISION in Carlos' place, since that was all he could manage. He had been taking any drug he could get to ease the pain, and now, four days after the 'attack', the oozing and the bleeding had stopped. Television helped. If the program interested him, he could forget what happened. Like the nurse said, there had been blood in his piss, but it had lessened and now, everything was almost as it had been. He ate and watched television, but would not go out.

Carlos had gone to Angel's room and picked up the few possessions he had accumulated, some clothes, a few old Life magazines, stereo tapes and money. The stereo tapes surprised Carlos. Aside from the some Salsa and Rock, there were several operas and a good deal of church music. There was also more than three thousand dollars.

Fed up with the show he was watching, Angel put on the stereo earphones and listened to a tape with many people singing and many instruments playing. Carlos had told him the name of the music, but he had forgotten. He loved the way the music left spaces for the singers and how the singers blended with the instruments. He was soothed and deeply moved by the sounds and once tried to explain how that felt to someone, but couldn't. All he managed to say was that the music and singing made him feel good.

A few times he tried to sing along with the tape and was happily surprised he had been able to keep up. After hearing any tape more than once, he knew what was coming and was able to join the performance. He was simultaneously pleased and ashamed that he could do that or even want to do it and never spoke about it.

With Carlos at work and not to return for several hours, there was nothing for him to do but watch television, listen to music, and look at magazines. He loved the large colored magazine pictures and Carlos said he was like a little

65

kid looking at animals at the zoo. He was surprised when Carlos told him a zoo was close by, right in Central Park.

He often thought about animals locked in cages and when he did, he wondered if they cared about being locked up. He had spoken to guys who had been in jail and they all said jail was terrible. They said being locked up like an animal was awful. They hated it. Did the animals hate it? They said there was nothing to do in jail; they fed you and you sat around. Trying to stay alive was all you did. He wondered why all the guys he knew who got out, got arrested again and went back. Angel figured that even though they said they hated jail, they did things, stupid things, so they would get caught and sent back. Angel supposed some people needed other people to take care of them. They didn't know how to be people themselves. Were the animals like that? Did they like being in cages? He wondered if they would leave if the cages were opened. One day he would open some and see for himself if they were afraid to come out. Were the animals like the jail guys and really needed to be in a cage? When I get better I'll do that, he promised himself. I'll go to the zoo, open a few cages and see what happens.

At that moment, he was in a pot-dream mood and watching a show about lifeguard girls on a beach someplace. He watched them wishing he could know girls like that. He wondered what you say to girls like that. He never talked to the ladies or girls he laid and liked the ones he paid best, for they knew what to do. They were better than the ones he screwed when he broke into places. It was better when they wanted to do it.

He stared at the TV-girls in their red bathing suits, with their big tits and round bottoms. He reached down to this cock and touched it through his pants. It was limp, dead. He massaged it with his hand trying to get a hard-on. Nothing happened. Before, those bathing suit girls always gave him a hard-on, so he knew something was not right. Concerned and bewildered, he put on the earphones, closed his eyes and leaned back letting the music and the pot take him away. I'll get a hard-on later, he told himself. I'll tell Carlos to go to the bar on 43rd and bring back that girl with the red hair. He had once paid her fifty bucks and she made him feel good.

He saw the red haired girl in his mind. She was small and pretty. He didn't like big girls because he wasn't big. His mother was big. He saw his mother in his mind, but she looked far away. It had been a long time. When he was little she went away and never came back. He lived with his mother's sister for a while and then lived alone, sleeping wherever he could and taking whatever he wanted. He learned that to live you had to have money and he learned how to get money. He didn't like to steal, but didn't know another way to get things. If he didn't steal and take money from people, he would not be able to live. He had learned how to get things because he wanted to live.

Angel stayed in the apartment even though Carlos had tried to get him to go out for food or to a movie. He had constantly refused, but two weeks later he told Carlos he wanted to go to a church.

"Whadaya mean go to a church?"

"Man, I want to go to a church. I want to go and see it all. I been listen' to that music and I want to hear it for real. I want to hear it without earphones... for real."

"I don't know if the church on 47th got music like on the tape. That tape music is for big churches with plenty of people."

"I don't give a fuck. Please find out where is that music. I don't know how to find out."

"Okay, okay, man. Take it easy. I'll find out. I'll call the church on 47th."

Two days later, a Sunday, they walked into St. Patrick's Cathedral. Neither knew what was happening, but the magnitude of the building, the windows, and the crowds of people struck them. Angel thought it was going to be like Yankee Stadium when he heard the first organ notes, but when the chorus joined, he knew it would be different. He was transfixed.

Listening to the chorus, he lost track of where he was. The singing was magic. He felt the music in his bones. It was in him. He closed his eyes and let the throbbing organ and the swirl of voices move through his body. The sounds pulsed in him, blasting from one leg to the other, from one arm to the other. It was like the wind rushing through his chest into his head down his arms and into his fingers. He thought he saw bolts of lightning shoot from his fingers- bolts of lightning shaped like musical notes. The music was in him, coming out through his fingers. He wanted to stay forever and become part of it. He wanted to take the music in and keep it. How could he keep it in him? How could he do that?

Unconcerned with his lack of understanding of the Mass, Carlos sat amidst the crowd. To him, the words and music were bullshit and he thought about girls who had come into Marty's the day before. They were from the neighborhood and wanted harmonicas. He had waited on them and sold them Hohner Marine bands. One of the girls, a blond, really turned him on and he was sure she was also getting hot. He was hoping she would pass by or come into the store after school on Monday. Thinking about her was giving him a hard-on that quickly dissolved when he realized where he was. He looked at the people in the church. What did they want here, he wondered. They didn't come for the music, like Angel. He glanced at his pal and thought he was getting a little weird with all this shit about music. What the fuck are we doing here in this goddamn church, he asked himself

Glancing to his right, he was surprised when a few people he eye-contacted smiled at him. Most of them were focused on a robed guy in a little box that stuck out over the seats. That guy didn't look like any priest Carlos had seen before. He wore some outfit. It was gold and white and shined. Probably silk, he thought. Expensive. He had once tried to buy a silk shirt on 42nd, but had to pass because it was too expensive. If that guy up there—if his clothes are silk, then he's a big time dude. He probably made plenty—and it was a great gig—with only one Sunday a week.

He looked at the interior trying to put a price on the sconces, murals and fixtures. He knew Marty could make a good buck from this stuff. Then he thought of the book—the book Angel took from the priest. It had all that stuff about priests screwing around. He remembered what he had told Angel that these church people don't want the world to know about bad priests. It would upset and piss everyone off and the Church didn't want these people pissed off. The Church wants them happy, 'cause when they're happy they give bucks. Keep them happy. Keep them givin'.

He had not yet worked out a plan for doing what he said he would do. He thought about bringing Marty in, but he knew Marty would win big and that he and Angel would lose. Sitting in the pew, with the chorus praising the Lord, he decided to do the deal himself. He was ready and he was smart enough to bring it off and make a big score without Marty or anyone else.

He looked at Angel and saw his pal's eyes were closed and he was swaying with the music. It was hard to accept that such a hard-nosed killer would be so gooey about church music. Watching him, he considered and then rejected cutting Angel out of any deal. He would do right and give him half the dough because that's fair and because Angel made him nervous. It wasn't wise to fuck with a guy who'd stab you as quickly as he'd buy you coffee. Also, he knew Angel was the perfect guy to watch his back.

With his mind made up, he was able to look around with a confidence normally absent. He recognized why people were so fucked up about religion. The priests were smart—they ask who put everything on Earth and where did it all come from? Since nobody has answers, any wise guy who comes along and says, "I got answers and I got questions you ain't thought about yet." When someone comes along with a con like that, people buy it. They say, "Wow, I have no answers for anything, so if you say you do, I better listen." Damn, you listen long enough and they got you. Once they got you, that's it. From that point you believe what they say about everything.

Energized, Carlos listened to the guy in the box and realized he was putting all these people down. He was telling them they were sinners and that they needed to get a grip and they could be great if they ousted sin. He wondered if they believed the bullshit? All that crap about heaven, hell and sin. He remembered his mother telling him God told priests to eat fish on

Friday. She smacked him when he said it was a crock. He asked her why would God, who was so cool and powerful, get involved with little pass-ass things like fish on Friday? He remembered asking her why such a cool God would let there be war and junkies and poor people all over the fucking place? His mother freaked and threw him out of the house. Religion was never again mentioned.

Now he knew he was ready to deal with religion. Now he was going to score some dollars. As he looked around the church, he grew envious. This is some place and some racket. Start a new religion- make a bundle. Then it hit him that the guys on TV didn't start anything new, they just joined in and jumped on the gravy train. You don't have to start anything new, he told himself. All you do is tell people they are great and that God loves them and they'll pay so you can keep on telling them. Not a bad game, he chuckled to himself. It's a fairy tale for kids. The mom tells the kids they're sweet and wonderful and everyone loves them and the kids want to hear that story over and over. It doesn't matter if the story is a damn lie. As long as the story makes people feel good, they'll want to hear it again. He almost laughed aloud. It's like smokin' dope. As long as you feel good, you're ready for more. It's the kind of thing a guy like Marty would dream up.

When the service came to an end, Carlos and Angel filed out with the beaming audience. Near one of the 5th Avenue exit doors, a young priest was saying good-bye to those leaving. Carlos figured this was a good time to start his plan. When he got to the priest, he asked, "I wonder if you could give me some information?"

The Priest smiled. "What sort of information?"

"Well, if I had something important to the Church here, who would I talk to about reachin' a price for the item?"

Surprised, the Priest asked, "What sort of item? What do you mean?"

"That ain't important. What is... is who would I talk to? Who makes big deal decisions?"

"I don't understand you. Do you mean a painting or a statue?"

"It don't matter what I mean. All I want to know is who could say 'yes' to payin' money for something the church might want? I need the name of a guy with clout."

Perplexed and mystified, the priest said, "To be honest, I don't know, but I can find out. Why don't you give me your name and number and I'll call when I find out."

"That's cool," said Carlos. "But I think it'd be better if I call you. You give me your number."

The priest took a small card from his jacket pocket. "Here... this is the

Church's general number. Call and ask for me, Father Barry. I should be able to tell what you want to know by tomorrow."

"Fine. I'll call you tomorrow."

Though obviously uneasy, the priest said, "It's been my pleasure," as Carlos and Angel walked past him into the street.

When Carlos started speaking to the Priest, Angel wondered what was going on, but it took merely moments for him to realize Carlos was talking about the book. After walking a block in silence he asked, "You was talkin' about the book I got, right?"

"Right you are, Angel, and I know we can turn that book into cash, but we got to be smart. We can't let them know where we are or who we are 'cause they'll come and zap us and take the book. We got to be nice and sweet and very, very smart."

"Do you really think that book is worth money?"

"Angel, I got no idea, but I'm gonna call and talk to the big guy. When I tell him what I got and that I want cash for it, he'll tell me what it's worth."

"Hey, Carlos, what the fuck? What if the guy tells you he don't give a shit, but because he's a nice guy, he'll give you ten bucks for it? Is that it? We get ten bucks?"

Carlos stopped and turned to face Angel. "Listen to me. If that guy speaks to me, it means he's interested. And if he's willin' to pay me ten bucks or even five, that means he wants that book. If he'll pay ten dollars, he'll pay ten thousand."

"You think so?" Angel asked, his voice filled with admiration. "You really think so?"

"Trust me, pal. Trust me."

CHAPTER 11

WHEN LEO GOT TO his desk he found a message. "Leo- call Dep. Chief Reynolds, NOW." Leo knew Reynolds had info about the new assignment to Public Security. He was still not sure if he wanted out of Ballistics and into Dignitary Protection. What was that? He wondered. Babysitting wives of UN big shots while they play poker at a private club? No sir, I'll stay in Ballistics if that's what it is.

O'Brien, Reynolds' Sergeant, put him through when Leo mentioned his name.

"Leo, my boy, it is a distinct pleasure to hear from you."

"Good morning to you, Chief. How can I help?"

"That's the attitude, Leo, not 'waddyawan', but 'how can I help'. Leo, with a thousand like you, this Department could really do the job. Christ, we'd be the best friggin Department in the world."

"I think we do a pretty good job already."

"Well, I won't argue with ya, my boy. Let's just say we ain't knockin' a hunnert percent in every area, okay?" Not waiting for a reply, he continued. "Leo, I want you to report to Dignitary Protection, today. The people over there are waitin' for you with an assignment."

"You understand, Chief, that won't give me time to clear out my desk."

"Not to worry. When the assignment is finished, you can go back and clean out."

Willing to give it a try, Leo said, 'Okay, but there is one other item needing attention."

"You are referrin' no doubt, to the gunplay from last night and to the Shootin' Review Board's looksee, right?"

Leo smiled, realizing why he respected the man. He was one smart cookie. "Right you are, Chief. Your finger in every pie...right?"

"Well, Leo, let's say I like to know what's goin' on and people know that, so they ship me summaries of every goddamn thing that happens, no matter what. Everyday, without fail, I know what happened the day before."

"That's something I won't forget. With your memory and the summaries, I bet I can ask you anything and get an answer."

"I always said you're a smart boy. I'm more positive about that now."

"Are you sure the Shooting Review is not going to be a problem?"

"I'll take care of them for now, although you'll eventually have to give a statement."

"No problem. It was straight forward... no fatalities. I even managed to say 'Drop that gun.'"

"The reports I have describe it exactly as such. By the way, what gun did you use? Did it comply with Department specifications?"

"How come you ask?"

"Well, the policewoman who found the casing said it didn't look regulation to her, was it?"

"Technically, it is."

A slight pause. "Now... what does that mean?"

"I shot the perp with a .357 auto I carry."

"A .357 auto? I didn't know there was such a thing."

"It's a custom job I had made up. A very sweet shooter and most important.... 357 is still technically .38 caliber."

"Once again I tip my hat."

"Throughout my life, Chief, I have tried hard not to create problems for myself. There are always enough without me adding to the pile."

"My sentiments exactly.... So... as I said, I'll take care of the Shooting Board, you get over to the new unit and check in with Captain Hoffheimer."

"I don't know him."

"He's a quiet sort. European background. Came here, got a Ph.D.- taught at Baruch for a spell, then jumped to the force. First rate. Speaks more goddamn languages than anyone I ever met. Go to dinner with him and let him order. No matter what joint you're in, he orders in that language. Gets all sort of free stuff. Lotsa fun."

"I hope this works out, Chief. I wouldn't want any screw up to reflect on you."

"Don't be talkin' like that, Leo. Believe me, you're goin' to love this assignment. It's an intellectual challenge- that crowd out-thinks the bastards. They do not go around like cowboys and shoot it out in the streets.... they use their noggins."

Cowboy shootouts—if the shoe fits, Leo thought. "I do hope they're armed."

"Now, Leo. I didn't mean that personally. You aren't John Wayne and yes, they do carry guns. They are real policemen and women."

"Okay, Chief. I'll wrap up here and go over, but before I go, I want to make sure I thank you for thinking of me. No matter how this turns out, I want you to know I am deeply appreciative of your interest and faith. You've always been in my corner and knowing that has helped me in my career and also, most important, knowing you think well of me helps when I think about myself. You've been a friend and I thank you."

After a pause, the Chief said, "Leo, it's easy to be your friend... go see Hoffheimer."

It was simple turning operations over to Sullivan, since Ballistics rarely responded to emergencies. While in charge, Leo developed procedures that were so sensible not following them was difficult. All his work and planning had actualized and he was pleased to be leaving a very efficient operation that would run itself as long as no one tinkered.

When Chief Reynolds first mentioned Dignitary Protection, Leo needed a Department manual to get the facts on the Public Security Section. The manual said its mission was "to provide the Department with intelligence information and recommendations in order to preserve the peace and deploy manpower for conditions which may impact upon the operation of this city, including the protection of public officials, visiting dignitaries, and members of the service assigned to covert investigations. This section is comprised of the Dignitary Protection Unit, the Protective Research Unit, and the Special Services Unit." Additional details covered the Section's liaisons with government agencies and the diplomatic community, which, Leo guessed, were the feds and international police groups. He was legitimately impressed with the description, but most intrigued with its task of recording, evaluating, and if necessary, eliminating threats to officials and dignitaries. That sounded like real police work.

As he left the Ballistics Unit for uptown, he had James Bond movie moments running through his head. He didn't expect desk jockeying to be involved and then had a disturbing thought. What if that's exactly what they want? What if they want him to smooth out Dignitary Protection as he had Ballistics... he hoped that was not their plan.

He wanted some action and wondered if the recent shooting was the impetus. Street action was okay, but Leo really wanted some brainwork. He wanted to think perps into custody rather than shoot them into a grave. "It's the routine." he said aloud and sheepishly looked around. None on the street heard or if they did, they didn't show it. It is the routine, he thought, the seductive comfort of ably doing your job. Once you've got the routine, the challenge is gone. Then it becomes comfortable... a velvet trap. He thought of something he recently read- if you're doing the same thing for twenty years, it's time for something else because whether you know it or not, you're bored.

That's true, he thought. He wasn't burned out and most who say they are aren't either. They are merely bored out of their minds. They lack the challenge, the risks, the unknowns that existed when they started whatever it is they're still doing. He remembered the excitement of each morning's line up when he first joined the force. It was a great, endless adventure. It was fun. But suddenly, it's no longer fun. It's sameness that kills.

As he walked, he studied the people he passed. Some of them looked eager and coiled, ready to leap. So many others looked like they were marching to their death. I guess they are, he thought. And probably, many know it, but they're afraid to make a change. "Fear doth make cowards of us all." Shakespeare hit it. What's the prize for living on the safe side? Afterlife or not, death is at the door. Variety can't hurt. He realized that he owed Reynolds more than a thank you. Was he that smart? Did he see me heading for a sad and lonely retirement? Did he push this reassignment to save me from sitting on my ass waiting for death? Maybe he is that smart. Well, I hope so, Leo thought, because I'm ready for Hoffheimer and Dignitary Protection... whatever the hell it is.

The Dignitary Protection Unit was located on First Avenue across from the United Nations Building. Its location was generally secret and the building itself looked like an ordinary, well-maintained townhouse. He walked in and showed his ID to the plainclothes guy at the door who was trim and fit and looked like a movie cop.

The entrance foyer led to a long corridor. To Leo's immediate right was an elevator and a small windowed door to a staircase. Further on there were doors on both sides of the corridor. In front of each was a different color mat. There was blue, gold, and brown on the right and red, black and green on the left. Six doors- six offices? The floor was black and white marble and the walls were dark wood paneled. Gold-framed paintings, individually lit were centered on the panels. What furniture he could see looked antique and well preserved. Aside from the wall sconces, there was a small crystal chandelier. This was obviously not a South Bronx police station.

He was surprised that as he studied the interior, the plainclothes studied him and his ID. That surprise was replaced with pride. This unit dealt with serious, international situations and was as different from shooting crazies in the street as Velveeta was from Brie. The plainclothes doorman was young, polite, and could have been on the Cambridge rowing team. This is the movies, Leo thought.

"Captain Hoffheimer is expecting you, Lieutenant Flower. You can get to his office via the stairs behind you or you can use the elevator. He's on the second floor- first office to the left of the elevator." Leo nodded.

"You can call me Smitty." When Leo remained silent, he added, "I'm a Sergeant." Smiling, Leo said, "That's exactly the question I was asking myself."

"You know, sir, that after being on the door for a while, you get a sense of what people are going to ask or say. Their choices are more limited than you'd imagine."

"Limited?"

"Well... you could have asked anything at all, but that's unlikely. You might have asked about my tie, or suit, but I don't think so. The surprise on your face when I studied your ID was the same as it is for every new arrival. They're expecting a typical precinct house with stray dogs, and bleeding perps in the reception area. This unit is different. We are not typical. I knew you realized that and when I saw it in your face, I knew you'd next be thinking about me. Who is this guy? A civilian, a regular PO, an auxiliary volunteer, who? Right?"

Leo smiled. "Did all that show on my face or are you just very, very smart?"

"I'd be a fool not to say 'yes' to both choices." Saying that, he smiled and resettled himself on a tall stool that allowed him to rest his weight on its edge.

"Are you alone at this post?"

"Not exactly." His eyes moved up and Leo followed them to see four small TV cameras at the ceiling corners.

"Smitty, I've a feeling this is going to be a very interesting assignment."

"No question about that, Sir. None at all."

Leo turned and opened the door to the staircase. He expected to find creaking wood, instead he found concrete and steel treads and steel railings. Two short fights and he was at a hardwood door with a brass 2 at eye level. Going into a narrow corridor, he passed the elevator, knocked and opened the door. It looked like a military orderly room. A desk to the immediate right, two more to the left, bookcases and file cabinets in the remaining space, and windows on the far wall. The two left side desks had men at them. Seated at the desk to the right was a very pretty young woman who looked up at him and smiled.

"Lieutenant Flower, I'm Officer Melendez. The captain is waiting for you. That door." She pointed to a door at the back left. Leo walked to it nodding to the two men at the desks. They nodded in return and went back to the paperwork as he passed. He knocked, heard "Come."

Entering, he saw a suave looking, almost bald man of about fifty seated at a large desk. He wore a light gray suit, beige shirt and slate gray tie. As Leo walked to the desk, the man rose and with hand extended came out from behind the desk. "Good morning, Lieutenant Flower, I am Henry Hoffheimer and I'm delighted you are to be with us. Please sit." Leo headed for a small leather sofa Hoffheimer gestured to and sat. Hoffheimer sat across from him in a chair covered in similar leather and asked, "Well, what do you think?"

Leo glanced around the office taking in the drapes, the leather furniture, the massive desk, the brass lamps, and the book cases filled with leather bound volumes. "I think I walked into a movie set, since my office at Ballistics is all Army surplus. It must have been like this for troops who left Viet Nam, went to sleep there and woke up in San Francisco."

"Yes." he said softly. "I see how you might think that. We're not typical City police. We are almost an extension of Interpol and fortunately, have what most European police forces have- money. As they, we are select and see no gain from scrimping. If every moment is possibly the last, it should be a good moment- eh?"

"That's a cheery thought."

Hoffheimer laughed. "Don't let me upset you. Ever since this unit was formed, there has never been an actual bombing or threat on our offices. In fact, most of our playmates have no idea where we are located."

Leo extended his arm and rapped three times on the side table. "Let's hope the luck stays."

Hoffheimer stood, walked to the window and then turned to face Leo. "Let me explain why you have been assigned to us. Chief Reynolds keeps alert for a good prospect, since we need smart people who can think on their feet, who are good deskmen, able administrators, who are equally at home with a pistol or a computer, who can organize and analyze well, who are good planners, and maybe most important, people who are loyal and dedicated to the morality we represent. The chief assured me you are all that and more." He abruptly stopped, came back to the chair and sat.

Leo was pleased, but knew he wasn't Superman. Hoffheimer smiled. "Your face tells me you do not think as highly of yourself as others do. Avoid those feelings, Lieutenant, you are a very able policeman and we need your talents." Hoffheimer stood and continued. "Everyone in this unit is intelligent and capable. You will like to work with us... come outside and let me introduce you to some of the others."

The two men and Officer Melendez stood as Hoffheimer and Leo came through the door. It's like I'm back in the Army, thought Leo. He was introduced to the three. Officers Rose, Gottlieb and Melendez. As Hoffheimer mentioned some of their responsibilities, Leo noticed a long strip of paper on

Gottlieb's desk. Following Leo's eyes, Hoffheimer asked, "Why do you find that strip of paper interesting, Lieutenant?"

"I've seen something like that before." Looking at Gottlieb he asked, "Where'd you get it?"

Gottlieb looked at Hoffheimer, who nodded. "We found it in the pocket of a dead man who we think was a courier for an organization bringing in guns and narcotics. They are a Central American group and they've vowed to kill any elected politician who opposed their objectives."

Leo picked up the strip and examined it. It was about thirty-six inches long, an inch wide and had English letters running its entire length. The letters made no sense to Leo as he stared at it. Hoffheimer came alongside and said, "We presume it's some sort of code, but no one understands it. The cryptographers know it's a code, but haven't yet broken it." Leo looked around the room and then at Officer Melendez.

"Officer Melendez, would you do me a favor?" She looked at him and nodded.

"Please come over here, take off your jacket and roll up your sleeve."

She approached Leo taking off her jacket as she walked. "Which sleeve?"

"It doesn't matter." Leo answered.

When she was alongside him, he reached down, took her arm by the hand and held it out. Then he took the strip of paper and starting at her wrist, wrapped it around her arm in a spiral until the paper reached her bicep. The four of them stared at him.

"What exactly are you doing?" Hoffheimer asked.

"I may be breaking your code problem, Captain." Then after a quick look at Melendez's outstretched arm, Leo said, "No. I'm wrong. I have broken your code problem."

"Broken?" the four of them said almost simultaneously.

"Yes, take a look." He held out Melendez's arm, making sure the series of letters were visible to Hoffheimer. Rose and Gottlieb spun around to get the same angle. Running down Melendez's arm was the series of letters that now, made sense.

BKLYNNVYYRDMAYTWOONEAM.

Hoffheimer stared at the letters and then he looked at Leo. "How did you know about this?"

"Cryptography is sort of a hobby and when I saw that strip of paper, it reminded me of something I read a while ago. This is a very early piece of cryptography. I think it is called a *scytale*. Invented by the Spartans. If you wind a length of paper around a round object and then write your message from the top down, it can be read when you rewind it around something similar. If you fill in other letters, the original message disappears amongst them until you wind it around an object similar or close to the original object. I figured they used something round to make the original and Melendez's arm seemed the smoothest, roundest thing here, so I guessed lucky... and I was lucky the message was in English."

Hoffheimer, still staring at the message said, "Lucky? I think not, Lieutenant. You have just given us the edge for which we've been searching. This is vital, truly vital information." He turned to Leo. "Lieutenant, if you do nothing else while you're here, that'll be fine with me."

He unwrapped the paper from Melendez's arm and headed for his office. Talking over his shoulder as he walked, he said, "Stay here, all of you. I've got to make a telephone call and then I'm taking everyone to lunch. Lieutenant Flower is the guest of honor."

CHAPTER 12

LEAVING ABE AND CARLOS in front, Marty lounged in the back dreaming of his steady customers, the ones who showed up Friday nights and all day Saturday, ready to sell anything for some weekend cash. The regulars who made it their business to 'acquire' the stuff Marty bought for very little money.

Having a good idea of the worth of almost any item, Marty bought it at a fraction of the retail price. The sellers, of course, always had a choice. Leave with what they brought in to sell or hand it over for peanuts. Legitimate sellers were insulted by Marty's offers, but the sellers of swag, the petty thieves, didn't care about being swindled—they were after cash. They took what he offered and left smiling. Marty did very well buying and selling watches, guns, instruments, electronic gear, office machines, jewelry, cameras, golf clubs—anything that turned an immediate dollar.

Few from Madison Avenue bothered to check the efficacy of their ad campaigns. Marty was an expert. He knew which ads worked and which did not. Thieves would never steal a Brand X anything no matter how easy. Brand X items lacked the recognition that equaled desirability. An item not coveted was worthless. Because of that, the knock-off industry was running full tilt. During a run on name brand watches, Marty and Abe agreed that the only right place to buy a Rolex was at the factory in Switzerland. Buying anywhere else left you open for a counterfeit. When Marty started, his basic plan was to buy low and sell high. Now, he added another element to that business plan- know the difference between real and fake or get screwed.

The major swag hauls that got TV and newspaper space never mattered to Marty. He handled the missing typewriter, the VCR that vanished, the walking TV camera and the hundreds of similar items that were lifted and turned into smiling dollars. As in every major city, the New York police were unable to keep track of the thousands of items stolen daily. It was a rare item that was returned to its original owner.

Very few people kept track of what they owned. The police need a serial number to track and reclaim anything stolen, but few noted that number. At one time, serial numbers were etched onto an item and made tracing easy for the police. Of late, however, serial numbers were on a removable metal tape and when it was pulled off, all identification potential vanished. With the serial number removed, every camera looked like every other camera. One might think the manufacturers were making it easy for the crooks.

Many victims had seen their merchandise in Marty's windows, but were unable to claim it, since with no serial number they couldn't prove ownership. Marty's records proved he bought the item "as is"- without a serial number. It was legal, but sometimes, when the victim brought the police and made a scene, Marty would relent and offer to sell it back at a meager discount from his asking price.

But since it was Monday, Marty left everything to Abe and Carlos. At the moment, Abe was standing to the left of the front door with Carlos to his right. They looked like guards. Carlos was hanging around the front so he could watch the lobby area. He was waiting for the schoolgirl he had seen on Saturday. Abe merely liked to watch the crowd as people made their way up 8th.

As was his style, Abe stood with his hands clasped behind him as he slowly rocked front to back. He was dressed in his usual work outfit. Dark brown slacks, dark brown wing tips, white silk shirt, tan silk tie, and brown and white hounds tooth jacket. Everything custom tailored, for he had long before learned it was impossible to carry a pistol or hold several cigars in a jacket that was not specifically designed for such details. Off the rack clothing lacked the style and fit he demanded. Since Abe was never without a .38 auto and a pocket of Cuban cigars, he wore hand made clothes and kept custom tailors constantly working. Quite unlike Carlos, who was happy to wear the latest fad item.

Looking at Carlos, Abe asked, "Hey, why the hell are you hanging around the front all day? Are you expecting a delivery of something? You're watching every female that goes by like she had winning lotto numbers written on her legs."

"Don't be a pain in the ass, man. I'm waiting for a chick."

"What woman in her right mind would waste time on a spic like you?"

"Hey man, don't you call me a spic. I don't like that."

"Be serious. What does it matter what I call you, you're still an uneducated and nutty spic who wants to do nothing but get laid, right?"

Carlos smiled and waved his hand. "Abe, you are one fuckin' crazy bastard."

Abe stepped closer to Carlos and they watched the 8th Avenue crowd pass by, but paid closer attention to those who stopped to look into the merchandise crammed windows. Suddenly, a group of young girls stopped to look at the jewelry and watches. The young blond was among them and Carlos went on point like a well-trained dog.

"Oh, that's it," said Abe. "You're looking for twat. Hey, you like that little chippie?"

"She's cool, man, I think she's great."

"Carlos, she's a baby. Why do you want to waste your time with a little girl? All you can do with that is go to jail. Are you crazy or stupid...what?"

"I want to get laid, man. That's what I want to do with that. What do you think?"

"I think you're nuts. Screwing' little girls is not what sex is all about."

"Hey, old man. Don't be tellin' me about sex. I think you better have a good memory if you're gonna talk to me about gettin' laid." Carlos said, bending at the waist and laughing.

As Carlos stared, the blond girl walked to the door, smiled at him and then rejoined her girlfriends. As the little group walked away, she turned, looked at Carlos, and mouthed, 'I'll see you tomorrow'. Carlos lit up with a big toothy grin and smacked Abe on the arm.

"You see that, man? You see that? I'm gonna stick it to her this weekend. You wait. That little bitch is mine."

"Screwing little kids is dumb. Why don't you go upstairs to the hookers. They know what to do."

"I ain't gonna fuck no hooker. I want a virgin."

Exasperated, Abe backed up a step and bit down on his cigar. "Tell me something... all you do is fuck every girl you get your hands on and all you do when you're not screwing is tell me that you want nothing but virgins. Are you nuts? If you and your crazy spic pals don't stop, there won't be any virgins on the entire West Side."

Carlos laughed. "Don't you worry, Abe. There's always a lot of virgins... always." He hesitated for a second and then added, "Shit man... I'm gonna marry a virgin, you'll see."

"Marry! You? With that?" Abe almost shouted. "You think you're going to marry that little blond, huh? That little girl hasn't the brains to come in from the rain. Marry? Come on."

"I ain't gonna marry that blond. I'm gonna fuck that little blond. I'm gonna marry a virgin. That bitch ain't no virgin."

"Well, well that's interesting." Abe blew smoke in the air. "Tell me, how are you going to find a virgin if all you do is spend time with little girls like that. How are you going to meet a virgin, enroll in nursery school?"

"Very funny, very funny." Carlos said, smiling. "Look, Abe...I ain't got no answer for that, but I know what I'm gonna do. Believe me, I'm gonna marry a virgin."

Angel had watched two soap operas and in the middle of the third, wondered why he couldn't live like the people he was watching. What was it, he wondered, that made those people so lucky? Why were they able to get that stuff... all those beautiful clothes and the beautiful women? Everything was pretty. He looked at the chair he sat in and the other furniture in Carlos' living room and wondered why Carlos didn't have stuff like on the TV show. Then Angel realized it wasn't just money. He thought of the thousands of dollars in his box in the bedroom. "I got money," he said aloud. "I got money to buy things."

A character in the program had just entered a room and slowly walked to and sat in a soft chair. Angel stared at the chair. I got the money. I could buy a chair like that lady is sitting in, but I don't know where to get it. I don't even know what color to buy. "It's not just the money." He said aloud. "It's that I don't know shit."

Since he had been at Carlos', he had done nothing but watch television. Never before had he done that. He was usually in the streets, in the movies, in the poolrooms and bowling alleys, passing the day with no thoughts about anything. Occasionally, he would pick up girls, take them back to his room and get laid, but that was before he got cut. Now, he realized he didn't want to go back to his room. It wasn't even a room. He had carved out a living space in the basement storeroom of a restaurant. The people from the restaurant had worked a deal with him. They would let him use the space if he would wash dishes when they needed extra help. They didn't charge him for the space, but they didn't pay him for the work. He thought he got the better of the deal since it was always warm in the kitchen and he ate for free. Anyway, most of the time, he hung out in the back of the restaurant, so it all seemed okay to him.

Television was making a difference in his life, he realized. One of the stations had a kids program on in the morning with big puppets—he thought they were funny. Each morning he watched that program. Some of the things they talked about reminded him of school and he was surprised that he could remember and say the alphabet. Lately, he found he was beginning to understand how words were made with letters and he had memorized a few of the sounds and was happy he could remember what letters you used to make those sounds. Carlos laughed when he told him about the program, but said it was good that Angel watched it and that Angel would learn to read if he watched it every day. Learning to read had never mattered, now he thought it did, but didn't know why. He sat watching the pretty lady on television wondering why it mattered.

He had avoided thinking about what happened, but each day he felt he should think about it. It cost a lot of money for Carlos to get a doctor to come to the apartment, but they worked it out and the guy came and removed the bandages and took off the cast. In his entire life, Angel had never met a guy with no balls. He heard about some guy whose wife cut off his cock, but nobody said anything about balls. What is going to happen to me, he wondered. What does it mean to have no balls? He recalled the Doctor telling him that injections could fix things. He had no idea what that meant, but the doctor didn't seem worried. In the hospital, they talked like he had cut his finger. No big deal, they said, but he still had never heard of any guy with no balls.

Maybe it was a big deal. Since it happened his life had changed. He didn't want to go to his place. He wanted to stay with Carlos and he wanted to go back to the church to hear more music. He was watching TV and learning things. Many things were happening that didn't happen before. Maybe it was a big deal to get your balls cut off.

The program he was watching ended and another began. He pressed the remote and searched for something else. The number of programs amazed him, and he watched all day and night. There was always something to watch. He stopped when he came across a man sitting at a piano. The man was telling someone about the songs he had written and he played some of them. Angel listened and watched and thought one song was very beautiful. The man hummed along as he played and Angel joined in and hummed along also. He took deep breaths and hummed louder. It was fun and it was easy, since he knew what sounds were coming. He heard the song only once, but knew what sounds were coming and didn't have to think about it. Maybe he could learn to sing and read. There was so much he wanted to learn. How would he do it? How do you learn, he asked himself. Could he go back to school? Was that possible?

The night before Carlos had asked him if he wanted a new knife and he said he could pick one up at the store or buy one for him. Angel said he would let him know. He had never been without a knife, but now he wasn't sure he wanted to do all that anymore. The more he thought, the more he realized all of this was a big deal. That something really had happened. His balls had been cut off and his life had changed. He knew that now. Now he wanted to learn things. He wanted to sing. He didn't care about a new knife. He had changed, but no longer knew who he was.

CHAPTER 13

THEY WENT TO *THE Bagatelle,* a small Italian place on East 43rd between First and Second. It was new to Leo, but matched many places he did know with its carpets, soft lighting, piano jazz, and theatre types handling everything. He always thought these places oblivious to real time. At two in the afternoon or two in the morning, they looked the same, sounded the same, even the customers were the same. Leo was happy to see Hoffheimer wasn't a cheapskate.

Looking around as they entered, he saw quite a few small tables with cooing pairs huddling close. They all looked married, but just not to each other. Even the staff looked guilty, since they knew they would immediately quit if a decent role came along. Leo liked this sort of place since he thought it the real New York City—what the tourist doesn't see. At that moment, he knew Broadway was jammed while the street outside *The Bagatelle* was deserted.

"Are you fussy about food?" Hoffheimer asked. "No." Leo answered.

Hoffheimer signaled a waiter and said, "The usual."

No one was talking and Leo figured it wasn't his part to generate conversation, so he watched. Hoffheimer sampled some wine from a bottle of red with a professional confidence an amateur endlessly seeks. When he nodded, the waiter filled glasses, but before Leo could sip, he heard a soft ringing sound. Hoffheimer put his glass down and took out his cell phone. He listened and then said, "We'll be back in about forty-five minutes."

"That was Smitty checking in." He announced to the table. They nodded and Leo presumed it was standard procedure to know where everyone was all the time. No doubt about this being a different type of unit. Hoffheimer swallowed some wine and said, "Leo, before you leave today, don't forget to check with Smitty for an equipment package- that is- if you intend to come on board." Leo started to respond, but Hoffheimer put up a hand. "Don't answer now. Later this afternoon, you can tell me your decision." Leo nodded.

Hoffheimer took another drink. "Leo, this is not the usual police unit. However, our work is not necessarily any more dangerous than the usual. It is different and it demands a different protocol and a different operative." He gestured to Rose, Gottlieb and Melendez. "These people are hand picked. They are loyal and dedicated to our task." Then he paused, smiled at them and they smiled back. This is like a little family, Leo thought. Is that why Reynolds moved me over here? Are these people the replacements for my loss?

"I'm quite good about people," Hoffheimer continued, "and you seem to be the perfect candidate. Chief Reynolds said you are bright, imaginative, not afraid to venture a guess, willing to be wrong, and capable of assuming leadership. I have seen nothing to contradict and much to support his assessment. What I haven't seen and cannot see are your desires."

He was about to speak, but stopped as the waiter approached. After the salads were distributed and the waiter moved away, he continued. "Susan," he smiled at Melendez, "would you tell Leo a bit about us?" Leo thought Susan Melendez was a very nice name.

She put down her fork and looked at Leo. I bet she's going to smile, Leo thought. One happy family. Everybody smiles. Everybody's happy. Is all this bullshit?

She looked him straight in the eye- no smile. "We regard what we do as serious business. It isn't a fun job, but it's satisfying. That is of course, when we win. It's like a chess game. Sometimes we score an easy win, sometimes we don't. Our major problems are international terrorists. They are unafraid, dedicated, and often seek martyrdom. The key word to describe us all- them and us- is dedicated."

"Yes." Hoffheimer interrupted. "Dedication is exactly the right word. You see, Leo, the typical City police officer is married and a parent. Because of that circumstance, many of them are less than willing to leap from bed at three AM. I will not call them nine to five policemen, that would be unfair, but they work their shift and want overtime if they go beyond. That's fine. Simply put, we do not operate that way."

"That's true." Rose said. "No one in the unit is married, but being single is not a requirement, it just worked out that way. We don't put in for overtime and work when necessary. Hours are not a criterion- assignments are started and they are completed." He had a rough, low-pitched voice that sounded like he'd been at the stadium drinking beer and cheering longer than he should have.

Leo held up a hand, stopping Rose. "Look," he said, "let me set you guys straight. If I was top dog here, and one of you was coming to work for me, I would read your personnel file. I would probably have my first assistants read it also. It would be smart for everyone to know the entire history, since their lives could be involved." He stopped and sipped some wine. "I'm guessing, of course, but I'll bet every one of you has read my file and probably knows more about me than I can remember." He stopped again and watched them. Hoffheimer, Rose and Melendez looked impassive, but Gottlieb looked a little uncomfortable. "But," Leo continued, "in case you haven't, let me hit the high points." He drank a bit more wine.

"I am sixty years old, and an orphan. Two people who were like parents to me were recently murdered. I am not married. I have no family. I am alone. I have little in the way of a social life. I could retire at any moment, but don't want to because the Department is my family, and if I did, I wouldn't know what to do with myself. Reading is my main hobby, but I go off on tangents- cryptography was a recent tangent. That's it. That's the package." He drank more wine.

Hoffheimer stared at him for a moment and then spoke softly, "Leo, if you stay with us your family will be smaller. There will not be any parent figures, but there will be sisters and brothers. We can all be that for one another." Sister and brothers, Leo thought. I never ever considered there could be sisters or brothers. My search has always been for a father and mother. 'Sisters and brothers'—it was a pleasant thought.

No one spoke, then suddenly, as if by signal, they began to eat. He wondered if his straight talk had been taken as accusatory and embarrassed them with the talk about his file. Then he realized it didn't matter; either they accept him, and he they, or it doesn't mean anything.

An excellent pasta dish with Portobello mushrooms was the main course. Coffee and midget canoles for dessert, and they were on their way back by two. Smitty greeted them and mentioned the equipment pick up to Leo- if he was coming on board. Leo thought that maybe he should think it over and decide that night. Then he laughed. Look at me making believe I have alternatives. Don't be a schmuck, he said to himself, jump at this chance. Even if everything is a lie and it becomes real drudgery, at least it'll be new drudgery. I really have no options.

"Smitty, you get that package of whatever it is ready right now. Since this unit wants me, I'd be an ass not to grab the opportunity. From what I've seen of the NYPD, this place is the brass ring."

"Glad to have you on the team, Sir. I really am." He extended his hand and Leo shook it. "Thank you." The others had heard the exchange and stopped moving to the elevator. Hoffheimer walked the few steps back. "Are you sure? You haven't given it a good deal of thought."

"Two and two is four. Right?"

They walked back into the main office. Rose, Gottlieb and Melendez went to their desks leaving Leo in the middle of the room. "Susan," Hoffheimer said, "put Leo in twelve and show him around, okay?"

"Certainly." She stood up and motioned for Leo to follow. As they moved to the corridor, Hoffheimer called, "Leo, before you leave today, come and see me."

Leo turned, nodded, and then followed Melendez to the last door on the other side of hallway. There was no number on it. "You're office is eight, right?"

"That's right. One through six downstairs, seven through twelve on this floor."

"What's on the third floor?"

"Let me get you set here, then we'll tour the building."

They entered number twelve and Leo flashed back to the MP Army units he knew so well. All gray or olive- a plain desk, a bookcase, three chairs, three tables and three lamps."

"Kind of plain."

"What's plain?" she asked.

"The furniture. Not you. You are certainly not plain." Her eyebrows went up. "Your file had no 'Lady's Man' entry that I recall. Are you making a pass?"

"Me? No- at least I don't think so. I wouldn't usually- I think."

"Well, you sure do sound like the man of action."

They both laughed. "Susan, I am definitely old enough to be your father and maybe even your grandfather." He hesitated. "Look, I've never been handy with women, so I'm saying I wasn't making a pass, but... it isn't a bad idea."

"Leo, you were right about us reading your file and also, while you may not be pleased to hear it, you are older than my father. "

"Oh, that's great... really great... much older?"

"No." she said, smiling.

It took about five minutes to cover what there was to say about his office and then she took him to the third floor. There were the same three numberless doors to a side, and like the other floors, there were paintings, carpets, antique tables, lamps and benches. Leo noticed the benches had a striped fabric that picked up the colors of the carpets and wall paint.

"Was this place decorated? Everything's much too coordinated to be City issue."

"The Captain did it all himself. After visiting some European groups housed in real castles, he came back and demanded more than a cement bunker. Funds were provided and he watched over everything. Generally, he gets what he wants."

She opened the first door on the left and Leo saw it was a conference room with a very large dark wood table with about twenty chairs around it. They went through a door in that room to a lounge that held a bar, soft furniture, a pool table on one side, and a Ping-Pong table on the other. Leo enjoyed looking at it. Few in the Department would believe any unit was housed in such luxury. Across the hall were two rooms devoted to technical ends. One was filled with snazzy looking electronic communications gear the other was a workshop.

"The basement is a dormitory style sleep-in with a large kitchen."

"I can't get over this," Leo said. "I could live here."

"Gottlieb and Rose almost do. When they get involved in an operation, they seldom go home. Rose says this place is nicer than his apartment. He wouldn't leave if the Captain didn't demand it."

Leo chuckled. "You know this is unexpected, but if I thought about it, I'd have realized it had to be this way. With the UN, the President, and half the world wanting to be in New York, there had to be heavyweight protection."

"We coordinate with the Secret Service, the FBI, other police and military units from all over the world. With the big radios, we can talk to anyone anywhere." She paused. "Lieutenant, it's all very glamorous, but it is hard work and at times, dangerous."

"Call me Leo..." She nodded. "Is there much activity from the UN?"

"In general, they're our biggest headache. Guarding the Federal VIP's or foreign royalty is a snap. Most problems are with UN people from little countries who are permanently pissed off 'cause they're little. They come here and try to throw their weight around. The worst of them are the ones with a religious following. They're convinced God sent them and they treat everyone like dirt." She suddenly stopped. "Maybe I shouldn't be talking so much. It's just that I never have a chance to tell anyone about all this. Everyone here knows it all."

"Please. I'm appreciative of any information and whatever you tell me goes nowhere unless it's supposed to." She smiled at him. He wished he were thirty.

As they walked down to the second floor, she told him about the gym and a private 25-foot shooting range in the sub-basement. They got back to the main office and Leo waited to talk to Hoffheimer. About ten minutes later, Hoffheimer came out of his office, saw Leo and waved him in.

"Well, Leo what do you think?"

"From what I gathered, the building and the unit are pretty much your handiwork."

"When I came on, this operation was a rest camp for drunks and misfits. The mayor and City people who needed protection had their own, so this place housed people who didn't fit anywhere. Then we had some Latin American assassinations and it became clear we needed a unit like this. I came along at just the right time."

"How will I fit in?"

"From what I've gathered, you are one of the ablest administrators in the Department and you still have street cop smarts. We need that combination in planning. What Melendez said at lunch about chess is a good analogy. We can't outshoot the crazies, but we can outthink them. Tomorrow, I'll give you some material to consider. Try to empathize and figure the other guy's moves."

"The moves...?"

"Well, let's say you're an opposition party member in a country with a newly elected prime minister and you want that guy out. How do you do it? Maybe you wait for him to come speak at the UN and you set up a scene with hookers, porno flicks- anything that will make him look perverted and discredit him back home."

"Does that sort of thing really happen or are you creating a good example?"

"Oh, no, that happens. Eating pork may be meaningless to you, but to a devout Muslim it's a disaster. Governments have toppled for less than that."

"This is very interesting. I'm glad I like puzzles; from what you're saying, I'm going to be knee deep."

"Absolutely, and more interesting is that most times you won't know what's going on. You'll know the players, the stakes, but none of the rules- and what's worse- you won't know if you were right until the game is over."

He got up from the desk and walked to the window. "Leo, if you're like the rest of us, you'll love it." He crossed back to where Leo was sitting and extended his hand. Leo took it in a firm clasp.

"Don't forget, see Smitty and pick up the equipment before you leave. We'll see you tomorrow." Leo left Hoffheimer's office and after saying good bye to the others went downstairs to pick up the mystery package.

It didn't prove to be a very interesting pile of stuff. Leo was expecting paraphernalia "Q" routinely gave to James Bond, but all Smitty gave him were some books, a cell phone, and a new ID card. Leo was offered a new pistol, a nine-millimeter, which he turned down since it wasn't mandatory. He left the building, caught the downtown bus on Second and then a cross-town on Fourteenth.

CHAPTER 14

ON THE BUS LEO reviewed what had happened and decided he was pleased. He thought he knew why the family appeal was so attractive. Being familiar with the slow toll solitary life demands, he hoped this new job would ease his isolation. At Ballistics, he worked alone in his office and when he went to hang around the labs just to talk to people, they got nervous. Most didn't like the 'boss' hanging around. He couldn't tell the guys he just wanted to talk. As a friendly gesture, he would go back to his office.

As the bus bounced along Fourteenth, Leo pictured John and Ilene. He missed seeing them less than he missed being able to talk to them. It was their voices he missed most. Their slight brogue was special, so uniquely them. He wondered if having videos would be a remedy? But if he had any, he knew he'd over-watch them, memorize every bit of sight and sound and eventually avoid them. He decided memories are better since they slowly develop into nodding smiles.

The bus screeched to a stop at Seventh and Leo walked the block to his place. Nothing in the mailbox. His phone rang as he shut his door. He answered it and heard what seemed to be a familiar voice. "Hey, Leo is that you?" He asked who was calling.

"Leo, you don't recognize my voice? I'm hurt, deeply hurt. To think I am rejected so early in our friendship." Going through the lists of voices he kept in his head, he came up blank, but felt he should know.

"Please," he said. "Let's not play games. Who is this?"

"Leo, it's Abe Rosenberg." There was a pause. "Abe from Marty's place."

"Right. I knew the voice, but I couldn't find the name."

"Am I calling at a bad time?"

"No, that's not a problem... how'd you get my number?"

"Marty gave it to me. He said you wouldn't mind- do you? Am I disturbing you?"

"No... I just wondered... What can I do for you?"

"Well, there are two things. First, I want to congratulate you for not killing that punk the other night. The papers said you had the choice."

"They were right. I could have if I wanted to."

"I knew you were a good guy. Most coppers would have finished him... nice you didn't."

"Is he a relative or a pal?"

"Nope... don't know him from Adam... just feel you're playing the cops and robbers game as it should be... following the unwritten rules."

"Lots of cops would say the rule is to finish jokers who pull guns on police."

"I can't disagree... but the guy was an amateur... a dope."

"Abe, don't forget the bullets in his gun were real. There are no amateur bullets."

"That's true, but I miss the old days when everybody knew what was what."

"I do too... now... what's the second thing?"

Abe laughed. "You're all business."

"Not really. I just didn't want you to forget you said you had two things to talk about."

"I don't forget shit. I've got the memory of a twenty year old." He paused. "You should stop smoking those things. They're not good for you." Another pause. "Not bad...how'd you know I was lighting up?"

"I'm an old timer like you and I know the telephone brings out the smokes."

"I surrender, Officer... I see a phone and I get the urge." He laughed. "You're a smart guy, Leo. That's what Marty said."

"What else did he say?"

"Amongst other pearls, he offered, was 'watch your ass with Leo'. He ain't no dummy and he'll put your ass in jail no matter how old you are.'"

"Good old Marty... okay... we covered that... now, what's the second thing?"

"Well... I thought that if you didn't have other plans, I'd take you to dinner. You pick the joint." Leo was surprised and tried to recall the last time someone took him to dinner.

"Why do you want to do that?"

"Boy oh boy, are you a cop.... No subversive motives... just a friendly gesture and a chance to make sure you grow up big and strong."

Leo thought it over. Why not? "Okay, you got a date. What time?"

"I'll pick you up at seven."

"I'm at 177 West 13th... corner of Seventh.

"I'll have the cabby honk."

"No need... tell the doorman... he'll buzz me."

"A doorman building...well... cops are doin' better than I thought."

"Sure, we're all up there with Trump."

"Heh, heh, heh... yeah.... me too. Okay... seven."

Leo hung up and thought about the call. That old guy seemed to be one sharp cookie. This could be an interesting evening.

Carlos stared at the telephone. He wanted to call, but was afraid.

"Go head, man. Call the fucker. What the hell. That book ain't doin' us no good the way it is."

"It ain't that easy, Angel. I can't say I got a book that maybe the Church'd like to buy"

"Why not? That's the scene, ain't it?"

That's just like him, Carlos thought. He knows only direct action...smart enough to know what to do.... can't see the problems...but, he's right. I got to make the call.

"Look... Carlos. I know you don't feel good about the call, but fuck... you get nervous or whatever... hang up. You're okay with your mouth. Don't sweat it... call."

Carlos smiled. He's right, man. I can do this. Looking at the card the priest gave him he dialed the number. Angel watched him... he knew it would be a big score. He smiled at Carlos.

Carlos stared at the card, then he said..."Yes, I'd like to speak to Father Barry, please."

"Please hold on."

He gave the thumbs up to Angel. "Father Barry? This is the guy who spoke to you on Sunday...remember?"

"I gave you my card, right?"

"Yeah, that's right."

"You said you had something to offer and needed a decision. What is it?"

"Look, like I said, it don't matter... all I want is the name of the guy who can pay money for somethin' I got." Carlos picked up a pencil.

"Call Monsignor Healey."

"Say that again."

"Monsignor Healey... the same number, extension 237. He can decide"

"And I can call that guy now?"

"Yes."

"Great."

"What did he say," Angel asked. "What?"

"He gave me the name of another guy... a guy who, he said, can make decisions."

"You know, these guys got a good thing and they're gonna be pissed off for us buttin' in."

"No, man, it ain't like that. They won't snuff us. They got plenty of dough and if they want that book, they'll pay. It don't mean shit for them to spend. You saw that place Sunday. All them people. They are makin' big dough. It never stops comin' in, just like Vegas."

"Vegas? What's that?"

"You don't know about Las Vegas?" Angel shrugged.

"Never mind. I'll tell you later. I'm gonna call the other guy." He dialed and waited.

"Yeah, hello. I want to speak to a Monsignor Healy. Is he there?"

"What is the nature of your business?"

"Never mind what it's about. It's private. Tell him Father Barry gave me this number."

Carlos waited as he heard clicks on the phone. Then he heard a voice and he asked, "Monsignor Healy?"

"Yes. Who are you?"

"It don't matter who this is. I think I got somethin' you want."

"What is it?"

"It's a book."

"What kind of book – can you describe it?"

'It's black. It got a zipper around it and it got a cross on the front and it got stuff about Priests doin' things they shouldn't be doin'."

"Tell me where and how you got it."

"It don't matter where I got it." Do you want it?"

"I'd have to see it, first."

"You ain't gonna see it until you own it. Right now I own it and I can see it. If you want to see it, you are gonna have to pay."

"Pay? We are a poor church and can't afford to pay for what you have."

"Don't bullshit me that the Church ain't got no money. I see the operation you guys got. You got plenty."

"It may be impossible to pay you for the book."

"Hey, look. If you don't want it, that's okay. I can sell it to the papers or the TV. They'll pay for it and you know it."

"Okay, okay... when can we make an arrangement?"

"We can make a deal right now. You got the money, you can have the book."

"How much money do you want for it?"

"I want a hundred thousand dollars."

'Angel couldn't believe what Carlos said. A hundred thou for a book? If the book was gold, it wouldn't be worth that. Carlos is gonna fuck it all up.

"That amount is very high… that's a lot of money."

"Yeah, I know that's a lot of money."

"We cannot pay that much… we won't pay that much."

"Well, what can you pay? What would you pay so you won't see those idiots on TV makin' fun of your Priests?"

"Fifty thousand dollars."

"That ain't enough, 'cause I ain't in this alone. You're gonna have to raise that so I can see my partner smile."

"Okay, we will pay seventy thousand dollars."

"Yeah. That's better. I want the dough in small bills. Put it in a small case and give it to Father Barry. I know what he looks like."

"Where is he to deliver the money?"

"You tell him to go to the 59th Street entrance to Central Park, to stand right in the middle of the sidewalk. I'll give him the book when I see the dough in the case."

"When do you want to do this?"

"Now, man. Let's do it now."

"We will need more time to get the money."

"Okay, so it'll take time to get the money. When?"

"Nine tonight."

"Nine. Okay. You got it straight? Father Barry and the case across from the Plaza Hotel."

"There can be no slip-ups."

"Don't worry, man. You'll have your book back and no worries about the papers or the TV. And one more thing…. If the money ain't all there or if there are cops…. I will get that book to the people who will fuck you over the most… so no games."

"There will be no problems."

"Okay. Nine.".

Angel looked at a sweating Carlos with a level of respect he never offered anyone. Man, he thought if Carlos can do that… Imagine, askin' for a hundred g's. Ha! I hope he got ten. That would mean five for each.

"How much will they pay? How much?"

"Angel, my man," Carlos leaned back in the chair. He's cool, Angel thought. Looks like guys in the movies when they pull off a big deal. Looks like he wants to jump up and scream.

"Angel, my man," Carlos repeated. "Those Church guys are gonna pay us seventy thousand dollars. You hear me… seventy thousand big ones."

"What?" was all Angel could say. Seventy thousand dollars—that was impossible. That was crazy. Why would they pay that for a stinkin' book?

"You heard me. They are gonna pay us seventy. That's thirty-five for you and thirty-five for me. How's that for makin' a buck?"

Angel couldn't answer. He just repeated over and over... seventy thousand dollars. Then he asked, "Can we trust these guys? Are they gonna try to fuck us?"

"I don't think so. They got money and they want that book. Screwin' around will lose the book and the guy seemed nervous when I talked about the papers and the TV. They win if they pay. They lose if they don't."

"Yeah. I got it."

"Right. Now... we got to make a plan. I want it to be easy. So, we let's wipe our prints off that book wherever we touched it and put it in a baggy."

The plan was simple. They waited in the park across from the Plaza. When they saw Father Barry, they waited to make sure he was alone. Carlos walked up behind him and told him to sit on the first bench inside the park. Then standing behind the seated Priest, Carlos had him put the case on the bench and look away. Calmly, Carlos opened the case and counted the money. Satisfied, he signaled Angel to come and give him the book. He took it and handed it to Father Barry who opened it, studied it and nodded. Carlos took the case and backed into the darkness as Father Barry got up and walked towards the Plaza. Throughout, Carlos and Angel had remained unseen. Father Barry took the book straight to Monsignor Healy. Carlos and Angel went to count their small fortune.

Leo met Abe and they went to *La Hambra* on Greenwich and Horatio. During the week the restaurant was a neighborhood eatery. On weekends it was filled with tourists from New Jersey and Westchester who wanted to experience the Village. The food was Spanish and good. Nothing special, but Leo liked the place because he had never gotten sick after a meal.

He wore a sports shirt and jacket and was a bit embarrassed when he saw Abe in a very fancy and fresh looking suit. Since Leo was a regular, the waiter treated him with great deference. They were shown to a booth and after ordering wine, both he and Abe settled on the Scampi.

"They know you here. "Abe said.

"Yes. I'm here often. Close by and decent food."

"Did you ever get sick after eating here?"

"No. Why? Are you allergic to Spanish food.... the spices?"

"Nah. I can eat anything. It's just that some of these tourist places in the Village will give you stuff that's been hanging around a bit... not yet green, but not all that new."

"They know me here. I wouldn't worry."

"Yeah. I can tell they know you. The waiter carried on like you were a partner." Leo smiled, took some wine and looked around. Four occupied tables. For Monday that wasn't bad. Abe sipped the wine. "Not bad." Then he looked straight at Leo. "You like being a cop?"

"It pays the bills."

"Don't lay that on me. I'm not a Rabbi on a first date. Lots of jobs pay the bills, but most don't come with a gun and street shootouts. Being a cop can be dangerous."

"That's true, it can be risky, but that's why I joined. I don't think much about that now. If I was on the street, it would be different."

"Marty said you ran Ballistics. You work in an office, right?"

"I just got transferred from that. Let me tell you, running Ballistics was like running a trucking business. Material comes in, gets tested, and goes out. Not very glamorous."

"I know about the trucking business. Had a couple years ago. Used to run booze."

"You were a bootlegger?"

"Let's say I was involved. I was four when Volstead went in, but I was eighteen when it was voted out. Spent my youth drivin' trucks filled with Canadian before you were born."

"Have you always been in the rackets?"

"Don't say it like that, you're gonna make me feel guilty." Suddenly, he glanced to the right, stiffened, the smile vanished and his right hand went inside the left front of his jacket. When he saw it was the waiter, he relaxed.

"Well..." Leo said. "That was like watching a Jimmy Cagney movie. Is somebody after you?"

"I doubt it, but movement off to the side makes me jumpy. Too many guys I knew got it when they weren't watchin' their flanks."

"You got a gun in there?"

"And I got a permit. It's legal. I'm legal. I have never had a conviction and never been in jail."

"What would you have done if it wasn't the waiter?"

"Never mind. You remember about eleven, twelve years ago, two old guys, maybe each is over seventy, are walking down 8th, they see each other, whip out rods and start blasting away."

"I remember that... made all the papers."

"Sure. It's what the assholes call noooooze. Anyway, I knew them both. They used to be with different gangs here in the City. Enemies from way back... being old means nothing. If they would have plugged each other when they were thirty, they'll do it when they're ninety."

"Are there many old timers still wandering around?"

"Certainly. Guys like me are all over the place. You know... advisers... consultants... they aren't pullin' jobs, but they're around. If you have the smarts, they always apply." He took a drink. "Good." he muttered. Then he took some bread, dipped it in the wine and popped it in his mouth. "Like I said on the phone, these days, the stick-up guys, the strong-arm guys are all amateurs. Not trained at all. In my day, nobody got killed in a stick-up. You waved your rod, got the cash and took off. Now the crazies are killin' everybody. Ha! The real crooks are workin' easier action. They don't need guns anymore."

"What do you mean?"

"Look, it's no secret the racket guys got some good things going. The best one I've seen lately is an operation on Long Island. The new electric plant.... can't think of the name..."

"I think you mean Southshore."

"Right." He leaned forward. "Now... from what I've heard it's a no-no to run an atom plant unless you have a way to evacuate the locals if the plant screws up. That's a Federal law. Never mind that say the big guys, and they go ahead and build the plant. Must have cost a couple of hundred million. Now... who benefits from building a thing like that?" He paused and Leo thought he wanted him to answer, but as Leo was going to speak, Abe continued.

"Right. The unions. The builders. The suppliers—all the usual guys who build this expensive, but useless thing. Why useless, you ask? Because, like I said, you can't operate it if there is no way to evacuate the local population. So... the racket guys involved with the building are makin' big bucks putting it up even though they know it can't be used. They knew that before they bought one brick or one quart of cement."

"I never thought about it that way."

"And that is not all, my boy. About three weeks ago, I heard that since the plant is useless, it should be torn down. Now... who do you think is going to get those contracts?" Leo didn't answer. "Right, the same crooked bastards who put it up. They made millions puttin' it up and they'll make as much takin' it down." He hunched his shoulders and smiling, leaned back. Leo remained silent.

"You might think you got a good racket. Ha! There's nothing as good as the way those guys operate. All legit. Millions passing through hands which would have broken your head for a double saw buck thirty years ago."

"I guess that explain why it's amateur night out on the streets."

"Right you are. There's nothing left for the dopes to do but break heads and shoot people. They're too lazy for school and too lazy for construction, all they can do is sell dope, use dope, and shoot each other. Sometimes I feel sorry for them and think I should open a crime school."

"Not a bad idea."

"Yeah, I can see it now... the Rosenberg School of Safe Cracking, Forgery and Breaking and Entering. Hell, I could be a professor."

"I've met many professional criminals who are very bright guys." Said Leo.

"Oh yeah, I knew guys who could open any safe... they were well-schooled and learned a trade... like plumbers or electricians. Any asshole can pull a trigger." Stopping Abe from proceeding was the arrival of the Scampi. In the next twenty minutes neither said more than a word or two. They ate and drank hunched over their plates, straightening only when the waiter came to remove the debris.

"Leo, that hit the spot. I was hungrier than I thought." Agreeing, Leo nodded.

Abe glanced around—obviously looking for something. "What is it? Do you need something?"

"Well, two things.... a No Smoking' sign and the John."

"Easy. This is the smoking section and the John is right there." He pointed. Abe smiled at him the way a father smiles when his kid hits a Little League home run. "Super... be right back." He got up and headed away.

Leo wondered if all this was what it appeared to be. Was he being treated to dinner because he didn't kill some thug? Or was something else going on? So far—it's a blank—it's two guys out for dinner.

When Abe returned, he had a lit cigar. Leo liked the smell. It was an old-fashioned odor. At one time, cigar smoking was ordinary and butts were common on the sidewalk. Many men spent the day with an unlit stogie clenched in their teeth. Things certainly have changed. A good cigar used to be common after a good meal, now it happens in private clubs. Was it an example of society's split? Activities available only to those sophisticated enough to know of them? Items unavailable to the masses... the commoners totally ignorant of the great wines, great foods, and good cigars. Like the late 1800's where the poor and the ignorant lived alongside a world they only heard about. In Abe's day, money could help bring a person into a world of luxury. Not now. Leo had seen pushers with enough money to buy a Caribbean island, live dull, stupid lives surrounded by ignorant people.

They used money for bigger cars, bigger TV's, awful clothes and electronic junk. There were a lot of rich and very stupid crooks.

"I asked you before." Abe said. "Do you like being a cop?"

"Yes, I do, always have. The force was like a family... I never had a family."

"Yeah. I know what you mean. I'm alone also. I have no one. That's one of the reasons I wanted to take you out tonight. If the idea isn't crazy, I thought we could do this every now and then. I live alone... in a hotel and that's okay, but it's living in a hotel, you know what I mean?"

"Oh, yes. I've traveled for the Department. After dinner it's the bar or the TV in the room. Gets dull in a couple of days."

"On the money. The people at Marty's don't help me. Marty is okay, but a loser. The kid, Carlos isn't stupid, but he's ignorant. The kind who'd win the lottery, get a dame with big tits and buy her a wet T-shirt wardrobe. I spend some time with them, but that's it. When Marty told me a little abut you, I got interested and I hoped you wouldn't mind going out once in a while."

"Abe, consider it a done deal. My new job may steal more time, but when the chance comes, I would love to repeat tonight."

"That's great. I need to talk with somebody or my brain'll go stale." He gestured for the waiter and ordered a Cadiz and a coffee.

"What's a Cadiz?" Leo asked.

The waiter told him it was a dessert drink made with sherry, blackberry liqueur, triple sec and cream and had fewer calories than the Flan Leo usually ordered. Leo laughed and ordered one. The waiter brought their drinks and coffee and as Abe sipped, he asked Leo about the new job.

"Well, I can't tell you much, because it is new for me... Dignitary Protection."

"Hey, that could be interesting. You'll probably get to meet a lot of foreigners. That's good. They know how to live. The average Frenchman lives better than the average Yank. Almost all of them know about wine, cheese, and good food. In France they all know. It kills me that in this country there are so many smart people who are so damned dumb. I see guys at the hotel bar—rich guys—good schools—good families—they have burgers and beer and think it's a gourmet meal. What went wrong here?"

"That's a question I wouldn't even begin to know how to answer. Maybe... America is the home of the common man..."

"Bull!" Abe growled. "The Schools don't teach the right stuff and it's advertising. Tell people often enough a burger and beer is great food and they'll believe you after a while." Leo laughed.

Abe signaled the waiter and pulled out a wad of bills when the check was presented. He peeled a single hundred from a larger number of them and smiled at the waiter. "Keep the change, Amigo."

As they walked out, Leo said, "You know, you remind me of Jimmy Durante."

"I knew him well." smiled Abe. "He was a real gentlemen, a very aristocratic guy... very cultured and very bright. He used to stay at the same hotel where I live."

"Where's that? What hotel?"

"I have rooms at the Regency. The one on Park."

"I know where it is. That's a classy place... very expensive."

"Money is not a problem. I have plenty of money. What I look for is an interesting way to spend it."

They walked up Greenwich to Seventh and Leo waited with Abe until a cab came. As he entered the taxi, Abe said, "I'll be in touch. Enjoy the new job."

Leo crossed the street and went upstairs. He had a message and hit the recorder button. It was from Monsignor Healy. Leo dialed the number and heard that familiar voice.

"Monsignor, this is Leo Flower."

"Oh, Leo...good... only two quick items. First, a great 'Thank you' for Aptin's book and second, but most important... before the night is out we will have the book Father John was working with. I am glad to say there is no longer any problem."

"You'll get his book?" exclaimed Leo. "That means you'll get the killer. Only the killer could have that book."

"While that may be true, it is not our concern. Our primary concern is the book. We must primarily think of the Church and the negative image that book would create."

"How did you get it?"

"Believe it or not, we were contacted and made a deal. We'll pay a lot for it."

"But the killer took it and now you'll pay a murderer—a double murderer. How can you do that? What about Father John?"

"Leo, Father John is with the Lord. He's in better hands than we are."

"But damn it, you can't let a murderer get away. Is there a way to make a capture?"

"Leo, as I said, that is not our concern. The Church's image is our priority. Paying money to protect it is vital and anyway, the killer will burn in hell."

"I'd like to see him in a cell. I'm not overly concerned with eternity."

"Be that as it may, I just wanted to give you the news. Good night to you." Leo stared at the phone. "Sonofabitch." he muttered. They're concerned with image and let a double killer get away. "Sonofabitch." he said again, and dropped the hand piece into the cradle.

A half-hour after leaving Central Park, they were drinking beers and gaping at the money.

Broadly grinning, Angel said, "Carlos, you are one wild fucker. When I heard you say to the guy you wanted a hundred g's, I said 'shit' to myself. I figured you were goin' to fuck everything. Then you go and tell the guy you'll take seventy and he says OK and there it is." Angel pointed. But as he did, the smile faded from his face. "Carlos... do you think maybe they fucked with us? Do you think the money ain't real?"

"I thought about that, man. I really did. But I didn't want to say nothin' 'cause I figured you'd worry. But...nah... the more I thought about it, the more I'm sure the dough is good. They didn't have enough time to get phony dough. If we had to wait a week, I'm sure they'd fuck us over, but no, I can't believe they got phony money just sittin' around."

"Yeah, I see what you mean." Angel lifted his eyes from the case. "What do we do now?"

"Waddaya mean?"

"What do we do? I mean... I mean look at the money. What do we do with it?"

"Well, I'm gonna tell you. The first thing we do is say nothing to nobody. Right?" Angel nodded. "The second thing is we do nothing." Angel stared at him blankly. "Listen, man, if you and me went out with our pockets filled and bought clothes, girls, or whatever, it wouldn't take no fuckin' genius to figure we got our hands on some real dough. Those fuckers would be up here in a rush, probably knock us off and take all that with them." he pointed to the case. "What we got to do is live exactly as we did before. I am goin' to work tomorrow like I always do and you, well... I don't know about you. What are you gonna do?"

Angel shrugged. "I don't know. Before I got cut, I would sleep all day and then go out and get money. It was that or hangin' at the poolroom. I didn't do nothing, but I want to do something now, I want to be different."

"Angel, that is 'Fuck You' money. As long as you got it, you can say that to anybody. If Marty fucks with me and I don't want to take his bullshit anymore, I can say 'Fuck you' and walk."

"Fuck you money.... Hey, that's cool, but I don't got nobody to say that to. I ain't got nobody but you."

"Don't sweat it, man, your life is goin' to change. I can feel it."

"I know what you mean. Since I got cut, I don't feel the same about jumpin' people."

"But that's what you do. What're you gonna do if you don't do that?"

"I don't know, man. You gotta help me."

Carlos looked at him in a new way. Previously, there was never any need to see him as anything more than a vicious little street killer. But since Angel had nobody, because he was alone and only a kid, Carlos treated him like a cousin- like he was family. Now, he had a lot of money. If Angel went on the street with it, he'd blow it in no time and bring attention to them both. Carlos realized he had to help the kid and protect himself at the same time.

"I tell you what we're gonna do. You are gonna go to school. You are gonna learn to read and write. Once you got that, you can do anything."

"Oh shit, Carlos, I can't go to no school. Don't be crazy."

'Man, don't you be crazy. I know you can't go to no regular school. I mean you are gonna learn to read and write and I am goin' to find you a teacher. You know... private lessons. You'll learn that shit in no time.... I even got somebody in mind."

"Who is that?"

"There is a guy who comes into Marty's all the time. He got somethin' to do with music. I heard Marty tell some guy he's a copier. There's some special name for what he does, but I don't know it. Anyway, he works for musicians and they hire him to copy music parts for the different instruments. I seen some of the stuff he does and it's somethin' else... really beautiful. This guy is quiet and he's smart and knows all about everything. He could teach you."

"Do you think he'd want to?"

"Angel, you see that pile of money? We give that guy twenty a week and he'll teach you. I heard Marty say the guy is like an artist, and I know one thing about artists, they never got a fuckin' dime. Believe me, this guy will always need dough and we got some. Don't worry, he'll teach you and when you got that down, we'll go on from there. Okay?"

Angel stared at him. "Man, I don't know what to say to you. Nobody has ever done anything for me. Nobody! Everybody is always rippin' me off or hurtin' me. You are the only guy who's ever helped me, ever."

"Hey man, I like you... and just like you, I got no family either so maybe that's it. Maybe that's why we're together right now. Maybe we're supposed to be together."

They sat on the floor finishing their beers and then they went out for Chinese. Later that night, they watched a television movie and went to sleep.

When Father Barry returned to the residence, Monsignor Healy was waiting. "Do you have it?"

"I guess so, but I have no way of knowing if anything was removed."

"Come with me."

Healy led him to his private rooms- a bedroom, a sitting room and an office. The rooms looked like they were done by a theatrical set designer. Large overstuffed leather sofas and chairs, brass nail heads on everything, heavy wood pieces, lamps with darkened shades, hardwood floors and Persian rugs.

An essence of Scotch and cigar smoke hovered like mosquito netting. The sole feminine item was on a small side table: a doily under an ashtray.

"Father, sit down and tell me everything that took place."

The young priest related what had transpired. Healy listened intently only interrupting when Father Barry described the person who took the money. "You mean he was young?"

"The one who took the money looked twenty-three or four. I got only a glance at the one who brought the book to the bench, but I would say he was much younger. I think the older one was Hispanic, but I can't be sure. It was dark and I was nervous."

"You had a right to be nervous. Anyone with a lot of money in hand is in jeopardy in New York. But the money is a trifle. This book..." He took it from his lap and held it so the light reflected from its covers. It looked like the room, orderly, important and masculine. "This book is directly involved with the deaths of two people."

"I've heard rumors about that and also about what it contains."

"What have you heard?"

The young Priest looked at the floor. "Well...it's supposed to provide details of homosexual activities of some of the local Priests."

"That's exactly right." Healy laughed. "You know I'm always at a loss to explain the accuracy of the Church's grapevine. Nothing is ever a secret—just too many eyes and ears—too many inquisitive and interested parties."

"If I may ask, what are you going to do with it?"

"I will think about that long and hard, but right now, I have Church work to do so I will ask you to excuse me." Both men stood and Healy escorted Father Barry to the door. "I do thank you for what you've done tonight. My boy, believe me, it will not go un-noticed. You have performed a great service for the Church."

"I'm not seeking a reward."

""Don't concern yourself. I will do what should be done."

When the young man left, Healy locked the door and went to his desk. He opened the book to search for the one piece of information he prayed would be there. When he found it, he sighed and poured a half glass of Scotch. Near the front was a note from Father John... it said the one civilian working with him was Aptin. That meant only two outside books and now he had them both.

For the next several hours, he copied out the pertinent information-names, dates, events and parish affiliations. Then he went to the basement. When he found a metal bucket, he slowly and deliberately tore each page from each book and burned them. One after the other, the pages flared, curled, then blackened as they attacked other pages floating down. When he was finished, he stood over the ash filled bucket holding the leather covers. He tossed them into a furnace and was glad to be rid of every shred of evidence

As he walked from the basement to his rooms, he promised himself he would not fail to do what must be done. He would personally visit every priest mentioned in both books and calmly tell each to curtail their activities or risk harsh punishment. That would hold things for a while. What else could anyone do?

CHAPTER 15

LEO HAD BEEN MAKING the trip to Ballistics for so long, he was walking to the subway before he realized work was now a bus ride. As he waited for it, he wondered if things were moving too fast and maybe a waiting period would be wise. Then he reproved himself for his doubts and brought out his learned defenses to ward off insecurity. I am able. I am capable. I would not have gotten anywhere if I were a bum. I haven't been rewarded for anything... I've earned everything I ever got. Nobody ever gave me a damn thing.

Feeling more determined than he'd been for a while, he got on the bus ready to make a go of this new job. He sat in the back, feeling every jarring thud as the bus bounced along Fourteenth hitting every pothole in its path. Leo wasn't sure if he would be able to handle such a kidney buster every morning. Maybe a taxi would be better.

When the bus dropped him at Fourteenth and First, Leo got a cab. Getting in, he saw that the space reserved for the driver's name on the hack license was not long enough to hold his entire name, so the last five letters had been hand written over his picture. His name was Alipha Nahatnariansingh and he was all smiles. Turning, he asked Leo something impossible to understand, so Leo said, "Forty-first Street. I want to go to uptown to Forty-first Street."

The driver, now no longer smiling, said something else. Leo couldn't understand that either.

"Do you understand English?" Leo asked.

"Ah." the driver said, "Eeeengleeeesh, ahh, Eeeeeengleeeesh. No, I no spik it."

"Wonderful. Look... just drive straight... go." Leo pointed to the front, flicked his hand and said, "Drive that way... go." The driver dropped the car into gear, threw the meter and swept out into uptown traffic. Since First Avenue is one-way uptown, Leo knew he would eventually reach the Forties.

The ride lasted about eight minutes and in that time the driver cut off three cars, a bus, and roared through two red lights. At Thirty-ninth Leo told him to stop. When nothing happened, Leo yelled, "Stop!" With that, the driver stood on the brake and skidded to a halt. Happy to have landed, Leo threw a five over the seat and jumped out. As he walked away, he heard the driver repeating, "Thankayou, thankayou."

Looking around, Leo wondered if this morning's trip was an omen or merely an introduction to a new routine. The Ballistics commute had been so automatic, nothing penetrated during that trip. Now, he had a new journey and a new section o the City with which to deal. Looking around, he thought the streets were cleaner then the Village. Maybe they just looked cleaner because of the sunlight.

First Avenue was broad and open and the sun hit everything. He could see the sky without looking straight up. An image of Father John flashed into his mind. Is he up there? Is that where heaven is? How could they be so cold-blooded? We have his book. We have Aptin's book so screw you. Father John is in heaven and the killer will boil in Hell for his sin. Damn!

He thought of the street shooting the other night. What if that sonofabitch was the killer? What if that guy killed John and Ilene? I wouldn't have wounded him if that were the case. I would have blown his head off without hesitating. Why the hell do I carry guns? Damn, I may never shoot to wound again. I'll kill every street perp I can and maybe that will settle the score. If I kill enough of the bastards, will I manage to get the creep who killed them?

"Doubtful," he muttered. "Doubtful."

Crossing First, he made his way to a coffee shop on the corner of 43rd. He walked in and sat at the counter. The usual was always coffee and a roll. Only on a farm did people eat like television commercials… eggs, bacon, toast, pancakes, and French toast. It was the labor- they worked it off. Eating like that and working at a desk would have you looking like a guest on an afternoon television show in no time.

Leo finished, paid, and went around the corner to the building he would call home for a while. As he entered, Smitty told him the Captain wanted to see him so Leo made his way to the main office. Rose, Melendez and Gottlieb were there. As he eye contacted Melendez, she nodded at Hoffheimer's door. Leo knocked and entered when he heard, "Come."

He was on the phone with the hand piece balanced on his shoulder and was making notes as he thumbed through a small book. He gestured Leo to the sofa. A minute later he gently hung up and stood. He was wearing a dark blue suit with perfectly flat shoulders and lapels so sharp they looked like needles. In general, Detectives dressed well. The suit and tie were trademarks of a job that demanded brains rather than muscle. Detectives were like the

Meister Mechanic at a Mercedes dealer who wore the same white coat, as a medical diagnostician. A uniform was one level, the business suit quite another. Cops in blue got dirty, mechanics in gray got dirty, detectives in suits stayed clean. Leo figured he'd need new clothes; if he, like Hoffheimer, was going to directly deal with oil rich Princes.

"Good morning, Leo."

"And a good morning to you, Captain."

Hoffheimer smiled. "Two things. One, I have placed some information on your desk. Study it and provide me with a list of the possible outcomes you envision. Two- In approximately thirty minutes, a Security Officer I want you to meet will be arriving. He is from one of the UN's newly admitted African countries and is out making his security needs plain to everyone and anyone who will listen. I'll say no more, since I want your evaluation of him and what he has to say. I'll let you know when he arrives." Leo nodded and went to his office.

There was a cardboard box on the floor by his chair. As he picked it up, he noticed a red folder on his desk. The box contained personal items from Ballistics. Some books, some ornaments, pads, pencils, and the like, and a picture of Ilene and John. The meager pile that constituted his treasure trove saddened him. Some would need a moving van for the accumulated stuff a similar number of years would produce. Leo hoped the mark he left on Ballistics was more telling than the amount of material he took away. It took two minutes to put the box's contents in a new place and with that done, Leo opened the red folder. It contained two sheets of paper. The first said:

In four months, (August), the pope will address the General Assembly. Intelligence maintains two groups have targeted him for elimination on American soil. Nothing is known of their specific plans. What is known is contained herein. **Your task is to formulate plans to carry out the assassination. Every potentially successful plan will highlight weak security points.** If possible, develop more than one plan.

The second page was divided in half. The top was headed, "The Mighty Fist of God" and included names and addresses. The bottom heading was, "Sons of the Merciful God King" and also listed names and addresses. Since the names and addresses of these people are known, they are probably not a threat. Leo almost smiled. Two groups bent on eliminating the pope and both had names that read like the pope's favorite charity. Like Abe, Leo preferred crooks and gangsters who called themselves crooks and gangsters. When the crazies regarded themselves as messengers of God and intended to carry out their version of his wishes, that's when things got very sick. When martyrs are involved, suicide attacks are plausible and adequate protection becomes very, very difficult. Killers who wanted to stay alive are always easier to handle.

So, Leo said to himself, my first assumption is an assassination without an escaping killer. Before he could put any ideas on paper, his intercom buzzed. Melendez said the Captain wanted him.

In his office, Hoffheimer told Leo he was just notified from across the street, the security chief from Gabon Leone was on his way. "Leo, follow the conversation as well as you can- some of these security people use abbreviations you may not know, but keep track, I'll fill you in after." Leo nodded. There were two beeps from a pager. "That's Smitty, Hoffheimer said. The guy has arrived."

Moments later, there were three knocks. Smitty opened the door and escorted in a very tall black man in banker's gray. He looked like a pro basketball player, from the custom tailoring to the custom shoes.

"Captain Hoffheimer, this is Inspector Guy Magalana."

Hoffheimer thanked Smitty and came from behind the desk to shake hands. Inspector Magalana offered his as if he expected it to be kissed, but Hoffheimer grabbed it in mid-air, and shook it twice. Then he introduced Leo who also shook hands; Leo thought Melendez had a firmer grip.

Inspector Magalana sat on the sofa and began speaking in a thick British public school dialect and rather than casual conversation, he started listing requirements.

"Captain Hoffheimer, I want to make clear that while you may regard my country as not terribly significant in the overall pattern of world affairs, Gabon Leone is a full-fledged member of the United Nations and I demand the same respect and compliance you would offer to dignitaries from other countries with similar status."

Hoffheimer glanced at Leo and then looked at the tall black man. "Inspector Magalana, rest assured the New York City Police Department is fully prepared and willing to provide whatever services you deem necessary and appropriate."

Slightly surprised, Magalana said, "Well, I must say your attitude is refreshing and quite enlightened. I will take what you say at face value." He removed a very large gold cigarette case from inside his jacket and popped the cover. The cigarettes were custom- red barreled with black filters. He looked for an ashtray, seeing none; he slowly closed the case and pocketed it.

"We will work with the security team at UNHQ and help in every way we can to ensure your country's leaders a productive and safe visit to this City. By the way, there has recently been a law enacted here that just about prohibits smoking in public places, particularly restaurants."

"Captain, the ridiculous and barbaric banning of smoking aside, I must say it is refreshing to hear words of cooperation spoken so openly. Last year, in London, my leader's son, and I were treated as if we were tradesmen. It was a most irritating encounter. The British will not see my country's flag any time soon. We are not to be treated as commoners."

Hoffheimer opened a white folder on his desk, looked at a sheet of paper in it, and then looked at Magalana. "Inspector, information about the episode to which I presume you refer was provided to me by Major Farnsward of the UK CID. His report states that you and Prince Putenyaya were swept up in a raid on a hotel catering exclusively to homosexuals. You were caught, it seems, with your pants down."

Leo had never seen a black man blush, but the Inspector did so as he leapt from the sofa.

"How dare you refer to that incident? That was an arranged smear to make the prince appear less than the man he truly is."

"Please understand my position, Inspector, I have no way of knowing what is the truth. All I can deal with is the information provided to me by Interpol and other agencies."

"Interpol is nothing but a pack of mongrel hounds intent upon keeping the Black man in one place. I would offer little credence to the information they provide. What they say is worthless and specifically designed to embarrass my Prince and myself."

For the next several minutes, Inspector Magalana railed against Interpol, the UN, British aristocracy, South Africa, diamond mine owners, and the Canadian Government. Leo was surprised because he had never heard of anyone being pissed off at Canada. Also, it struck Leo that Magalana's ranting sounded like a drag queen (not in drag) complaining about being harassed by precinct cops. This was not the sort of security chief Leo had expected to meet.

Throughout Magalana's tirade, Hoffheimer had not moved. Composed and unaffected by the display, he sat and watched. When the Inspector had calmed and once again was seated, Hoffheimer stood. He very slowly walked to the window and then turned to face the seated man. The light from behind framed him and provided a halo like luminescence.

"Let me fill you in, Inspector, I have the report from Major Farnsward. I have a report from UN Central and another from Inspector Berghoffer of the South African CID. I have information from the French arm of Interpol and I have a document from The Brazilian government. Each attests to your unabashed homosexual activities." He paused, but kept his eyes fixed on Magalana. "Inspector, these reports do not concern me. Your personal sexual business is your personal sexual business, but... I am concerned with any activity that might result in a security breach while your government's representatives are here in this City."

Again, Magalana erupted from the sofa and drew himself to his full height. Leo thought he was going to start swinging. Hoffheimer stepped toward Magalana, speaking slowly, with his voice emotionless and his words evenly spaced, he said, "Sit down and do not say another word." Magalana stopped short, stared at Hoffheimer and then half turned and glowered at Leo. The drama had so captured Leo; he was surprised when Magalana looked at him. Nonetheless, in that instant, he wished Roberto's play had possessed similar drama. Then, Leo did what he had seen a street-wise cop do in a South Bronx bar when the tension had peaked; he asked Magalana if he would like something to drink. There was silence and then Magalana smiled, "Yes. A drink would be nice. Would lemonade be available?"

As Leo stood in the middle of the room, Hoffheimer said, "Lieutenant Flower, tell Gottlieb to get it." Leo left the room.

At Gottlieb's desk, he said, "This may sound odd, but the Captain wants you to get a glass of lemonade for our guest." Gottlieb got up smiling. "When you been here a while, Lieutenant, you won't consider any request coming out of that office as... odd."

Leo chuckled and returned to Hoffheimer's office. Entering, he saw a changed scene. The two men were no longer glaring, Hoffheimer was at his desk, Magalana was on the sofa holding a lit cigarette and there was an ash tray on the small table alongside the sofa. His voice soft and without rancor, Hoffheimer said, "Inspector, you must understand my position. Your personal desires do not concern me, nor do I care how you and your prince entertain yourselves. However, I do not want your need for unrestrained pleasure to bring harm to you or your prince while in this city. Do you understand?"

Blowing a shaft of perfumed, blue smoke in the air, Magalana nodded. Before Hoffheimer could continue, there were three raps on the door and Gottlieb entered carrying a small silver tray and a glass of what Leo figured was lemonade. In one sweeping motion, he placed the glass on the table by Magalana and turned to leave. Hoffheimer stopped him.

"Sergeant, what would you do if I told you it was important to keep this man out of trouble whether or not he wanted close supervision?"

Gottlieb squared his shoulders. "Well, Captain, if you were serious, I would deposit this man in a hotel room, handcuff him to the bed, fill him with sedatives and watch him sleep for as long as you wanted him to stay out of trouble."

Hoffheimer said. "Thank you, Sergeant." Gottlieb nodded, turned and left the room.

"Do you understand what I am saying to you, Inspector? If I have to, I'll order Gottlieb to do what he just described. You and your prince will remain unconscious long enough for me to have you shipped back to your starting point." Then he got up, came around the desk to stand in front of the seated man. "Decide to play around on your own while you're here and you will regret it... it will be wise to follow the advice I will offer."

Magalana's expression changed and he looked at Hoffheimer with interest as he repositioned himself on the sofa. Leo was surprised as Hoffheimer sat down next to the tall Black man. "Inspector," he said, "believe me when I say I am a sophisticated man. I recognize your needs and also, believe me when I say I am in a position to provide entertainment you will not soon forget. New York is a city with a very active nightlife... leave it to me to select from available resources the fulfillment for your desires. If you trust me, you will not forget your trip to New York."

Magalana killed his cigarette and sat up, a smile forming on his lips. "Captain Hoffheimer, what you say warms my heart. I absolutely will respect and trust your decisions. I will throw my Prince and myself into your care." He paused and looked at the floor. "Please forgive my earlier behavior, if I had an idea of your worldliness, I would have sought your advice before we arrived."

Now Hoffheimer smiled. "Inspector, do me a favor. I want you to create a list of, well, let me call them activities, and a list of people, performers, if you will, who would help you enjoy those activities." Hoffheimer sounded like a father telling his son he was going to buy him what he had always wanted. "Inspector, trust me to provide you with whatever you desire." Magalana's face lit up. He knew he was going to get a new bat and ball.

Leo was surprised and impressed. Hoffheimer was probably going to supply this guy with happy times.... a crew of arbitrary sexuals, excellent dope, liquor, and good food. Leo smiled to himself, hell; I'd behave myself also if I could have my list of fantasies come to life.

Magalana stood now brimming with good feeling. "I will go to my Prince and relate this most astounding conversation. When I have ascertained his desires, I will contact you."

"Wonderful," Hoffheimer said, as he escorted him to the door. Leo jumped up, shook the tall man's hand and opened the door to the outer office. Gottlieb rose from his desk chair ready to take Magalana downstairs to Smitty. "We will be expecting your call, Inspector." Hoffheimer said to the departing man. "Thank you, Captain, for a most enjoyable and civilized conversation."

When they were once again alone, Hoffheimer asked, Well, Leo, what did you think of that?"

"I'm a little surprised to see an overt homosexual as a nation's security chief and you becoming some sort of a pimp."

Unperturbed, Hoffheimer said, "Leo, I know you wonder why you might have to risk your neck for the likes of him, but you have to understand the game. Magalana and the Prince do not mean very much. They are replaceable parts... as are most diplomats with whom we deal. What is important- what is vital to me is the game. It's us against them."

"Who are they?"

"I have no idea. They constantly change. Tomorrow it could be the "Swift Avengers" or a group of militant rednecks. Who they are does not matter. What does count is outwitting them. I want to defeat them. I do not want their plans to succeed."

So it is a game, Leo thought. Chess, checkers, bridge, poker, no difference. It's Vince Lombardi come back to life. "Winning is the only thing." Though Leo spent years in Ballistics, he still saw himself as a cop, a guardian dedicated to protecting the goods guys and catching the bad guys. Now, things were a little different. Now, losing a pawn becomes an acceptable part of the game. "So Magalana doesn't matter?"

"Leo, don't get worked up over a guy like him. I bet he and the Prince got their power by knocking off the guys who preceded them. That's the way this game is played. Two years from now, there will be a different Prince, a different Security Chief and a different group of self-serving bastards who will keep the country in poverty so they can dance until dawn in Paris. Leo, these guys are in for the fun and the authority."

"So UN diplomats are pieces for our board game?"

"That's the idea. They can be sacrificed. If we catch terrorists, put a stop to a movement, then hundreds, maybe thousands, are safe. Losing someone is unfortunate, but we are at war."

"This is a game for grown ups, I still see police work as the good guys versus the bad guys."

"It is, but not quite... A precinct cop feels bad when a local citizen gets done in. He should feel bad. We do not enjoy having victims, but we refuse to waste much time on them. We expect a casualty and we regret loss of life, but our total and primary focus remains on the perpetrators."

"Putting it that way makes it sound like that's what police work is supposed to be."

"Let me ask you a question, Leo, do you think it is possible to prevent a presidential assassination?"

"No. He's too much in the open. You could prevent it, I guess, by locking him up."

"Right. If he wants to 'press the flesh,' he has to be out there with them and he knows it. He knows he's a target and he knows there is no real protection. So we focus on the situation and try to outthink the killers before they act. That is far more difficult and challenging than merely chasing them after the fact."

"So get Magalana and Punteyaya out of the way."

"Right. There is no need to waste time. Give them some grass and some sweaty bodies and they're happy." Once they're happy and under our eyes, nothing will happen to them." Leo sighed, "Well... this has been an interesting morning, Captain."

"Leo, this is only the beginning... By the way, any other thoughts about Magalana?"

"I admire his tailor... That was a great suit he wore."

"Yes, the internationals all go to Hong Kong. Have you been?"

"Me? No."

"You will,"

Leo smiled and when Hoffheimer told him there was nothing else, he went to his office to think about the Pope.

CHAPTER 16

VINCENT DIMANNI STROLLED UP 8th Avenue as he did every Tuesday afternoon. He was coming from lunch at the White Rose Cafe on 43rd where the Tuesday special was fresh corned beef and cabbage. To him, the midday meal was crucial since he firmly believed it would influence the remainder of his day and the quality of his afternoon's work. For weeks, he would eat at a different place, cautiously selected from the hundreds available, and then, carefully, he determined which local restaurants provided the best lunch. He selected his favorites based on the freshness of their food, the quality of the cooking, and for him, the most important element, their consistency.

All his friends were pleased with his even temper and his soft-spoken, unflappable demeanor. He never uttered a bad word about anyone or anything; keeping whatever negative thoughts he did have, to himself. It was impossible to dislike him and no one did.

Continual leaning over a desk had left him round shouldered and stooped, making him look older than forty-four. However, all thoughts about age dissipated when speaking with him, since his white blond hair and pink skin suggested youth. His work had taken a toll on his eyesight and he wore thick, dark framed eyeglasses that enlarged his clear blue eyes making him seem even friendlier than he was. He was a person others immediately trusted and it was rare if he walked a block without being asked for directions. Those tangled in the web of streets would spot him and know he would help. He often smiled at people he passed and they smiled back.

Years of careful work had earned him a reputation as one of the top music copyists in the City. But a meticulous nature prevented him from turning out anything but supreme work and that took a good deal of time. The upshot was a constant need for money. To partially solve that problem, he sought out quality musical instruments in shops throughout the City. Generally, he resold what he found unless he was working on a direct commission to find a specific item. In addition to music copying and instrument buying, he also taught music. Being exceptionally ethical, he taught only to the limits of his ability and then spent time finding other teachers for his better students.

He visited Marty's at least once a week; since it was close to his apartment and there was no way to ever predict when something good might turn up. As he opened Marty's door that day, Abe hollered, "Well, well, look who's here. How are you Vinnie, my boy? How's it going?"

"I'm feeling fine, Abe. I hope you are well."

"Vinnie, I never felt better in my life."

After a quick look at the instruments that were visible, he asked, "Is there anything worth anything?"

"As a matter of fact, there is. Marty picked up a viola that has very good sound and only needs a slight refinishing."

"Oh, that's great. I have two buyers lined up and I've been looking for something decent. What does Marty want for it?"

"He bought it cheap. Offer him seventy-five and he'll do a back flip."

"Can I see it?"

"Vinnie, does Pinocchio have wooden balls? Of course you can see it. I wouldn't mind if you even played it. I love the viola. Let me get it." Abe went into the back of the store as Carlos came in the front door.

"Vinnie, I got to talk to you. I need your help."

"What is it? Is something wrong?"

"No, nothin' is wrong, but I need somebody who can teach. I got a friend, a guy I know. I got to help him 'cause there's no body else that will. He needs to learn to read and write."

"Read and write? I don't teach that. I teach music."

"Music...schmoosic. Teachin' is teachin'."

"I don't know about that, Carlos. I never taught anyone to read. I don't know how you do that."

Hey, Vinnie... what do you get to teach music?"

"I charge twenty an hour although I usually spend more time than that."

"Vinnie, I'll give you thirty. It'll be a snap."

Smiling, Vincent said, "Thirty? That's a lot. Hell, for thirty I'll give it a try." Abe emerged from the rear carrying a sleek, black case. "Well, well, look who's here. Hey, Carlos, did you go to Philly for a chicken steak? Where you been?"

"What's a chicken steak?" Carlos asked, looking first at Vinnie and then at Abe.

Abe laughed. "What're we going to do with a goof like this? What's a chicken steak?" While still muttering, he opened the case and took out a dark looking viola. He handed it to Vincent as he extracted the bow from the case top. Vincent hefted the instrument, looked at the front, the back and then peered inside. "It says Stradivarius in there, right?"

"Sure it does, Abe, Antonio Stradivarius, Hoboken, New Jersey, USA."

Abe and Carlos laughed as Vincent placed the instrument under his chin. His left hand plucked the strings and a mellow sound emerged. Then he placed the viola on the counter and picking up the bow, turned the screw to tighten the frog. When everything suited him, he put the viola under his chin and ran through some scales. The instrument had a full, rich sound, far more beefy and masculine than a violin. Abe was enthralled. The few people standing in the lobby area moved closer to the door and listened with their heads tilted toward the interior.

When a guy slipped inside and held the door open with his shoe, people walking by on 8th heard the unmistakable sound of live music and drifted into the store. Looking up, Vincent realized he had an audience and decided to offer them an after lunch mini-concert. He played some Tchaikovsky and then segued into Gershwin's "Bess, You is My Woman Now." The crowd loved it. After a diet of television's two-inch speakers and jukeboxes with pop crap, a real musician playing real music drilled them in their souls. When he stopped, they applauded and insisted he go on. However, Abe, as much a listener as any one of them, took a different route.

"Hey," he called out. "This is not Carnegie hall. Come in and let me sell you something or get back out there and go to work." A few in the crowd laughed as most filtered into the street.

Vincent put the viola back in the case. "Abe, I'll take it. When Marty gets in, tell him I'll go seventy-five. If he's reluctant... I'll go a hundred. I already got it sold."

"Consider it done, my boy. I'll take care of it." Abe put the bow back in place and headed for the rear. When he was out of hearing, Carlos said, "Look Vinnie, I got to talk to you about this teachin' thing. When can we meet?"

"How about tonight. I'm free."

"Tonight's great. You want me to call you?"

"Sure, here's my card. I'll be in, call when you want to meet. We'll go for some food at the Embassy, all right?"

When Abe came back, their talk turned to food. Vincent told them about the neighborhood's offerings until he had to leave. When he did, Carlos was still trying to get Abe to tell him about chicken steaks.

At seven that night Carlos called Vincent and they agreed to meet at the Embassy. The Embassy Inn called itself a hotel, but really was a motel. In any other city it would be a hotel since it had six floors and covered an entire city block. It looked like the Holiday Inn that's at every airport. Red brick, functional design, lunch and breakfast diner, a dinner restaurant, and parking on premises. But hotels in New York are different. Most have at least twenty floors, high styling, superb restaurants, and elegant guests. The Embassy catered to West Side tourists who were at home at any Holiday Inn. These were people who liked to wear shorts and tank tops, who needed beds capable of supporting excess weight, and most important, these were folks who ate more hot dogs in a week than might be sold at a Yankee ball game.

As Vincent was being escorted to a table in the Ranchero Room by the hostess, he looked at the tourists and wondered how they could get sunburned walking the streets, since New York's air had visible chunks floating in it. People sitting around outside for any length of time would find numerous, unidentifiable fragments had settled on their skin, yet many of these folks were lobster red.

At eight, Carlos and Angel stood in the Ranchero Room doorway looking for Vincent and spotting him, headed for his table. The fellow with Carlos Vincent had never seen before. He was small and looked 13 or 14 years old, but as they got closer, he noticed something and revised his estimate upwards to 16 or 17. They sat across from Vincent when they got to the table.

"Vincent, this is Angel, my pal. He needs to learn to read and write."

"How do you do? My name is Vincent DiManni." Angel appraised him with a crooked smile. "You can teach me to read and write."

"Angel, I must make something clear... I'm really a music teacher. I was never trained to teach reading and writing."

Carlos jumped in. "Vincent, I told Angel that and he said it don't matter. He thinks like me- if you can teach music, you can teach." As Vincent looked at Angel a bit more carefully, he revised his age estimate downward. This is a kid, he thought. He can't be more than 13- maybe even younger. He wondered why the kid's image didn't hold still. He looks young and old at the same time. "Angel, how old are you?" Vincent asked.

"I don't know." Angel answered.

"You don't know? How come you don't know? Why don't you ask your parents?" Staring with blank eyes, Angel said, "I ain't got no parents."

Vincent realized why he was confused about Angel's age. He looked young, but didn't act young. He doesn't fidget like a kid. He isn't nervous or embarrassed. Saying he had no parents didn't faze him.

"You don't have parents? Well, then, how do you live? Where do you live?"

"I get by."

"Did you ever go to school?"

"Do you got to know that to teach me?"

"Well...no, I don't. I just find it hard to understand why you never learned in school."

"Vincent," Carlos interrupted, "look... it don't matter if he went to school or if he got any people. All that matters is he don't know how to read and write and you can teach him... right?"

"Of course, that's all that matters. I'm not being nosy. It's just surprising to meet someone who never went to school."

"Can you teach me?"

"Sure...well, at least I can try."

"Okay... do it."

"Here? Now?"

"Yeah... here, now. What's the matter?" Vincent stared at him. This is going to be very interesting, he told himself.

"Like I said, I don't know how to teach reading, but I know how to read and I know music, so I think I'm going to try to teach you to read by using music."

"I like music." Angel said. "I really like to sing and I love the music in the church."

"Oh, yes, Church music is beautiful. What pieces do you like?"

"I don't know nothin' like that. I just like the music and the people singin'."

"You go to church a lot?"

Angel looked at Carlos. "How many times we been there, two three?"

"We been there two times."

"And I was there two times by myself." Sensing this was a good moment to see if Angel had any math knowledge, Vincent asked, "Okay, you've been there how many times all together?"

Not comprehending for a moment, Angel stared at him. Then his face lit up. "You teachin' me now, right?"

"That's right and I'm asking you how much is two and two."

Angel smiled. "That shit I know, 'cause I know money. Two bucks two times is four bucks."

"Okay, Angel... you just passed your first test."

A bus boy brought water and menus. Vincent held the menu for Angel to see. He pointed to a line of print. "Angel, what you see there are words and the words are made up of letters. Right?"

Angel nodded. "Okay. Now the letters stand for sounds. When you want to make a certain sound, you write a certain letter. People who read know when they see this letter or that letter they make one sound for this one and another sound for that one. What I must do is get you to know which letters go with which sounds."

"I understand that."

"Good. Now, look at this word. Vincent pointed to 'soda' and said, "That is the word 'soda.' It has four letters. Each letter has a different sound and a different name. The four names are ess, oh, dee, and ay."

"You mean whenever I see that letter, the 'ess', I say ess?"

"Well, no, not exactly. In this case the 'ess' sounds like a snake hissing."

"Other sounds are different, right?" Vincent nodded. "How are they different?"

" I'm glad you asked me that. There are two different kinds... vowels and consonants."

"What's the difference?"

"Well, vowels are open sounds, like musical notes. They come out of the throat."

"Teach me those first." Vincent chuckled... maybe he could do this after all. "The vowels are ay, ee, eye, oh, and you.- say that."

Vincent did not realize it, but when he said the vowel names, he sang them in a descending order. Starting on about middle C, he sang them down to F. Angel repeated them effortlessly. Not only did he use the right names, he sang the same pitches. That was something Vincent did not miss. "See if you can do it this way." Now he sang them in ascending order and Angel again mirrored them exactly. Vincent was now becoming intrigued. "Angel, see if you can sing this." He hummed the opening phrases of a Bach invention, about ten or twelve notes. Angel listened, and then repeated them exactly. The phrasing was correct and the pitch was right on.

"Hey, man, what're you doin?" Carlos asked.

"You know, Carlos, I think Angel has real musical ability. I think he has perfect pitch. That means he is able to produce the musical sound he hears exactly the way it was made." Carlos stared at him.

"Well, it doesn't matter, I guess, but if he does have good pitch, I think it'll be easier to teach him to read. Writing is another matter."

Looking at them both, Vincent sensed that Angel had a better understanding of what was happening than did Carlos.

The waitress arrived and they ordered. While they waited, Vincent tested Angel by asking him to reproduce some songs and series of notes. In a short time, Vincent was convinced that Angel was some sort of musical freak. He was able to sing the exact notes in the exact time. As long as the material was in his range, he had no trouble reproducing the exact sounds he heard.

"You know what, Carlos. I'm going to try and teach Angel to sing as well as teach him to read and write."

"You can teach me music?" Angel asked.

"Angel, that's what I do. Teaching you music will be easy."

Angel was about to say something when their food arrived. Carlos and Angel had burgers Vincent ordered a salad. As he was putting on a blue cheese dressing, Angel asked what kind it was. Vincent told him it was blue cheese and that many people liked it although it was an acquired taste.

"An ark-wired taste? "What does that mean?"

"Angel, I didn't say ark-wired, I said ah-quired."

"Ah-quired," said Angel, his face breaking into a wide grin. "An ah-quired taste."

"That means it may taste strange at first, but if you have it enough times, you'll probably get to like it."

Angel put down his burger and grabbed Vincent's wrist. "You gotta understand. I feel like I never had no chance. I don't know nothin'. I sit in Carlos' place all day and watch television and I see stuff I never saw before. I don't know what they're talkin' about a lot... you gotta help me. You know things. I can tell." Then he looked at Carlos, who was staring wide-eyed at his friend. "Carlos tries to teach me, but he's like me. He don't know too much either."

As did Carlos, Vincent stopped eating and stared at Angel. Never before had he met someone who was so completely aware of what he did not know. Vincent wondered if other kids, even adults, realized they were empty. The kids he saw in the street were almost always in groups... each one not that much smarter than the other. Solidarity protected their ignorance, making it hard to step away from the group. But this kid had no one but Carlos... his only friend. He must be very smart to recognize his own ignorance, his own shortcomings.

Vincent remembered something his mother would say when talking about the neighbors. 'Your eyes are good enough to see a speck on somebody else', she would say, 'but they're not good enough to see an elephant on yourself' Vincent knew that was true. Criticizing others was a snap, but introspection, self-analysis- that was hard, maybe impossible for some. But this kid sees the speck on himself. This is a special kid. At that moment, Vincent knew he would help Angel come out of the void and into the world.

CHAPTER 17

LEO SAW A CAB waiting for the light at 13th and 7th, so he jumped in. The driver crossed 7th, went straight up 8th to 42nd, then over to First. It was an easy ride. The only drawback was the number of messages plastered on and in the taxi. There was a plastic lump on the roof sprouting ads, and more ads on a smaller lump on the trunk. Inside, both doors had advertisements mounted on them and there were ads on the back of the front seat. One was for McDonalds with a photo of pancakes and the picture gave Leo a yen.

Pancakes always sounded good in his head, but they rarely turned out. As a kid in the orphanage, he loved the idea of them- perfectly formed circles of batter, cascading waves of thick syrup and slowly melting butter. But orphanage pancakes were mean, hard, and thin with curled edges. The syrup and melted butter tasted like motor oil. It was like eating round pieces of heavily greased corrugated cardboard. He still could taste them. Nonetheless, he was still trapped by the image and still thought of them as they looked in ads. He had been pursuing the perfect pancake ever since. Every IHOP, every Perkins, and every new diner was always a test site. Maybe once or twice a year he got what he wanted and now, he thought, this was a good time for a new test.

He paid the cabby and headed straight for the coffee shop on First and 43rd where he sat at the counter and ordered a short stack. There was no need for three...if two were good, there was always tomorrow. Looking around, he saw the diner was not typical. It didn't have a grill behind the counter. Rather, it was behind a wall that had an opening and a shelf. The grill cook finished the dishes and placed them on the shelf for the waitress to grab and serve. Leo was a little sorry, for he wanted to see the grill cook work. Years before he had seen a real artist at work in a diner on 20th and 6th. That guy never wore an apron and dressed like he was going to the ball game or a movie—casual, decent clothes. He never got dirty, never spilled anything, could keep seven or eight orders going at once, and carry on conversations as he turned out absolutely perfect eggs and pancakes. He was the consummate grill master. People who understood what was going on would come from all over the City, not only to eat, but also to admire his coordination, skill, and his effortless control of the grill. In that diner you could order eggs anytime of the day or night and they would never taste like hamburgers or have strange looking, unidentifiable dark specks on their edges.

That guy kept one side of the grill hot and cooked the pancakes over that special spot. Their edges would roll, not up, but under, and the center would pull up and away from the grill. That left a beaded edge crisper than the center. Each was an eight-inch slice of heaven. That guy used standard mix, never any private mill stuff and never, never, any nuts, berries, or other things. Just plain flour, egg, oil and milk and the smarts to make them come out right. Where was he? Leo wondered... where was he now?

As he dreamed about perfect pancakes, the waitress brought his coffee. A few moments later an oval dish in front of him smelled the good smell. The plate held two dark tan ovals with deeper colored edges, each almost three-eighths of an inch thick. Could it be possible? Gaping at them, he cut off an inch with his fork and saw the air holes in the cream colored center. Then, without syrup or butter to cloud the issue, he slid the piece into his mouth and smiled. Symphonic music would have been appropriate. His smiled changed into a broad grin and he was happy.

He took the butter from the little paper cup and spread it on the top pancake, added a touch of salt and a dribble of syrup—real maple—and started to eat. It was a delight, a morning's joy. It was water in the desert... good wine in Italy. The waitress offered more coffee. Leo smiled and nodded. The coffee added to the wonder of it all. It took seven minutes and two cups of coffee to finish the pancakes.

"Mister, you really know how to eat breakfast. I ain't never seen nobody get a rapture from pancakes." Leo looked at the waitress. Like some who work around food, she was thin, but not athletic thin—she looked anorexic. Had on white sneakers and a white uniform that contrasted with her flaming red hair. Not the red hair of the runway model, but the red hair that ladies change from... not to. She could have been the over-fifty cover girl for the Irish Times.

"Darlin," Leo said slowly, "that was the best plate of pancakes I have had in a long time. I was hoping they'd be good, but these were better than good. They were absolutely fabulous." As he took another sip of coffee, the waitress turned and went behind the walled off section. A second or two later, she came out with the grill man. He was Chinese and looked like he never stopped eating. A fat Chinese guy with an apron so white it hurt Leo's eyes. The waitress pointed at Leo.

Walking over, he asked, in perfect English, "You like my pancakes, huh?"

"Damn right I do. They were great. Where did you learn to cook like that?"

"Went to cooking school. Learned from Teddy Millman, the greatest grill man ever. One day, I'll be like him... I'll get rid of this damn apron."

Unbelievable, Leo thought, absolutely unbelievable. "Apron or no apron, the pancakes were great. I'll be in here a lot and get to know all your specialties."

The guy smiled. "Cool... my name is Fred and I don't like to cook Chinese."

"My name is Leo and that's perfectly okay with me." Leo shook the extended hand and got up. He paid the bill, left a dollar tip and walked out with a lilt reserved for special mornings.

After exchanging a few words about Fred's diner with Smitty, Leo went upstairs. No one was around but Gottlieb, who didn't look well. "What's wrong? Are you sick?" Leo asked

Gottlieb's eyes flicked at the ceiling before settling on Leo. "No, I'm okay... it's just I got this damned assignment and Rose called in sick. It's a duet so I can't do it alone. I'm gonna have to get help from downtown on this one... all our guys are busy."

"Can I help?"

"Would you? I wanted to ask, but I thought that being a Lieutenant and being new, you'd probably turn me down."

"Hell, no. I want to get involved. The planning I'm doing I can do anywhere." Leo pulled a chair to Gottlieb's desk, sat, and then leaned across. "What kind of assignment is it?"

"The category is called personal protection. We call 'em PP's and sometimes they can be very interesting, but I think this one is going to be a pain. A U.S. senator's wife and the UN French Ambassador's wife want to go shopping. Usually, that's none of our business. UN or French security would normally handle it, but this trip includes the Mayor's wife and he put the word out that the NYPD is going to provide protection and that's that."

"But won't the other agencies be involved?"

"Of course they'll be involved. They'll probably be all over the place and that's what bugs me. We have to escort them, tend to their whims while their regular security will be watching and laughing their balls off as we open doors, get coffee and guard dressing rooms."

"Is there any danger for the women?"

"That's hard to say. There's always the possibility that some asshole will want to kidnap one of them or kill them all- who can say? You know what goes on in this City."

As Gottlieb talked Leo wondered if he wanted to be involved in this sort of thing? Traipsing around town with three high-powered ladies... but it's a new job and maybe I should get involved. He decided he would play along.

"I'd really appreciate it Lieutenant, if you could see your way clear to join me. Were you serious before?"

"Sure I was. I've never escorted anybody's wife anywhere. Always a first time..."

"That's the spirit... Look, I probably painted a dark picture, but that was because I didn't want to work with someone outside the unit. Workin' with you will be super." As he finished, the hallway door opened and Hoffheimer walked in with Melendez. "Leo, he called out... just the man I want to see."

He spoke as he came up to the desk. "Leo, we have a little problem this morning and maybe you can help out. I won't order you to do it, but it would be a problem solver if you say 'yes'."

"Say 'yes' to what, Captain?"

"Rose and Gottlieb were scheduled to escort some ladies today, but Rose is out of it. That leaves Gottlieb and..."

"Captain, excuse me for interrupting, but I spoke to the Lieutenant about helping me and he agreed. There's no more problem."

"Great... that makes things easier, but that's not all of it." Gottlieb's eyebrows shot up. "As I thought about the assignment, I realized there might be a situation where two males might have a problem."

Hoffheimer paused and, as if planned, the three turned to look at Melendez who was already getting up from her desk and reaching for her jacket. "My mother didn't raise a dummy. C'mon Gottlieb, let's hit the road."

"No." said Hoffheimer, holding his hand like a traffic cop. "You mean the assignment is canceled?" Melendez asked.

"It isn't canceled... I need Gottlieb for a meeting, so it's you and Leo for the PP." Melendez shot Leo a big, broad smile and he had a feeling the day would match the morning's pancakes. "Are there any questions, Leo?"

"No, Captain and I'm ready... shopping with four ladies could be a treat, at least I think it'll be fun."

Hoffheimer gave Leo a long look and then handed him a sheet of paper he took from his jacket. "That's the itinerary. You pick them up at the Plaza at 10:30. Shopping at Bergdorf's, Prada, and the Armani Boutique. Somewhere in there the ladies plan a lunch."

"Captain...what about transport?" Melendez asked.

"The usual. It's arranged."

"The usual?" asked Leo.

"You'll see," Melendez said, walking to the door. "Come on, Lieutenant, this may be a day you'll long remember." As Leo followed her he noticed that Hoffheimer and Gottlieb were smiling.

As they passed Smitty, he asked, "Are you two handling the shopping trip?"

"That we are, Smitty. It's Bergdorf's or bust."

"Hey, Lieutenant, you've got a better spirit about it than Rose and Gottlieb usually do."

"Hey, yourself, Smitty, wouldn't you want to spend the day with Officer Melendez?"

Outside, there was a gleaming limo parked at the curb. "Is that the usual?" Leo asked.

"Yes." she answered "Comes complete with security who knows how to drive."

This is class, Leo thought. When people think limo, they think Cadillac or Lincoln and they think black or white, but the one at the curb was a large Citroen with diplomatic plates. It was deep maroon with a light tan interior; very elegant, completely custom and odd-looking in that regal French way. Leo sensed Melendez was equally impressed. He looked at her and said, "I've never done this sort of thing, what's the drill?"

"That sounds like a line I used to use."

Leo smiled, thinking he was the virgin of the Personal Protection game. "Whatever happens, will you respect me in the morning?"

She laughed. "I never said anything like that."

"Seriously, what is the game plan?"

"You sit up front with the driver. I'll be in back with the ladies. Since there's room for six back there, you could join us if they want it that way."

"I think I'd rather ride up front. "I'd be a little uncomfortable with four ladies."

"Four?"

"Well... you may not consider yourself on a par with the Mayor's wife or Mrs. French Ambassador or Mrs. Senator, but I think you are."

"Leo, that's sweet. Thank you."

He noticed there was no stammer, no blushing, just straightforward confidence. She was quite a girl. The driver's door opened and a man came out to where they were standing on the sidewalk. "If you please, your ID." There was a slight accent. "Are you Rose and Gottlieb?"

Leo explained the situation. The driver listened, took their ID, opened the curbside door to use the radio. Three minutes later- it was okay. He got out, returned their credentials and opened the rear door. As they got in, Leo asked, "You work for the French, the UN or the City?"

"I work for the French, Lieutenant. I come with the car." I'll bet, thought Leo. This guy was too young, too good looking and fit, probably French security. Wouldn't make sense to have their Ambassador's wife depending on a Pakistani cabdriver.

They settled in the rear as the car floated from the curb. It felt like a jet taking off with the forward thrust pushing them deeply into the plush seats. There was a sense of great power and speed, but not a sound. Leave it to the French to build a real luxury car.

They cruised up Third and cut over on 59th. It was morning by the Plaza with the usual taxis, and limos out front, and the homeless drifting out of the park. The driver placed their car at the side entrance and when he got out, so did Leo and Melendez. They waited as he went inside to announce their arrival. Leo scanned the street. Central Park South had to be one of the great streets of the world, the serene looking Park on one side and some of the City's most prestigious buildings on the other. It was not their architecture or facade design that elevated them to high status; rather it was how those buildings fit into, or perhaps, how they created a true urban ambiance. The width and breadth of Central Park South lent those structures an elegance they would not have had if located elsewhere. They were just tall enough to make them almost invisible to strollers on the same side of the street, but crossing to the Park side allowed a complete view of their lush stonework. The more distant the viewer, the more elegant they appeared. It was like a clever painting.

Even the tourists, who might not know the reputation of the Plaza, walked in awe as they recognized the area's majesty. Leo was certain it was due to the open space, which provided visual freedom and a broad, clear view. One block south of the Plaza and a viewer was in a valley between buildings. A ravine, whose narrowness not only cut off sunlight, but eliminated a sweeping view of the street or any specific building. Because of the narrowness, a glance would not permit an appreciation of the width and height of any building. Looking up eliminated the ground view, focusing on the lower floors eliminated the upper floors. Streets were too narrow, viewers were too close, but not on Central Park South.

He wanted to say something to Melendez but didn't know what to say. He was trying hard to get away from the Vegas one-liner wise crack. Living alone drove his need for conversation, but the same isolation had stunted natural action. He had learned nothing at the orphanage except to mind his own business and keep his mouth shut. The Army was no different. Then, as now, he lived inside his head. So often, he scolded himself for not giving voice to his thoughts- a compliment, a complaint, anything that would release his emotions. Though he felt his silence to be almost natural, he fought it and wanted to make innocent conversation as others so easily did. He always felt like a dancer who had learned the steps an hour before.

The driver, standing to the side, opened the Hotel's side door. Living in New York enabled Leo to see many elegant women, but the two coming down the stairs in front of him were truly special. Both wore trim, tailored suits of a light colored cloth that matched the tone of their shoes and handbags. Each had long, flowing hair that gracefully swayed as they moved. Their unmistakable confidence and self-assurance were as visible as the gold sparkles from wrist, neck and ear. With erect carriage and unhurried movements, the two strode down the steps and across the sidewalk to the car. Leo thought they looked like poised, elegant award recipients, slowly crossing an enormous stage, unconcerned with the millions of gaping eyes. Neither was young, but their ages didn't matter. These were schooled, polished women- probably good at everything. The driver led them to the car.

"Lieutenant Flower, Officer Melendez, permit me to introduce Madam Rousault and Mrs. Henderson." Everyone smiled and Leo offered a feeble bow. Melendez looked at him as if to ask whether he was going to click his heels and also lay his jacket on the sidewalk. Leo acknowledged her look with a wan smile.

"How very good to meet you both." Said Madam Rousault. "I am certain I speak not only for myself, but also for Mrs. Henderson, when I say how delighted we are to be under your protection. It is most reassuring to know our safety is important to others." She spoke like an actress with a low-pitched and fully resonant voice. Leo learned later from Melendez that Madam Rousault was a famous film actress before she married the current ambassador and that he was her fourth husband. As Leo stared, he thought some vague recollections attached themselves to her face, but he could not remember if he had ever seen her before. Certainly, he thought her beautiful enough to be a star in any country, but realized he was at a loss to describe her beauty. He wondered if it was her skin, the shape of her face or lips, the size and color of her eyes, the slope of her eyebrows, or the way her hair framed her face. In a flash, he decided he had no idea why she was beautiful, just that she was. There was a symmetry and tightness to her features that made it incredibly easy and pleasurable to look at her. That's why she was a movie star, you idiot, he said to himself. You're just one of the many men who melted when they saw her. Nonetheless, a flowing warmth filled him and he realized he was in love with a woman he did not know and had seen for less than two minutes. It was like loving a photograph, a snap shot of a person. What would a psychiatrist make of his instant infatuation? Arrested development, would seem a likely diagnosis.

I don't think I think like a mature man, he said to himself, as he simultaneously mumbled an almost sub-sonic, "You're welcome."

As one, they advanced to the car with Melendez getting in back with the ladies as Leo got in the front. Heading east and uptown, the driver kept the partition between the front and back lowered and Leo thought it a nice touch- gave the expedition a family outing feeling.

Turning the corner of 86th, they saw the crowd in front of the mayor's residence. Not a large group, maybe fifteen or twenty, but all were behind the established police barricades. With some carrying colorful signs, they walked in a tight circle and looked almost festive, as if they were elementary school kids playing a game. He glanced to the back and saw the ladies did not share his view. They looked nervous and frightened.

"Damn these people." said Mrs. Henderson.

Madam Rousault spoke softly, "Alice, do not forget this is a democracy and people have a right to peaceful protest. Here they carry signs, I have been in places where they blow things up." Then, turning, she said, "Officer Melendez, I think it wise if we do not exit the vehicle."

"I certainly agree."

The driver pulled the car into a side entrance by a porch. A uniformed cop opened the left rear door and the mayor's wife came bounding into the car. Leo had seen her on television and thought her attractive. Now he saw the TV did not do her justice. She was very pretty and looked as wholesome as the other women looked worldly. Not only was his head swimming from being so close to so much femininity, but also the collective odor from the mixed perfumes absolutely blurred his senses. What a trip this is going to be, he thought.

As the driver slowly moved the large car into the street, Leo saw two vehicles waiting that had not been there when they pulled in. He pointed and the driver said, "Secret Service- French and American... nice to have friends around."

Limousine drivers generally pay little attention to parking rules, but those piloting cars with diplomatic plates don't pay attention to anything. This driver stopped the car on Fifth directly in front of the store as if there weren't hundreds of other cars behind him that had to swing out to get around. He owned the street and Leo realized it was the only way to drive in New York.

The driver exited and opened the sidewalk-facing door. Leo jumped out of the front and took a position between the car and the building. Melendez was opposite, about twelve feet away as the ladies prepared to exit. Leo watched them get out, first was the mayor's wife, next the senator's wife, last was Madam Rousault. Her legs entranced him. Long and smooth, and shining in the sun. He stared dumbly wondering about the color of her underwear.

Red? No. Pink? Possible. White? He was instantly blasted from his blissful reverie by a shout. A man next to him started yelling. Leo looked at him wondering if he were a nut case yelling about private lunacy or was he yelling specifically at the women, who now, along with everyone on the sidewalk, stopped to stare?

The answer was immediately apparent when the man raised his arm and Leo saw the knife blade flash in the sunlight. In a loud, frantic voice, the guy yelled "Vive L'Algerie, Vive L'Algerie!" as he stared directly at the wide-eyed Madam Rousault. Then in one quick step, he moved directly in front of Leo. At that moment, the ladies slowly started to move toward the safety of the building, but he specifically noticed Madam Rousault never took her eyes from the man who was about seven or eight feet away. Simultaneous with the ladies motion, Melendez shifted to intercept the guy who was about an arm's length in front of Leo. The guy must have been oblivious to where he was and what he was doing, since he never looked around and never stopped yelling.

Quickly, Leo judged shooting to be impossible since the bullet would go through the guy and do additional damage. He hoped Melendez realized the added danger shooting would create. Bullets flying through the entrance to Bergdorf s at 10:30 would be as bad as whatever this crazy guy intended.

Time compresses in emergencies and for Leo, watching the guy's right hand with the knife was like watching stop motion photography. Every movement was slow and seemed to go on forever, but suddenly the man moved. Throughout, he had remained frozen, his arm raised and his eyes glued on Madam Rousalt, but when he took a step in her direction, Leo made a quick decision. Rather than pull his gun, he reached for the blackjack he carried attached to his belt. With one sweeping motion and with great energy, he whacked the man behind his right ear and the fellow crumpled to the ground. There was no way to keep track of time, but afterwards, Leo figured the entire incident took less than two minutes.

It had started and ended so rapidly, many didn't realize what had happened. However, others were fully aware, but like true New Yorkers, pretended they were deaf, dumb and blind. Those people had learned that to stop, to be concerned, to offer eye contact, involved them in the ongoing event and that could be dangerous. It was wiser, thought certainly less humane, to keep going about your business and let those involved do whatever they planned. No one reacted to the man's shouting and no one reacted to the loud "bonk" when Leo hit him. It was like a movie where a character starts dancing and singing in the street and everyone keeps on walking and talking as if people singing and dancing in the street are as commonplace as lampposts.

Leo stared at the unconscious man on the sidewalk and became aware of the driver at his side. Then other men appeared. There were sounds of voices coming from radios. Was this a full-scale attack? At Melendez's urging, the ladies moved from the sidewalk into the store. When Leo realized those around him were security people, he relaxed as much as the adrenaline in his system would permit. The guy Leo knocked out was quickly scooped from the sidewalk and taken to a car. As that was happening, the driver told Leo to stay with the women.

Leo entered Bergdorf s and saw the four women looking at him. They weren't staring at him, but at his right hand. He grinned like a bad copy of Gary Cooper when, following their glance, he saw the ugly, but extremely efficient blackjack still dangling from his fingers. As he walked to them, he replaced it in his belt. Carrying one had been usual in his old, uniform days, and he never got out of the habit. Used properly, a sap was as effective as a bullet and better for situations like what had just transpired.

As he drew closer to the ladies, he realized fear was still in their eyes though the incident never seemed exceptionally dangerous. If the guy had a gun and had started shooting, that would have been different. But, luckily, a nut with a knife was not a problem and Leo was not going to get involved with speculation of what might have been.

Madam Rousault stepped to him and touched his arm. Leo could see the warmth and appreciation in her eyes along with the diminishing terror. "Lieutenant Flower, a moment ago you saved my life and I will always be in your debt." Before Leo could reply, she continued. "How quickly you acted. How decisively you acted." She looked up at him, her green eyes moist and lovely. Leo wanted to kiss her. "Thank you." She said softly. "Thank you for my life."

The others closed in and Mrs. Henderson asked Madam Rousault if she wanted to cancel the shopping and return to the hotel. Without hesitation, that suggestion was turned down and the three ladies, Melendez, Leo, and the driver went shopping.

CHAPTER 18

ABE AND MARTY WERE able to handle the buyers and the sellers, since it was a day of usual traffic. Drunks selling whatever they could for the price of a drink; students seeking typewriters; photographers needing another camera; workmen replenishing tool chests and musicians searching for that incredible find.

Abe was having a good day. He had sold two shotguns- a Remington, and a Browning; three cameras, one Leica, and two Canons; three Omega watches; two sets of golf clubs, and a Swedish music box that played ten-inch brass discs. Of all those items, he admired the music box most. He loved the tinkly sound.

When they were alone in the store, they occupied 'stations'- Marty was always in the rear alongside the cash register and Abe always stood in the front, on the left side. Because they were about ten feet apart, they spoke with raised voices and seemed to be endlessly arguing. However, when they did argue, which was rare, each became so exasperated they refused to speak.

As Marty was congratulating Abe for today's take, Carlos and Vincent came walking in.

"Well, well," Abe said. "Look who's here... and on his day off. Can't live without us, right?"

"Abe, don't be a schmuck. I ain't workin'. Me and Vincent was passin' by and we thought a 'hello' would be nice."

"For sure, it was Vinnie's idea."

"Very funny, very funny."

"Hey, don't you guys ever stop?"

"Vincent, you got to understand what's it like to work with a numbskull like this kid. All he does is stare out the window at the girls. He tells me he wants to get them to his place so he can inspect their moving parts."

"No disrespect, Abe, but I think Carlos and Angel are two serious and respectable young people."

"Angel? Who the hell is Angel?"

"Angel is my pal, my buddy. I take care of him since he ain't got nobody else."

"No parents, no home?"

"Abe, he ain't got shit. Ever since I know him he is alone... all by himself. No people. No friends, but me. And to top that, he used to be real bad. I heard he did nasty things and believe me, we don't want to know about what he used to do."

"What? Did he boost rubber erasers from the five and dime?"

"I ain't shittin' you man... this kid was bad. He iced people all over town. Marty knows him. Marty used to buy shit from him all the time."

"You mean that little kid who'd come in here and drop off purse-snatched swag?"

"Yeah. That's the kid, but he didn't get most of his stuff from old ladies in the street. He would ice people and loot out their places."

"Okay..." said Abe. "So we're dealin' with a summa cum laude from the Charley Manson School of Social Deviation. So what? If this kid is so bad, why are you his pal? Ain't you nervous he'll do you?"

"He's changed, Abe. He don't do that stuff no more. His whole life has changed."

"Why- did he win the lottery?"

"Yeah. That's right. He come into some cash. I guess you could say he won the lottery."

"Abe, what Carlos is saying is true. Angel is very intelligent and very talented. He has a unique musical gift. He really is special."

Abe nodded. "Well... that's different. Carlos' taste I don't trust, but you... you I believe." Interested now, Abe reached into his jacket for a Cuban. They watched the lighting-up ceremony and when he had it going, he asked Vincent. "What does the kid do... play guitar like the rest of them?"

"No, as a matter of fact, he doesn't, but I bet he could in a couple of days. He's probably a prodigy. Right now, I'm teaching him to read and write and also, I'm guiding his singing development."

"Read and write," Abe yelled out. "You mean the kid can't do that?"

Carlos sounded like a father defending his son. "Abe, you got to understand. Angel was turned out when he was little and he managed to make it. I don't know how, but he got by. He looks older than he is and he acts older, but he's a kid. You spend time with him and it slowly dawns on you that he's young. It's really weird."

"I'll vouch for that. When I first met him, I couldn't guess his age...I thought he was older, maybe 16 or 17, but I'm with him every day now, and I think he's 12 or 13. Truthfully, I have no idea and neither does he."

"This is one for the books." Abe said, and puffed out a cloud of smoke. "What kind of music is the kid into, rock and roll shit?"

"No. I've been teaching him music. I have been teaching him how to develop his voice and he learns so fast, I'm continually amazed. I haven't focused on anything specific, but he's in love with Church music. I think he wants to sing in church." Vincent looked at Carlos. "What do you think?"

"Oh, yeah. I took him to St. Pat's and when the chorus sang, he just about flipped. That was one of the big changes. When he was with me in the church, he ... well... it was like one person went in the church and another came out."

Abe, pulling on the cigar like he was in a contest to manufacture ashes, blew smoke in the air. "What kind of plans have you got?" What do you intend to do with this kid?"

"Plans?" Vincent asked, surprised at the questions. "I don't have any plans. Carlos asked me to teach him to read and write. The music thing was a surprise."

"Well," said Abe. "It seems you got your hands on a magical kid. A kid who is a musical genius, who don't have no family and who loves the Church." He paused and knocked ash from the cigar. "Look... if what you're tellin' me is true, then this kid is worth a fortune."

"Fortune? What kind of fortune?" Carlos asked.

Abe stared at him and Vincent like a third grade teacher stares at a slow class. "Look, you two... if what you say is true and Angel is a lost soul who had an evil past, but now walks a new road and is a church-goin', psalm singin', child prodigy... well... don't you think those dumb talk shows that are on all day would fall all over themselves to get this kid on screen? Can't you see it?"

He walked from behind the counter and in the middle of the store, used his cigar to punctuate his words. "There is Angel, all neat and clean, tellin' the world about how he used to do bad things... and then he went to church and heard the music... and was touched by God... and after that, he could make music and then he proves it by singin' a song that has them cryin' their eyes out. Are you crazy? This kid is a gold mine. The country needs a kid like this."

Carlos frowned. "But Abe... Angel can't go on television. He's wanted. If people see him, they might ID him and he'd be in jail in a minute."

"Maybe, maybe not."

"Waddaya mean?"

"Well, if what you say is true and he did ice the people he stole from, then no one alive can identify him. All the 'witnesses' are pushin' daisies."

Marty had been standing to one side, intently listening and now, he spoke up. "Look, the first thing we got to do is hear this kid and if he can really sing, then we got to sign him to a personal contract. We can form a partnership. The four of us and Angel... and if you guys aren't talkin' smoke, we'll be rich. With all the world turnin' into brown shit because of dumb-ass rock and roll, here comes a young kid who sings for the Church and does it after being touched by God."

Abe jumped in. "There could be concerts, records, Hell... there are good Christians everywhere who'd pay to catch some of the Angel's action?" Then he almost yelled. "Did you hear what I said? Did you hear? The kid is already named right. 'Angel.' Unbelievable, absolutely unbelievable." He stalked around the store pointing at what he named. "Are you kidding, look... there could be Angel guitars, Angel radios, Angel harmonicas, Angel everythings and Angel anythings." He stomped on the floor. "Jesus Christ, people are always ready for magic... always ready for some hokum about miracles." He smiled. "Believe me, it won't be hard to sell this kid. There could be millions of kids wearin' Angel outfits when they go to Church on Sunday.""

Marty looked like a hungry dog eyeing the supermarket meat counter. "Take it easy, Abe, take it easy. The first thing is to hear the kid sing." He turned to Vincent. "Is that possible? Does the kid sing in public? Would he come here or go to a rehearsal hall and sing?"

"Gosh, Marty. I don't know. We've never talked about anything like that. He sings because he loves to do it. I don't think he ever thought about singing for money."

"Hey, you guys," interrupted Carlos. "I been with him for a long time and he has changed from how he used to be, but he ain't changed that much. Angel ain't gonna become no TV nut promisin' people a talk with God. No sir. Angel wants a big-ass Caddy to ride in, same as me."

Marty smiled. "That's it Carlos. Don't you ever lose sight of what America can offer."

The four of them stood in a small circle staring at each other.

"Listen," Abe said. "We got to make some plans. Vincent, could you get the kid to sing where we could go and listen?"

"Sure, that wouldn't be a problem. I bet I could arrange it... St. Mary's is right here on 46th. I bet I could swing it for tonight."

"Do it!" insisted Abe.

"Yeah," said Marty and Carlos almost simultaneously.

"Look," Vincent said. "When we stopped in here, we were on our way to Carlos'. That's where Angel and I run through stuff. We'll go there now and talk to him. If he likes the idea, I'll call St. Mary's and if it's okay with them. I'll call you, Okay?"

"Perfect." Said Abe. "That'll be perfect."

A few moments later, Carlos and Vincent left and Abe and Marty went back to their stations.

"Do you think it can be done?"

"Don't you worry, Marty, I know people who can get any operation into gear. If this kid's got what Vincent says, concerts and records and public appearances are just the tip of it."

Leaving Marty's, Carlos and Vincent walked up 8th towards Carlos' apartment. Both could recognize bull when they heard it, but what Abe said made sense and did seem possible. The pop music industry was shabby enough to exploit anything for money. Nothing was out of bounds, not mental illness, not sex, not illegality, and certainly not religion. Vincent figured it was the right moment in time. With politics demanding a catering to the religious right, Angel's niche was perfect. The only immediate problem he recognized was the material. Straight ecclesiastical music would never be a mass-market item. Young people needed a beat to match their pulse and that made him think of what Richie Valens had done with *La Bomba*- took an old Mexican folk song, added rock rhythms, and Bingo! The material is the key. With Abe and Marty handling the business end and Carlos being Angel's go-for, my end, he thought, is the music.

As they walked, Carlos was thankful for Vincent's silence. He was hoping what Abe said would come true. If they could make money with Angel, then he could have all he ever dreamed of. There would be concerts filled with groupies who would be happy to bed down with Angel's main man. It would be great. He would really score, since Angel was no longer a star in that department. Carlos imagined himself in one of those round television beds surrounded by lots of pretty little girls. He closed his eyes and wondered what more could he want.

When they got to the apartment, Angel was not watching television. He was practicing a piece Vincent had prepared for him. It was part of Palestrina's *Missa pape Marcelli* and Angel really had it. The purity of his voice and the simplicity of his approach were breathtaking. Carlos was completely overwhelmed by Angel's talent- transfixed by the tonality and smoothness. He had no idea of the music's history or any way to compare Angel's singing with similar singing, but he understood the serenity and pleasure the singing generated. The more he listened, the calmer he felt. Before they interrupted Angel, Carlos whispered, "Vincent, when he sings that stuff, I get chills up my back. It is so great."

"It isn't only you. When he sings that song, I get chills up my spine, too."

Sensing their presence, Angel stopped and turned. "Hey, Vincent, how do you like that? Do you like the way that piece is comin'?"

"Angel, your voice is just beautiful, it really is. You're singing that piece exactly as it was meant to be sung. Maestro Palestrina is smiling."

"I am doin' exactly what you tol' me. I am breathin' full and slow and payin' attention to how I hold my mouth. Man, it is all happenin' like you said it would. When I hear that sound comin' outa me, I dig it... I really do." He put down the music, picked up a copy of the Daily News and pointed to the headline. "How about this shit? 'Man kills wife for their Anniversary'- waddaya think of that? I can read the shit outa this paper."

Vincent smiled. "Angel, that night when I said I would try to teach you to read and write, two things went through my mind. First, I thought since I didn't really know how to do it, you wouldn't learn anything and all that we'd lose is some time. Then when I realized you had a flair for music, I thought maybe I could accomplish something." He crossed the room and placed a hand on Angel's shoulder. "But now... I listen to you sing and I listen to you read and I am filled with wonder. It seems unbelievable, yet it's happened." He paused as if searching for the right language. "But it is important you should not think me a great teacher. You did it. You did it all. You have magic in you. With little help, you've learned to read and write and your singing... well, it is so beautiful; I cannot understand how it can be... But it is and I don't really care about how..."

They looked at each other until Carlos broke the silence. "Angel, my man, we got to talk. Vincent and me, we just come from Abe and Marty and we got a deal cookin'."

"Deal? What kind of deal?"

"Vincent and me, we was passin' and we stopped to say hello and we got talkin' about how great you sing and well, Abe and Marty, when they hear about you... man, Abe lights up like a Christmas tree and starts makin' all kinds of plans." Angel stared at him, a puzzled look on his face. "Oh, yeah... I just realized you don't know Abe. Well, he works there in the store and he's an old fucker, but he's smart and Marty told me he got plenty of dough..."

"What kind of plans?"

Vincent broke in. "Abe suggested you could make records and earn a good deal of money. There might also be concerts and television. You know... you could be like the Rolling Stones or something."

"I ain't gonna sing no rock and roll."

"Angel, that's the point." Carlos said. "We all want you to sing what you were just singin'. If we feel what you're doin' is so cool, so will other people and they'll pay to hear you."

" Ya mean Abe and Marty think I could make money singin' Church music?" He paused, turned to look out the window, and then turned back. "Vincent, do you think I can make money singin?"

"Yes, I do. I think your voice is as pure as any I have ever heard. It is clear and warm and people will love it... and they'll love you, also."

"That's right, man. Abe and Marty, they're willin' to put up money. With their dough, this can happen, man." Carlos looked first at Vincent and then at Angel, all the while, nodding furiously.

Angel stared at them. "How?"

"It can start tonight," said Vincent, "... if we can get into St. Mary's on 46th. I'm going to call and arrange it if you want to do it."

Angel shrugged. "Why not. I got nothin' to lose."

It took Vincent 15 minutes to arrange everything. Once before, he had provided music for that Church and the director, Father Taylor, knew him and went along with the idea. Being Episcopal, St. Mary the Blessed had a long tradition of music for the Mass so they were quite willing to go along. Since Vincent intended to provide the accompaniment, everything was set for 8:30 that night.

Later that evening, they met outside the church and waited as Vincent located Father Taylor and had the doors unlocked. They marched into the vestibule, which opened directly into the sanctuary. It was not a large Church but it had high ceilings, masonry walls and acoustics Vincent admired. While Carlos and Vincent set up some chairs, Abe and Marty sat in a front pew.

"Abe, aren't you a little uncomfortable?" Abe turned to look at him. "No, Marty, I'm right at home. Being deeply involved with Judaism, I come here every Friday night for services."

Marty's eyes widened and Abe paused long enough for his eyes to widen even more. "Hey, what kind of shamooz are you? All I know about religion is that it's a great racket." He paused again. "Are you nervous about bein' in church?"

"Yeah, a little."

"Forget it. If there was a God who got pissed off at wise guys like you and looked to get even, he'd be so busy there'd be no time for anything else. Guys like you get a free ride." Marty stared at him. A trifle exasperated, Abe explained. "Look... God's too damn busy with this world and with the universe. He don't give two raps for your penny-ante operation. In fact, if this scheme works out, we will do more for religion than Bingo. Ha!" He laughed aloud. "Can you see it? Can you picture it- you and me bein' declared heroes of the church. Me gettin' 'The Jew of the Month Award'- a tee shirt with a target on the back- and you gettin' a plaque from the bishop sayin' you're an okay guy. Hell, you could put it in the front window. Probably help you sell more golf clubs to the priests."

"You don't really believe in God?"

Abe smiled. "Marty, I'm too old to believe in God."

Carlos slid into the pew alongside Marty as Vincent opened a guitar case and took out a beautiful old Gibson E-5. "Hey look at that..." said Marty. "I sold that to him years ago. Gave him a good deal."

Abe laughed. "Marty we all know you're a prince... now shut up and let the kid sing." Vincent announced the first song Angel would sing would be an unaccompanied piece by Palestrina. Turning to Angel, he asked, "Do you want warm up?"

"Maybe I sing a scale or two. Do that thing with the guitar." Vincent played a few chords and then hit a major. Angel sang up and down the scale, then Vincent raised it a half step and Angel sang that scale, they did that for about five minutes.

Abe noticed the ease and amazing range of Angel's singing. How simple it seemed, he opened his mouth and the sound came out. He didn't strain or arch his back and his neck muscles were completely relaxed, unlike so many singers who looked like they might explode. Clearly, it was easy for him. Abe remembered seeing Steve Lawrence in Vegas where he noticed the same relaxed ease, the same lack of tension. It was like talking. All you had to do was talk in key, give the words feelings the audience can catch and stay with the rhythm.

He looked around the church. It was old. All the wood was dark except where people had worn away the finish. That beautiful smoothness of well-handled wood always impressed him. It didn't matter if the wood was an instrument, a banister or furniture. Years and years of human contact took away the burrs and the imperfections and smoothed it out. Abe remembered wood he had touched that felt as smooth as glass.

Vincent asked Angel if he was ready and Angel nodded and started to sing a chant-like song. It had a melody of notes loosely strung together. There was room for Angel to sustain tones, giving them color with twists of volume, quality and pitch. The listeners were carried away. Father Taylor, in the last pew, closed his eyes letting himself drift into a tranquility he usually got only through prayer. As Angel sang, they all floated into a world of serene quiet. Even Carlos was calmed.

Angel sang the piece twice and stopped. No one said anything. Immediately, Vincent began a song by Couperin with which he had taken some liberties. Rather than follow the melodic line to completion, he had inserted a repeat which when followed by a second repeat, established a rhythm pattern that had a contemporary feel. Angel sang the beginning lines letting the guitar follow. At the first repeat, Angel stopped and Vincent played the rhythm. Then Angel sang, only now, he followed the steady beat Vincent had developed.

The melody was not in a pop song pattern and seemed to go on and on. With the guitar playing a steady pulse behind the ever-changing notes, Angel sang, and a trance-like state was evoked for his audience. At one point, Vincent stopped abruptly letting Angel sing up an octave to a note that was sustained. With no additional breath, Angel sang down the same path, ending with a note in a baritone range. Then Vincent started the rhythm and Angel followed in a low register, coming finally, to a series of notes high in the scale. He held the last note until Vincent played out the rhythm pattern, which had become an integral part of the song- an inseparable melody and beat. Then suddenly, they stopped and there was silence.

The silence continued. Usually it's easy and comforting to speak after a performance by mediocrity. The quicker the conversation, the faster the short-term memory releases the previous input. Enough talk and the recollection of the 'presentation' will vanish. At this moment, Angel's audience hoped for the opposite. They sensed if no one spoke, they would be better able to hold onto what they had experienced. In a world of sham, it is rare to be exposed to real and wonderful talent. Everyone who had intently listened to Angel realized it was an important moment.

Marty was the first to speak. "Damn, that was fabulous...really great. I never heard anything like that before. "Abe... wasn't that wonderful?"

"For once, Marty, you got it right."

Vincent watched them and saw their appreciation. Throughout the years, he had seen many audiences and was able to read their signs. Like so many other groups Vincent had seen, Abe, Marty, Carlos and Father Taylor had no idea of Angel's musical genius, but it wasn't necessary for them to know anything at all to appreciate what they heard. People are able to recognize quality when they hear it even though they are completely ignorant of what is involved.

Father Taylor slowly got to his feet and walked down the aisle. "Vincent, I want you and Angel to bring my congregation the pleasure and revelation you have brought to me. I want you here on Sunday." Vincent looked at Angel who was smiling. Turning to Father Taylor, Vincent asked, "What time?"

"Be here for the ten o'clock. That's the Mass most come to and I want as many people to hear what I have heard- to experience the inspiration and the quiet joy." Turning to Angel, he said, "Young man, you have a talent God wants you to share. How wonderful for you to be the instrument to bring us closer to him."

Angel beamed at the man. "You like it, huh? You thought it was good?"

Father Taylor had been at St. Mary's for over ten years and in that time he had been exposed to many Broadway types, like those with real talent to star-struck wannabes who thought they were gifts to humanity. Some were good; a few had real ability and the humility of the great, but none matched this young boy, who obviously had no idea of the enormity of his greatness.

Slowly and softly, Father Taylor said, "I thought it was more than good. You have brought to me an opportunity few have. People come to this church every week, some come every day. They want to believe and need help to keep their faith. You have given me the chance to bring to my congregation the proof they seek. When they hear you sing, they will know it is as they hope. Your voice is from God- anyone who hears you sing will know. I will be honored to have you sing in this church, next Sunday or any day."

"Well, how about that? How about that?" Abe pushed his elbow into Marty's side. "We have ourselves a winner and we are in the money." Then he asked Vincent, "What was that song? Was it Catholic? Protestant? What?"

"Both of those pieces are usually considered Protestant, but it doesn't matter. They apply everywhere."

"Well, it might be stretchin' it a bit to push them in a Temple, but that's not the point. Can you teach Angel some general stuff, songs that are acceptable to everybody?"

"No problem, Abe. When you go back far enough, it all sounds much the same. Add some pieces in a Minor key and you cover everything and everybody."

"Now you're talkin'." Shifting to Father Taylor, Abe asked, "Father, would it be possible to bring some recordin' equipment in here for Sunday so we can get the first performance on tape? It won't be in the way."

"I don't know you, Sir, but to answer you're question... It won't hurt anything. We've done that before. We've had Jazz services and many recordings have been made here- the acoustics are very good. Also, if recordings mean more people will hear Angel, the last thing I would do is stand in the way."

"Father, I think you'll be very happy when you see the money basket on Sunday. This church is going to be famous!"

Abe was true to his word, on Sunday, three technicians placed microphones, and he had also arranged for a blitz of ad flyers announcing *Music at St. Mary's,* to be placed in neighborhood mailboxes. The local TV news shows were called and two of the four showed up.

Vincent had worked out thirty minutes of material with Angel and they agreed to repeat two of the pieces if everything went as they hoped. As it turned out, Angel had to repeat the entire thirty minutes and then add the two-piece repetition. While Vincent shifted from guitar to keyboard and back, Angel sang almost nonstop for close to seventy minutes. Throughout his performance, no one in the congregation moved, coughed, fidgeted, or regretted their attendance. When it was over, they looked liked people with fulfilled dreams... like little kids who had long pined for a Christmas present they had just received. Abe thought some looked like they had been sexually satisfied, so complete was their rapture. The congregation looked pleased, refreshed, a little tired, but overall, inspired and happy.

Vincent had prepared pieces by Allegri, Schulz, Vaughn Williams, and Ontario, in addition to the Palestrina and Couperin. As Angel sang, the assemblage followed every syllable and every nuance. After the first selection, the audience unconsciously matched Angel's breathing. Vincent was amazed to see hundreds inhaling and exhaling together. All of them, from little kids to the eldest worshippers, metered in air and gradually let it out, as Angel sang. They became one large being, almost one living organism. Most had their eyes closed and ecstatic smiles on their lips.

Vincent's arrangements bore slight surprises such as Angel singing down the scale to an obvious and expected final note that he never sang. Instead, he changed key and modulated to another song. As all were mesmerized and soothed by his voice, he too was affected. Thoughts of his past were in his mind and in response, tears streamed down his face. While not understanding what he was singing, Angel did recognize a quality of repentance and sought that feeling as he sang. He tried to sing an apology.

When they finished there was silence, since no knew the appropriate response. Father Taylor seized the opportunity to speak of God's blessing, telling the gathering about Angel. How, in a short time, he had developed the amazing ability to sing God's music. Everyone understood, for they felt as God had been with them.

A man in one of the front pews stood, as if in Sunday school, and asked if Angel would return the following Sunday. Father Taylor looked at Angel who was looking at Vincent. When Vincent smiled, Angel nodded to Father Taylor. The man looked past the Priest and speaking to Angel, said, " I know I speak for everyone here when I tell you how wonderful it was to hear you sing. I will be here next week to hear you again." Then he started to applaud and all in the church joined until there was a heartbeat like pulse of appreciation.

Father Taylor called for silence and invoked the final prayers. As people slowly moved out they filled the 'poor box.' Abe had put in a one thousand dollar check on his own to make certain the church benefited. Now, as he and Marty stood in the rear watching the money accumulate, they realized what they had hoped for was going to be true. Angel was going to be a major star.

That night on the late news, two channels got about 30 seconds of the story aired. 'Young singer mesmerizes church audience' was the lead on Channel 4. They showed some of the crowd, got some comments and played about eight seconds of Angel's singing. Even at that time of the night, they got 73 phone calls. Abe hoped the newspapers were watching and would run it the next day, providing some additional free publicity.

CHAPTER 19

LEO WONDERED HOW HE could have considered retiring. More action had come his way in the last three weeks than in the past three years. Maybe the job molds the person, he thought. I had a desk job-I became a desk job.

His thoughts stopped with the elevator. A few seconds later, he was in his apartment and finding it stuffy, opened the window nearest his still unmade bed. After all the years in the orphanage and then the Army, a disheveled bed represented work unfinished. For him, it was the same as stopping running water, answering a ringing phone, or turning off the lights. It had to be done. He was convinced he envied people who could leave water flowing, phones ringing and every light bulb they owned, blazing.

Finishing the bed, he stared at it, and saw Madam Rousault on it, a satisfied smile on her face, her arms stretched above her head and her hair spread on the pillow. He stared until the image vanished. Then shaking his head, he turned from the bed. Plummeting back to reality, he looked around the apartment; everything was where it should be. Glancing back to the bed, he shrugged at its flat, bland neatness. He crossed the room, turned on the radio, and headed for the shower. Ten minutes later, he came out to some good jazz- sounded like Horace Silver. Hearing that music put him in the mood to hear more, so he decided to eat light and go to the Vanguard. He loved to carefully plan his time and truly cherished the real freedom doing so provided. So many thought it was easier to make no plans and be free to whatever came along, but that was not freedom. Live that way and you became a victim of whatever did come along. Leo believed that absolutely free choice led to paralysis. People stalled out waiting for the perfect choice to turn up, but it never did... and those people always had to settle. He remembered hearing that as the hour grew later, the girls in the bar got better looking.

As a kid at the Friday dances the nuns used to chaperone; he watched the girls refuse to dance with this boy and then that boy and then another. They were waiting for that perfect guy. He never showed and they never danced. Some told him it was better that way, but he never believed that. It was the same now in the bars. He watched attractive women of all ages pass up guy after guy waiting for 'Mr. Right.' Unfortunately, he never got there and the ladies settled for a schmuck or went home alone. Guys were even worse. They passed up wonderful, appreciative women while they waited for a combination of Madame Curie, Mae West, Zeta Jones and Meg Ryan. If such a woman existed, I'd wait for her also, Leo thought, but that model was not in production.

Making plans and carrying them out without interruption—that was the essence of freedom. You decide what and when to do something and then do it. Living like that put Leo in control of the happenings in his life and he loved the security and the comfort. It was the answer to the uncertainty in his past. It was a barricade against the memories of intrusive institutions... the "Leo do this, Leo do that" years. It wasn't much better in the Army. "Sergeant Flower is to report to Lieutenant Smith."

"Flower—go there, come here, get this, get that." Now it's different. Now I decide what I'll do. Tonight, I will eat and then go the Vanguard to hear some good jazz.

He put on chinos and a sweatshirt while he thought about food. In the kitchen alcove, he looked through his cabinet of cans, choosing tuna. He added a salad and while the coffee dripped, he ate and listened to public radio to get in touch with the day's events. Glancing at the newspaper, he saw no mention of what had taken place that morning—too soon—maybe tomorrow. Then again, it might not get a mention anywhere. It was over so quickly people who witnessed it would probably never connect it to an attempted assault. Most would swear it was just a local street nut that got 'removed' by the cops when he acted up a little more than usual.

The paper mentioned little it hadn't mentioned the day before, so he put it aside. The radio was playing a feature by a reporter who covered the northern United States by train. He talked about the towns, the people, the history and the potential of the areas he passed through as the train followed the tracks west. It was fascinating radio and held Leo's attention as he finished his meal. Maybe one day, he thought, I'll take a train trip across the country. That would be marvelous. Flying made the trip itself meaningless. Flying got you where you were going so you could be there; trains made the going important. On a train, travel became an end in itself. Yes, he thought, maybe the next vacation I will take a train across America and see those small towns and talk to people. I want to see this country, he realized.

He was washing the dishes when the lobby intercom buzzed. "Yes?" he said into the wall unit. "Lieutenant, this is Roberto. There is a limousine driver here who wants to know if you are at home and would appreciate a visitor."

"Roberto, that depends on the visitor."

There was a silence, then Roberto's voice. "The driver said the party is French and you would understand."

"Send whoever it is right up," Leo responded.

He went to the door figuring it was someone from the Embassy who had come to shake his hand and give him a medal for that morning's efforts. As he heard the elevator start up, he smiled at the thought it might be the French ambassador himself, who would present a bottle of decent wine, kiss him on both cheeks, say, "Merci et Au Revoir" and beat it. Leo chuckled. When the elevator stopped, he opened his front door and took a half step into the corridor, enough to see who was getting out. What he saw made him freeze. Stepping onto the corridor's carpet was a slim foot wearing a beautiful and graceful, high-heeled shoe- a combination of black suede and pearls. As more of the figure emerged from the elevator, Leo saw it wasn't the French Ambassador or some minor functionary, it was, as if in response to his secret prayers, the Ambassador's wife. She looked to the right then to left and met Leo's eyes.

As he gaped, she smiled. "Lieutenant Fleur, you do not mind the intrusion?"

Leo was too stunned to reply. He wondered if there could be a more astounding surprise- a more wonderful and heart-stopping wish fulfilled. Lurching into the corridor, he said, "Oh, please come in, come in, Madam Rousault. You could never be an intrusion."

"Oh, please, call me Jacqueline," she said, pronouncing it, Zhacklean. "You are no longer on duty." Smiling, she walked past him into the apartment and he almost staggered. Her perfume hit like a taste of exotic food. First there was nothing, then there was something new and nameless. He stood in the hallway looking at her, astonished at her real beauty. She was no product of a make-up factory or a Brazilian plastic surgeon. She had a genetic beauty with a bone structure that offered a perfectly formed face. Shifting his eyes, he instantly concluded her graceful, athletically slim figure was a product of the ballet academy rather than the gymnasium.

She turned and looked at him still standing in the hallway. "Lieutenant, you are not coming in?" He felt stupid and childish. He had never encountered a woman like her and felt terribly inadequate as he lurched into his apartment and closed the door.

"I'm sorry... you're the last person I expected to come out of that elevator. I'm kind of stunned."

Looking serious, she said, "Yes, I guess I should have called, but I was afraid if I did so, you would have found an excuse and we would be unable to meet."

Surprised, Leo asked, "How do you know I wouldn't want to meet with you?"

"I did not, but I had my suspicions." How right she was, he thought. I would have chickened out, for sure. She's out of my league. Hell, I screw up dates with secretaries, how could I deal with her? Aware of his silence, she asked, "Lieutenant, are you all right?"

Sighing, he said, "I'm fine. It's just that I know you're right. I would have made some stupid excuse to avoid a meeting." He paused. "How did you know that? How did you guess that after meeting me only once?"

"I know men, Lieutenant. You are a policeman and know criminals. I know men."

She wasn't wearing a coat, but a suit of iridescent material that changed color as it reflected light from the windows and lamps. He guessed her jacket had moderate shoulder pads for it formed a perfect vee to her waist. Her skirt, which ended at the knee, was the exact right length to frame those great legs. She was really something to look at.

"You are certain I am not intruding?"

"Oh no, not at all. Please, sit down and let me get you something- coffee or a drink? I have some wine." She placed her bag on the table and sat on the sofa, facing him.

"Some wine will be perfect." He had recently bought a bottle of white zinfandel. The guy at the liquor store said it was tasty and pleasant. Leo took his word, for he had never developed a taste for wine and knew zero about it. He came out of the kitchen with two glasses and saw her standing by the bookcases.

"Have you read all these books?"

"Yes I have. I read a lot."

She looked around the room. "I see you have no television. Why is that? Do you need the time to read?" Before he could answer, she moved back to the sofa and he sat on the facing red chair. He looked at her as he placed the drinks on the table. What a picture she made. The dark wood of the bookcases behind her created a frame-like setting as the light from the copper lamp reflected the maroon of the sofa onto her suit. It was easy to see how good looking, pretty people steal your eyes. Visually avoiding them is impossible. Who's to say whether it is their satisfying physical symmetry or the viewer's lust that creates the subtle magnetism? Leo could have looked at her for hours. She was like a painting, poised and carefully arranged.

"You know, that's funny. I had a TV, but just got rid of it. Tossing it out was like giving up smoking- took a lot of strength. So now, I don't have one- mainly because I think it's a waste."

"What do you mean?"

"I have a theory, but I don't want to bore you or keep you. You didn't come here to hear my views about the evils of television."

"You are correct, Lieutenant."

"Please, call me Leo."

"I will... now what is your theory about television?"

"You really want to hear about that?" Leo asked with innocence and surprise. He knew she would say 'yes' and he knew he would tell her even though he wanted to kiss her and make love to her. Why else did she come?

"As I see it, it appeals to the worst in people. It satisfies the seven deadly sins."

"The seven deadly sins... is it that bad?" She asked, sipping some wine.

"Yes it is. The food commercials cater to gluttony and sloth, the trashy movies to lust and anger, and the soap operas to envy, pride and greed. It's not a very good influence."

"I have never thought about it that way. It sounds terrible." She paused, took another sip. "Have you ever seen any of my movies on TV?"

"No, but I'm sure I've seen one or two in the theater."

"Did you like them... me?"

"I think you're a very good actress, but I remember having trouble with the subtitles. I was so busy looking at you, I didn't read them and the plots escaped me. I didn't know what was going on. I'd rather look at you anyway." He swallowed... "you're so very beautiful."

She shifted her weight, moving a little closer to the edge of the sofa. "You almost seem afraid of me... are you?"

He could feel sweat break out on his upper hp. What could he say? Of course he was afraid of her. He was always uncomfortable one-on-one with women. He always felt dumb and stupid. "It isn't that I'm afraid of you.... it's more that I don't know how to be with you. I wasn't brought up in a family situation. I don't know how to act around women."

"Why not?"

"I was raised by Catholic nuns in an orphanage and believe me, they were no help and neither were the priests."

"Were you not in the Army?"

"I was, but that was no help either. I met women in bars, drank with them, had sex with them, but never got beyond barroom talk. I've never had a long term relationship with a woman."

"I'm surprised. You're an attractive and competent man. I bet a lot of women you met would have been thrilled to be with you or stay with you."

"Maybe, but that doesn't matter anymore. I'm too old to..." Interrupting, she asked, "too old? How old is too old?"

He had no answer so he retreated to a swallow of wine. They sat, with the little table between them as time passed. Suddenly, she asked, "What were your plans for tonight? What were you going to do before I arrived and ruined your evening?"

"Oh, don't say that. You haven't ruined anything. I cannot tell you how thrilled I am that you are here... It fills me with pleasure to look at you... and meeting you... having you sit there across from me is like magic. There is no way on earth you could ruin any plans I might have had."

"What do you mean you don't know how to talk to women? What you just said is complimentary and a pleasure to hear."

"I'm just telling you the truth... what I feel."

"And that is all you ever have to do. Tell every woman you meet exactly what you feel. There is no reason to hide. If you feel passion, say so. If you do not, say nothing. Telling the truth makes everything so very easy." Then she smiled at him and the room lit up.

No longer being able to control himself and seeing no reason why he should, he stood and took the wine glass from her hand. Reaching for her other hand, he gently raised her from the sofa. Pulling her to him, he kissed her. Equaling his passion, she pressed her body against him. With her face inches from his ear, she said, "You saved my life today and I will forever be in your debt."

"I don't really think I saved your..."

She placed a finger against his lips. "What you think does not matter. I think you did and that is sufficient." She kissed him again and he felt an overwhelming passion.

"I want to make love to you. I must make love to you." he whispered.

"Come." She took his hand and they walked to the bed. He sat and then got up. "What is it?" she asked. "The lights- should I turn off the rights?"

"Do you want to?"

"Oh, God no. I want to see you."

"Then leave them alone."

He kissed her once again and felt light-headed. She took a step back and began to unbutton her jacket. He smiled as he saw her bra... it was navy blue. He had never considered that. She tossed the jacket onto one of the chairs and they kissed again. Then she pushed him and they fell onto the bed in a tangle of arms and groping hands. He was amazed to realize her passion was as great as his.

Their lovemaking was slow and elegant... like being on a train, he thought, don't rush ...enjoy and relish the trip... you'll get there. She enraptured him with her smell, with the music she brought to his soul. He didn't know what she felt, but he knew she was as passionate and needy as he and they fit together well.

Later, sipping wine and talking, she asked him why he liked being a policeman and he told her it was important because he believed in order and in keeping the chaos under control.

"Have you ever been in jail? Do you know what it's like for those you arrest?"

Smiling, he said, "As a matter of fact, I was, but only for one night."

She moved her head back a little as she looked at him and he knew she wanted to hear all about it. "It was when I was in the Army. I was stationed in Texas and we used to cross the border to Juarez whenever we could. I got drunk one night and fell into a... into... ugh...."

"Into what?"

"It's kind of embarrassing."

"That's very obvious. Tell me... into what did you fall?"

He sighed. "In Juarez they had an open sewer.... a pit... that ran through the part of town where the bars were. I fell in and started yelling my head off. As you would guess, a crowd gathered and everyone had a great time... until a cop showed up. As I tried to climb out, I got his pants wet with the slop that was all over me."

"For that, you went to jail?"

"It's clear you've never dealt with the Mexican police. In border towns they're the Supreme Court and God rolled into one."

"You didn't like jail?"

"Hell, no! Even drunk I knew a cage was no place for a human being."

She leaned against him and put her glass to his lips. He sipped and then took the glass from her hand and put it on the floor. He kissed her and slowly ran his hands over her slim body. Then they made love once again.

Leo knew he was dreaming because the face in the mirror of Juarez's *Black Cat Bar* was his 'now' face. It wasn't the face of a twenty-year-old kid filled with Tequila. His eyes shifted from the mirror to movement on the staircase at the side of the barroom. Coining down the stairs in a slow provocative glide was Jacqueline dressed in a nun's habit. She smiled at Leo and he walked to meet her. They sat at a small table and drank. He wanted to ask her why she was wearing that outfit, but didn't. After more drinks, she took his hand and led him upstairs to a small room. When the door closed, she tore off the nun's clothes and revealed a navy blue dress covered with glittering stars. Then there was a burst of flamenco music and she began to dance. He jumped into the beat and danced with her. She circled as he glared at her in a pretty good imitation of Rudolph Valentino. They teased each other in time to the music and when he was too aroused to continue, he threw her on the little bed, tore off her clothes and made love to her while she bit his flesh. Suddenly, he was awake. "You were dreaming." She said.

He told her his dream and she laughed. "I have a dress like that. Next time I will wear it so you can tear it off."

He couldn't believe what she said. "Next time?"

She shook her head. "What is the matter with you? Of course, next time. Do you think I would be here if I didn't share your feelings?"

It was like waking up and finding you're the King of France. "I don't know what to say. It's been so fast... so wonderful. Is it still the same day?"

"Yes, my love... it is..." She kissed him. "We will have good times."

"What about your husb.... the ambassador?"

She laughed. "He would thank you for entertaining me, since I think he is happier with his government friends than he is with me. All day and night, they sit and make plots. He tells me they are creating scenarios to better understand the world's problems. I tell him he's wonderful because the world needs saving." She laughed and leaned over to kiss his chest. "We will be good for one another... we will discover each other... but now... I must leave."

He took her hand, "I have much to learn... not only about you... but about me."

"You will, Cherie, you will." Her use of that word stunned him. It was a word from books and film, not from a living person inches away... and certainly, he never expected 'Cherie' to refer to him. "I can't believe this." He said. "It's another dream and I'll wake to find you never existed."

She came up against him and while they kissed, she grabbed his testicles. "Dreams don't do that, do they?"

He laughed. "None of mine... ever."

Girlishly giggling, she jumped from the bed and went into the bathroom. In less than 15 minutes, she emerged with her hair and make-up in place. She wore her clothes except for her jacket, which he helped her put on. "I will call you tomorrow. What is a good time?"

"I'm usually here at six... but you never know. Can I call you?"

"That will be difficult. There are many people between the telephone and me. I have a large staff."

He went for his clothes. "Wait, I'll have to get you a cab. You can't be alone in the streets."

"There is no need. My driver is waiting."

"Your driver?"

"That's right... but don't think about it. He is loyal and very French." Standing with only a towel around his middle, he felt foolish, since she once again looked as cool and serenely composed as she had when she arrived. He didn't know what to say. "Jacqueline. I..."

"Cherie... I feel the same. There is no need to say anything. We have had a wonderful moment and we will have more." She turned and walked to the door and opening it, stepped into the hallway... A moment later the elevator arrived and as she stepped in, she blew him a kiss. Back inside, he looked at the clock and saw it was half past ten,. Four hours, he was amazed. It seemed moments. As in a trance, he walked to the bed and dropped onto it. He slept peacefully and did not dream.

CHAPTER 20

WHEN HE OPENED HIS eyes to the light, a trace of her perfume floated from his pillow. Staring at the ceiling, he thought about the previous night and knew no one would believe such a tale. A world famous actress... an international beauty had come to his apartment to thank him for saving her life. He laughed when he recalled Ilene once telling him, that after a favor, a thank you card was vital and should never be forgotten. A card would have been nice, but last night's thank-you was far better.

With her still in his mind, he showered, shaved and headed uptown. Breakfast was coffee and a roll carried to his desk. He had been thinking about the task Hoffheimer dropped on him and realized assassinating the pope would be a supremely stupid act. It would provide no benefit for anyone, and if some lunatic did manage to do it, who would embrace him? And if some group did do it and was dumb enough to admit their involvement, they would also be shunned. There was nothing to gain from killing the pope; except for the thrill some nut would get from killing someone special. That bothered Leo, since there is no way to protect against those people except by eliminating the opportunity. That means bulletproof cars, bulletproof glass and the inspection of everything- from the air to the toothpaste... and that demands tons of money and plenty of troops.

Potential danger is not a secret and all public figures know it exists. Being a target comes with the job and certainly even the Pope knows that to be true. Leo likened the Pope to a painting in a museum. Little would be gained from its destruction, since demolition gave rise to another hung in its place. Six months later, a memory exists, nothing more. Kill the man, there would be another. As with Kennedy, the bastards killed him, but they couldn't kill the Presidency. It is then same with the Papacy. The man is but a moment in time.

Leo turned on his desk computer and prepared a report of his thinking knowing Hoffheimer would carefully consider his estimations. With that done, he completed another report covering the events of the previous day. He carried them to Hoffheimer's and was surprised to find only Melendez. "Hi," he said, as he walked in.

"Leo... just the man I was thinking about..." He stared at her.

"I wanted to make sure I tell you that I thought your action yesterday was as smooth as anything I have ever seen. You turned off a situation before it got started and that's really cool."

"Look, I didn't do anything special. The guy was right in front of me."

"Say whatever you want. You were great... and ... I may add, shopping at Bergdorf s and the boutiques is one great way to spend a day. Now I know how the other half lives."

"You're right about that," he said, wistfully. "Those ladies are special." A moment later, he snapped back from his thoughts and asked, "Where are Gottlieb and Rose?"

"Over at the UN."

"Is he in?" he gestured at the door. She nodded, and then asked, "You want to lunch later?"

"Sure, if he doesn't tie me up." He walked to Hoffheimer's door, knocked and entered when he heard, "Come," from inside. He was at the window when Leo came into the room, but he strode over to shake Leo's hand.

"From what I've been able to piece together, you really saved the day yesterday. The cloak and dagger boys who observed the action were all compliments. None of them realized there was a problem until it was over."

"Captain, it happened in a moment. The guy was real handy and I whacked him when I saw the knife."

"Did you hit him with your hand?"

"No. I always carry this." He opened his jacket so the strap handle of the blackjack was visible. Hoffheimer stared at it. "Doesn't that thing get in the way? I mean... doesn't it slide around to the front and hit you in the balls?"

"It did once, after that I had elastic loops sewn into the side of all my pants. The sap stays in the loop until I pull it out. It's really handy."

Hoffheimer smiled and walked around the desk to his big leather chair. "Now, what else can we talk about?"

"Well, I'd like to talk about the assignment you gave me... about the pope." Hoffheimer leaned back in his chair and Leo started talking.

"I don't believe any group, no matter their position, would benefit from his death. If you have a gripe with GM and you kill the CEO, it does no good. They get a new one in hours. You can't kill an organization by killing its head, at least not an organization like the Church. No group I considered, no rival religious groups, no atheist group, no Middle East terror mob, no one would gain... and frankly I don't think any of them really give a damn. Whatever they want, killing the pope would not get them closer to it. It's a non-event." He wanted a drink of water. "But... on the other hand, a solitary nut with a personal mission is hard to defend against."

"Oh, yes," Hoffheimer said, "The Kamikazes could be shot down because you knew what they were and you could see them. A lone killer in a crowd of thousands is not visible until after his act. So... are you saying we have to do what's always been done, separate the public from the target?"

"Exactly, and I don't see a major role for us... what with Vatican security, the UN and the Feds. I think there might be more security than worshippers... maybe we should all go to the movies."

"Yes, that would be nice, wouldn't it."

"But I want to add, Captain, I'm working on some other ideas."

"Leo, anything that can keep fingers off triggers is fine with me."

Leo got up. "I guess that's it. I've typed my thoughts about all this and yesterday's events for you to read. It's all here. He placed the papers on the desk and when Hoffheimer nodded, turned and exited the room.

Rose, Gottlieb, and Melendez were at their desks. As he passed Melendez, he asked, "Lunch?" She nodded and said she'd meet him downstairs at eleven forty-five and added that he'd gotten two phone calls while he was with the captain. When Leo got back to his desk, he looked at the messages. One was from the French Embassy; the other was from Abe Rosenberg. He had been told it was impossible for anyone outside special personnel to get the number of this outfit. How the hell did Abe get it? Looking at the other slip made Leo squeeze his groin muscles. He thought he could still smell her perfume as he dialed the number. He was connected to the Limo driver who told him there was to be a major dinner that night and everyone was deeply involved. Attendance was mandatory and that went for the ambassador's staff and family. He asked Leo if he understood the message. Leo said yes, thanked the driver and hung up.

The driver is *her* driver, he realized, and he could probably write a full-fledged expose. That must be one loyal guy. I wonder why? He asked himself. What does he owe her to keep her secrets? What has she done for him to ensure his silence? Interesting questions. Maybe I'll ask him one day, since he not only has secrets about her, he now has secrets about me, also. Feeling a little more paranoid than usual, Leo called the number Abe left. It was the number for the Regency Hotel and when Leo gave his name, he was immediately connected.

"Hallloooo, who's that?" Abe bellowed into the phone.

"Abe, it's me, Leo."

"Leo, my boy. How good of you to call back so quickly."

"Abe, how did you get this number... the unit is supposed to be secret."

Abe chuckled. "Leo, I can get anything your little heart desires. It wouldn't matter if it was secret, illegal, or a mortal sin- I- have- connections." He spaced out the last three words for emphasis.

"I'll bet you do... Now, what can I do for you?"

"I want to do for you. Let me take you to dinner tonight- a special treat for a New York boy."

"What kind of treat?"

"Hey... first say you'll come and then... maybe I'll tell you." He would have preferred dinner with Jacqueline, but... "It'll be my pleasure, Abe."

"Fine. Fine. Come over here to my place whenever you're ready to eat. Just ask for me at the desk."

"Okay... see you later."

Replacing the receiver, Leo thought about Abe. The first thing was the Regency. Leo had been there once for a very elegant and really expensive Sunday breakfast. Eggs and the usual for about thirty bucks a plate. Dinner must be outrageous. A real first-class hotel and the guy *lives* there. With money like that he could live anywhere, so the hotel must fit his style. And he does have style. Everything first rate. Smokes expensive cigars. Works for fun and eats out... a real New Yorker... a real wise guy. Was he joking with the talk about his criminal past? He carries a gun and got the number of this unit, so he has connections in the Department. Leo glanced at the computer screen on his desk and wondered... could I check him out?

He found the manual for the Department's internal network and after several attempts managed to get the Records Section. After entering the password from his manual, the screen revealed a menu that asked for names or aliases. Leo typed in Abe Rosenberg' and waited. In less than one minute the monitor showed a picture of Abe. He looked like a kid. Obviously, an old picture. Other screens had information that went back to the earliest days of the records unit. He had been arrested about twenty times between 1930 and 1940. There was nothing from 1940 to 1948 when he was arrested once again. The last arrest was 1953, after that nothing.

Abe had been picked up for arson, attempted murder, hi-jacking, smuggling, racketeering, arson again, racketeering again, attempted murder again... it went on and on... all those arrests and not one conviction. He had never spent more than a couple of days in jail. Reading Abe's record was like reading the history of crime in New York. He had been into everything, but never got caught with enough evidence for a conviction. One smart cookie.

Drawing Leo's interest were the periods of inactivity. Why nothing from 1940 to 1948? Career criminals don't take vacations. Leo doubted Abe was in the Army, but when he read through the arrest records and the intelligence information, he was surprised to see references to the War Department and then the initials OSS came up. Well... I bet he was a spy during the war. There had been rumors about the Feds using gang guys to do wartime dirty work. That stuff was still going on- Leo thought about Kennedy, Castro, and the boys.

What kind of spy could Abe have been? He certainly wasn't the typical suave operative. It was almost comical to picture him bouncing around Europe with his New York dialect and taste for good cigars. But then, audacity was always a winning hand. Playing it safe was great if you had lifetimes to spare... if not, rashness and insolence were the cards to play.

He wondered if Abe would get pissed off if he learned Leo was poking around in his past. After a moment, he realized Abe would have expected him to do it and that Abe is probably proud of his past. Well, I'll find out tonight.

He shut down the machine and went to meet Melendez. They managed to get away with no more trouble than promising to bring Rose a sandwich. Leo took her to Fred's and in great detail, told her of the magical moments with his pancakes. She thought it was hysterical.

"What's so funny about that?" he asked.

"Leo... sophisticated guys- even cops- like to boast they know wine, Thai cooking, or that they can recite an entire Chinese menu, but I never heard a guy get misty eyed talking about pancakes."

Slightly taken aback, he said, "Look maybe I am not a great sophisticate, but let me tell you, a well-made breakfast is more important- to me- than a lobster drowned in butter."

She laughed out loud and turning to face him, looked at him in a way that made him wish that thirty years before, a girl had looked at him the same way. If there had been one, would his life have been different? Impossible question.

Suddenly, he was thinking that fifty-nine seemed young while sixty seemed old. He thought of Abe being eighty and couldn't fathom what that meant. He knew he wasn't concerned with death. He had killed people and seen others die. He had lost Ilene and John. It wasn't about death, but it was about death, since every breath could be the last. That's true every moment of every life, but at forty or fifty, it isn't a recurring thought. At sixty it starts to seem to be more at hand. Everyone knows death is inevitable, yet they fear it. What do they fear? Pain? Not knowing how or when? What happens after? Not being? "After you, sir."

"What?" Leo blurted out. "I'm sorry, what did you say?":

"I said 'after you' since we are at Fred's and I'm holding the door open even though your head was obviously someplace else."

"You got me. The way you looked at me a moment ago really sent me into fast forward. One thing then another and I'm a million miles away. Do you do that?"

"To some degree, but I think you probably have a better imagination."

He figured she was right. It is his imagination that runs wild, with fantasy after fantasy building on the previous and then catapulting to something new. As they walked in, Fred came out from behind the counter.

"Leo, good to see you. Who's the friend?"

"Fred, this is Susan Melendez. She's hungry."

"Came to the right place. Take a seat."

He walked back behind the counter after he spoke to Irene. She brought water, silver, and napkins. "No menus?" Leo asked.

"Fred said you will eat what he cooks."

Melendez laughed. "Wouldn't have it any other way." Leo said.

Less than ten minutes later, they were served a dish new to both. Sliced lamb interspersed with sliced potatoes, covered with an apple and mint sauce. Somehow, Fred had managed to slice the lamb and potatoes thin enough for microscope study and then laid them on some sort of flat biscuit. Hot food on hot plates, Leo could have kissed him. He glanced at Melendez as she tasted a piece of meat. "Leo, this is great. What is it?"

"Couldn't even guess, but I think lamb."

A moment later, Irene brought plates of vegetables. Each held rows of thinly sliced carrots and string beans, side by side, with green peas placed at their bottoms. "Leo, look at the veggies. They look like exclamation points."

He had never felt responsible for the books, movies, or restaurants he recommended and had armored himself to ignore complaints from people unhappy with his endorsements. He also liked to think he wouldn't take credit for a successful recommendation, but that wasn't the case. As Melendez gushed compliments, Leo smiled as if he had done the cooking.

Being no dope, Fred came out from behind the counter to get what was due him. Seeing him, Melendez, said, "Fred, this is great... what is it?"

"It's lamb and potatoes."

"I know that, but what do you call it?"

"Lamb and potatoes... Leo, what's wrong with her... she got a hearing problem?"

"Very funny, very funny." Melendez chortled. "Do you like it?" Fred asked.

They both nodded. "Good." Fred said, "I'm going to name it after you both. Now... it's a dish called 'Susanleo.'

"Are you really going to call it that?" she asked.

"Sure. Why not. If you leave a big tip, I may even take your picture to put on the wall. You'll be famous." A bell sounded twice and Fred looked toward the counter. Irene was in a classic pose: one hand on hips, one foot tapping, a glare on her face and an order in hand.

"Time to go. More starving people to feed."

"Leo, this is great food. How great to have it right next door. I don't understand why I never came here."

"You better limit your trips or you'll have to use Fred's dressmaker."

They finished, had coffee and a dessert that Fred said had fewer calories than fat-free yogurt. Leo would have bet it was more in the order of three thousand, but how can you argue?

The sandwich they brought back for Rose was the lamb dish on a roll. When he finished it, he went out for another. Fred's cooking was much the subject of that afternoon's conversations.

Leo spent the remaining hours getting onto paper the beginnings of a strategy to defuse the plans of the wise guys who wanted the pope out of the way. "Just got to tell 'em what they want to hear." He muttered as he worked.

CHAPTER 21

LEO FELT GOOD AND relished the joy and ebullience that came from a total refusal to let the funk of the past get to him. He knew it would be a great night, yet had no idea why he felt so good. Maybe it was Fred's food, lunch with Melendez, or starting his pope plans. Two clear successes and a third with winning potential. The key is to keep positive. "As a man thinketh, so is he." Who said that, he wondered- Keats? Shelly? Doesn't matter—keep good thoughts and don't give in to the darkness.

His mood fit him into a new suit he was saving for a worthy occasion, and this was it. It wasn't a suit he'd normally wear because it was not typical of his gray and black work clothes. This one was a dark tan and even though it fit well, he never would have considered buying it, if it hadn't been for a lady in the store. He saw her leering reflection in the mirror as he was trying on the jacket. She liked it and him, but since she was with another guy and he couldn't take her home, he bought the suit.

He added a spread collar shirt, paisley tie, dark brown shoes and socks- and there was a guy who didn't look sixty staring at him from the mirror. Wondering if he should wear the suit to work, Melendez popped into his mind. She's too young for me. Maybe I should set her up with Roberto. I bet they'd hit it off. He won't be a doorman forever. Very satisfied with the mirror, he hit the lights and left.

Getting a cab was a snap as was getting uptown. The Regency is at 61st and Park- a nice neighborhood. People walking in the street had purposeful strides and looked able to handle the next of life's chapters. None had that searching, vacant look. The cab u-turned at 63rd and stopped in front of the hotel. More limousines than he could count. Looked like a Funeral Director's convention. A uniformed doorman hustled to the cab and whipped open the door. Leo paid the driver, tipped the doorman and walked into the hotel like he owned the patent for television.

The lobby didn't look like a hotel lobby. There was a separate concierge station to the right of the front desk and plush sofas and chairs facing the main entrance. Passages and elevators were to the rear. Marble floors and walls and lots of mirrors. All well planned and very sedate- a cross between Grand Central Station and the Public Library. The help wore dark green uniforms and were all smiles, courtesy and assistance. When Leo said he was Mr. Rosenberg's guest, people jumped. That meant Abe was special, since he didn't match the celebrity of typical Regency guests. Leo was escorted to a bank of three elevators. The first two were labeled 'local and express' the last was 'express and penthouse.' He was taken to the last.

"Sir, Mr. Rosenberg is in Penthouse A. This car will go straight up."

The elevator was like everything else, silent, beautifully maintained, and fast. He didn't get a good look at the numerals, but he guessed the penthouse was on twenty-one. Not bad for an old hood.

When the car stopped and the door opened, Leo was surprised to see no sign on the facing wall with directions. Instead, woven into the deep maroon carpeting were navy blue letters —"A" and "B" with arrows going left and right. No clutter on the walls here except for a painting that looked like a Klee. As he admired it, he thought that Warhol could have added to his fame if he had painted a series of 'Penthouse A' and 'Penthouse B' directions—would have sold well.

The door to Penthouse A was polished, dark wood. A snazzy custom cover for the steel fire door the City's building code demanded. Leo was impressed before he got inside. He pressed a button and waited. A moment or two later, Abe opened the door. As Leo stepped in, he thought he heard a sound like on electronic watches- a little beep, but wasn't certain.

"Leo, my boy, come in, come in. It's good to see you." Abe gestured to his left and Leo followed him into a room that was at least twice the size of Leo's entire apartment. There were chairs and sofas everywhere. "Sit. We'll have some wine, okay?" Leo walked to a long, beige sofa. "The restaurant is around the corner, so there's no rush. I mean... if you aren't starving and would like some wine?"

"Some wine would be fine. I had a great lunch so there's no rush." Abe was wearing a dark suit and looked comfortable and assured, much more at home here than at Marty's. Leo was able to quickly sense the enormity of the apartment. There were doors and hallways in every direction and from where he sat; he could see a piece of a grand piano and more furniture in another room. The painting, the rugs, and furnishings he could see, matched a typical spread in an up-scale decorator's magazine devoted to a glimpse of how the landed gentry lived.

"Abe, is this place rent controlled?"

"Heh, heh, " Abe chuckled. "Not quite... but, it's only money." Abe sat in a chair facing the sofa. "Red or white?"

"I'll have whatever's open."

"Hey, do you think I live in a bar? There's nothing open."

"Then I'll have red."

Abe pressed a button on a dark wooden box on the chair-side table, and said, "Red." Then he looked at a puzzled Leo. Abe gestured to the box. "It's an intercom to the kitchen. I have one of the hotel staff here when I have guests... makes it easier for me."

"Abe, I have to confess, I didn't have you figured right. This place, the hotel, and the way the staff straightened when I mentioned your name. This is luxury...it's like you're Duke of Windsor in disguise."

"Leo, I told you money is not a problem for me."

"Yeah, Abe I know, but what I've seen so far has nothing to do with money. There are plenty of heist guys with plenty of dough and no one's got more money than the dopers, but this place is not only money; it's taste and you can't buy taste."

He smiled, "I'm going to take that as a compliment."

Hearing footsteps to his right, Leo saw a middle-aged man wearing hotel colors carrying a silver tray with a bottle of wine and two glasses. He placed the tray on the table next to Abe who nodded. The waiter poured and served them both. Saying he would need nothing more, Abe dismissed him.

Leo sipped the wine and was rewarded- a smoothness he always hoped for. He scanned the room and noticed an object on a table by the entrance. The table had those reversed turned legs, like claws bent inwards. It looked old and very sturdy. Abe followed his stare. "You like that table?"

"It's really beautiful. Is it an antique?"

"All the wood pieces are antiques."

"What's that box on that table?"

"Why do you ask about that?"

"Well- everything else in the room is... how do I put it, everything is explainable. The intercom, there, and the other things look like their supposed to look... lamps look like lamps, furniture looks like furniture, the piano looks like a piano, the frames and the paintings look legit... but that box," Leo pointed. "It doesn't fit. It's the only enigma in the room... besides you."

Abe laughed. "Leo, you're a cop with a good eye. Not many people notice that box... if they do, they pay it no mind, but you're curious, right?"

"Yes, I am. Now..." he laughed. "More than ever."

Abe got up. "Watch that box. I'm gonna walk to my front door and then come back in here. You watch the box." He turned and walked into the hallway that led to the front door. As he got close to the door, Leo heard a beep and saw the box light up. The dark glass surface was actually a screen that glowed red with the outline of a person. On the outline, at chest level, was a dot. The dot and the outline glowed for about ten seconds and then faded. By the time Abe got back to the chair, the glass surface of the box was once again dark. "Okay... what is it?"

Leo smiled. "I don't know what to call it, but I have an idea of what it is. I heard a beep when I came in. When you got to the front door, it beeped and showed a dot on your left chest. So... I think it's some sort of detector that can tell if the person in the doorway is carrying a gun. And, if they are... it shows where. Right?"

Abe smiled. "Leo, you are a smart sonofabitch. But... you missed a couple of points. It goes after lumps of metal. It'll pick up a blackjack, a knife, and any gun... if it's one of those new plastic jobs, it'll pick up the ammo. It is one smart machine... not perfect, but I know who's carrying when they come in."

Leo laughed out loud. "I don't know what you call it, but I would put it up there with my favorite bumper sticker- 'Paranoia Saves'."

"Goddamn right it does. Nothing wrong with knowing what's goin' on around you. I can remember a guy named Freddy the Frisk... with Dutch Schultz's mob. His one job was to frisk everybody who came near Schultz. He would pat you down and find whatever you carried as fast as that thing does."

"Where did you get it?"

"Some guy came into Marty's a while back... wanted to know if anybody needed any custom electronics... said he could modify anything to do more than it's supposed to do, and of course, Marty threw him out. He's such an asshole. Anyway, I followed the guy, got his card and after about ten conversations, he built me this thing. Said it's a copy of a unit they got in the Pentagon. I said it's like the airport metal detectors and he almost crapped. Got real insulted... said it's a hundred times more sensitive."

"Does it have a name?"

"I call it 'Freddy the Frisker'. The kid who built it didn't call it anything ... said that it was a natural offshoot of the MRI." He sipped some wine. "You into electronics?"

"Not really. I have a good stereo and a computer at the office, but that's it. No need."

"Hey! I love all of it... the newer the better. The stuff that comes into Marty's is amazing. The swag-men boost stuff even before it gets advertised.

We've bought things without knowing what it was... and after, we try to figure out what it does. It's like a game."

"Is that why you work there?"

"That's one of the reasons. I also get a kick out of being where there's some action. Can you imagine me sitting up here all day and night- watching TV, getting stock quotes from my brokers. I'd go nuts in no time."

"What else do you do?"

"I hit the museums, the movies, the opera, you name it. This city is paradise if you got the time and the bucks."

"I understand all that... but why Marty's?"

"There are many reasons, Leo. First, I got a piece of the action there, so I'm protectin' my investment. Second, it's a funny place. Lots of people who cruise in are not quite from this planet and there is no way I could meet up with them if I was workin' in some legit joint. Can you imagine a kid like Carlos and the 8th Avenue crowd gettin' past the Tiffany doorman?" He left the question hang in the air as he sipped some wine. "You remember that TV show, *The Millionaire,* the one where a guy goes around and gives people money?"

"Sure... I can remember sitting in the orphanage hoping he'd give me something."

"You wanted money?"

"No, I wanted family... wanted to be part of something. When you have no one, it doesn't take long to realize nobody's thinking about you. You learn fast that day or night, summer or winter, nobody's there... nobody even dreams about you. It's like you don't exist."

"Yeah. I can remember thinking like that. I have no family either."

"Why did you ask about the TV show?"

"Oh yeah, what I was going to say is that sometimes I play that scene. When a couple comes in the store, really up against it or someone shows up who really needs help... I help out... give some cash or make a connection... I like helping people."

"How come your so generous? Most people won't give you spit."

"Yeah. I used to be like that," he said simply. Then he stood. "Come on, let's go eat. We'll talk as we walk." Leo followed him to the door. As they passed the hidden sensor, the beeper rang out. "I'm gonna talk to that guy and see if he can change the beep into a tune- that'd be great."

Opening the door, Abe waited for Leo to move past him, then he said, "Lock." In the silence, Leo heard the door click. Surprised, he looked at Abe.

"Same guy. I say 'lock' and it does. I say oh-pee-ee-en and it does. That's the only word I got to watch. A pisser, huh?"

"I'll say. No more keys."

"Yeah... and it only works to my voice." They walked to the elevator. "The only problem is electricity. No juice and I got to use a key. Right now, electricity is hot, but you wait. Sooner or later, the bastards are gonna figure out how to sell us air- they're already sellin' water. When they start sellin' air, we'll be one step from the middle ages. The elite will have it all, the rest will be lucky if they live to thirty."

The elevator came and they got in. Moments later they were downstairs. Strutting through the lobby, Abe lead the way and Leo enjoyed watching him walk. It wasn't a boastful saunter, nor did he do anything specific. He just walked slowly enough so he would have to be noticed. A casual, deliberate pace that quite clearly stated he was in no hurry, and, if people or events were waiting, they'd just have to wait. Leo loved that walk.

Outside, it was dark enough for the streets lights to make a difference. It was that magical moment in New York when streets took on the mystery and beauty seen in photographs. It was after work, but before evening... a moment of preparation, like a runner getting set in the blocks. It was all potential, outcomes yet to be decided.

Abe turned the corner at 60th and in the middle of the block Leo saw a large sign jutting from the smooth building facades. *Goldberg's* it read, in large, white neon letters. If they were going there, Leo knew it wasn't going to be a Chinese or Thai meal.

"You see that?" Abe pointed to the sign. "Not too many people move to Park Avenue and expect to see a sign like that. I paid for that goddamn sign... wanted to make sure they understand just how Jewish this city really is."

"You paid for that sign?"

"Well, why not. I got a piece of the action in the place and I wanted to make sure people knew it was there. Let me tell you, this place could give the lower East Side a run for their money with pastrami. And... I made sure it's a no heartburn pastrami, so have no fear."

They walked into *Goldberg's* and, as in the hotel lobby, everything stopped. Waitresses, waiters, managers, cashiers, they all came to say hello. The guys behind the sandwich counter raised their greasy carving knives in a salute.

Goldberg's is a New York Kosher delicatessen. What they serve is unmatched anywhere in the world and many try to copy it, but few succeed. If the meat isn't prepared just so, it will never have that special seasoning and taste which makes Kosher deli extraordinary. There's a place in Montreal where they spell pastrami with an 'o'- a pastromi sandwich. No way it could taste right. Leo could remember from his Army days going into stores marked 'Deli' seeking a kosher hot dog or corned beef sandwich and finding instead ice cream and milk. What a let down. Almost a perversion. It was like learning Marilyn Monroe was really a drag queen.

Abe led the way to a round table in the middle of the front room. He sat and beckoned Leo to sit opposite. Before they were fully settled, plates of dill pickles, potato salad, pickled tomatoes and peppers, coleslaw, and rye bread appeared. It was a parade of essential side dishes. Looking at it all was wonderful, smelling it was even better. Leo could remember the first time he had a Kosher frankfurter. It was after a ball game and one of the priests took the team for a bite at a neighborhood deli. They had franks and French fries. Amazing tastes. If there had been a rabbi in attendance, he could have had a converted infield in minutes. To this day, franks and fries were still one of Leo's secret passions.

"You ready for a dish or two? I hope I won't need to twist your arm?"

"Abe, be serious. I love this stuff. I deprive myself until I'm ready, and then bingo..."

"I know you were brought up in a Church orphanage and ate what they gave you. I'm sure Kosher deli wasn't a menu item."

"Right, but that doesn't matter. If you're a New Yorker, you're Jewish. Remember what Lenny Bruce said?" Abe shook his head. "Well, best as I can remember, it was, 'In New York everybody's Jewish. Even the Cardinal is Jewish. Go to Des Moines and you'll find the head rabbi is a goy.'"

Abe laughed. "That's right. That's right."

A waitress appeared who was not a young woman, and was fighting that obvious fact with heaps of make up and red hair.

"Darlings," she gushed, "you know what you want? Yes?"

Abe ordered first. "I want a plate of meat. Have one of the carvers put two or three lean slices of all the meats on a plate. I'll start with that. Leo?"

"I'm going to have a cup of matzoh ball soup and then half an open-face tongue sandwich with the clear gravy and you can bring a nosh plate like his for me too... Okay?"

"Such darlings you are. Soon you'll be fat like pigs." She murmured, as she trundled back into the kitchen.

"I love it in here. Like the lower East side... if you don't get insulted, you feel left out."

"Is that waitress a regular or is she filling in for someone else?"

"Leo, that waitress is probably the most regular thing in here. She's been slinging salami for years and years. I think she's really funny... always makes me laugh.... always feel better after I've been in." He looked to the kitchen just as the swinging door opened and the waitress came slithering toward their table loaded with plates. "Finally." Abe said aloud. "I thought you had to send over to the Stage to get my order. Certainly took long enough."

"Well, pardon me, Mr. Prime Minister, you didn't tell me you were in a hurry to get to Tel Aviv for a conference. If you did, I would have packed all this to go, so you and your Kosher bodyguard would be able to stuff yourselves on that special jet the Israeli Air Force has parked around the corner... with motors running."

Abe smiled. "Hey, come on... you know you can't park a jet on Park Avenue."

"I don't know nothing like that, my friend. For somebody so very important like yourself, I would think they would double park."

Smiling and trying not to say anything that would bring her very obvious wit down on his head, Leo asked. "Do you really think I look Jewish?"

She stared at him- ran her eyes over his face. "Well, boychick, let's say there was this Roman soldier screwing lots of pretty Jewish girls in the old days. Without a doubt, you are one of his tax exemptions. With a face like yours, you have to be Italian or Jewish.... but so what... those two are the same thing." She efficiently placed the plates on the table and continued. "Back there in the kitchen from hell, there is a Jewish delicacy called kreplach. In Italy they call the same thing ravioli. Now... Mr. Rabbi-face... when you get two items that are the same, you don't have to be an Einstein to come to the conclusion that there is more here than meets a kettle of Gefilte fish. Take it from me, kiddooo, you're as Jewish as Mr. Big Mouth here."

Leo smiled, looked at Abe and wondered if it could be true. Sixty years ago they took kids off the street. Could I be Jewish? Abe stared back. "She's got you thinking, huh?" Then, turning back to the waitress, Abe said, in a voice of mock complaint, "Now look what you've done. I bring my nice altar boy pal for some Jew food and you go and upset his apple cart by tellin' him he's not what he always thought he was. Bein' told you're Jewish can give you indigestion if you ain't ready for it."

The waitress raised her eyebrows and disregarding Abe, said to Leo, "Don't you worry, darling, I won't charge you extra for your dinner... and, if you can eat such wonderful food while looking at him and not get indigestion, your kishkas have to be made of iron. You have to be Jewish."

"That's amazing," Leo said. "Considering myself Jewish is something I never thought about once in all of my sixty years. Jesus, do you think it could true?"

"Leo, stranger things happen every day." He speared a pickled tomato and in between bites said, "And if it's true... who cares? What does it matter? You're pecker ain't gonna fall off, right?" He swallowed the last of the pickle and speared a slice of beef tongue. With the thin slice of red meat dangling from the fork, he asked, "By the way, Leo, are you circumcised?"

Staring at the meat on the end of Abe's fork, Leo thought the question really funny. But he did no more than smile. "As a matter of fact, I am."

"Well, my boy, I guess the Church got you after the Rabbi finished. What do you think?"

Laughing, Leo said, "I must've been asleep- I don't remember a thing." Popping the tongue into his mouth, Abe looked up at the waitress and nodded. She looked at Leo and also nodded, then Leo nodded and the waitress smiled. "I'll go and get the tea ready. I know you boys are gonna have tea... it helps your little stomachs deal with all that fat and spice." As she slowly walked toward the kitchen, she said, loud enough to be heard, "Oy, such a mommy I am. Such cute little boychicks. Without me they'd be eating tuna fish right from the can."

Leo smiled but didn't stop eating, since every spoonful of soup and every bite of matzoh ball were to be savored. Having this food every day would make it ordinary and meaningless. Deprivation is the key to appreciation. That thought led to a question.

"Abe, if critics were locked away and deprived of the stuff of their criticism, would they be better at their game?"

Abe stopped eating. "That's an interesting question, Leo, but I think you gotta drown them in it. If you feed a guy chicken soup all day and night for a week, he'd probably get to be a champ at recognizing good chicken soup. Deprive him long enough and he'll think warm piss is haute cuisine." Leo nodded and both of them went back to what was in front of them. A little later, they ordered one combination sandwich, two franks, a side of French fries, and a bottle of cream soda, all to be shared.

As the waitress delivered the items, she asked, "Does all this sharing and half a sandwich craziness mean I am going to get half a tip from you two heavyweights?" Before either could answer, she turned her back and retraced her steps to the kitchen.

Abe chewed slowly, like he was trying to separate the spices for identification, but he stopped for a moment and asked, "Leo, do you like music?"

"Music and books are the mainstays of my life. I don't know which is more important."

"What kind of music do you like?"

"Jazz mostly- modern, not Dixieland, but I'm not that fussy. I like most all of it."

"Do you like religious music?"

"I've been involved with Church music since I was a kid. I even sang in the Church choir."

"Good. Let me invite you then. Marty and I are involved in a deal with a kid who has a really beautiful voice- sings heavy Church music. He's gonna be singin' this Sunday... you should come."

"I'd love to. I have a real warm spot for that music, but tell me about this deal with Marty."

"Ahhh, the whole thing is strange, but what happened is the kid Carlos, who works in the store... he got this friend, a little Spanish kid called Angel who got nobody, no relatives, parents, nothing. The kid lived on the street until Carlos took him in. Anyway, Carlos wants to do the kid a favor and teach him to read and write, so Carlos gets a guy named Vincent, who we know from the store, to do the teaching. Now, Vincent is a really schooled musician and while he's teachin' the kid to read finds out the kid can sing and has got a magical voice. One thing leads to another and now the kid can read and write and sing like a fish in water. The end result is going to be a record and plenty of money. The kid can sing anything... hears it one time and sings it back better than what he heard. We had a try out at the church and the congregation flipped. They thought the kid was marvelous. I did too, to tell the truth."

"So this street kid turns out to have a golden throat. Did he ever have music training?"

"My boy, you don't understand. This Angel kid is the real thing. He lived anywhere he could and did some nasty shit to get bucks. He was like from another planet until something happened. I don't know what it was, but then the kid changes. Carlos said all of a sudden he wants to learn stuff and before you can whistle, the kid is singing Church music. It's like a TV show."

"You know, it's funny, but as you were talking, my singing with a Church choir popped into my head. I remember I really liked it, but I stopped going."

Abe stared at him. "Why'd you stop?"

Leo hesitated, and then slowly said, "I was too ashamed, I guess. I took some money."

"Why'd you do that?"

"Best I can remember, I wanted a new baseball glove and there was no money... so..." Frowning, Abe said, "Shit, Leo, kids are always doin' crap like that."

"Maybe, but from that day, the choir was out and the Church too... sort of."

"Normal guilt, is all."

"I know that, but all the same I wonder what it meant in my life." He paused. "Abe, I owe my life to a Priest who took me out of the orphanage. I loved him, but the Church... the Church is another matter. He slapped the tabletop. "Dammit."

"Be angry if it'll make you feel better, but the Priest you loved was a specific man...like a father. The Church is general...lots of people...some okay and some not. Make a choice. Then... well, it's never too late for the department shrink. No reason for you to be carryin' a load from fifty years ago."

Leo did not reply, but just when the silence was ready to become uncomfortable, he said, "Well, this has been some dinner. In less than one meal, I find out I'm Jewish and recollect memories I've buried for years. I can't wait for dessert."

"That's the spirit, Leo. That's the way to think. Fuck it and they can't lay a glove on you. If you get frightened and live scared, you live half a life. What happened, happened. You can't change anything. All you can do is change how you deal with it."

"You have a philosophy? A way of looking at life?"

"Sure it's simple. I got it from Shakespeare- don't ask me what play-I don't even know if I'm quoting it right." Leo sat back, "What is it?"

"It goes... 'A man can die but once. We all owe God a debt and let it go which way it will, he that dies this year is quit for the next.' Badda-bing, badda boom. Nice and simple. Fear is the enemy."

"But there are two kinds of fear. I'm not afraid being a cop. It's the other stuff. The stuff of life not involved with being a cop- that's what I'm afraid of. Off the job, I run to the books and my apartment —to my hideout." He paused. "That's right, that's exactly right- to my hideout."

"Leo, my boy, you hang around with me, maybe you'll get a handle on life that'll help with the years you got left."

"Abe, do you think about death. Are you afraid of dying?"

"Of course, I think about it, but I ain't afraid. I've seen people die and it never seemed so terrible. I remember the old East Side- West Side wars... guys got shot up... they were alive and then they were dead. Seemed like a blessing for some of them."

Looking at Abe, Leo wondered, maybe he could help me live better. Maybe he could provide guidance... be like a father to me... show me the way. Father John said to rely on the Church... that never helped.

"What are you thinking about Leo, dessert?"

"That and a lot of other stuff."

"Forget the other stuff... it can wait. What do you want for dessert?"

"I heard that." Yelled the waitress as she approached their table. "Don't even think of anything. I will bring you dessert. A dessert I have made with my own hands."

As she started to pick up the empty plates, Abe asked, "And what if I decide I don't want that—or what if my Italian-Jewish dinner partner wants none of what you have made and wants instead a plate of stewed prunes garnished with whipped cream. What about that?"

"I will waste no time responding to such mishuginah nonsense. You will eat what I bring and you will shut up. Believe me, I will plotz if you don't kvell from what I will bring."

"Is it that good?"

"Does Irving Berlin's wife have a fur coat?"

"Okay, okay, it'll be too marvelous for words."

"Not a bad song, if I remember correctly. I used to sing it when I was the featured chantoosy at the Ridge Mountain Country Club, a Catskill resort of significance."

Abe raised a hand as if directing traffic. "Please... let us not get into nostalgia. I do not want to hear about the time you sang for the crowned heads of Europe or the Cohen heads of the Catskills. Just bring more tea and some of that irresistible, nourishing, incomparable, never to be equaled dessert so we can judge its quality."

"I will bring two portions even though I know it is like tossing pennies before swindlers. Neither of you will be able to appreciate my dessert because you are both victims of Sara Lee." She leaned closer to Leo and loudly whispered, "Don't tell him," she gestured to Abe with her chin, "but Sara Lee was really Sadie Lazarus... but what're you gonna do? America is a hard country."

She continued to stack plates as she talked, and also somehow managed to sweep the crumbs away with a tiny whiskbroom. When she turned back to the kitchen, the table held nothing but two tea cups. In what seemed like seconds, she returned with a jug of hot water, additional tea bags and two plates of pastry. Since they were watching her, she took her time getting back to the table.

"That looks like strudel," complained Abe, "plain old apple strudel."

"Oy vey, like an arrow to my heart. 'Plain old apple strudel,' he says. Dunce, dimwit, like the Hope Diamond is a piece of coal." She placed the plates on the table. "Eat, then talk. Take a bite and tell me it isn't the best strudel you have ever tasted and- in your heart- you know it is the best you ever will taste. Eat! Go ahead, eat!"

She stood looking at them as they cut off pieces and almost simultaneously slid the morsels onto their tongues. Leo expected the heaviness of damp dough and syrupy apples like the strudel he occasionally had, but this was not weighty at all. It was lighter by half and had a tart, yet sweet taste. His delight showed, for she immediately looked at Abe and hollered, "You see, he loves it. Everybody loves it. What about you, Mr. Big Shot? Are your taste buds so dead as a doornail that you can't taste perfection when you confront it? Well?"

Abe looked up at her and with a big toothy grin said, "You know something, this isn't bad strudel after all."

She snorted in triumph and while walking back to the kitchen said, "Like I said so many times, it's like casting perfume before sneezers."

They laughed and they ate. There was more tea and more strudel and Leo couldn't remember a day filled with as much warmth and honesty.

Eventually, they walked back to the Regency, had cognacs at the bar and talked deep into the night. As they spoke, Leo fully recognized his great need to speak with an older man and listen to views of life different from his own and the Church.

CHAPTER 22

NO EXTRAVAGANT BREAKFAST TODAY. Leo brought a roll and coffee to his desk, for this was going to be a workday—a day to move ahead with his plans. The best information from Department Intelligence and UN Security indicated an attack on the pope would come from a non-aligned Islamic terrorist cell. The basic problem was that no one knew how many such groups were operating in the country or in the City. Moreover, it was not known whether any of them would consider killing the Pope worthy of their time and effort.

Leo had managed to get in some reading about martyrdom and found it wasn't an exclusive concept. As a kid he was taught about the first Christian martyrs, St. Stephen and St. James. He once had to write a report about the apostle martyrs, SS. Peter and Paul. The intervening years had not dimmed the memory. Rome was always the villain and Clement of Rome had described the apostle martyrs as athletes contending for the heavenly prize. The kids in his class used to compare them to the 'Babe' and the 'Iron Man' and viewed it all as a race for the MVP in heaven.

As he had learned more about other religions, he saw that all of them had their martyrs, though the Jews probably took the prize, with a history of endless persecution and help from the Nazis. That era seemed simultaneously incomprehensible. Before Hitler, the German people were ordinary folk living ordinary lives. Then Hitler gave them the opportunity to go completely insane and far too many jumped at the chance, like they were competing for a prize given to the most psychotic.

In the present, Leo couldn't find any religion sponsoring or advocating martyrdom outside of Islam. Within that religion, the designation *Shahid* is equivalent to the Judeo-Christian concept of martyr. In addition, Islam's Hadith literature says those killed in a holy war, a *Jihad,* can achieve the rank of *Shahid* and stand nearest the Throne of God. He saw it as an old story- set out a prize and watch the contestants try for it. Learning whether a local cell member was going for the prize would not be easy.

Leo knew he needed a contact—the right contact—if the scheme he was planning was going to work. A morning of phone calls had produced nothing and he was ready for lunch at Fred's when his phone rang. It was Jacqueline and her voice was like the beginning of a song. How wonderful to have this moment, this affair... whatever it was. He knew it had to be short-lived and eventually she would not be available, but while it lasted it would be magic.

"Leo, are you able to talk? Am I disturbing you?" After a moment, he said, "Yes, you disturb me, but not the way you mean."

"Oh, Leo you are such a romantic... so much passion in you." His groin had come alive and he longed to hold her. "Let's not talk about being overwhelmed... you have no idea"

"Oh, Leo... I am calling because I am free tonight and hoped it would be possible for us to be together." Dreams come true, he thought.

"I'll be at my place by six. Want to go out for dinner?"

"Certainly, I do have to eat, you know."

"I know that. It's... well... I thought being in public might be a problem."

"I will be at your place at seven."

"Wonderful... but before you go, would you be able to go to a concert on Sunday?" He explained what he knew and added it would be perfect cover, since there isn't a much more respectable event than a Church concert. Laughing, she agreed to go and he was flying. Then, before he hung up, he realized she might be able to help in another way." Jacqueline, I have a delicate question for you."

"I would think we are past that point."

"We are, but the question concerns my work." He explained his difficulty getting reliable information about terrorists who might be planning an action against the pope and that possibly she might have access to intelligence at the Embassy. She said she would inquire and call back. "Until seven." he said, and added, "Adieu, mon amour." The last thing he heard was her deep, throaty laugh.

He felt like he was back in high school and just got a date with Miss Cheerleader. His thoughts flashed to the first 'date' he ever had with a 'nice' girl. Every week, his church would arrange a teen dance so the kids would not go totally insane. He had first seen her at one of those dances. She was blond, blue-eyed, slim, Catholic pretty- a Saturday Evening Post good girl. As soon as he spotted her, he asked her to dance and they danced away that Friday night. The next Friday the dance was at her church and being on home territory, she took Leo to a dimly lighted area by the Church organ. He was the perfect example of teen-age-boy-stupid and couldn't understand how they would dance in the small space of the organ loft. But when she eagerly began to play his organ, his stupidity vanished in spasms of blasphemous joy. It was from her he learned that girls like everything boys like. That information was the bedrock of his teenage social life.

He closed his eyes and thought of Jacqueline. What was her magic? Certainly, arriving with movie star billing and an international reputation didn't detract from her allure, but it was more than that. She had style. It was the way she got him to notice little things. He had never focused on a woman's jewelry, but she wore pins that he admired. The way she held her scarf and handbag made him see them. Maybe it was from the films. Maybe she had learned how to direct an observer's eye to what she wanted them to see.

He recalled a woman from years before who managed to make a cleft lip almost disappear. She had flaming red hair and wore it upswept in an organized, disorganized way. Her eyes were heavily made up and she used very little lipstick. Her clothes always showed a good deal of her breasts and her smooth, beautiful skin. There was so much going on, so much to look at, no one noticed her lip, but if they did, they never lingered. Clearly, it was a matter of directing the eye away and it worked beautifully. Leo decided Jacqueline's style was not accidental for education is no accident.

He sat at his desk with closed eyes and drifted into the evening. Where to eat? Cafe Brigitte would be fun, but it wasn't elegant enough. As he mentally walked the streets near his place searching for a restaurant, the phone rang. It was Jacqueline.

"That was fast."

"I asked my driver. I think he is a spy. He knows something about everything and everyone."

"What did he say?"

"To summarize, he said you should look to Africa since the Islamic revolution is creating more stir there than in other parts of the world. He suggested you contact, if it's possible, someone from a small African nation. He feels they would have first hand knowledge and may be willing to direct you to a resource in this country." She paused. "Does that help?"

"More than you realize and I think I know just who to ask."

"How wonderful, Cherie. I will see you at seven."

With the phone still at his ear, his mind jumped to Inspector Guy Magalana and his Prince Punteyaya. Gabon Leone certainly qualifies as a small, new and restless African nation. Maybe it would all fall into his lap.

He dialed Melendez and got Magalana's number. While he had her on, he invited her to the Church concert and told he knew a guy who would be a great blind date... if she wanted. "Why not?" She replied immediately.

He planned to call the Gabon Leone Embassy as soon as he got Jacqueline out of his head. Thinking about her brought him such pleasure; he wondered how he would deal with his life if he had married a woman who excited him as she did. Would he spend time thinking about her or would his thoughts eventually cool and find him, like others, having affairs? He thought about the few times he had worked undercover. They were exciting times... the adrenaline flowed, everything just seemed to be more. Weren't those secret affairs the same? Take away the secrecy and the dash and they go into the toilet. Forbidden fruit is sweet. Nothing like a Catholic background to develop a taste for what you should avoid. By the time he was thirteen, he had compiled a menu of Church banned places, books, and movies he intended to devour.

The more available something is the less people want it. So many guys he knew had these heavy romantic adventures with other cops or people they met while working. As soon as their divorce went through, everything cooled. It was funny. Maybe I had the best of it, he thought. Maybe never getting married allowed me the joy of deception. I'll guess I'll be secretly pleased when Jacqueline dumps me...maybe the next romance will be around the corner. He shook his head wondering if he was very nuts or very sane.

He dialed the Gabon Leone Embassy where the operator told him Magalana was not available, but he would get the Lieutenant's message to Magalana as soon as possible. When Leo heard that, he left for lunch. Fred's was crowded and Leo feared the word was getting around. The place had existed without notoriety, would it survive being discovered by those- 'in the know'? What would happen if it became a chic place to eat? Would Fred convert it into a nightclub?

He sat at the counter looking at the plate of food Fred put there. It smelled wonderful, but didn't look like a photograph in Family Circle. Leo tried it- tasted good. "Fuckin' place is gettin too crowded." Fred growled. He had come out from the grill booth and stood in front of Leo.

"If it is, you're to blame. Don't cook so well. Fix it so someone gets sick at the counter. Nothing will turn off a crowd as fast as someone throwing up their food. It works on planes."

"Hey, that's not a bad idea. I guess I could hire somebody... you wanna volunteer?"

"No thank you. I like your cooking and I have trouble making myself heave." Leo ate another fork full... "Hell, Fred, you'll have no trouble if you're serious. You can rent people in this town who will do anything. Vomiting is small scale."

"I got to think about this, Leo."

"By the way, what am I eating? What is this?"

"What do you care?"

"I don't really, just curious. Whatever it is, it tastes great."

Fred leaned as close to Leo as his girth and the counter allowed. "Leo, answer me this... what would be the most repulsive dish you could imagine?"

Leo thought, fork poised in mid air, brain working overtime. "Person. I don't think I'm ready for humans as food."

"Me too, but the problem ain't moral or ethical. All over the world people eat other people. I doubt there's a recipe, but they've been doin' it since hot food began." Leo took another mouthful as Fred spoke. "I thought about this a lot and the problem is the supplier. Unless you are goin' to create your own source, you'd have to deal with some character who was willin' to keep the menu entry available."

Leo dropped a piece of bread into the gravy. "You gotta understand, Leo, anyone who would sell you human meat might sell you spoiled human meat. Who the fuck could you complain to- the Board of Health? Can you imagine that phone call?" Fred leaned back. "This is a tough issue. The damned supplier got you over a barrel."

"No question about that, no sir." Leo finished the last of his dish, mopping up the gravy with a shard of bread. "Now... are you gonna tell me what I just ate?"

"Meat."

Leo stared at him. "That's great, Fred, just what I wanted to hear."

Fred smiled, turned, and heading back to the grill booth, waved his arm. "See you tomorrow, Leo. There'll be another surprise for lunch."

Frowning, Leo paid and walked back to the office. He really didn't expect it, but Magalana had called back and left a number that was not the Embassy. Leo dialed. After three rings, a deep voice answered. "This is *Below the Equator.*' To whom do you wish to speak?"

He introduced himself and asked for Inspector Magalana. There were hushed voices in the background as the phone was passed from hand to hand. "Lieutenant Flower, this is Inspector Magalana, what is it you want?" He spoke with a deliberate air of theatricality clearly designed to impress those nearby.

"Inspector, let me thank you for returning my call, I know you are busy."

"Think nothing of it. How can I help?"

Rather than pussyfoot around the subject and give Magalana a chance to speculate, Leo figured the best way was to jump right in. "I need some specific information about Islamic revolutionaries and I was told you and the Prince might be able to offer some assistance."

"Who was it that told you we might be in a position to help?"

"It would make little sense for me to say, since I got the information third hand, but I can tell you another embassy is involved."

"So you have asked a UN contact... well, that is not a problem. Whatever the case, can you be specific about what it is you want to know?"

"The matter is too delicate for a public phone. If it would be possible, I would like to meet with you, but I don't know where you are, I've never heard of the place called *'Below the Equator'.*"

"It is a place recommended by your Captain Hoffheimer, a truly sophisticated man."

"Would it be possible for me to come there? When you hear what I want to know, you might put in a good word with your Prince."

"Lieutenant, the Prince is here with me. Please wait a moment." The phone went almost silent as a hand was placed over the mouthpiece, but Leo could just about make out Magalana asking the Prince if Leo could meet with them.

"The Prince says it would be fine if you came here. He said he is looking forward to meet you since you work so closely with the captain."

"Wonderful. Where are you? Where is *'Below the Equator'?*"

"It is on 64th Street- 89 East 64th Street to be exact. Use the street level entrance."

"I'll be there in twenty minutes." Leo straightened his desk and headed out.

As he bounced in the back of the cab, he wondered about *'Below the Equator.'* His first thought was tropical rendezvous with blue-green ocean and white beaches. His second thought started with Magalana's reference to Hoffheimer's sophistication and then leaped directly to human anatomy. As the cabby drove through a red light to make the turn onto 64th, Leo saw 89 East was a small, but very beautiful building.

It was an example of a simple little bachelor's place straight out of one of those Doris Day-Rock Hudson movies. All over red brick with white marble trim around the windows, doors, and roof line. A large second floor window showed a wall of books, the top of a sturdy looking brass lamp and a small part of the ceiling that met the ornate edge molding of the wall. The ground level windows were heavily curtained and barred. It was a very classy place- a one family long ago- no way to tell how many tenants now.

Sunlight bounced from the highly polished brass work on the street level door. There was enough for a full days work, what with an oversized knocker, large doorknob, exposed carved hinges, kick plate and plaque that read 'Private'. The door itself was painted a deep purple. As if that was not impressive enough, there was a garage door to the left of the main entrance painted similarly. The main entrance at the top of the white marble steps looked like polished mahogany. All the brass up there was equally gleaming. A super building in a super neighborhood with pruned trees, trimmed plants, trash cans with covers, and no dirt at the curb. Leo checked the address since there was no sign and the place looked like a residence. The address was correct.

He used the knocker and stepped back as the door was opened to show a face that had seen a good many referees and left hooks- only the refs had been friendly.

"Yes Sir, may I help you?" The voice and the manners did not match the nose.

"I'm Lieutenant Flower- to meet Inspector Magalana."

"He is expecting you, Sir. Would you step in and follow me?" Leo sidled into a small space as the main door closed. It was like walking into a closet. There was a wall to the right, the front door behind, a wall straight ahead and the guy with the broken nose on the left. Turning to face the doorman, Leo saw a door behind the guy and realized he was in some sort of a closet.

"This is a very impressive entrance. Whose idea was it?"

"I thought of it, Sir." His smile showed a missing tooth. "You see, I was very good on the ropes and in the corners and when it is necessary for me to prohibit someone's entrance, I am at my best in a small space."

Leo blinked. "I can see the ex-boxer, is there also a degree in architecture?"

"Almost. I have one year remaining."

"That's far better than a cold compress."

"Right you are... and you're one of the few who recognizes the utility of the entrance. So many others bitch about the size."

"I am very impressed. It isn't common for middleweights to change into architects."

"Light heavyweight," he said, smiling. Then turning, he opened the door to the larger room behind him, and stepped aside. Leo walked past into an entrance that looked like the foyer of a high-style nightclub. Dark walls and ceiling, low voltage lighting, a young girl in a cloak room for the coats, and everything muted and subdued. Beyond the entry was a bar with a dining room beyond that. There was no one at the bar so Leo walked toward the dining room. It had booths on three walls and several tables alongside a small stage. Magalana and another man wearing full African tribal dress were at a booth. In an instant, Magalana jumped to his feet and came to up to Leo.

"Lieutenant Flower, how good to see you once again." He extended his hand and Leo shook it. "Come, let me introduce you to Prince Punteyaya." He walked across the open space with Leo close behind. As they approached the table, the Prince stood. He must have been at least 6' 5". He was a giant of a man and in good shape, judging by the flow of the robes as he stood. There was no potbelly or massive girth hidden by the cloth.

"Lieutenant Flower, it is my pleasure to meet you. Captain Hoffheimer has spoken highly of you and I most certainly respect his judgment." The voice matched the physical. It was deep and soothing- Gregory Peck with a British accent. He waved his arm to the booth. "Please join us and tell me how I can help." Leo felt like a kid walking between the Prince and Magalana and wondered how weird it must be to live with a professional basketball or football player.

He slid into the booth. The Prince sat opposite while Magalana sat on a chair at the end of the table. Before Leo could speak, a waiter appeared and inquired about a drink. Leo assumed he was the waiter due to the drink request, though his uniform was not standard, since all he wore was a G-string. Looking more closely, Leo saw it was not all. He also wore a small, black bow tie around his neck. A tiger print G-string and a black tie- not quite a Disneyland uniform. Trying to be cool, Leo said "Scotch and soda." The waiter vanished as the Prince and Magalana giggled. Leo tried not to fall apart.

"This place is a most refreshing change from the usual, Lieutenant. Have you ever seen such a cute waiter?"

Leo laughed. "Well, Prince, a change from the usual is exactly right. I thought guys like that work as dancers on ladies' nights."

"Every night is ladies night here. *'Below the Equator'* is not for those seeking the 'usual'."

The waiter reappeared with Leo's drink and after setting it down, slithered away. The Prince watched the waiter leave and then turned to Leo. "Lieutenant, I do hope all of this does not disturb you, I would not want you to think we are uncouth."

Looking at him, Leo said, "Prince, that would be the last thing I would think. You are probably the most couth person I've met today."

Magalana laughed and the Prince smiled a yard wide. "You see, Guy, it is impossible for him to work for Captain Hoffheimer and be a vulgarian." Magalana nodded his agreement. Picking up his glass, the Prince sipped from it and asked, "How can we help you?"

There was no way for Leo to know if the Prince would consider his request far-fetched or impossible, so being coy made no sense. He figured it best to be direct. "Prince, one of my responsibilities is refining protection for the pope during his upcoming visit. As best as can be surmised, the only people posing a threat are some renegade Islamic terrorists. I want to get in touch with them.

Is there a way you can help... maybe steer me in their direction? I want to talk with them. That's all of it. That's what I'm after."

"Aha," said the Prince. "That is a tall order. Some of these people are quite rabid in their philosophy and once set upon a course of action, will not bend from that decision."

"I realize that. That is why I want to meet with them early... maybe before they have finalized a plan. Once plans have been made... they may not be willing to talk about anything."

"That is true."

"Do you think it might be possible for you to help? Get me a name or arrange a meeting?"

"Anything is possible, Lieutenant Flower. And, fortunately for you, I do have some connections amongst the people you describe. Nonetheless, I would think you are wondering why I would even consider coming to your assistance in this matter... is that not true?"

"Sure it's true and also... there's no doubt I would appreciate any help I can get, but help usually comes with a price. I'm wondering how you would gain from assisting me."

"To be frank, I myself am not yet quite sure, but I do not think constructing a meaningful friendship with the West can hurt me or my country. As you must realize the political world is one of *quid pro quo-* we help you, you help us. Therefore, I envision the following. We assist you and whatever plan you have works out. We gain. If your plan does not work out, we lose nothing or... we gain for bringing the matter to their attention. Furthermore, helping you could put us in a favorable position with the terrorists and the people they represent... and from that situation we also gain. So... because we lose nothing and stand to gain quite a bit, I would be foolish to at least not say... Lieutenant... I may be able to help."

Smiling, Leo said, "That would be wonderful."

"Fine Lieutenant, but now...is there a chip you can give me for the game... can you promise something specific... something concrete?"

"Officially, absolutely not, but privately... I may be able to arrange something they evidently seek. I may be able to get the pope to meet with them."

"You can do that?" The Prince asked in amazement. "You can make a promise for the pope?"

Leo nodded. "I may be able to do just what I said."

"Unbelievable, totally unbelievable." Prince Punteyaya looked at Magalana whose mouth was hanging open. "Did you hear that, Guy? Did you hear that Lieutenant Flower can make arrangements for the pope?"

Magalana finished the remainder of his drink and then picked up Leo's. "I toast you, Sir. When we first met you did not deeply impress me. Then, when Captain Hoffheimer alerted the Prince and myself to the underground bliss here in New York, I revised my opinion of him. Frankly, I did not think about you. But now... now you come and tell us that the pope will act as you direct... that is amazing. Such power deserves a toast." He finished Leo's drink in one gulp.

Leo wished he deserved the toast. "Prince, do you really think you can help?"

"Lieutenant, for the most part, your countrymen see me as less than I am. In Africa, I am held in esteem and I should be able to arrange a meeting with little trouble."

"I would be indebted to you."

"Could you get me an audience with the pope?"

"If things work out as I hope and plan, I don't see why not."

"Do you think he would like this place?" the Prince asked. Leo burst out laughing. A moment later the Prince joined him. As they laughed, the lights suddenly dimmed and their nearly nude waiter leaped to the dance floor. Music began and he started to gyrate. Other people came into the room. At first, only men, then several women. Hands clapped in time to the drum beat music and the waiter performed what Leo judged would have been a mating dance if he had had a partner. Watching intently, Leo thought of Jacqueline. Closing his eyes, he let his libido drift until the music stopped. When he opened his eyes the room was dark. Slowly, the lights returned to their low glow and looking around Leo saw every table now occupied. Asians, Blacks, and Whites- it looked like a UN afternoon tea, but the onlookers' sweaty faces proved it was no tea party. "You did not know such a place existed, did you Lieutenant?"

"Prince, as I sit here with you I am still not certain such a place exists." Both Magalana and the Prince chuckled. Figuring it was a good time to exit, Leo said, "Prince, I don't want to take up more of your time. I hope you will contact me as soon as you have information."

"Fear not, Lieutenant. I can move mountains."

Leo got up, bowed slightly to both men and walked back to the entrance area. When he opened the door, the boxer was still on duty. "Quite a place, huh?"

"That's putting it mildly," Leo responded.

As the door closed behind him, he walked into the brightness of the late afternoon sun. Standing on the sidewalk trying to adjust his eyes and his head, he turned and looked at the building. It still looked like the mansion of someone who made big money in insurance- as straight and legit as any building on the block. As he walked to the corner for a cab, he wondered what was going on in the other buildings on that nice, quiet, respectable street. New York, New York... like someone once said, "It's a helluva town!"

181

CHAPTER 23

LEO GOT BACK TO his place around six and was showered, shaved, and changed by half past. He was like a high school kid getting ready for a hot Saturday night date. For a long time, he had been getting ready for women coming over. How long could it continue? How long has it been? He looked in the mirror and said aloud, "thirty years." He had been entertaining various women in this exact way for over thirty years. He shrugged; fully aware of the game he was playing... the only one he knew.

He put on the new suit again, hoping Jacqueline would like it and marched around the small apartment like an expectant father in a hospital waiting room. Then, checking his restaurant list, he selected *La Hambra* because of the continental food and because it dark and romantic. There wouldn't be many tourists and maybe the guitar player would be working. He was walking around the apartment like a caged lion.

Calling the lobby looking for Roberto was a diversion and when he realized it was Roberto he was talking to, he invited him to the Sunday concert. Like Melendez, Roberto agreed with no hesitation. Leo offered some details, a little about Melendez, and was surprised when Roberto asked about her figure.

"Is she fat?"

"No. She's built slim... very athletic looking."

"Good. My mother wants me to marry a woman the size of a small house. I avoid them like the plague."

"Why is your mother hung up on size?"

"She's real old country and convinced thin girls get sick. To her eye, health and weight go together. You know that kind of thinking- if the medicine tastes good, it can't possibly work. If the horse dies, hook the wife to the plow. It's all that back woods Latin stuff. I stay away from large women in case I might find one attractive."

"Hey," Leo laughed, "I had no idea you had it so rough."

"Some day, I'll give you an earful- my father's discourse on acting, for example... Hey, I gotta go... a fancy car just pulled up." The intercom clicked off and Leo checked himself in the mirror. He jumped when the intercom buzzer went off- it sounded like a bomb.

"Lieutenant... a lady is on her way up and, if I may say, wow! "

Leo went to the door when he heard the elevator stop. A moment later she filled the doorway. 'Wow" was exactly the right word. Her suit was almost the same color as the door on 64th Street... a blackish purple with touches of suede and leather on the pockets and collar. "You look fabulous." He said.

She walked across the room to kiss him. "Good evening, my love." His mind raced as he held her. Why can't she be mine, he asked himself. If she really loved me she would leave her husband. He heard a smirking voice in his head. "That's right, ding-dong, she would leave him for you. Right. She would leap at the chance to surrender international fame and acclaim, recognition all over the world, unlimited expenses, cars, drivers, mansions- right- she would give it all up to move into this Junior Executive Three, Two- whatever the hell it is- move in here and be at the door when you come slogging home after a hard day. She would stand by the door with a bowl of steaming chicken soup- chicken soup?- maybe you are Jewish. She would be covered in flour after baking 5 loaves of bread. Her floral, print dress would need darning, but it must wait, she says, your socks come first. She would love you and never again think of the fashion trips to Paris and Milan. Your love would be powerful enough to overcome everything."

He actually heard a cymbal- a CLANG- then silence, then the little voice once again. 'Right... she would give it all up for you?' The next words he heard were slow and clear. 'Be happy with what you got. Don't be a fucking moron.' He gripped her tightly and kissed her back.

"I'm thrilled to hold you."

"Leo!" She pulled away. "Leo, we must eat. If you touch me again, I will drag you to bed. I waited to have dinner with you. I am hungry."

Like a lion surveying dinner at the waterhole, he realized the feast was guaranteed. It was just a matter of patience. "You're right. Say no more."

When they got to the lobby, Roberto handled the doors with a flourish. Outside, the limo was double-parked. Leo gave the driver a salute and told him they were going to a place two blocks away. That cut no ice, he insisted they ride and they did. Pulling up to the restaurant in a car that took up half the street was noticed from inside and when they walked in, they were greeted like rain in a drought. The manager recognized Leo, but fell all over himself when he recognized Jacqueline. From that moment on, Leo knew he would be treated like royalty. If nothing else, a beautiful woman is a great shill. Everyone shows respect, even other women- especially other women.

They sat at a dark booth and ordered light- Jacqueline, because she probably never ate much. Leo, because he didn't want a full gut hindering his lovemaking. They ate and talked. He told her about the concert and she seemed genuinely interested. Like him, music was a large part of her life. For a moment, he thought about a quick trip to the Village Vanguard, but was too greedy to share her. There was music in the apartment.

The *La Hambra* guitar player was working that night and dedicated every tune to her. Her fame preceded her and Leo realized attention from others was normal for her. Maybe she expected everyone to notice. Maybe she would be hurt if there was no fuss. Never having been in the spotlight, he had no way of knowing if it was desirable. Those he read about said they hated the lack of privacy and longed to be able to walk un-noticed in the street. Leo thought that was bullshit. They love the attention. Has there ever been a 'star' that relished obscurity? Maybe- but he couldn't think of one.

Our age is based on celebrity and everyone wants a piece of the action. It was like dealing with an atheist. Since they deny God and religion, you'd think it would be far from their mind, but that was never the case. Every atheist he ever met talked endlessly about religion. You would know their views before you knew much else. That was their shtick. That's what made their alarm bells ring. She was probably the same. "I vant to be alone..." (but... not totally—dahling).

That's okay, he admitted. She's entitled. Considering how many were killing themselves to become an international movie queen, let her bathe in her achievement. In the long run, it does matter. He knew he would certainly remember his moment with her. It might be his crowning glory. At some future time, when a rocking chair and porch would be all he could handle, he would bathe in private recollections of these moments- private- because no one would believe any of it. Not that it would matter, it was his dream. They can get their own.

They ate simply, wine, scampi over rice and espresso. He passed on dessert, but she had Flan—took three bites. Leaving the restaurant was more of an event than arriving. The manager promised him the meal of a lifetime—on the house, if he brought her back. That happened while she was repairing makeup. When they left, they walked out to the waiting limo and Leo thought it was not a bad way to get around. No bus, subway or taxi. Just flop into the back seat and announce the next destination. Not bad!

Back at the apartment, they had more wine and he decided against music because he didn't want interruptions or the wrong song at the right time and certainly, he didn't want strange voices from the radio. As things turned out, he wondered if he would have been able to pay attention to anything else anyway.

It took moments for them to undress and embrace. His passion was unlike what he usually experienced. It was unselfconscious and free and he was able to recognize the lack of honesty involved in his usual gambol. Those other moments were certainly fun and accomplished their purpose, but there was always a part of him separated from things. Now, it was totally liberating and he reveled in the pungent and sensuously fervent moment.

Afterwards, when he thought about that evening, he was surprised at how little he did recall. He figured details didn't register because of the ecstasy of the instant. It was all 'now' with no past or future.

Both of them lingered in bed. She said her legs were so weak, she would not be able to walk and he understood, for he felt the same. He closed his eyes trying to absorb every impression. He touched her and slowly moved his hand over her... his fingers drifted, touching and caressing as much as he could. She stretched and tensed and he felt her muscles contract and shimmer in spasm. His last recollection was her hand between his legs and her body looming over him.

When he awoke, she was gone. Never before had he fallen asleep after making love. He reprimanded himself and felt awful. Overpowered by the moment, he had let himself drift away. What a dope. He looked across the apartment to focus on something other than himself and noticed a piece of paper on the sofa. It was a sheet of her perfumed stationery. Does she carry it in her bag? He smelled it then read it.

Leo, my love. How wonderful for you to be so good for me. Tonight was magic.

I am thrilled you were able to sleep. I am going to think I sent you to dreams. It was signed with a florid "J".

Good for her? Shows what you know, wise guy. All these years acting like you had a handle on the big picture. Two thoughts pushed into his mind. One was a song. "Love is better the second time around." the other, "it's better to give than to receive." He finally understood both.

Rising from the bed, his legs still weak, he slowly, clumsily, picked up his clothes- then decided not to brush his teeth or shower. He wanted her with him as long as possible. Getting back into bed, he was as self-satisfied as he'd ever been. Turning on the small radio by the bed, he listened to an all-news station. It was going to be great, he thought, to drift off to sleep listening to continuous slices of human tragedy while he felt so God-damned great. Smiling, he said aloud, "Leo, you really are one lucky son-of-a-bitch."

CHAPTER 24

IT WAS WEDNESDAY AND Leo strolled into Dig Pro as if he owned the rights to Happy Birthday. When he first conceived his plan, he never thought he could pull it off, but now, with Punteyaya hopefully putting a word in the right ear, things might just work- and what would that mean? Primarily, he figured nobody he'd contact would make a try for the pope, but what about others? There was no way to tell. For a reason he couldn't grasp nor explain, the thought of two or more totally separate cells going after the same target just didn't seem likely.

He stopped in Hoffheimer's office to tell Melendez he had set her up for Sunday and when he said the guy's name was Roberto Colon, she got antsy.

"Right now, he's a doorman, but he's an actor. That's what he's after."

"Is he one of those a macho assholes expecting his 'woman' to scrub floors on her knees and have ten kids in ten years between services for his majesty-Don Supremo?"

"Hey, wait a minute. Wait a minute. I'm only getting you two together for a respectable date. I'm not promising anything." She stared at him. She won- he continued.

"Look, I don't know how he lives or wants to live. He seems modern, educated, cultured and ready for the same kind of woman. I have no idea if he has screaming Macho genes. I don't know if he needs a hunchbacked midget spraying him with chocolate syrup while he has sex. I don't know a thing about his private story."

She was still staring at him, but now there was a smile in her eyes. "A hunchbacked midget spraying chocolate syrup? Where did that come from?"

"This very morning, during breakfast, I read about it on the back of the cereal box. 'Horny Flakes' is running a series for kids about sexual dysfunction and vitamin deficiency. It's been very interesting. You want the box when I'm finished with the cereal?"

"Never mind the smart ass, just make sure this guy is not one of those Pancho Villa types who expects a woman to develop a heart murmur when he takes off his shirt."

"Look, Roberto is a sweet guy and you're a dynamic and sweet lady. The two of you should have a great time." He paused "My hunch is..."

"Your hunch is what?"

"My hunch is- don't let him introduce you to his family and don't take him home to meet yours." She laughed, "You got that right, Leo."

Leo got back to his desk and stared at the phone. C'mon, he urged it- ring, ring. It didn't, so he turned on the computer and ran through the procedure to check his e-mail. He was more than a little reluctant to admit his growing fondness for the device. As much as he would like to remain safe and secure in his ignorance, the machine's power was amazing. Information just poured out.

The menu on the Department's information program had a listing for City Records that Leo had never checked out. Curious, he ran the program to see if he could identify the legal owner of that building on 64th Street. In less than five minutes he had it. It was deeded to the United Nations in 1989. That is a very interesting idea- the same thinking produced USO Canteens where soldiers relaxed when they came off the front lines. Keep their minds off the big battle and they won't get restless or crazy.

Whenever he learned something like this, something about the 'real' world, he had a good laugh on himself. For many years, he thought himself cool and up on what was happening. Now, little by little, he was learning he knew zero about what was going on- and worse, he was shocked by some of the things he found out. If anything, the 'shock' proved him far less sophisticated than he thought he was. It was hard to admit naiveté, but maybe I should be less hard on myself, he thought—at least I admit I'm ignorant.

"The phone rang, zipping him from his self-congratulatory reverie back to his desk. "Lieutenant Flower, here."

"Ah, Lieutenant, you sound fresh and eager this morning." It was Punteyaya. That deep, resonant tone was unmistakable. "Are you ready for the meeting you asked about?"

"Good morning to you and you bet I am. My God, I can't believe you actually managed to set it up. I'm grateful and awed."

"When I say I'll do something, I do it. There is little I cannot accomplish."

"It's all fantastic. Where's the meeting? When is it?"

"Oh my," Punteyaya laughed. "You are eager so let me tell you. To make things easier for all, I suggested we sit down to lunch at my embassy. In that way, everyone is on safe, protected and neutral ground. You understand?"

"Absolutely and I fully approve. That's a smart move. If I were in their shoes, I wouldn't want to meet in the McDonalds on 42nd Street."

"Oh my... that is funny. That is very funny."

"Why?"

"The McDonalds on 42nd was their very first suggestion."

"You're kidding."

"No. They thought a busy place would be a safe place. You must realize they do not know what you want and of course, they do not much trust anyone."

"I wouldn't trust me either."

"We will meet at the embassy for lunch at one-thirty. Satisfactory?"

"I'll be on time."

"Excellent. I will see you this afternoon."

Leo stared at the phone and knew what it feels like to volunteer for a suicide mission. Once you're in- you're in. If he was following Hoffheimer's plan, he could object, abstain, or screw it up, but this is his plan. How do you back out on yourself? Once I have this meeting, it's in the works and there's no backing out. After a minute of reflection, he realized this was the time to let Hoffheimer in on what's going on. He dialed Melendez and arranged a meeting. Five minutes later, Leo was explaining himself.

"You really think you can pull that off?"

"Why not? When it came to me, I knew I had to give it a try."

Hoffheimer stared at him. "What if it backfires?"

"Captain, I'm going to handle this very simply- it's all from my desk. No one else is involved and no one has any idea of what I intend except you. If I'm successful, then I'll be successful. That'll be it."

What if it gets around you screwed up"

"No problem for anyone but me. I was almost ready to retire before I came here, so if I screw up you can toss me to the wolves." Leo got up and walked to the window. He stared out for a moment, and then turned back to the seated man. "Captain, what can they do to me? If it blows up, I'll say you and the Department were not involved, which is the truth, and I'll go further, if you want... I'll say I never told you what I was doing."

Hoffheimer sighed. "Well, I don't know... but I won't stop you. Make sure you keep me posted. I want to know what's going on."

"You bet." Leo headed for the door, went back to his office to run through exactly what he wanted to say to the people at Punteyaya's."

After an hour of writing carefully detailed notes, Leo had a firm hold on the approach he would take. Since so much of his idea depended on the upcoming conversation, there was no way to work out the complete picture. He wondered if he would be meeting one man or several. He figured several, but anything was possible.

In the taxi, Leo wondered if he had gone a little crazy. What he was doing was out of character, since he rarely took chances. Risks were not part of his repertoire. Through the years he had met his share of bold and brazen guys. Most were nutcases who didn't care about anyone or anything- guys that didn't care if they lived or died- the undercover guy. Compared to that crowd, Leo felt like an IRS auditor. Now he was out of character. He thought of the expression, 'You get too soon old and too late smart.' If that was true and he was finally 'getting smart', then maybe there would be something different for him in the end. Maybe he wouldn't fade away to a beer bar bullshitting about the 'good old days'.

He stopped the cab at 72nd and while walking the two blocks reviewed his approach. The Embassy was a typical neighborhood brownstone, an old one with old line class, heavy stone work, metal gates, and shrubs treated so carefully, individual leaves looked hand scrubbed. In the middle of a spotless main door was a highly polished, engraved brass plate that read, *'The Embassy of Gabon Leone'*. He pressed a bell button and counted to three before a large black man who looked like the Hollywood actor, Rex Ingram, opened the door.

"Yes sir, how may I help you?"

"I am Lieutenant Flower, Prince Punteyaya is expecting me."

"Do you have photographic identification, Sir?"

He inspected Leo's ID slowly and carefully and when satisfied, said, "Follow me please." Leo stepped into a hallway that he guessed, looked much as it did when the house was built, except for a new looking floor of green and beige marble squares. The polished oak woodwork was definitely not new, since similar wood was quite rare. Leo couldn't tell if the wood had been stripped and brought back to life or whether he was looking at a hundred years of appropriate care.

In the center of the entrance hall stood a table that was clearly a one of a kind piece of art. It had a beautiful marble top that was completely overpowered by the four wooden legs. Each was a carving of a horse's leg and showed what was probably every sinew and muscle the eye would take in. Each leg was different, but the similarities indicated one carver had done all the work. Leo was struck by the work and wondered where and how you get such an item?

"Ah, Lieutenant, you like my table. Everyone who comes here loves that table." Said the Prince as he walked into the room.

"It's amazing. Who did the work?"

"A craftsman from my country made it for me when he learned of my affection for horses. It was his way of showing affection for me."

Punteyaya was wearing robes that would look foolish on other men. He made the voluminous folds of cloth appear comfortable and appropriate. Leo's gaze shifted from the Prince back to the captivating artwork. "Much as I hate to drag you away from my table, I must remind you Lieutenant, you did not come to admire my furnishings."

"Forgive me Prince, but you're right... when are they going to arrive?"

"They are already here... upstairs, waiting for you. Shall we?"

Prince Punteyaya led the way to the second floor where two men were standing in front of a double door. One looked like an Arab, the other was a duplicate of the fellow who opened the front door. As Leo and the Prince approached, the doors were opened enabling them to step into the room without breaking stride. Once inside, Leo quickly scanned the room. A large conference table with many chairs filled the room's center. Alongside it, on a small sofa, sat three men. Each man was dark, thin, and mustached. Two chairs were facing the sofa. Leo followed the Prince and when he sat, so did Leo.

"Gentlemen, this is Lieutenant Leo Flower of the New York City Police Department."

Leo nodded at the expressionless men. "Lieutenant," the Prince continued, motioning to each man as he introduced him, "this is Aram Singh, Saleh Lor, and George McGinty."

Unable to contain himself, Leo laughed. "George McGinty? Funny, but you don't look Irish to me."

In perfect, accent free English, McGinty said, "That's okay, Lieutenant, you don't look like no fuckin' rose to me either."

Everyone laughed except the two men sitting alongside McGinty. They looked like their shoes were too tight. Leo decided he would not focus on them, figuring they were brought along as guns or they were the big boys and McGinty was their translator. Whatever the case, Leo was gong to talk to whoever spoke to him. The decisions would be made by the man in charge no matter who he was.

"Would anyone care for some food or drink?" the Prince asked.

"Yeah. That'd be nice." McGinty said. "Can we order in sandwiches?"

"You may have whatever you want." The Prince motioned to his man by the door that moved to a desk and took what looked like menus from a drawer and brought them to the seated men.

Staring at the menu, McGinty asked, "Is this a restaurant or a neighborhood deli? "It is a traditional delicatessen," the Prince answered.

"Great. We'll have three corned beef and pastrami combinations on rye.

Plenty of half sour pickles and a couple of sides of French fries. Two cokes and a hot tea for me." Leo said to make it four sandwiches; another side of fries and another hot tea. The Prince nodded, said something to his man who went to the desk picked up a phone and gave the order to someone at the other end.

"Now, Lieutenant, what exactly is it you want? All the Prince told me was that you were interested in talking to us." McGinty talked like he was the one who did it all the time. Never once did he look at the other men or hesitate.

"Okay, Mr. McGinty, let me be frank. I told the Prince I wanted to talk to some people who wouldn't shed a tear if the pope were sent to an early visit with his commander-in-chief. That's what I told the Prince and he invited me here to talk to you gentlemen. So... I am inclined to believe the name McGinty does not really mean you are a good Irish Catholic, but rather an alias of convenience."

McGinty smiled and sat back. "First, the name is legit. Second, I appreciate the candor- that will make it easy for all of us." He gestured to the other men. "My friends here and me- none of us would feel great sorrow if the pope died. As the chief representative of a multi-billion dollar business, which has captured the hearts, and minds of millions, the pope is truly an important man. We know that and we also know that if he was killed, there would be a new pope in a matter of weeks." He shifted forward to the edge of the sofa. "Lieutenant, the man who is pope is not important... the position, the office is another story. Anyone who could manage to swing it- manage to knock off such a well-protected and important guy would really get a big rep with people who care about things like that." He stopped, sat back, satisfied with himself. Leo noticed tiny smiles at the corners of the mouths of the men alongside McGinty and he figured they obviously understood English and also, they approved of how McGinty was telling their story.

Leo was both surprised and pleased by what McGinty said because now things made sense. "You are telling me," Leo asked- "that taking out the pope is not the issue... the point is taking out someone who is hard to take out? You are talking about doing a job with the world watching... and if the job is done successfully... there will be admiration for the doers of the deed?" Hit men? Leo asked himself—is that what they are? A Middle-Eastern Murder Incorporated?

Smiling, McGinty said, "That is exactly right except I must correct one point, that the whole world would be thrilled, only certain people would be delighted. Other people in other places would not be overjoyed."

"Let me ask you then, why not the president of this or another country—why the pope?"

"Lieutenant, a couple of kids with a good rifle could take out any president. All these political egos are so busy with the citizens; it is impossible to protect them. But the pope- that's another matter. He is not so public and not so available and he is a tough job. Only real professionals could manage that job." The two guys alongside him smiled a bit more.

"So you guys are really not that political. You work for the money?"

"Better you should look at us as being very, very political."

Confused, Leo said, "Please, you're going to have to explain that for me."

"Well... let's say you want to knock off the Head of Syria or Libya. We won't do that and we won't do certain others. It's not that we have principles, it's just that we don't do everybody and anybody."

"Okay, okay, the picture is clearer, but I need help with you. You sound more like a McGinty than Danny Boy sounds Irish. How come?"

"Lieutenant, a full bio ain't important. What I can say is I was born in Brooklyn, but that means crap now. When the Dodgers left I gave up my Brooklyn allegiance and I am a man without a team, so I find a team. One that has deep connections to my roots. Now I am part of a team and the Dodgers can go screw."

Leo laughed. The Prince laughed, but with some hesitation. Leo was sure the Prince wasn't up on baseball and wouldn't know the Dodgers from a Mercedes Benz.

"Tell me, Mr. McGinty," the Prince asked. "Would you have embarked on your present journey if only the Giants had moved from New York and left the Dodgers in Ebbets Field as the sole representatives of the National League?"

"Prince, that is a very interesting question. Off the top of my head, I would say nothin' would have changed. Livin' in Brooklyn, as I did, made it impossible to be involved with the Giants. It'd be like asking W.C. Fields to run a day care center." Leo laughed at himself. It was clear he wasn't a modern incarnation of Sherlock Holmes.

As if it were timed, the double doors opened and a black man in tribal robes wheeled in a teacart laden with the ordered food. As he was placing it on the table, the Prince said, "Gentlemen, we can continue our talk as we eat." He stood and was followed by the others to the table. The Prince sat at the head—Leo sat to his right, McGinty and company sat across from Leo.

Almost simultaneously, the five of them scooped up a sandwich half. The Prince had ordered the same as the others: five corned beef and pastrami combinations, fresh rye bread, and some dills along with the half sours. How wonderful it all smelled.

"Tell me, Prince," Leo asked, "When did you develop a taste for this kind of food?"

"Yes, Lieutenant, I understand. You find it a bit off-putting to see an African Prince melt at the sight of Kosher deli."

"Well, I would not have bet my paycheck you were a pastrami fan."

"I acquired the taste while I attended McGill University in Montreal. For almost a year, I ate at a local delicatessen and though they called the meat pastrami, I managed to develop a relish for it and all the accompanying delicacies."

"I been to that place." McGinty said. "Tile floors like a big men's room, but decent food."

"Oh yes, easily seat a hundred or more."

"Yeah, I really love this stuff also." Said McGinty.

Leo was finding it fascinating. If it were on television- five men eating at the conference table at the Gabone Leone Embassy- Leo would presume the conversation to be about world events, arms trading, economic policies, and the like, but here they were talking about pastrami.

McGinty's pals dug in like converted vegetarians. Neither one made a sound except one who belched after a swig of soda.

"You also like this food, Lieutenant?" the Prince asked.

"Yes I do... but my favorites are hot dogs... they're my major weakness, but I like it all."

The door to the conference opened and Inspector Guy Magalana walked in. He surveyed the group, but seemed to focus more on the food than anything else. "Lieutenant, it is good to see you once again." Leo made an effort to rise, but Magalana's huge hand on his shoulder kept him in his seat.

"There is no need for ceremony here, Lieutenant, not with that scrumptious sandwich in front of you. From what I can see, if you divert your attention, one of these vultures will steal it away without a word of apology." As he said that, he rolled is eyes and everyone smiled, even McGinty's men- who obviously understood English.

"Gentlemen," the Prince announced, "I have an appointment in thirty minutes so I would appreciate you reaching whatever conclusion you desire within that framework." McGinty nodded as did Leo and each chewed a little more vigorously. A minute or so later, Leo said, "Mr. McGinty, let me explain what I can do for you." McGinty and the two other men straightened.

"I can get you an audience with the pope. I can arrange a videotape of you and your entourage meeting the pope. The tape will be yours to do with as you please. In fact, you can handle the camera yourself, if you prefer."

"And for that... what do you want?"

"I want your promise that no one will make an attempt on the pope."

"Well, I can speak for myself. I don't know if I can speak for other people."

"You will have to speak for others. I can put you in a video, but you have to guarantee no hits."

McGinty looked to the men at his sides. The one to his right got up and gestured for the others to follow. They went to a corner of the room. After several minutes, they came back to the table. "Now, let me get this straight. You are promisin' that you can get us a videotape of us meetin' the pope. Sittin' close enough to him so I could put my spoon in his cup and stir his coffee?"

"Exactly." The three of them smiled broadly. Heads nodded. "But..." Leo said. The smiles vanished. "He's a tea drinker." The smiles returned- broader than before.

"You're on, Lieutenant. There will be no attempt on the pope, but you have to do exactly what you said." He paused. "I gotta add, I'm afraid, that if you don't produce what you are guaranteeing- you might have a problem."

"Don't worry. All over the world, your friends will be able to see that you could- if you wanted to- eliminate the pope as easily as you did the pastrami."

"Okay. When will this audience take place?"

"I will have to arrange the time. How will I get in touch with you?"

"I will take care of that, Lieutenant," said the Prince. "You gentlemen can depend upon me to work as a go-between so that your arrangements will proceed smoothly."

Leo smiled and with sincerity in his voice, said, "Prince, I have no way to thank you except to say I will be in your debt."

"Yeah," said McGinty, "us too."

The Prince rose and the others followed his lead. Everyone shook hands and ten minutes later Leo was on the street looking for a taxi. As he walked to the corner, he searched his mind for the answer to a nagging question- How the hell am I going to arrange what I just promised to arrange?

CHAPTER 25

VINCENT'S MAJOR PROBLEM WAS deciding what songs Angel would sing on Sunday. His minor problem had been Marty who felt compelled to play producer and offer answers to questions asked and unasked. After one call to Abe, Marty ceased to be a problem. Abe was a godsend for Vincent and he recalled how thrilled he was when Abe allowed him complete freedom to do whatever he thought best. It's all in my hands, he thought. Carlos is busy with the little girls, Abe will keep Marty's nose out, and Angel is happy to do what I tell him to do.

As the weeks had passed, Vincent tried to teach Angel what he could, but it was almost unnecessary. Angel seemed to know things. Somehow he managed to guess right. He figured out word meanings from their context. He correctly guessed pronunciations whether the involved words were Latin, Spanish, Italian or everyday American English. Vincent was in awe of him. The few students Vincent had over the years who were actually talented couldn't match Angel in any way. He had to remind those kids to practice; to be on time for a lesson; to take care of their hands, their voice or themselves. That never happened with Angel. Tell him once and that was it. But discounting the growth, the maturity, the entry to the world of light, Angel was more an enigma now than when they had met.

When Vincent thought about Angel and Carlos at that first meeting, it was like watching a movie in his head. Carlos then was Carlos now. He looked the same, sounded the same, and had the same ever-present lustful glint in his eyes. The only real change was new clothes. Comparing the images, Carlos remained the same, but Angel was a totally different person.

His clothes had changed gradually. The jeans, tee shirts, and boots gave way to trousers, shirts with collars, and loafers. The wild, hunted look vanished. He had his hair cut regularly at a beauty salon and the ladies fawned over him.

Slowly, he had become confident and almost charming. He provided answers to questions in words rather than grunts. When he mastered telling time, Marty presented him with a gold dress watch. Several days before, he had come to Vincent's carrying a sleek leather briefcase, which he said he bought at a fancy store on 5th Avenue.

"You see, Vincent," he said, "it isn't a case like everyone carries. It's just big enough for an inch of paper... big enough for music or contracts. You can't put no lunch in it."

When Vincent admired the luxurious feel of the leather, Angel pointed out the monogram. "You see that, the 'A M', that's not only for Angel Martinez, it's for me. It's 'am.' It's me-I am. That's what the 'A M' stands for. Now I am somebody, Vincent, You have made me a person."

Passing Angel in the street, no one would take him to be anything less than a well-heeled kid from South America- the descriptive pejorative, 'New York Puerto Rican,' no longer fit.

During some of the past weeks, Vincent felt like a well being drained. A teacher needs to have a student who is willing to learn, willing to do whatever work is necessary to learn. A teacher needs to be able to plan learning from lesson to lesson so that continuity can be established and maintained. All that went out the window with Angel. You tell him one thing, he knew two, create a pattern and he jumped to the next step no matter how obtuse.

So far, Angel had left all musical decisions to Vincent. His sole suggestions concerned key changes and the order of the songs. Vincent was most amazed by his key change ideas since they involved knowledge of music theory Angel had not yet formally learned. More mysterious was that every choice was not only complex but absolutely correct. Angel had an ear that imagined unconventional sounds. If it were all jazz, Angel would be a combination of the greats, and like Parker and Gillespie, he was capable of forging a new music. There would be no name for it, no formal procedure- just a series of harmonics and feelings that he could bring out. It amazed Vincent when he considered that other people like Angel were roaming the street. Dirty kids who probably could do the most amazing things if given the chance. How strange that Angel had fallen into his lap. A Street kid who wanted to learn to read. Before he finished his learning, Angel might very well reshape the world of music.

Picking Sunday's songs was less of a problem than Vincent thought it would be. Aside from the standard pieces, Angel wanted to include some material with a Spanish flavor. They had talked about including other pieces and finally decided to include a song for every religion that might be in the audience. Several Asian pieces rounded out a set that included European Church music and religious music of the Far East, the Middle East, and various combinations of church music that no longer had a specific home or clear-cut lineage.

Vincent found himself with little to do in the way of actual musical support. So much of the music was chant-like, there was little needed from him beyond opening notes or mood settings for the next piece. Essentially, every performance was a solo venture by Angel with the full weight and strain of its outcome solidly on his shoulders.

Angel did not understand what was happening or what had happened to him. Each day was new and all too often, seemed a part of someone else's life. This person he had become looked like him as he remembered his appearance, but yet it wasn't him. Now, he was wearing gringo schoolboy clothes and shoes. On the first day without boots, he wondered where he would put his knife. It took time for him to understand he no longer needed a knife. Now that he had money he didn't have to cut people to get some.

Several days before, he had walked into a store two doors from Tiffany's and bought the slim leather briefcase. The salesman, who looked like a television actor, had smiled at him and asked if he was buying it for himself or as a present. Angel told him it was a gift to himself. The salesman loved that idea and offered to put Angel's initials on the case for free. While Angel waited for the initials to be applied, the salesman asked if he was going to school, "Yeah," Angel answered, "I'm going to school. I'm learning to be a singer. The case is going to be for my music."

"Are you going to Julliard?"

Angel didn't know what he meant, so he said, "No."

"Oh, you must be studying privately. That's the best. You don't have to be with others- just you and the teacher, right?"

"Yeah, just Vincent and me. He knows everything about music and what he knows, I'll know soon."

"That's wonderful."

The conversation ended when a young kid came back with the case. Seeing the golden initials 'A M' on the leather was unreal, like watching television. He looked at the kid who had brought the case from the back of the store. He looks like me, Angel thought. With a super smile, the salesman asked if Angel wanted it wrapped. The kid tilted forward a bit since he'd have to wrap it, but Angel said, "No. I'll take it like this."

Then the salesman moved to the register and asked, "Cash or charge?" Ever since Angel walked in, the salesman had treated him as he would any customer with no hesitations or signs of doubt. But now, Angel saw a flicker of indecision in the salesman's eye. The guy was nervous. Biting into his friendly demeanor was the possibility that Angel was bullshitting and would walk out saying he had changed his mind. Angel glanced at the kid and thought he looked like he was hoping that would happen. But not because the kid was hoping the salesman would look stupid, rather, Angel thought the kid resented him coming in as a customer. However, everything changed when Angel pulled out a fat wad of bills- now the kid looked proud, quite unlike the salesman's look of envious greed. Angel handed over money, put the receipt inside and gripping the thick leather handle, walked out. He strode up 5th broadcasting his worth as a human being to all.

Angel loved to walk in the daylight now. When thoughts of the West Side and his search for victims filled his head, he smiled. It was like thinking about a movie he had seen months before. Now he belonged in the daylight. He belonged on 5th Avenue and he knew it wasn't merely the money in his pocket—that was only a part of it. It was more that he could talk to anyone who asked a question. Maybe he would sing to them. The thought amused him. If someone asked a question, he would sing the answer.

When he thought about the robbing and killing, he thought about his balls. Taking a leak, he tried to look in the bathroom mirror to see what he looked like and it was strange to see his prick with nothing under it. There was no pain, but he was still afraid to touch there. When he took a shower, he let the water flow there on its own. Except to piss, he hadn't touched his cock in weeks. It was a quiet nightmare. He wouldn't let himself think about girls. He was afraid and wouldn't take the chance. When he thought about getting a hard-on, he froze and tried not to think about it. He knew he would never be able to get a hard-on. Singing allowed him to put it out of his mind. Don't think about it, he told himself. Don't think about it and it won't be there.

He thought about the television girls surrounding rock and rollers and how they tried to touch the musicians. Those girls would do anything to be with those guys. They would fuck them and suck them. He heard about it. What if he became famous? Vincent said it was going to happen. He said that after Sunday, after the concert, he would be famous and rich. There would be girls trying to touch him. What would he do? If he wasn't afraid, he might ask about it, but whom could he ask? Carlos didn't want to talk about it and Vincent would lose respect when he found out he was teaching a freak.

There was no one and there was nothing but the music. It had saved him for the moment, but he knew he'd have to pay. He knew the good guys win and the bad guys lose. He knew that from movies and television. He had been bad and he would have to pay. Getting his balls cut was the beginning—there would be more.

Seeing trees in Central Park, he decided to walk to them and sit, but the benches in front of the Plaza caught his eye, so he headed there. He never usually looked at buildings, but always at people because people were always the solutions to his problems. But now, with a pocket filled with money, he didn't have to look at people trying to figure how much they had, whether it was worth it to hit on them. He didn't have to do that anymore. Now he could look at anything.

He sat on a stone bench and looked around. The Plaza Hotel stood like an advertisement in the bright sunlight. There was just enough breeze to gently move the flags that waved at the tourists. He watched the horses pulling the carriages, but his attention shifted when he became aware of the sweet smell of perfume. Like a dog on scent, he pushed his nose at an up-angle and twisted his head sniffing. A girl had sat on the other end of the bench. When he saw her looking at him, he felt stupid.

"Do you like my perfume?"

He was afraid to answer. She was beautiful and young. He stared at her taking in everything in a flash. She was wearing new shoes and shiny dark stockings that emphasized her perfectly shaped legs. Her clothing was smooth, the cloth looked thick, but not winter thick. She wore a little jacket and carried a small bag. Her hair was long and dark like her eyes. She was looking at him, smiling. White teeth. A television girl. Her head was tilted to one side. She asked him once again, this time in Spanish.

"¿Le gusta mi perfum."

Her question so surprised him he answered her. "I speak English."

"Oh," she said. "I am sorry. I thought maybe you did not understand me. You see, I am learning English and I am not yet so very good with it. So...let me ask you again. Do you like my perfume?"

He thought she was very beautiful. "The perfume smell is pretty- like you."

"You are very sweet to say that. Those who know me might say something nice to make me feel good. You have no reason."

He stared at her. He had never had a conversation like this. The girls he usually spoke to asked if he had money and wanted to get laid. But now he was talking and before he could stop himself, he said, "I would not lie to you. You have life in the palm of your hand."

Her smile slipped away and she tilted her head. "What do you mean I have life in my hand?"

"You will get what you want. How could anyone not give you what you want?" Angel stared at her like she was an alien sent only to visit and he wanted to cry.

"What a wonderful thing to say." She pointed her chin to the left and quickly twisted her head to settle the long shank of her hair. "I wish I had more time to talk with you, but I am meeting people. Will you be here later? Are you staying at the hotel?"

"No. I stopped only for a moment."

She started to say something, but stopped and stood. "The people I am meeting are there at the hotel entrance. I must go. Thank you for your sweet compliment." Then with long, measured steps she walked toward the hotel. Staring at her, he imagined her turning and walking toward him, her clothes melting away as she walked. He gaped at her swaying breasts and at her slowly moving hips. Looking at her face, he saw her smile grow. With each step she drew closer and finally stopped in front of him. She was naked, close enough to touch. She was so beautiful, he didn't now what to do. She was 100 feet tall. There was so much of her. His hand groped in the air.

As his hand clutched the air, he sensed his cock getting hard. Quickly, he put the case on his lap and felt under it. As if paralyzed, his breathing stopped as his hand groped the stiffness of his cock. His mind was swirling. It was a gift from heaven. His fears had been so great, he was unable to speak, but now he had an answer. But how could it be? With no balls, how could he have a hard-on? Mystified, he felt the tension subside and his cock grow soft. The hardness of the stone bench came through to him as he sat bewildered, unable to understand what had happened.

Confounded, but excited, he got up from the bench and walked west. Wait 'till I tell Carlos, he thought. Will he be surprised? Angel knew Carlos avoided talking about the 'accident' because he thought Angel no longer a man. But now, being a man was no longer a problem. Angel smiled as he thought of the girls who would want to be with him. He laughed out loud.

Now, days later, Angel sat at the window of Vincent's apartment looking into the street, thinking about the concert. He could not understand why he might be rich and famous because he could sing. Singing wasn't anything. It was easy. Maybe that was it. Maybe because it was hard for others, they thought who ever could do it was a big deal. Is that the answer? Do people go nuts over somebody because he can do something they can't? Do they pay a guy a million dollars because he a guy can hit a ball from here to there and the people watchin' can't? Is music the same? I can sing and they can't so they'll pay money because I can and they can't? That's crazy, Angel thought.

"Vincent, answer me a question."

"Sure."

"I can't figure out why people will pay money to a guy who can hit a baseball or make me rich 'cause I can sing. What's the big deal about bein' able to hit a ball or sing?"

"I don't have an answer for you, but I do know it isn't just singing that's involved. People will pay money to anyone who makes them feel good. If they like the way you sing and it pleases them, they'll pay to hear you. With the sports stuff, a lot of people are pissed off about things and they need a way to fight back, to win what they can't win. So they pick some guy or a team and become a fan. When their guy or the team wins they feel good, when they lose the fans feel bad."

"But why do people need somebody else to make them feel good and why do they gotta listen to me or somebody else sing? Why don't they sing to themselves?"

"Like I said, Angel I don' have the answer, but I think it's like an artist painting a picture. When a person can do something others can't do, that person is admired." He searched for a better example. After some silence he said, " Say for instance, there's a place where everybody hunts with a spear, the guy who can make a strong and good spear is admired by everybody. They'll pay him to make them a spear or they'll study with him to learn how to do it. Because he's good at it, he becomes a big shot. It depends on where it all happens. Here, we don't care about spears, but we do care about singing and music,- you know, show business. Sports is show business, too. You understand?"

"I think so."

"It's funny you ask, because the other day I heard a guy say something that really fits what we're talking about. There's an old saying- 'There's no business like show business.' do you understand what that means?"

"Yeah- that show business is different."

"Right- but what I heard this guy say, was- 'There's no business but show business'- you see the difference?"

"Yeah... I gotcha. I know what you mean. Like on TV- it's all a show."
They talked a bit more and then got back to their rehearsal for the concert.

CHAPTER 26

THE STREET OUTSIDE THE church looked no different at seven that morning than it did any other morning, except for the three vans parked in the "No Parking" zone. Each had discrete door markings identifying it as property of a TV network which, depending upon the channel, provided either the 'latest news,' the 'most recent news,' or the 'up to the minute news.' In keeping with the industry's desperate need for individuation, the vans were referred to as either 'Roaming,' 'Rolling,' or 'Roving' remote facilities. Interestingly enough, the only time these three hot rods were not bumper-to-bumper covering the same 'news,' was when one of them rear-ended a sightseeing bus and became grist for the others' mills.

From each vehicle a bleary-eyed reporter and camera operator emerged and authoritatively delivered an on-camera piece identifying the church as the probable place for an outpouring of people. They spoke of rumors that the church was the location for a free religious-music concert expected to occur later that morning. Rumors had spread and they had grown in intensity and therefore, veracity. The police, victims of rumor to the same degree as the local population, turned up about twenty strong to handle the potential crowd. The rumors had managed to reach even the chief's office and since both the chief and the police commissioner were professional Irishmen, neither wanted to be left out. Attention to this event would guarantee each the television publicity they craved.

Wooden barricades were placed to the right of the church's front doors in order to contain the expected crowds. By eight, there were about fifty people on line. By half past, there were over three hundred. At eight forty-five, Abe, Marty, Carlos, Vincent and Angel arrived in a limo. Angel was wearing a long, monkish robe Abe had insisted upon. At first, Vincent thought it foolish, but now saw it to be the right touch. He was convinced by the collective

202

'ooooooh' from the crowd when Angel stepped onto the sidewalk. By nine, it was impossible to estimate, but an authorized guess said the crowd was at least a thousand.

Most viewing Angel's arrival immediately presumed him to be an actual monk. Their primary evidence was what he wore- an ankle length, flowing brown robe with a hood that was sufficiently oversized to completely obscure his face. He looked monkish- mysterious and spiritual- exactly the look Abe sought.

Father Taylor who was overwhelmed by the growing crowds, the police, and the television crews met the group at the front door. Years of running a small church were no preparation for what was taking place. As they stepped from the sidewalk into the church, Abe slapped the astonished priest on the back. "Well, Father, Angel is going to cure your attendance problem this morning." The priest returned Abe's joy with a twisted smile and a vigorous nod.

A moment later, a reporter asked a man at the head of the line what the group entering the Church said. The man replied, "Well, best as I could make out, the distinguished white-haired gentleman told the priest, 'that the Angel was going to cure the attendant's problem this morning."

"Are you saying, Sir," the reporter asked, now fully alert to the possibility of a hot story, "Are you saying the white-haired man said those attending would have their problems cured? Is that the word he used, 'cured'?"

"Yes Ma'am, that's what he said. He said the Angel was going to cure problems this morning, no matter what."

The cameraman shifted the camcorder and closed in on the reporter who was now staring at the lens with the practiced sincerity that got her an "A" in acting. "We have just been told that a man claiming to be an Angel has entered the church and that he intends to cure those in attendance."

The reporter also got an "A" in Voice class and her projection carried a goodly distance. The first fifteen or twenty people in line heard what she said into the microphone. A man with a cane pushed his way forward and loudly announced he wanted the Angel to cure him. Upon hearing what he said, a short woman with a blue hat started to sing, "Nearer My God To Thee." At that moment, the reporter spied a man who was stooping to re-tie his shoe lace, but thinking he was hunch-backed, she rushed to him and asked if he thought the Angel could cure him of his affliction.

Straightening, the man asked, "What affliction?" Abashed, the reporter smiled and apologized saying she thought he had a hunchback, but now she could see it was not the case, he was fine. People behind the man, jostling to get closer to the television camera, misinterpreted what they heard and passed along to those behind them, that a man's hunched-back had already been cured as he stood on line waiting to enter the church.

Within fifteen minutes, the crowd, now almost three thousand people standing four deep in orderly lines, had convinced themselves that a real angel had come from heaven to cure all of their ailments.

The regular parishioners who normally arrived at ten were dumbfounded as they approached the church. Their first shock was seeing the crowds, the police, and the TV crews. Their second shock was being refused admission and told to take their place at the end of the line. No amount of protest would sway the police at the door whose instructions were clear- no one enters without proper authorization. Unfortunately, no one expected what was happening to take place, so no one had the foresight to discuss who would be allowed in and what was proper authorization. As a result, no one had the proper authorization and the likelihood of chaos was high until Leo arrived.

He had easily gotten a cab and headed uptown with the smooth travel of a Sunday morning. As the cab neared the forties Leo noticed more than a few Department cars headed in the same direction. When his cab turned the corner and Leo saw what was happening, he felt some of Oppenheimer's reaction when the bomb went off. He exited the cab, flashed his badge to the police at the church door and went inside where he saw Abe, Marty and a priest. He rushed over. "Abe, do you have any idea what's going on outside?"

"Sure Leo, sure. We saw the crowd when we came in. not that many."

"You better take another look. They're standing four abreast all the way down to Ninth. There are thousands out there."

The priest, doubting Leo's estimate, walked toward the front of the church. In less than a minute, he returned the color drained from his face.

"Mr. Rosenberg, he's right. What shall we do? The church can't hold all those people."

As they pondered the priest's question, the police commissioner and the chief of patrol came inside. "Who the hell is in charge here?" the commissioner asked and then reddened when he saw the priest in the middle of the group.

Before anyone could answer, Abe asked, "And who might you be, sonny?"

Laughing inside, Leo jumped in before the commissioner saw any need to push his weight around. "Abe let me introduce Police Commissioner Brougham. Commissioner, this is Mr. Abe Rosenberg, the concert's promoter." Turning to Abe, Leo asked, "Right?"

Abe smiled and said, "One hundred percent correct, Leo and well put." He shook hands with the commissioner. "This is Father Taylor, Commissioner. It's his church we're in and we are all here to bring some free music to the congregation. We did it once before... they liked it, so we are gonna do it again."

"That's fine, Mr. Rosenberg. I'm glad, but... what are your plans for the thousands in the street who are quite obviously not going to fit inside?"

At that moment, Vincent, Carlos, and Angel, who had been at the front of the sanctuary, came to find out what was happening. When Vincent heard what the commissioner said, he casually said, "No big deal, we'll do the entire service outside in the street and let 'em all take part." Turning to Father Taylor, he asked, "Father, can you do a Mass in the street?"

The priest smiled. "Young man, I can do Mass anywhere... and that's a wonderful idea. All I need is a public address system and I'm ready to go."

"There are three news vans outside," the commissioner said, "I'll get them to park mid-street and we'll supply what's required. Will that be all you'll need?" The priest nodded as Vincent said, "A single mike will be fine for Angel also." Abe and Marty smiled, both recognizing the free exposure this would provide.

The Commissioner turned to Chief Reynolds. "Who can we get to swing this into action? I want it all done as quickly as possible. The size of that crowd makes me nervous."

Chief Reynolds said, "Commissioner, this is Lieutenant Flower of Dignitary Protection. He's one of our best." Turning to Leo, he asked, "You can do this, Leo?" Leo nodded as the Commissioner said, "Lieutenant, you know what has to be done- do it!!"

"Give me fifteen minutes." Leo strode up the center aisle, went outside and located the assigned Traffic Unit Commander. In less than fifteen minutes, 47th Street was closed at 7th and 8th and the people who were between 8th and 9th were escorted to an outdoor parking lot in the middle of 47th.

Over a loudspeaker from one of the TV vans, a reporter read a short statement saying there was insufficient room inside the church so the morning Mass and the concert would take place outside. All would be able to see and hear- no reason for anyone being upset. He concluded saying when everyone was settled the Mass would begin. A rock concert crowd would probably have rioted, but this crowd obediently and almost immediately filled the sidewalks and the street. People stood shoulder to shoulder in almost a solid body, but room was provided for those who wanted or needed to sit. The front ranks were filled with people in wheel chairs, on crutches, using canes, wearing splints, and sporting bloody bandages. It looked like a television emergency room.

Someone located and placed 'special guests' folding chairs to the left of the van selected as the 'pulpit.' A ladder led up to the van roof where a small lectern and public address system was placed for Father Taylor. New York City has always been a city filled with surprises and today's unforeseen element was the unexpected silence greeting Father Taylor as he opened his arms to the crowd and offered a blessing.

Leo stood off to the right and listened to the words he knew so well. As he silently prayed for the gentleness of people to be more visible, he noticed a Citroen limo stopped on 7th. Walking to it, the rear door opened and Jacqueline got out. She was a movie. A yellow and white suit with ivory shoes and a bag that immediately made him think of Audrey Hepburn. What a fashion sense Jacqueline had. Turn her lose in boutique and she'd find the best-looking items. Leo didn't believe that skill was learned... some just had the knack.

Since Leo was the only person moving away from the crowd, a cop on duty by one of the barricades noticed him. Before the cop could say anything, Leo flashed his shield and put his hand over the wooden barricade to touch Jacqueline's.

"You look wonderful." He said.

She smiled and said in a French accented version of Mae West, "You don't look so bad yourself, big boy." They stood smiling at each other like kids who discovered they have enough money for popcorn and soda.

"Leo, what is going on here? We had to circle twice to get close enough."

He sighed. "Best as I can make out, word spread about the concert and a great many people are evidently interested in religious music."

"That's not what we heard."

"What do you mean? What did you hear?"

"A man told my driver an angel had come from heaven to cure sick people."

"You don't believe that, do you?"

"What I believe is not important. Look at the people." she gestured with her hand. "They look like they are expecting more than just a few songs."

Leo turned and for the first time looked into the faces of those he could clearly see. They had that glassy-eyed look you see in Grand Central when people have been waiting hours for a train. He wondered how Abe managed it... how he got all these people to show up.

"Jacqueline, I don't know what they've been promised, but what they're going to get is a Puerto Rican kid singing some Gregorian Chants. "

"Leo, does it matter? If people believe something is true, then it's true. Look at them... those people are expecting a miracle."

Leo spoke as he looked at the eager, waiting faces. "Well, I don't know about them, but the only miracle I know is the two of us..."

She smiled and touched his face with her hand. "Yes," she whispered. "Do you want to get a closer look?" He asked. "Oh yes, I would love to."

He directed her to the end of the stanchion where the cop moved it enough for her to slip inside. They walked to the front of the church and stopped to the right of the seated 'dignitaries'. When Abe noticed them, he walked over and Leo introduced him to Jacqueline. Winking at Leo, Abe marched off, returning in a minute with a chair for her. As she sat, Father Taylor started the service.

The sun was gleaming and the morning air was still. A glance to the right, showed the traffic on 7th Avenue slipping by. On that thoroughfare, it was still a usual Sunday morning. Looking left, however, provided an amazing spectacle. Thousands of faces, all staring at a man standing on the roof of a black van. It was beyond strange, for there was nothing by which a comparison could be made. It was difficult to accept the simple fact that it was happening. It looked like a scene from a fantasy film

Standing next to Leo, Abe asked, "What do you think of all this?"

"I think it's great and I'd love to know how you brought it off. How did you start a rumor about an angel? And not only that... how did you manage to spread it so fast?"

Abe laughed. "Leo, I had nothing to do with this. We came this morning to do concert and I hoped we'd at least fill the church with more people than the first time. I didn't arrange any of this." He paused, looked at the crowd. "I wish I could arrange something like this. I would love to be able to get people to come out in such numbers."

In the silence that followed Abe's remark, Father Taylor's voice boomed from the loudspeakers. He was getting into it. After years of preaching to small crowds in a dark and silent church, he was ready for the street. The sun was shining and his white hair gleamed. His voice, usually wrapped in piety, blasted forth with a decibel level worthy of backcountry preachers.

Leo knew there exists a mentality that grows with the power it can use. Sit a meek man at the controls of a bulldozer and watch him slowly become a tyrant, pushing over trees, ripping out stumps, and moving tons of earth. It's simple- the people who run big machines become extensions of the machine. They start to think like bulldozers. It's the same with voices. Give a microphone to a guy with something to say and stand back. As the volume grows, the power grows, as the power grows, the self-righteousness expands and eventually, a booming voice self-proclaims expertise. Listening crowds tend to get taken in, thinking if it's loud it's got to be right.

Father Taylor loved the sound of his own voice. As he spoke, his connection to amplification empowered his delivery. After a hesitant start, he was now listening to himself, learning quickly how to move the microphone closer for an intimate, more sincere sound or further away as he increased his volume.

"This is a moment for repentance." He boomed. "This is the moment to look into your hearts and realize that nothing must be as it is. You can put down sin and achieve your place in the glorious hereafter. To be with him..." He paused and bowed his head. The crowd was silent. He was silent knowing full well that the longer the pause the greater the importance of the next remark. Five seconds. Ten seconds. Just enough time for people to get edgy, to grow a trifle nervous. Just long enough for them to wonder if he was all right... and then before anyone could move to check, He raised his head and stared into the many upward turned faces.

"You who believe will receive. You who believe will receive. You who believe will receive." Each time he said it; his voice was louder and slower. Some might have thought the booming voice was God himself. In the front ranks, people that had put crutches and canes on the ground, stood tall, ready for their miracle. Others sank to their knees with hands clasped tightly. "This is the moment," the electrified voice resounded. "This is the moment for Angel to sing."

Father Taylor hadn't enjoyed himself more in years. Broadly smiling as he climbed down from the van roof, his mind raced at the possibilities.... Seek a transfer to a larger church with an external courtyard... make a case for a public address system... get that Vincent fellow to give him some lessons. Reaching the ground, he played the real life version of Dr. Livingston in Africa as he walked into the crowd, touching people and offering blessings.

As Father Taylor swaggered amongst the sinners, Vincent and Angel climbed the ladder to the roofs decking. Vincent sat, Angel stood at the microphone. The crowd, fired with Father Taylor's piety, now grew silent as they gaped at the robed figure on the roof of the truck. There was silence. The only sounds were reverberations from the pulse of the surrounding streets. Then Vincent strummed a chord to set the key and Angel sang.

Later, those who recalled accurately insisted there was a hum that grew in intensity. It started low and rose to a level so high and clear few would think it was a person and not some electronic device. Angel had been working on range and he now had more than three octaves at his instant command. Vincent had played Yma Sumac records for him to demonstrate a multi-octave voice and Angel listened, smiled and said, "I can do that."

The hum segued to some Latin sounding lyrics and then to a rhythmic chant. The crowd already exposed and educated by rock and current 'pop' were ready to follow- and in a few minutes, they did- thumping, bumping, and grunting in time. It was amazing how quickly the crowd joined in. There were no waiting skeptics hanging back...the crowd wanted to take part.

Angel was electrifying. As he sang, he remained motionless, save for a slight swaying. With the hood of the robe obscuring his face, it was impossible to see his lips move and without being able to actually see him sing, the crowd regarded his tones as magical. His sound seemed to come from a mystical, black, empty space... from nowhere. People swayed, their heads thrown back, theirs eyes closed, wispy smiles on their lips. They swayed in unison, moving as a field of wind driven wheat... first this way, then the other.

Abe, standing alongside Leo, elbowed him in the ribs. "Well, what the hell do you think of this? Huh? Ain't this hot shit?"

Leo couldn't disagree. "You're right, Abe. Thousands in the street. Television news trucks, and that kid's voice... it's incredible."

Sitting in front of Leo, Jacqueline reached up and took his hand. Everyone was at peace. The commissioner and his family smiled. Everyone smiled. Carlos stood in the doorway of the church, his arm around a young, pretty girl he had 'rescued' from the crowd. His smile, more a leer, grew as he slid his hand to the girl's behind. Rather than pull away, she leaned back and pushed her hip into his crotch. His leer grew even more devilish. He too, expected a 'miracle.'

Angel's singing affected this crowd as it had the smaller group inside the Church. There was no difference. Those who wanted to sit on the pavement did and those nearest backed away so none were crowded. As Leo watched it taking place, he wondered if people could behave so decently without there being a well from which they could draw. There was no time for them to learn how to be decent. They knew. We all know, he thought. What we need is the opportunity to display what's in us. People responded to Angel's songs and selfishness diminished.

It was hard to explain Angel's magic, but Leo thought it was similar to hearing a great jazz solo. Everything fit. The pattern of the notes, the standard harmonies giving way to explorations. To Leo, Angel's singing was ultra-conservative. It explored no new territory. What he sang, everyone expected him to sing. What they expected, what they wanted, they received. Those musically sophisticated and those not so, managed to know when a phrase would end, how the next would begin, and when the song would end. He pleased all.

Later, Jacqueline would insist she heard and recognized tunes she sang as a child in France. Others felt similarly, yet they came from different parts of the world. Somehow, and maybe it was a miracle, Angel touched a musical universal. Somewhere deep in our chemistry, there is a memory gleaned from sitting at the fire, from treading in the forests or foraging in the fields, from huddling together waiting for the night to end. When we learned how to make our own music by imitating nature, we were ready to listen to the music in our souls.

CHAPTER 27

AT TIMES, AN ATMOSPHERE is created that can permeate available surroundings. Similar to radiation, it sidles unencumbered through what it encounters. It is impossible to deny its onslaught and only escape can eliminate its effect. During Angels' performance, no one wanted to escape.

Like Hollywood extras paid to stand still, the crowd focused their attention on the small, robed figure. They were ready for Angel's message. He said nothing, but effectively managed to erase the pious tension created by Father Taylor. The combat between Good and Evil was Father Taylor's war and he could not preach without establishing the lines of battle. But these people knew of the strife, reminding them of it was not essential.

Keep the congregants as children, the Church implores, for the more infantile and fearful, the greater is their reliance. Fear is the enemy of the people and the friend of the Church. To be bold is to end the parental control the Church greedily seeks. Self-reliance and fearlessness are the enemies of all religions.

Angel's singing made people fearless for he so thoroughly satisfied them they needed nothing more. Father Taylor's ravings against sin were seen as sham once the crowd fell under Angel's spell. He made them feel wonderful. He made them smile. He made them unafraid, and what is more, he gave them self-respect and therefore, respect for others.

Finishing, he fell silent. There was no "thank you" and no bowing. Standing upright and motionless, he stopped, turned from the microphone and climbed down to the street. No one rushed to him as he walked into the church. When Vincent followed, the crowd knew the concert was over and they slowly started to drift apart, to melt away. The police were amazed since they knew the larger the crowd the faster personal guilt vanishes. A massive group could do anything; commit any mayhem, with not one participant burdened by blame or shame. Now the police were silently joyous. Father Taylor would have liked one more chance to push his message, but this crowd had been over-sold. They were TV veterans and knew the last commercial was no different from any of the other self-serving sponsor messages.

Reporters flowed after the crippled that now walked with heads high. The buoyancy of their spirit was like the heat shimmering from the sidewalk. Some carried their crutches, others, like antiquated drum majors, swung theirs in the air. A few were pushing their own wheelchairs. Person after person related their miraculous cure. They said they felt the power run through them in the middle of a song. They said the Angel had cured them "Just look at me. Do I look crippled?" shouted one man. Everyone smiled.

Wondering what was happening, Leo watched the dispersing crowd. He had been so involved with Jacqueline; he had paid scant attention to Angel. The few times he did become aware of the throbbing music, his mind repulsed it and returned to Jacqueline. Looking down as he stood behind her, he closed his eyes and imagined the passion of her lips. Others also had stood with closed eyes, but Leo was unconcerned with them. If Angel was a virus, Leo was not infected.

As the police began to dismantle the barricades, Leo and the 'official' group went into the church. A short time later, the police commissioner and the chief said good-bye to those nearby and drifted out. Eventually, except for the addition of Jacqueline, the same little group that had been in the Church at the outset was again assembled. Abe slapped Leo on the back. "Goddamn, Leo, you swung it. The Commish says 'go do' and you go and do. I think we owe it all to you."

"Now wait a minute, Abe." Leo protested. "All I did was tell the cops to move some people here and put some barricades there. It was no big deal."

"Don't pull that modesty crap with me. You did it and we owe you—period." Then, turning his attention to Jacqueline, he slowly appraised her. "Leo, I think you should take your girl for a walk in the park... she looks lonely and unattached."

Leo glanced at Jacqueline, and then turned to Abe. "Lonely she isn't and unattached, she certainly isn't. Mr. Rosenberg, let me formally introduce you to Madame Jacqueline Rosuault, the wife of the French ambassador to the United Nations."

Abe bowed ever so slightly and then grasped Jacqueline's hand. As he took it to his lips, he said, "Madame Rousault, I am honored to meet you, et si je vows dire, vous êtes trop belle être vue avec une telle numero."

Looking at Leo, Jacqueline burst out laughing. Leo sputtered, then demanded, "Abe what did you say?" Then he turned to Jacqueline, "What did he say, c'mon, tell me, what did he say?"

She looked first at Abe, then at Leo. "He said that I am lovely and you ought to be proud to be in my company."

Leo smiled and muttered. "Sure he did and I'm related to Napoleon Bonaparte."

Vincent and Angel joined them. Abe introduced them to Jacqueline and then insisted everyone come to brunch at his hotel. As they prepared to leave, Leo asked about Marty and Carlos. Abe said they were busy, but would eventually join them. They started to leave the church, but were interrupted when Father Taylor stopped them. "Wait a minute, wait. What about next week? We must do this again." His face beamed with delight.

"Now, you wait a minute, Father." Said Abe. "All we did was ask to use the Church to see how a concert would go and we profoundly thank you for letting us do that. The idea was to see if Angel would do well with a large crowd and we found that out, didn't we?"

"But wait," pleaded the priest. "I haven't had an opportunity to preach to such a throng in my life. I want another chance."

Abe stared at him. "Let me put it this way. Now that we know Angel is a real success, there will be a fee for all performances. When we work out the price, we'll get back to you."

"Hire him?" the priest burst out.

"Father, charity may be the foundation of the Church and I gladly contribute, but as far as Angel's singing is concerned... he'll get paid whether he's singing here or in Las Vegas." With that, Abe turned and guided the group up the aisle. Once outside, they saw two cars at curbside, Abe's hired limo and Jacqueline's Citroen. Standing to the right of the Church were Melendez and Roberto Colon. When Leo saw them he smacked his forehead.

"What is it?" Jacqueline asked.

Gesturing to the couple, he said, "I invited them, but forgot about them with all the fuss. She works with me and he works at my building."

"I met her, don't you remember? We went shopping at Bergdorf s and I met him when I came to your apartment." He shook his head. "You know, when I'm with you I forget everything."

He apologized for being such a poor host and Melendez laughed, saying that anyone who's hosting a small party of thousands shouldn't be overly concerned if a guest is misplaced."

"How did you two find each other in this crowd?"

Roberto laughed. "Well, when I realized there was no way I could find you and since Susan and I didn't make careful plans about meeting, I just drifted around" He stopped and looked at Susan. "Then I spot this one and I figure the morning wouldn't be a total loss if I could pick her up, so I try."

"And- He was very successful." Melendez broke in. "It was only after we talked a while did we realize who we were."

"How about that?" said Roberto. "I manage to pick up the girl I have a date with." Jacqueline laughed. "If people are destined to come together... they will. It's meant to be."

"That sounds so romantic, so French..." said Leo.

"Don't forget, Lieutenant Flower," Roberto added, "Spanish and French are languages of love. English... it is the language for business."

Abe pushed into their circle. "If you saw the hookers on this corner every night, you might reconsider. English is the language of negotiated romance around here."

Jacqueline smiled. "Mr. Rosenberg, what you speak of is not romance... those negotiations are strictly business."

Abe smiled. "Touché."

There was silence until Abe announced, "Look, it's easy to see everyone is feeling good, so let's go to my hotel for brunch... my treat."

Roberto, Melendez and Leo rode with Jacqueline, the others went with Abe. In a short time they arrived at the Regency and flowed into the lobby. Angel, still in his robe, caused a scene until the staff realized he and everyone else were Mr. Rosenberg's guests. After that, treatment was first class.

They were escorted to a semi-private section of a small dining room and seated at a table set with ornate and expensive china. After they ordered, Abe asked how they felt about the concert. Jacqueline, Melendez, and Roberto were enthusiastic and Leo said it was the best he ever heard. Vincent, who had been silent, could no longer contain himself.

"Let me tell you, I have never experienced anything like that. After years of playing, teaching, and associating with musicians, I thought I would never accompany anyone who always did the right musical thing."

"You taught him well." Said Abe.

"No, Abe. That's not what I mean. Angel sings in key- hell, he's got perfect pitch. No. I mean that in my head I hear the music. I hear where the note is and I hear where it should go. Many singers and players don't go to the right place... lots of arrangers don't take the music to where my head wants it to go. It's like a reality and an imaginary reality- but with Angel... Angel always goes to the imaginary reality. He sings the notes I'm hoping he'll sing, but don't really expect it... so it's like magic. Hell, it is magic." He turned to Angel. "How the hell do you do that? How do you always pick right?"

Since they left the church, Angel had not spoken. The oversized robe so separated him from the others, they were almost happy he stayed silent. Leo thought the kid strange... sitting next to him, looking at him and then seeing him look back. There was something odd about his eyes and face. They didn't register nonverbal messages... they seemed vacant and empty. He didn't seem to register other people. It was like he lived in a private world.

Angel turned to Vincent. "How do I get it right? I don't know, Vincent. I open my mouth and the stuff comes out. I don't think about it... it's there. But everybody likes it, right?" He looked around the table and saw the answering smiles. Satisfied, he went on. "But let me ask you guys a question, okay? What do you do when you memorize somethin' and you want to go over it?" No one answered. "Like when you want to go from this place to that place and you memorize the way you gotta go to get there. What do ya do?" Again, no one answered.

Then Roberto spoke up. "Well... I'm an actor and when I memorize a role, I memorize it in relation to what other people say or ask. I know what I've got to say, but I know it in relation to the other characters. I don't think I could say all my lines... one after the other, like I was reading a poem."

"Do you have the whole play open in your mind?" Asked Angel.

"No. It comes out... like one word... or one sentence at a time."

"That's what I mean, man. I understand what you're sayin'. I don't do it or see it like that. When I sing, I see the whole song in my head, from beginning to end and all I do is go from one place to the next place. It's all there, all the time, so all I do is sing the note that supposed to come at that time and then go on to the next until there ain't no more."

"Do you sort of cross the notes off after you've sung them? " Roberto asked.

"Nope. I just go on. I don't look back there."

No one spoke since no one knew what to say. Finally, Abe broke the silence after a minute. "Speaking personally, I don't give a damn how you do it. I'm just delighted you do." Turning to the table at large he continued. "This little concert is just the beginning. Angel and Vincent are going to perform all over the world. Every country is gonna demand Angel. To say the least, I have some plans." He picked up a fork and used it as a baton to punctuate his words. "In about three weeks, the CD will be out."

"What CD?" Asked Vincent.

"The record, CD... whatever you call it... of what just took place. The concert at the church."

"You recorded it?"

"Vincent... of course I recorded it. As soon as I knew we were going outside, I told the people I hired to do whatever they had to do to get it all on tape." Abe laughed. "Heh, heh, they told me they hired the guys in the video trucks to do it for them and they got it all."

"What label is going to bring it out?"

"Vincent, don't you worry about that. The wise guys who run those record companies are going to be calling me. By Tuesday, my phone will be glowing."

Angel shrugged off the robe's hood and stared at Abe. "You mean I'm gonna be on a record?"

"Angel, in about a month you're gonna see CD's of *The Concert at the Church* all over the place. You are goin' to be so famous, you'll need ten Carlos' to take care of the girls."

"By the way, where is Carlos... and where is Marty? " Vincent asked.

"They are taking care of the loose ends with the recording guys." Answered Abe.

"Abe, how did you know it was going to be such a huge success?"

"Who the hell knew, Leo? I had no idea. I had hopes... I knew Vincent is a pro, but Angel is new to this... I figured I'd invest the money and see what happened. Anyway... you saw the crowd, they ate it up."

"Abe?" Angel broke in. "You mean I'm gonna have a CD with my name and picture on it?"

"Your name and picture and Vincent's name and picture also, but it's really all you, Angel. You are gonna be a star. You're gonna be able to fill every church in the world if you want. Or, if you'd rather, we can put you in theaters and you can sing regular songs. It doesn't matter. You're a hit. You'll be bigger than the Beatles, you'll see."

His fork poised in mid air, Angel's mind raced. Television had become real. He couldn't believe what he was hearing. He thought of the hours he had watched television people getting what they wanted... now he would be like them. They had clothes. They had cars. They had everything. Now Abe was saying he would have all that. Flashing through his mind were pictures of the people he had attacked to get money for food. Now he was holding a gleaming fork and eating food from a fancy plate in a dining room he couldn't have imagined a year before.

"Abe," Leo asked, "What did you say about the church?"

"What did I say? I said he's gonna be bigger than the Beatles."

"No, not that- about the church. What did you say about the Church?"

"I said that Angel would be able to fill any church in the world." He popped a piece of French toast in his mouth and while chewing said, "Christ, Leo, he's gonna be bigger than the Pope."

"You think so?"

"Do I think so? Are you crazy? Did you see those people?" He put down his fork and wiped his mouth with a napkin. "I don't know what it is people need from the Church and I don't care. What is clear to me now, is that less than two hours ago, thousands of people were standin' in a city street not makin' a sound and lookin' at this... at this... wonder man... hangin' on every

215

sound he made." He put down the napkin and leaned back into the soft chair. "I have never seen the pope in St. Peter's Square, but if Angel and the pope were there together, I wouldn't bet on who'd get the most attention."

As Leo ate some of the perfectly prepared eggs, he realized all of them at the table agreed with Abe's observation. No one offered even the slightest rebuttal.

Throughout the conversation, Leo saw that Angel gave only cursory attention to what was said. Most often, he ate and watched Vincent. When Vincent cut bacon, buttered toast, or speared eggs with his fork, Angel did exactly the same thing. It looked like Angel was learning far more than music from Vincent.

After most of the dishes had been cleared, Abe suggested, "How about you all come up to my place for coffee and dessert... it's right upstairs?" Like a grandstand wave at a baseball game, one after the other nodded a reply of "Why not?"

After Abe summoned the waiter and gave instructions for the food to be delivered to his apartment, he led the way from the dining room to the elevators. As they walked through the lobby, Leo took a good look at Roberto and Melendez and an idea started to form. He realized that if he didn't know them, he wouldn't be able too pin down their nationality. They certainly didn't look like Iowa farmers, but they didn't look Latin either. If a person didn't know their background, it would be hard to place them into a specific ethnic or national category.

As they rode the elevator to Abe's, Leo was toying with the germ of an idea. He figured Jacqueline could help, but exactly how she could do so wasn't clear, but it was nice to think about. Also, a pattern was forming involving both Melendez and Roberto.

When the elevator stopped, Abe led the way, positioning himself squarely in front of the massive wooden door. Then, as if he were a vaudeville Ali Baba, he proclaimed "Open!" To everyone's delight, the mechanism went 'click' and the door did as ordered. Everyone laughed when Roberto said, "There you go... automation's got my job."

Their laughter subsided as they entered the apartment. There seemed to be sky everywhere, like being in a plane with windows six feet high. Leo figured the drapes were drawn when he had been there, since it was a view not forgotten. He remembered moving into his place and after seeing the brick wall opposite, he had lowered the blinds- they're still usually down.

Jacqueline took his hand as they walked to the windows. "Here's a view of Manhattan most never see." He said.

"It's the same in Paris; unless you are high up, you miss the essence."

Then, without ceremony, Abe herded them into the dining room where two of the hotel staff was busily arranging coffee, tea, cakes, muffins, pies, and Danish pastries, everything a dieter is told to avoid. Leo shifted his gaze from the food to the furniture, the paintings, the silverware and dishes. Wealth was not bad provided you wanted what money could buy. In some ways the orphanage was a good training ground for appreciating what you had. He never forgot what Sister Agnes always said, 'a starving man thinks moldy bread a feast'.

Being alone, his pay was enough, but he often wondered how the guys with families managed the crushing need for money. It didn't surprise him when he heard cops were on the take. It was like the Army. You get a guy in, pat him on the back, tell him how much the country needs him and then pay him just enough to keep him poor. Asking soldiers and cops to put their bodies in front of a bullet and then denying them the money to send a kid to a good school was hardly the thanks they deserved. What would happen if one day the Army and the cops decided to leave for better paying jobs?

After they finished dessert, Abe dragged Angel and Vincent to his office saying they would be back in a bit. Roberto and Melendez went onto the terrace, leaving Leo and Jacqueline at the table.

"What are you thinking about?" she asked.

Leo looked at her, appreciating her beauty. Was it the symmetry of her face and the smoothness of her skin? He once read that bone structure was the key to beauty and now he could see the truth of it. Her face was perfectly balanced. Above a soft, yet firm chin was a broad smile and beautiful teeth. Then a slender nose and dark green eyes set off by arched brows. As he stared, he wondered why she would bother with him. Just when he thought he knew all there was to know about himself, she comes along and tells him he is not what he thought.

She had totally contradicted the hours he spent fighting tears thinking about what he did not have and never would have... the painful willingness to look at what had been and what would be... how he had lived alone and would probably die alone.

And then as if getting whacked by lightening, she was in his life. At the same time he reveled in good fortune, he waited for the other shoe to drop... for the moment she would leave. Until then... follow Sister Agnes and appreciate what you have.

"Leo," she poked him. "Where are you?"

"Oh, I was wondering why the gods brought you into my life?"

She nodded and spoke softly. "I have seen that look before. Please... don't get morbid and sorry for yourself... let's enjoy what we have while we can."

He took her hand. "It's hard for me, but I know you're right. I'm upset because there's nothing I can offer to make you stay."

"Leo, please."

"Okay, okay." Lifting her hand, he kissed it. Then, like turning a page, he said, "I may need your help."

"My help? What can I do?"

"I'm not exactly sure. My current assignment is to prevent an attempt against the pope. I think I found a way, but I need to see him. I need an audience."

"Everyone wants an audience with the pope, Leo. It's like meeting Queen Elizabeth."

"I know that, but I need to see him. I'm going through channels, but I don't think anyone will pay attention. I thought the ambassador could get word to the Vatican."

"I don't know about that."

"All I'd want him to say is that a New York City policeman has a plan to protect the pope but needs to see him."

"Why do you need to see him?"

"There are some decisions that he alone can make."

"What are you proposing?"

"It's complicated and I don't think this is the place to go into it." He took her hand. "C'mon let's go outside." They walked onto the terrace and joined Melendez and Roberto. The terrace was large enough for a full-scale celebrity wedding.... maybe even big enough for a regulation volley ball game. "How do you like this place?" Leo asked them.

Melendez laughed. "Are you kidding? You get a taste of a place like this and you want to jump rather than go back to your broom closet."

Roberto look surprised. "Does this kind of place mean that much to you?"

"It isn't that," she said. "It's like going to a museum. You see art that makes your mouth water, and then you go home to your framed prints. The real stuff is so different, you're better off never seeing it."

"Ignorance is bliss... is that it?"

"I don't know, Leo. I love my place and my prints, but seeing this place and thinking about how this old guy lives makes me jealous."

"Don't be jealous, it's a waste of time. If you and Roberto can hit it off and get a place of your own, having a terrace won't matter."

"Let me tell you, Lieutenant," Roberto said, "if I could come home to her every night, I wouldn't care if we lived in a coal mine."

Leo looked at Jacqueline with an "I'm a little cupid" smile on his face.

As he did that, Melendez said to Roberto, "Why do you think I would live in a coal mine?"

"I didn't mean that and you know it."

Wrapping her arms around him, she turned to Leo. "I think you did me a very big favor." Then she turned back and looked at Roberto in a warm and sexy way.

Suddenly, Leo asked, "Would you two help me with a plan I'm thinking out? It would mean you have to act tough."

"What?" they chorused simultaneously.

"Look... I'm working on a idea that will need two young people able to look cold and very tough. You two would be perfect."

"What would we have to do?"

"Nothing... as I see it, you'd have to stay expressionless until I say you're killers and then you'd have to look like you are."

"Leo..." Melendez said, her voice trailing off to silence. Roberto asked, "You mean we have to act tough, is that it?"

"Not really... you have to look willing... yeah, that's it... for instance, if I say you are a cold-blooded killer, you have to look like you are exactly that. By doing nothing, you have to convince someone that you could kill." They stared at him.

"Leo, you aren't making sense," Jacqueline said.

"Oh, no, don't say that." Roberto broke in. "I know what he means. In class we called that 'menacing'."

"You mean," Melendez, asked, "that we're supposed to fulfill the expectations of the people looking at us?"

"Exactly, exactly!" Cried Leo. "I will say you two are terrorists and you have to make them believe it's true. What you have to do is confirm what I've said."

"Who are these people you keep talking about?" Melendez asked.

"Don't worry about them. They're absolutely nonviolent. I don't want to elaborate until I have it all worked out, but let me assure you there will be no danger."

Roberto looked at Melendez who smiled. "You got us Lieutenant; I guess we are the principal players of the Flower Acting Company... right?"

Leo straightened. "You **are** the Flower Acting Company... entitled to all the rights and benefits there from."

"And what are those benefits?" Melendez asked.

"You get to pay me twenty dollars a week... okay?"

CHAPTER 28

BY MONDAY AFTERNOON, LEO made clear to Hoffheimer that his plan required a meeting with the pope so details could be worked out. Hoffheimer said the chance of a meeting was unlikely, but he would tell his Vatican contacts it was important. Leo also called Chief Reynolds, telling him there could be an attempt on the pope and an audience was vital. The chief promised to help, as did Jacqueline, though she wasn't sure anything could be done by the Embassy. With those calls in place, Leo still felt he needed more insurance, so he called St. Patrick's. He got through to Father Barry who told him the Monsignor was busy.

"I understand he's busy- we're all busy, but you tell him Leo Flower is calling and that he has a line on terrorists who intend to kill the man in charge."

"Why would anyone want to kill the Cardinal?"

"Forgive my language, but I wasn't talking about the Cardinal, Father Barry, I meant the pope." There was a pause and the phone was put down. About 15 seconds later, Leo heard a familiar voice.

"Now what is this all about, Lieutenant Flower? Father Barry told me you're talking about an assassination attempt on the Holy Father."

"That's correct, Monsignor. I have met terrorists who told me of their intentions."

"Why didn't you arrest them?"

"You can't arrest people for talking. In front of a judge, they would deny it or pass it off as a joke. There's no way to prove anything."

"How can you be sure they aren't joking?"

"I know they are serious. They aren't local goons fooling around or trying to impress me, they're international killers and they mean what they say."

"My God! ... But what would they gain? Another pope would be on the throne in a short time?"

"I asked that question and they said they weren't concerned with what made sense to me. They said their actions would make sense to the world after they acted."

"Unbelievable, absolutely unbelievable," Healy said, his voice flat.

"That's what I thought when I stumbled onto it, but these people are serious."

"Is it possible for me to meet with them? Could I offer them money or persuade them to change their plans?"

"I don't think that will mean much. Money is not the object and they aren't emotionally involved. They are working professionals who do the job they're hired to do."

"Hired? Who would hire them to kill that man?"

"People who think they'd benefit from it, but what difference does it make?"

Leo heard the Monsignor's breathing as he considered what he'd heard. After a pause, Healy asked, "Well... if what you're telling me is true, why are you calling me? You have all the protection at your end- UN and Vatican Security and your Department are our lines of defense. There's not much we can do here."

"I understand that, but I need something and you can help."

"What is it you need?"

"I have to see the Holy Father in a private audience."

There was a long pause, then Healy said, "I don't think that will be possible. I don't see how we can allow that."

"You don't understand. It is the one thing that will prevent the entire situation."

"I don't see how that could make a difference."

"It doesn't matter what you understand or don't understand." said Leo, with urgency. "A meeting is essential."

"Well..."

Leo cut him off. "Maybe it would help if you saw these people. I think I can get them to come to a meeting."

"A meeting? Is this teatime? You're telling me there are people who want to kill the Holy Father and they are willing to sit and talk about it?"

"No. I'm not saying that," said Leo emphatically. "I am saying that I have things I need to explain to you and I think I can get them to come with me. If you see them, you'll understand the seriousness of the situation." Leo paused, then added, "Monsignor, I can bring people who are involved... seeing them will help you understand the urgency."

After a pause, Healy said, "Well... I guess there's no harm hearing what you have to say." Leo snapped his fingers- he did it. "Are you sure you can bring these people with you?"

"I can probably get two to come... When can we meet?"

"Tomorrow... Is tomorrow satisfactory?"

"Tomorrow night. I'll have to contact them and get back to you. I'll call before eleven tomorrow morning."

"I'll be expecting your call." Healy hung up.

"Got you." Leo said aloud, a broad smile forming on his face.

He spent the remainder of the day fine tuning his plans and clearing Melendez's schedule with Hoffheimer. Since Roberto was on duty the next evening, Leo had to call the building manager to get him free for the night.

That evening, Leo went to the Village Vanguard to catch the Monday Night Big Band and loved it. He liked small groups, but seventeen coordinated players, all pulling together was better. A really good band had no place for individualists unless they were able to wear two hats at the same time. Basie's band managed it... great soloists willing to submerge their individuality in a group effort. Every successful organization was made up of people able to work alone and as part of the group.

As he sat and listened he was pleased to notice quite a few young people in the crowd. Like classical music, jazz demanded knowledge for true appreciation. The more you knew, the more you realized how much talent was involved. Like cooking, driving a car well- maybe it was like that with everything, he thought. The more you know about anything, the easier to recognize greatness. To an idiot everything is simple or a blur.

As Leo watched the band, Angel watched the girls in bikinis dancing on the beach and wondered if he would ever get on a TV show. When Abe said his picture and name would be on a CD, he imagined himself a guest on a show with great looking girls. As he watched the TV girls on the beach, his hand drifted to his crotch and his rock hard penis. It amazed him that he could get a hard-on.

Silently and slowly, Carlos opened the apartment door trying to catch Angel playing with himself. Almost every day that past week, Carlos returned to the apartment to find Angel watching TV and whacking off. Since he had been thrust into the role of brother, Carlos saw it as his responsibility to set things right. When he realized Angel could get a hard-on, he knew a girl would be needed.

So Carlos had brought two girls with him. Both had seen Angel at the Church concert and considered him celebrity enough for boasting to their friends. Both wanted Angel, but Carlos insisted the little blond keep her distance. "You're for me, man. Not him."

She nodded, but it made no difference. She knew she could have Angel **and** Carlos whenever she felt like it. After her stroll last summer, she knew men would do anything for her. She remembered that little walk. It was a Monday and she got her hands on a thin, white silk slip, a slinky, sexy, full slip with a plunging neckline. Looking at it, she got a bright idea. She undressed completely, put on the slip and went out for a walk. Just high heels and that white slip — nothing else. She knew enough to realize that with the sun shining on an angle, the material would be almost transparent. With the confidence that comes from good looks, she walked very slowly down Eighth Avenue. Just strutted down the street. The uptown traffic, heavy at the time, came to a halt- everything stopped. Cabs stopped, trucks stopped, horns blared, people gaped- everything paused. The world paused, took a breath, smiled and then leered as she very, very slowly walked past.

High heels, a slinky white slip, swinging hips, bouncing boobs, and a smile was a miraculous combination that had the entire neighborhood holding its breath. After she passed them, a few of the cabs tried to back up on the sidewalk, creating even more mayhem. When the cops finally came, nothing happened, since they joined the gaping onlookers. She thought it was great fun to see all those men just staring and panting and wishing. Men would do what she wanted. They always had and they always would. Angel would be no different. When she wanted him, she'd have him.

The three of them came into the room quietly and Angel didn't feel their presence until they were looking at him. He didn't jump or seem embarrassed- Carlos thought that was cool- all Angel did was look up at Carlos and smile. Then, still smiling, he looked at the girls. Maria, the girl Carlos picked for Angel, stepped to the front of his chair and cool as you please, put her hand on the lump in his pants.

"Carlos," she said, "I'm gonna take The Angel to the bedroom if he wants to come with me." Angel laughed, stood, grasped her hand, and together, they went into the bedroom. Carlos looked at the blond and smiled.

"See that, baby, you see that? That little guy is dynamite. He is so ready for her. It doesn't bother him that we caught him playing with himself. He is ready and she is gonna get it from him."

"Am I gonna get it from you? Or am I gonna have to get it from him after Maria?"

"Hey, baby, don't talk like that. I got plenty for you." He took her hand, intending to bring it to the front of his pants, but there was no need to lead her. She pushed his hand away, opened his pants and took his penis from the folds of clothing. Then she pushed him into a chair and dropped to her knees in front of him.

In the bedroom, Angel sat on the bed with his knees slightly apart, Maria stood in front of him. "Do you like me?" she asked, trying hard to copy the voice of a girl from a James Bond movie. "Do you think I got what you want?" Angel ran his hand up her thighs and under her dress. He could feel her crotch hair through the thin fabric of her panties, "You got what I want and you know it." She leaned on him, pushing him down on the bed. "You just relax, baby and I'll treat you right."

"I know that," he said. "I need you to do me right."

Kneeling on the bed, she opened his pants and pulled aside his underwear. "This is what I want," she said, as she wrapped her hand around his penis. Her other hand slithered inside his briefs in an attempt to stroke his testicles. Her intentioned caress became a search, as if seeking loose change in a coat pocket. Her hand darted left, then right. It moved to the base of his penis- a place of known anatomy- and stopped. She sat up and pulled her hands to her side.

"Where are your balls?" she whispered. The sexy quality of her voice was gone, replaced now by sincere concern. Before he could answer, she asked in a little girl's voice, "Why don't you got no balls?"

Angel took her hand. "I lost them, but that don't mean shit." He guided her hand to his penis, still rock hard with desire.

"I got to see." With surprising tenderness, she slowly removed his pants and underwear. Then, while gaping, she unbuttoned and removed his shirt leaving him naked except for his shoes and socks. Backing off the bed, she removed them as well.

Her usual involvement with "lovers" was not the Honeymoon Suite at the Waldorf. Rarely was anyone even naked. Sex for her was just a rearranging of clothes and at the most, a half hour of her time. But now, she confronted something new, a naked guy with a stiff and throbbing cock, but no balls. She stared at the vacant space between his thighs as she moved them apart with her knees. "Ohhhh," she moaned. "Look at that. Look at that."

Angel didn't know whether to be upset or happy. He reached for her but she backed away, but only for more room. Swaying from side to side, she began to unbutton her blouse and then let it and her bra fall to the floor. Angel reached for her breasts, but she backed away once again. Still swaying, she removed her skirt and her panties. Now naked, her swaying changed into a dance. No longer trying to imitate the girl in the James Bond movie, now she was the dancing girl in the sultan's harem.

Listening to the music in her soul, she danced. Her hips swayed, slowly at first, then with greater vigor. As she moved from side to side, she thrust her pelvis at him and then, cupping her breasts, she offered them as he sat gaping at her. She had never danced like this for a guy and she was enjoying it. Watching him get more and more excited was exciting her as well. She danced closer to him and then backed away. She tried hard to tease him. As she swayed and rocked, she copied the dancing girls from the movies and TV shows she'd seen. She was dancing for the sultan, for the pirate chief, for James Bond. She was doing the hula, the hootchy-kootchy, a combination of every rock and roll dance she ever saw and all of it was aimed right at Angel. Her growing excitement fascinated her. Usually, the guys she went with were so eager to screw, nothing lasted, but this was different. The excitement in his eyes was shared and she was equally aroused.

Suddenly, he jumped from the bed and grabbed her, but she did not stop moving. She thrust her body into him until he started to move with her. He crushed her to his thin frame and they swayed as one. Her hands slipped over his body and pinched and grabbed at his flesh. Then he spun her around until the bed was behind and then tightly holding her flopped onto it. He lay on top of her as she writhed, and then like opening cathedral doors, she spread her legs as far apart as she could. Her excitement had so drenched her; there was no resistance as he effortlessly slid into her. Gripping his body as tightly as she could, she never stopped moving. Matching her passion with his own, he matched her thrust for thrust until they were both vibrating.

Thoughts of who she was, where she was, and who he was, vanished from her mind. She clutched at him and he thrust and thrust until he sensed an orgasm coming. Then he started to moan and held her even more tightly. She realized he was going to come, but didn't understand how that could be. Her mind couldn't deal with what her body knew. With no balls, how can he come? She asked herself. There was no answer, for what little she knew could not cope with the question. Casting out the need to know, she relied on her senses and holding him, tried to match his movements. Faster and faster they moved until he arched like a fish trying to escape the hook as his hips slammed into her over and over. Then she climaxed and her muscles quivered and shook as her body convulsed. Unable to keep her legs from shaking, she shivered as if freezing.

The power of his orgasm amazed him and he felt like Superman. How could it happen? He asked himself. From all the street talk he had ever heard, he believed what had happened was supposed to be impossible. With no balls, he was still able to get a hard-on and have an orgasm that felt like his backbone had melted and come out of his dick. He was blessed, he told himself. There was no other way to explain it.

It was the music. It had to be the music. Singing to God had paid off and God was thanking him by giving him back his sex. God was wonderful, Angel decided.

Minutes later, Maria snaked over him and touched her lips to his chest and thighs. She spread his legs and kissed the scar tissue. Then she took his penis in her mouth and slowly roiled it on her tongue. By moving it to the side of her cheek, she took all of it in her mouth. To her delight, he started to grow and she sucked him until his full hardness returned.

Suddenly he sat up, pulled away from her and stood alongside the bed. She looked up, not understanding what he wanted until he reached for her hips and turned her around. As she scooted to her knees, he immediately entered her from behind. Like two impassioned animals, they sexed each other. He pushed into her and pulled out, first slow then fast. In response, she thrust backwards to meet him. The muscles in her neck were taught and her chin was high. Then, she could feel another orgasm happening, but he didn't stop and she didn't want him to stop. Every muscle in her body reacted. It was like a fist opening and closing, opening and closing. This was the first time sex had meant something for her. This was the first time she had ever come twice. His hands held her hips in a vise like grip as he thrust into her and then he came, bursting into her. She thought his cock was like a throbbing steel rod able to push everything out of its path. It was true, she thought, He is "the Angel." Nobody human could fuck like that. He has to be from heaven, from God.

Panting, he dropped to the bed alongside her. Without thinking of the reason, but wanting to love and appreciate him, she started to kiss his body. Like a bitch with her puppy, she slid her tongue over his skin. His glistening penis attracted her and she licked it like she was curing it. She kissed his chest, his face, and his arms. He relaxed in a way he had never known and eventually, he slept.

As he slept, she stared at him not fully believing what had happened. When Carlos said he could fix it so she could have sex with his friend, she wanted to do it because she knew the friend was The Angel. Getting laid was always fun for her and she thought doing it with the Church singer would be cool. She and her friends thought this strange little guy was magic. When he sang you felt the music in your bones and in your head. Now she knew he was magic. He had no balls yet he could have sex. It was crazy, but it happened, so it had to be a miracle. There was no other explanation that made sense.

Looking at him sleeping peacefully, she realized he made her feel things she didn't know she could feel. That, too, was magic. Suddenly, she grew nervous. The TV shows about people from space popped into her head. Was it possible? Could he be from another planet? Was she going to have a spaceman's baby?"

Becoming aware of sounds from the other room, she got off the bed and walked inside. Carlos and Ginger were on the couch watching TV. They had a cover over them, but she could tell they were naked. Unconcerned, she walked into the room. Carlos saw her and was surprised she would come in without her clothes. Then Ginger saw her and asked, "Maria, where are your clothes?"

Getting no answer, the two of them more attentively turned to her and saw the expression on her face. Carlos remembered seeing a similar look on a girl in a movie who had been visited by a person she thought dead. He wondered if she had fallen, hit her head and was still dizzy. She ambled over to the sofa and stood looking down at them. "Are you okay?" Ginger asked.

Maria stared silently and then burst out, "The Angel fucked me so good, I can't tell you. He's the best. I want to fuck him until I die. Nobody can fuck like him... Nobody!"

Carlos burst out laughing. "Sonofabitch... can you beat that shit? That little kid surprises the shit out of me. He's like from another planet."

"Yes, Yes." Maria cried. "That's what I think also. He can't be from here."

"Shit, Maria, I don't mean it like that. I don't mean he's an alien."

"No. No. But he's not from this planet. He's from heaven. He's 'The Angel'."

Ginger stared at Maria with a combination of envy and surprise. They had been friends long enough for her to know Maria was not crazy and had had her share of guys. But now she was behaving like a little girl who just got her first good screw. That little guy is probably one great fuck. Imagine that, she thought. Then, like a general planning a campaign, she began figuring how she could get a piece of The Angel.

CHAPTER 29

WHEN THE CAB STOPPED, Leo slid over to make room for Melendez and Roberto. They were wearing black and looked like a honeymoon couple from Omaha trying to look as New York as possible. The cab driver eyed them suspiciously, but said nothing.

"Are you ready?" Melendez stared at him. "Am I ready? Leo, you haven't told us what we're supposed to do."

"C'mon... I told you the other day. Don't do anything." Leo could see Roberto was not happy with that piece of news. "What I mean is that you don't have to do anything, but... you have to create belief in the audience."

"You mean you want us to act."

"Exactly." With that, Roberto relaxed, but Melendez still look puzzled.

"Look," Leo said, "I don't know if we're going to be in the same room. If we are, then you have to create and maintain the impression you're cold-blooded killers... matter of fact murderers who are beyond tough."

"What do we do if we're not in the same room?"

"You know, I can't believe Healy would put you where he couldn't keep an eye on you. But whatever, you'll still have the same job... to create the same impression."

"Have you told them we're killers?" Melendez asked.

"Oh, yeah, they have that piece of news."

"Then we'll be fine." She looked at Roberto. "Our job is to do nothing that might have them think we are not what they already think we are. They think we're killers, fine. By doing nothing, we'll confirm their belief."

"That's it." Said Leo. "That's exactly what I mean. Just don't do anything."

Still watching them with unrelenting doubt, the cabbie announced, "St. Patrick's" and pulled the cab to the curb. Leo dropped a twenty over the seat.

"We're in a play." He said to the driver, as they were getting out. The cabbie stared at Leo, but quickly grabbed the bill and sped away.

The three of them stood on the sidewalk staring at the building for a moment before Leo led the way to the entrance on 58th. There they encountered security and Father Barry, who escorted them to an elevator that took them to the administrative area. They walked down a corridor to a pew-like bench across from an oversized wooden door. The three of them sat as the young Priest knocked on the door. A moment later, when a small light built into the jamb glowed, he turned the ornate brass knob and entered the room, closing the door behind him. Sitting on the hard wooden bench, Leo surveyed the hallway. He could see no windows or reference points. It was all paneled walls, marble floors, and hand-carved wood. Suddenly the door silently opened, framing the priest in its opening.

"Lieutenant Flower, would you please come in." Leo stood and walked across to the doorway. As he entered the room, he saw Monsignor Healy behind a massive wooden desk framed by the sidepieces and mantel of an enormous stone fireplace. Walking the length of the room, Leo wondered what would happen if God turned out to be a woman who really didn't care for all this German-looking, hunting lodge decor, preferring instead, pink Formica? If that became true... would we see priests in sport coats, nuns in form fitting habits, non-sensible shoes, and lipstick? Would glamour help the conversion rate?

Healy stood and extended his hand. "Please sit in that chair." He said, pointing to one that would enable Healy to face Leo but also have a clear view of the bench in the hall, that is, if they leave the door open.

"Father Barry," Healy said, "Leave the door open and sit with those people." The priest nodded, walked to the bench and sat alongside Roberto. Monsignor Healy stared through the doorway at the bench. "A woman? These people use women?"

"Monsignor, you must understand how these groups operate. The people sitting there and those they represent make their own rules. They use women and they'd use children. They're the ultimate pragmatists and will do whatever is necessary to accomplish their plans."

"I guess what you're saying is true, but I find it hard to accept."

"You should expect no humanity from them. One I spoke to told me to view him as a surgeon from whom I might seek a life-saving operation. He said I shouldn't be overly concerned with methods as long as I get what I'm after- survival."

"That's so heartless."

"Maybe so, but we both know it's sensible from their point of view. They provide a service."

"They also look like normal people." He said, getting up from the desk and walking to the doorway where he stood, staring at them. "What's wrong with you people? Why must you kill?" Melendez and Roberto had seen him coming and responded in different ways. Feigning disgust, Melendez creased her brow and narrowed her eyes as she might if she had seen a mouse. Roberto smiled and offered a slight nod, as if to say, "You're welcome" to a typical "Thank you" he might get at work. It was absolutely perfect.

Healy stood there a moment before he returned to his desk "They do not look like killers."

"In their business," Leo said, trying hard to sound ultra serious, "it helps not to."

With searching and troubled eyes, Healy asked, "Do you mean to tell me those two young people out there would kill the Holy Father?"

"I don't know about that. I only know they were assigned to come with me so you would understand this is serious business. They could be part of a 'hit team' and then they might not be directly involved."

Leo watched Healy wondering how long this would go on and then a change came over the man- there was visible tension and then it was gone. Leo guessed a decision had been reached.

"You said you want to have an audience with the Holy Father. That's what you want, right?"

"Yes. It is essential I have a private audience."

"Why must it be private?"

"The matter is very delicate and concerns the Holy Father's life. I cannot add to that." Healy straightened. 'I'm afraid you're going to have to tell me. There's got to be more to this than what you're telling me."

"Of course there is, but I hesitate to tell you because you would think me crazy and not enable me to save the pope's life."

"Do you think I would do anything that might bring harm to him?"

"Of course not, but that's not the issue. You're going to evaluate my reasoning and if you find it less than valid, you might tell me to leave. The end result will be the Holy Father's assassination- because you didn't think what I told you made sense."

"I will judge what you tell me very carefully and I will not let my feelings about you or anything else cloud my vision."

Leo looked away. "I just don't know."

"Lieutenant... you can trust me."

Leo stood and slowly walked to the doorway. He stared at Melendez and Roberto and Father Barry sitting quietly on the bench. He stood motionless for thirty seconds and then turned back to Healy. "Can I trust you? Can I?" He asked, as he walked back to the chair.

"Why do you have doubts? I have devoted my life to the Church. I would do anything-1 would give my life for the Church." He leaned across the desk to Leo. "Lieutenant... you can trust me."

"You must understand, I don't doubt your devotion. I have doubts about your judgment."

Healy started to speak, but Leo cut him off. "You've been in power too long. You're too confident. It doesn't dawn on you that you might not have all the answers. You have become a real bureaucrat." Healy stared blankly at him as he continued.

"Everyday, you make decisions. You blindly follow your conclusions. Most times- at least with Church matters- you're probably okay. But this is not a Church matter. This is a matter of people wanting to kill the pope and you're out of your league dealing with it." Leo got up from the chair and slowly walked around the desk to within a foot of Healy. He leaned in close. "You must understand how serious this is and that I do know what is right. You don't know the right move in this case and you must not think you do. You must not let the years of obedience from those around you influence you now. This situation is not at all like others you've dealt with." Leo breathed deeply, straightened and walked back to his chair.

"Will you at least tell me the subject of the audience? Can you do that much?"

"Simply put, these people are ready to kill the pope unless they get what they want."

"Is it money?"

"No. They have all the money they could possibly want."

"Then what is it they are after?"

Leo hesitated then said, "They want a picture with them standing alongside the Holy Father. That's what they want and by granting that simple request, all threats will be eliminated."

Healy was stunned and glared at Leo with bulging eyes. "They want a picture of the Pope? Are you serious? A photograph?"

"Not a picture of the pope. They want a video of him and them together."

"Why? For what purpose? What would such a picture satisfy?"

"Strange as it may sound to you, they want that video to prove they can accomplish anything." Leo paused and tried to look confident. "You see, Monsignor, they **could** kill the pope, maybe anyone could, but... getting a video at a private audience- very few are capable of that."

Healy stared at Leo as if he said the earth was cream cheese. Slowly, he said, "So... if I understand you, a video of these people with the pope will spare his life?"

"That's correct."

Healy wrinkled his nose as if an ugly smell had flooded the room. "That is absolutely ridiculous. I cannot accept it nor can I permit it."

"I said you would find it hard to believe and I told you how you would react... Because it sounds ridiculous to you and you cannot accept it, the Holy Father will be killed."

Healy looked like he was entering the portals of Purgatory. "Wait... Wait. I haven't said it can't be done."

"I don't know what else to say. I have put the facts before you, as I know them. What I need from you is confirmation the audience will take place. I don't want to hear you cannot accept this or whether the terrorists' demands seem reasonable." Leo let his voice rise. "You must allow this or they will kill him. Can I make it any more clear than that?"

Healy sighed deeply and crossed himself. "All right... All right. It will be done. You have my word."

"I was praying you would see there is no other way."

"It is extortion. Nothing less."

'That may be so, but let's not forget all we're paying out is videotape. No matter how you cut it, a video for a pope's life is a pretty good deal."

Sneering somewhat, Healy replied, "I suppose you're right." He paused, and then burst out, "My Lord... this is so crazy."

"You're right about that, but we live in a political world where many things make little sense."

His shoulders slumping, Healy responded, "Yes... Yes. So what is it you want me to do?"

"I'll be in touch with the details. Please be certain to notify whoever has to know about this. There can be no slip-ups."

"Are you afraid I'll drop dead and you'll lose your permission?"

"Monsignor, people die every day... all day. I don't want you or the pope to be among those who reap the benefit too early."

For the first time, Healy smiled. "That's a nice way to put it... reap the benefit. I like that. Yes, I like that."

Leo stood as Healy came from behind the desk and they walked to the doorway. Leo stepped into the corridor while Healy stayed by the door staring at Melendez and Roberto. "You must relay my decision to your people... they will get what they want. Make sure your superiors understand that."

Expressionless, Roberto and Melendez stood and joined Leo. A moment later, Father Barry and a security guard escorted them from the building. Shortly thereafter, they were on the street breathing deeply of the night air. Leo felt as if he had won Olympic Gold... he had done it. His long shot had paid off. With admiration in his eyes, he said. "I owe you both a dinner. What would you like to eat?"

They looked at each other. "Anything but Spanish cooking." Said Melendez.

"Right," said Roberto. "I would love some Chinese."

"You got it," said Leo. "Follow me."

CHAPTER 30

LEO SAT AT HIS desk pondering the location for the meeting with McGinty and company. Punteyaya's Embassy? My apartment? Here at Dig. Pro's conference room? He wondered why he was making such a big deal about it and decided if he didn't come up with something, he'd let Hoffheimer pick the spot. He pushed it all from his mind and looked at the coffee container he held in his hand. It was white, had no design and bore only one word- *Fred's*-across its middle. No address or phone number, just the one word. "That's it," Leo said aloud, "Fred's."

The meeting at Punteyaya's came back to him with all that blissful talk about the deli. There was no question; everything else had come in second. Leo decided this meeting would also have food at its center. It took about four minutes to get to Fred's where Irene, drifting around tables like a trout in a stream, stopped when she saw him.

"Leo, whatsa matter? Ya didn't like the coffee?"

"No. It was fine. I have to talk to Fred."

"You know where he is." Turning away, she resumed her patrol. Leo slipped into the kitchen to see Fred stirring something in an enormous stock-pot.

"What's in that thing, soup for the month?" Fred turned slightly from the stove. "Hey... Leo... welcome to my world."

"Isn't that quite a bit of soup?"

"It's not for here."

"Not for here... for where, then?"

"I do stuff on the side for the big guys."

"The big guys?"

"Yeah, you know, the fancy joints with twenty-five executive chefs in the kitchen who are always too busy to bother with staples like soup."

"Then what are they doing?"

"They are knockin' off waitresses, writin' cook books, designin' desserts. All sorts of crap that leaves them short for the dinner crowd. I'm forever gettin' calls... 'Fred, you gotta help me. I need a main for twelve' or I need three appetizers' or 'Fred... the soup was magic. One more time, please, please. I'll never ask again... I promise'."

"That's incredible."

He stirred the soup. "Ahhh, the hell with them. What can I do for you?"

"I was going to ask a favor, but now I'm a little reluctant."

"Don't be a schmuck... what?"

"Well... I'm going to be holding a special meeting and your place would be perfect. What's more, I'd want you to prepare a special meal that will put my guests into such a good mood, they'll forget they can be disagreeable."

"How many people?"

Leo counted on his fingers. McGinty and crew, Punteyaya and Magalana, me... "Six for sure, maybe one or two more. I'll let you know the exact count this afternoon."

"When?"

"Wednesday."

"Time?"

"What's best for you?"

"Two-thirty, three."

"Two-thirty.... that's great." Leo turned to go, but Fred stopped him.

"Leo, wait, wait a minute... I need information." Leo stared. "Tell me about these people. Who are they? Where do they come from?" Leo continued to stare.

Mildly exasperated, Fred asked, "Leo... what are their countries of origin?" Now he realized what Fred was after. "I'm not sure of all, but there are two Black Africans, two from the Middle East... maybe Libya, one American with Middle Eastern allegiances and me."

"Okay, you got it. I'll give them home cooking... they'll think their mama's in the kitchen."

"Two more things, Fred... one, there is no expense to be spared and two, thank you!" Fred nodded, but he had already turned his attention back to swishing a ladle that looked like a canoe paddle in the soup pot.

Back at his office, Leo immediately called Punteyaya. He was out, but an aide said the message would be delivered. While Leo waited for a return call, he had a sit-down with Hoffheimer and filled him in. Hoffheimer was delighted that Leo was apparently going to bring off his idea and eliminate a real headache for the unit. While they talked, Punteyaya called back. Leo returned to his office to take the call.

He thanked Punteyaya for so promptly returning his call. "It is my pleasure, Lieutenant. Dealing with you brings me surprises. You are not like the others. With you- things get done."

"I appreciate the compliment and that's why I'm calling. I have arranged what I said I would and now I need to meet with the people I met at your Embassy."

With a combination of excitement and disbelief in his voice, the Prince cried out, "You have arranged it? You actually arranged an audience with the pope?"

"Yes, I have. They'll get what they want."

"Oh, Lieutenant, Lieutenant. You have no idea how pleased I am. Your accomplishment will raise my credibility beyond my dreams. These people understand the real world- they pay for everything. What you have arranged will mean millions and millions in aid for my country." He paused for breath. "How did you do it? I must know. We must meet before the sit-down so you can tell me."

"There may not be time, but I'll tell you eventually. I was hoping we could meet on Wednesday- if that's okay with you. If it is, you can call McGinty and tell him I have arranged a meal for us so we can fully discuss the audience."

"Wednesday is fine with me... I will call McGinty."

"Also, if you want, Inspector Magalana is welcome to attend. A special meal is being planned and I wouldn't want either of you to miss it."

"Wonderful. I will bring Magalana."

"Good. As I see it, there will be six, but that number can be altered if you wish. If you want to bring others, that will not be a problem."

"You are very kind to allow me to arrange the guest list, but I see the number as six."

"Fine. The restaurant is called Fred's and it's on the corner of 43rd and First- across from the UN."

"I know Fred's. How do you know Fred's?"

Leo was surprised, but instantly realized Fred's location across from the UN made it a convenient spot for the internationals. "Prince, I found Fred's the way a fisherman finds a great stream- sheer dumb luck."

"We eat there often. You will tell Fred I am coming for there is a dish he makes especially for me."

"You can count on it." Leo let out a breath. "Okay then... it's all set. Fred's at half past two on Wednesday."

"Perfect. I will notify Magalana and McGinty. If there are problems I will let you know."

"Prince... I hope you understand there is no way I can thank you."

"On the contrary, Lieutenant, I am thanking you. What you have arranged will make a difference in my country for years to come. Your country gives aid, but there are always strings. Those with money in Africa and the Middle East give it away more freely- that is, of course, if you do them a favor. What you have arranged will be good for my country."

"I glad about that. Now... let me say goodbye until we meet on Wednesday."

"Yes... a good day to you, Lieutenant."

Savoring the moment, Leo gently replaced the hand piece. Bathing in satisfaction, he leaned back in his chair. How wonderful when things went well. He wished it were possible to bank these feelings against the disaster loitering out there somewhere. Successes were so easily destroyed... why was that? What is it about our nature that makes us so fragile? Ten years, twenty years, a lifetime of good living wiped out by one episode of misfortune. Why are we so eager to suffer? He toyed with the idea of calling Jacqueline, but didn't. Instead, he called Abe and invited him to lunch at Fred's.

Later, when he told Fred the meal was definite and that Punteyaya and Magalana were two of the guests, Fred s smiled broadly.

"Leo, that's a big feather in your cap dealing with guys like them two. They are somethin'. The two of them came in one night just before I was closin' and demanded I cook their favorite Russian dish. They really duke out the moolah when they want somethin'. I love them guys."

"Did you say Russian dish?"

"Yeah. The two of them- they both went to spy school, regular school, graduate school and who knows what else in Russia. They've been goin' for years. You should hear the stories they tell. They sound like Nabokov and Tolstoy roiled into one." Leo stared at him... this was a surprise.

"Leo don't look so shocked. For many years, the Russians and the Chinese have hosted more Africans than the State Department. The American government pays almost no attention. It's really kind of stupid."

Since Leo had no idea what to say, he was happy to see Abe arrive. As usual, Abe walked in like he owned the space he occupied. He strode in, looking from left to right, making eye contact with everyone. Also, as usual, he was dressed impeccably. Whatever needed a crease had one and whatever was supposed to shine... did. He looked around, finally settling on Irene.

"Hey Red, ya got decent chow here?"

Irene, standing at the end of the counter, smiled at him. "We got the best of New York here and if you don't want some of it on your pretty suit, keep a civil tongue."

Turning to Fred, Abe said, "When are you going to send her to waitress school? If she'd be more friendly... hell, by now she'd be worth a bundle and could open a pub in dear old County Fork.

"Hey, Mr. Smarty Pants...." Irene called out. "That's County Cork." Abe's eyes opened wide in mock surprise. "Cork? Hell, I always thought it was Fork."

"All right, all right, you two," Fred interrupted, "don't get started." Then, with a big smile, he said, "Abe, good to see ya. How come ya dropped in?"

"I got invited by my pal Leo, here."

Fred shifted his bulk and appraised Leo. "Comin' up with Prince Punteyaya and Abe in one day puts you waaay out front, Leo. There ain't many people in this burg who know the right folks, but I'm suspectin' you happen to be one of 'em."

Leo was dumbstruck. "You two know each other?" Then realizing he already had his answer, he lowered his voice and asked Abe, "You got a piece of the action here, also?" Abe smiled, saying nothing, leaving Fred to answer Leo's question.

"Leo, it's a long story of how I got to Abe, but when I did, he was the only guy willin' to advance a fat Chinese chef enough dough to open an American diner... this joint, in other words."

Smiling like an Oscar winner, Abe asked. "What's for lunch, Freddy? I could eat a goat."

Fred hunched toward the kitchen. "You got it." He looked at Leo over his shoulder." "Same for you?" Leo nodded and followed Abe and Irene to a table in the rear.

After they were seated, Leo studied Abe, wondering if his elegant, tailored clothes came from a custom haberdashery in which he had a piece of the action. He probably owns half the City, Leo thought. Most of the old time hoods Leo knew were penniless. They were merely old guys that always lived, and still lived from hand to mouth. None could get Social Security because they never worked. A few did live well, mostly the bootleggers, but no one he ever met matched Abe.

Police records had shown Abe primarily an arsonist. You needed a fire, you called Abe and his pal, Georgie... but how do you wind up with all kinds of dough setting now and then fires?

Abe laughed, and then said, "Leo, I can read you like a book. You're sittin' there lookin' at me wonderin' where the hell did that old sonofabitch get all his money? What did he do in the old days that brought in so much cash that he can get a piece of the action all over the place...right?"

Leo nodded. "You hit the jackpot, but... I can't figure it out and I'm too embarrassed to ask."

"Well, I'll tell ya... that'll make it easy. It began when a guy comes to me and Georgie sayin' he needs a fire so he can collect the insurance on some Bowery rat-trap he owned." He paused to take out a leather cigar case and a gold lighter. After the lighting ceremony, he continued. "I figured real quick there was more than one way to make a buck burnin' down the guy's joint. Georgie and me, we got paid for the fire, took that money, bought the lot the buildin' sat on and then sold it for a nice profit."

"But what if the guy who owned that building didn't want to sell?"

"Well, we had a sit-down to discuss the issue and Georgie stuck his finger in the guy's face and said very quietly that we would use him as the torch for our next fire. Never failed. Georgie got 'em so scared they never figured we weren't serious. So they got the insurance and we got the lot and the burned-out joint. They lost nothin'." He pulled on the cigar and blew a column of blue smoke to the ceiling. "Eventually, we wound up with a very large chunk of New York and New Jersey. When Georgie died, I was the partner and now, I own everything we didn't sell. What we did sell, we sold for plenty...and that, Leo, is how I got my finger in so many pies."

"That's amazing."

"Oh, I don't know about that. You'd really be amazed if I named guys with a lot of dough who made it in the old days like I did. Hell, before there was income tax and all that crap, you could make a fortune in a minute. The only thing close now is selling drugs." He smiled and blew more smoke into the air as Irene brought silverware, napkins, and bread and butter. Several minutes later she was back with two plates. There were thin slices of brown meat covered with dark gravy, a scooped out orange half filled with what looked like pureed sweet potato. Tasting it, Leo found the potato to be mixed with orange. The last item was a pile of greens. It looked great.

"Ya ever eat goat?"

"Goat? Is this really goat meat?" Leo asked, poking his fork into the gravy.

"Goddamn right. Ya ever try it?" Leo saw himself as the old dog and new tricks were like new foods. There had been too many dinners of canned ravioli. Now, he was faced with goat. He was surprised and also as usual, he cursed himself for being such a coward. The meat resembled thinly sliced London Broil, but tasted better. He looked at Abe who was watching him. "I'm a real baby with food. If I didn't get pushed into it, I think I'd never eat anything but endless breakfasts."

"You're a brave guy, Leo, but you mustn't be a coward with food. There are so many great things to eat. Ya gotta try everything." He took a mouthful of sweet potato and savored it. "Christ, if what you're eatin' don't suit your taste buds, spit it out or puke. Be brave." He laughed.

When both plates were clean, Abe sat back. "Leo, how come you live like you do? Why didn't you ever get a girl, get married?"

How many times had he asked himself the same question? There was no answer. "I don't know, Abe. I really don't." He paused, "I wish I had back the hours I've spent asking myself those questions."

"You must've met plenty of nice broads?"

"The women were never the problem. I'm the problem. There's something in me or not in me, I don't know. I just can't put up with a woman for too long. It starts out great and then it dies."

"What about the Frenchy? The one you had at the church?"

"She's perfect. Intelligent, beautiful, as cultured as can be, but she's married. That makes her temporary. Sooner or later, she'll dump me."

"That seems like a real pain."

"Were you ever married?"

"Nah, but I used to have a girl when I was a kid. We went together for a long time, but she wanted to get married and I didn't, so she left."

"When was that?"

"A long time ago- 1930 or '35- who remembers? In those days, I was a West Side Romeo and there were plenty of girls, but every now and then, I think about that one. She was real sweet. Like you, I think how different my life would have been if I married her."

"No, Abe, there's a difference. You didn't want to get married, so you didn't. Me, I always thought I would like to get married, but I couldn't. I wanted to, but I was paralyzed. Being an orphan isn't the best way to get into family life. Me and women- it just wasn't in the cards."

"You know somethin', now that I think about it, the last time I heard from that girl was when she told me she thought she was pregnant. I remember I offered her money for an abortion."

"Did she have one?"

"I don't know. One day she turns up and takes the money and that's it. I never saw her again. I don't know what she did."

"You know... if she didn't have the abortion, you might be a father."

"Can you picture that? Me, a father?"

"They told me I was born in 1935. What if the girl was pregnant had the baby and put it in an orphanage? Christ, you could be my father."

"Of course, I'm your father. We both like pastrami and corned beef, don't we?" Leo laughed. "Don't you think we need a little more evidence than that?"

"Maybe... and then again...maybe not."

"Was the girl a Catholic?"

"Who knows? I never went to church with her, I can tell you that, and she never went to a Friday night candle lighting with me." He paused to relight his cigar. "Religion wasn't the cement of our relationship." He pushed the dishes to the table's center as he puffed on the cigar.

"Is that all you remember about her?"

"Leo," he said, with some exasperation, "it was lifetimes ago. I'm lucky I can remember anything from back there."

"Yeah... it is a long time ago." As he spoke, he realized the attractiveness of the thought that he could be speaking to his father. Next, he toyed with the idea of starting a search to see if any records do exist. Next, he thought the entire idea nutty, and a great waste of time.

"Hey," said Abe, "did I tell you about the kid, the singer from the Church?"

"No, what's going on?"

"Well, it's more than I can believe. Vincent got the tapes to a distributor who is already turnin' out CD's. You know, I thought I pulled off a few good scams in my day, but compared to record companies, everyone's an amateur. They told me the kid started a whole new category. They're calling it Religio-Pop."

Leo sat up in his chair. "Say... I just thought of something. You might be able to help me."

"Sure... what is it?"

"I have to arrange a meeting with some people to see the Pope when he visits, and I thought maybe you could help me by getting the kid to sing at the meeting."

"Sing for the pope? Are you kiddin'? That'd be the best. You talk about sellin' records... Religio-Pop would be over the top." He laughed. "Heh, heh,heh... I like that. Religio-Pop would be over the top. That's cute."

Seizing the idea, Leo said, "The more I think about it the better it gets. The kid could give the meeting a central idea. It would explain why the people would come together for a private audience. The kid would sing for the pope and my people would be there to listen."

"Hey, what're you doin' arrangin' a meetin' with the pope? Is that usual for the NYPD?"

"It's a long story, Abe."

"I ain't goin' anywhere." As they drank coffee and ate a dessert Fred personally delivered, Leo told him about the meeting with the pope.

"That's fantastic. You bet the kid will sing. Vincent is a strong Catholic. He'll faint when I tell him. The pope! Hot shit. Hey... I can tell Vincent, right?"

"Sure, but don't tell the others. Carlos and Marty are not my idea of secret agents."

"Them two... shit. Marty is all day droolin' over the record money and Carlos has been screwin' every little chickadee on 8th Avenue. The Angel kid is doin' the same thing. Vincent is the only one of them who's normal."

"Abe, this gets better as I think about it. Before it was a meeting, now it's a concert with all the trimmings."

"Heh, heh, heh. a meetin' with the pope. That is hot shit, Leo... Lemme tell you... there aren't too many people who could pull off a wing-ding like that."

Appreciating the compliment, Leo grinned. "Will you be home tonight? I want to call my Church contact and tell him about the concert. If there are problems, I'll have to talk to you."

"Don't worry about problems... the kid and the rest of them will do whatever I tell 'em. There ain't goin' to be any problems."

Later that night, Leo called Healy to tell him of the revised plan for the meeting with the 'terrorists.' When Healy heard of the concert with the Angel, he immediately approved. His only question concerned the Angel's management. He wanted to know if the contract was for sale. Leo told him that an Hasidic Rabbi led the Angel's management team and he didn't think a sale to the Church was likely. Nonetheless, Healy wanted the telephone number so he could contact the Rabbi. Just to get off the phone, Leo had to promise he would arrange a meeting for him with the Rabbi, so the matter could be discussed. Leo laughed when he thought of Healy trying to convince Abe to give up his piece of the action.

The day for the meeting had arrived and Leo was nervous. Hoffheimer looked at him. "Stop worrying. There's nothing that can foul up. You have both sides ready and they want to deal. Each of them see a gain- it's a win-win."

"That's how I see it, but I'm a born compulsive. I worry about what I didn't take care of."

"What didn't you cover?"

"Ahhhh, the magic question. If I knew that answer, I wouldn't worry."

"Take my word for it, Leo, nothing will screw up."

"I wish I had your confidence." Leo said fidgeting nervously.

"I wish you did also. You worry too much. Only in books can authors make their characters geniuses. No one is or could ever be as smart as Bond, Smiley or Karla. Most real-life operatives are dummies. The winners of the game have more luck than brains, believe me."

Leo hoped Hoffheimer was right. "Are the camera guys in place?" he asked. Hoffheimer nodded. "They'll get pictures of everyone and then they're gone. I want to get a good look at McGinty."

"How will you know who he is?"

"I won't. The picture guys will snap everyone who enters Fred's. Tomorrow you can fill us in." Hoffheimer was going to continue, but was distracted by Leo's tapping foot. "Look, you're acting like a house cat in a thunder storm. Why don't you go to Fred's and help set the table, make a salad or something. You're making me nervous."

"Good idea," said Leo, bounding out of the chair. "I'm on my way."

Upstairs, he checked his messages and then left the building. A few minutes later, he walked into Fred's trying hard to be cool and calm. Irene noticed him. "Leo, you're early."

"Couldn't stay away."

"Don't worry about the meal. Fred's got some stuff in the kitchen I never saw or even smelled before. When he starts usin' exotic ingredients, I know we're in for special dishes."

"Do you need any help?"

She tilted her head. "Leo, what would you say if I trundled into your operation and asked if I could help you with your job?"

"I get the point."

"Right... go get some sun... you got almost an hour."

Not a bad idea. He walked out, crossed First Avenue and headed for the gates in front of the UN. Leaning on the steelwork did not provide the pleasurable heat a wooden fence would offer. All he got was unyielding resistance.

The tourists were out in force and those he saw seemed undecided about the building. As a structure, it was impressive and they showed that in their first, long look. But then something changed their expressions... maybe when they started to think about what went on inside. Unable to keep leaning against the fence, he walked downtown to 30th, crossed and started uptown. Trying to kill time, he studied the display of every store window he passed, but could no longer contain himself. At a quarter past, he walked into Fred's and saw a large round table with six chairs had been set up in the back. It was separated from other tables by about ten feet of open space. As he stood staring at it, he heard voices behind him and turning saw Magalana, Punteyaya, and McGinty and his two pals exiting a limousine and loudly entering the restaurant.

Seeing Leo, Punteyaya called out, "Lieutenant Flower, there you are. We are here, as you can see."

Relaxing... finally... Leo said, "I'm glad you came."

Fred ambled from behind the counter and after shaking the Prince's hand, led them to the rear. At the table, Punteyaya said, "Let me arrange the seating." He indicated three seats. "Mr. McGinty, Mr. Lor, and Mr. Singh will sit there and I will sit here. Lieutenant Flower will sit next to me and Inspector Magalana will sit next to him. Satisfactory?"

Everyone nodded and then looked down to the table. It had been set with fancy china and sufficient glasses for a multi-course meal. As they expectantly studied what they could see, Fred announced, "Gentlemen, I know some of you and Lieutenant Flower has given me a very brief sketch of those I do not know." He smiled at McGinty and crew, who nodded stiffly. "Using that information, I have prepared a meal I expect you will enjoy." With that, he walked back behind the counter.

A moment later, Irene appeared with a cart holding, red and white wine, bottled water, some small dishes, and two rattan bowls of heavy looking, thick-crusted bread. The wine was poured and the water and bread distributed. Lor immediately went after a small dish of thick oil, and taking a spoon, dribbled some on a chunk of bread. His eyes shone, as did his smile, as he tasted the combination. Singh immediately followed suit. Leo tried it and was surprised to taste unknown spices and butter at the same time.

Singh said something that sounded like Arabic to McGinty who, smiling at Leo, also put some oil onto bread and tasted it. "I really got to hand it to you, Lieutenant. Finding a place serving Ethiopian spiced butter is not easy in New York. Both Lor and Singh were nodding and smiling.

"I'm glad you like it, but don't compliment me. Fred is the genius in this place."

"Maybe so, but you brought us here."

As they passed the spiced butter, bread and sipped wine, Irene and the cart reappeared. On it were six small bowls holding what looked like a heavy cream. The bowls were passed for sampling and Leo found the cream thicker than it looked and very bitter.

"Ahhh..." said Magalana, "it is homemade yogurt. Amazing."

"How do you know it is homemade?" Leo asked.

The Prince answered. "You can tell by the tartness. No commercial yogurt would be this tart. Few Americans would like it... do you?"

Leo smiled. "I don't think it's going to be the first thing on my mind tomorrow morning."

They laughed and continued eating. Leo was happy to see they were all relaxed, but obviously anticipating the next food items. Lor and Singh, so blank at the first meeting, were now visibly enjoying themselves. They poked each other and smiled whenever their eyes met.

Irene brought more bread and wine and stood aside as Fred came to the table. "Gentlemen, we will now move on to the main dishes. I have prepared three. One is Ethiopian, one is Lebanese, and one is Russian. A side dish you may all enjoy is Arabic." When Fred said the word 'Lebanese,' Lor and Singh snapped to attention.

"What is that dish?" McGinty asked.

"I have prepared Kibbe." As Fred named the dish, Lor and Singh jumped from their seats and embraced him.

Magalana poked Leo, "I have a feeling they have a soft spot for Lebanese dishes."

When the two men sat down, Fred continued. "There is sufficient food for all, so have as much as you like." With that, he waddled back to the counter where he helped Irene load large dishes onto the cart.

As it turned out, Leo thought Kibbe, a Lebanese baked lamb dish, was almost as good as the lamb and cardamom, which was Ethiopian. Magalana and the Prince were relishing the Beef Stroganoff. The Arabic side dish Fred had made was Baba Ghanoush. Each dish, though different, seemed to blend with everything else and that, Leo figured, was a sign of Fred's genius.

In a short time, every dish brought to the table had been finished, as had additional bottles of wine. Throughout the meal, Leo had been receiving congratulations, though he clearly felt the praise was going in the wrong direction, since the meal was clearly Fred's triumph. As he pondered the 'problem', Irene floated by clearing plates. A few minutes later, she brought coffee and three desserts new to Leo. He felt less the fool when Punteyaya asked Irene about two of them. With the proprietary tone of a mother displaying triplets, she said, "These here are Irish Almond Cakes which Fred baked because I told him to. The other stuff..." She pointed to each as she spoke. "...These he calls Chinese Pears and those things he calls Meringue Mont Blanc."

"Ahhhh... I have not had Meringue Mont Blanc since Paris," Punteyaya declared, leering at Magalana. "Do you remember?"

"Oh, I do my Prince, I surely do." As they privately relived a Parisian event, McGinty signaled Irene that he wanted the Irish Almond Cake. "Are you the one they call McGinty?" she asked.

"That I am." He answered.

Staring at him in disbelief, she said, "Don't be givin' me that Barry Fitzgerald movie talk. Talk to me the way you spoke to your mother." Listening to her, Leo's head filled with memories of the orphanage nuns giving orders.

"Forgive me Ma'am, I forgot myself." Both Lor and Singh looked surprised and Leo realized they understood enough English to follow that conversation. He wondered if maybe they came from Queens and had never been farther east than Jones Beach.

With her hands on her hips, Irene told McGinty, "As long as you behave and respect women and your elders, you'll amount to something."

"I'll do my best," McGinty responded. With that, her expression changed from concerned mother to the teacher of the best class in the district.

Later, after she cleared the table, they sipped port and enjoyed Cuban cigars Magalana produced from a small bag he carried. After a moment of silence, McGinty asked, "Tell me, Lieutenant... what's going on?"

"Well, I'm happy to say all has been arranged. You will meet the pope and you will get a videotape of the meeting. How you use that tape is your decision." There was silence.

Prince Punteyaya got to his feet and with great ceremony held a wine glass aloft. "My fondest hopes for our meeting have been realized." He turned slightly to Leo. "Lieutenant Flower, I toast you for being an honorable and ingenious man... a combination not usually found. *A votre sante.*" Glasses were raised and drained. Smiling, the Prince sat and Leo continued.

"I've tried to make it easy for everyone. I've arranged a musical event that the pope and all of us will attend. Prior to the actual concert you can make your tape." Leo looked at Lor and Singh. "Do either of you have a question about the arrangement?"

Lor said nothing, but Singh responded in perfect English. "Actually, prior to this meal, I would have wanted far more detail than you have provided, Lieutenant, but now, I feel you can be trusted to do exactly what you say you will do. So, Lieutenant, tell me... tell us all... what kind of concert is planned and where will it be held?"

"Half of that I can't answer. I do not yet have a place. It might be a church or a concert hall. Many places are possible."

"What music will we hear?"

"The music is religious in nature and will feature a new singing phenomenon named The Angel."

"I have heard of him," said Punteyaya. "He is the one who sang in the street on the West Side. From what I was told, he sings all sorts of religious music, not just Roman Catholic."

"Yes, that's true, but the Church people were very happy with the choice."

"How can you arrange such a thing?" Singh asked.

"I know the people, who manage him. They will accommodate our needs."

Smiling and shaking his head, Punteyaya said, "Lieutenant, you continue to amaze me. If someone had told me a month ago what has been planned would come to pass, I would have called him crazy. But... you have done it! I don't think there are many who could. You have my deepest congratulations."

As they lifted their glasses to toast Leo, he wondered if the praise was deserved. It had all been easy. Everything had fallen into place like pieces of a puzzle. It hadn't seemed a big deal, but he wasn't going to stop them from telling him he was wonderful.

"Lieutenant, you will call me when a location is decided upon?" asked Punteyaya.

"Of course, I will speak to the Church people and when a decision has been reached, I will notify you... and you can relay the information."

"Splendid... Mr. McGinty, that is satisfactory?"

Nodding, McGinty said, "Prince, that will be fine."

For the next half hour, they smoked, drank and exchanged tales. To a casual observer, they looked like alumni holding a small, informal reunion. Leo was delighted. All that remained was the place, and most likely, Healy would want to select it, so he could prove his involvement. Nothing was left but the location and the date. Things couldn't be better.

CHAPTER 31

DURING THE WEEKS THAT followed, Leo was continually surprised everything stayed under control. Good luck abounded. Every few days, Abe called with reports detailing the activities of his pop-culture kingdom. Angel was dicking every female he could get to come near him while Carlos was valiantly trying to match him in body count. Marty was watching the money roll in, as Vincent played conductor, trying to keep them all on track.

Angel's recordings were making sales history and were well regarded within the industry. The better music critics generally agreed that his music satisfied so many of the public's desires it would be impossible for it not to succeed. His music was everywhere. Aside from radio and television, it was used as background for the subliminal messages department stores used to remind customers that "honesty is the best policy" and "shop-lifting is illegal." It was successful in elevators by its effective, but inexplicable, ability to mask the fear that developed when citizens got too close to one another. On City buses, Angel replaced rap and salsa and helped people to smile rather than snarl. Only on the Uptown D train was his music a failure. Passengers rejected it because it lacked sufficient volume to compete with the strolling panhandlers, who like town criers of old, developed a rap-of-the-day to broadcast current community events.

A high spot was a achieved when Angel became the Channel Three offering on the intercontinental flights of American Airlines. With no words to complicate listening, travelers were able to snatch fragments of folk songs and musical religiosity recalled from their youth. Almost daily, Marty dickered with other carriers, promising them exclusive rights to specific hymns, operatic arias, American Indian chants, and anything else he could successfully isolate from the wonderful world of public domain.

Regular commuters between Italy's DaVinci and JFK or Newark could buy into a special Channel (two weeks advance notice required) that would accommodate specific requests. The Italian idea was Vincent's brainchild and it brought almost every traveler to and from the Vatican into contact with Angel's singing. In a short time, there emerged a top ten list of Catholic hits comprised of the "hot" hymns and psalms of the moment.

It was through the Italian arrangement, that Angel was introduced to the pope. The output of that special airline channel was hi-jacked by a visiting priest who managed to make a copy of the music. The tape he made was passed around the Vatican, eventually falling into the hands of the pope's chauffer who had it in the dashboard player as he drove the pope to an evening dinner at the American Embassy. Miraculously, of the several thousand melodies Old Pope Gregory gathered under his control, which are still regarded as official Church tunes, a chant Angel sang was one of the current pope's favorites. At the Embassy, he asked about the tape and was told of Angel's prominence in the United States. He promptly asked the Ambassador for a copy of Angel's most recent CD.

During the two days it took to get every one of Angel's CD's into the Pope's hands, Monsignor Healy, via a Cardinal Bonaventura, got word to the Pope that Angel was available for a private concert during the upcoming visit to America. After several days of listening to Angel's singing, the Pope personally spoke to and thanked the Monsignor for arranging the concert.

Within two hours of the call from Rome, Healy was on the phone offering Leo St. Patrick's Cathedral for Angel's performance. Since the Church would be closed to the public, Healy accepted the stipulation that the Pope's meeting with Leo's "pals" would also include meeting Angel and his entourage. On both sides of the Atlantic, everyone was smiling.

But at the moment he should be most satisfied, Leo felt like crap. As usual, it was empty for him. Sitting in his apartment, staring at nothing, he thought, okay, so let's say you carry this off, so what? What does it matter? Will it be on the gravestone?- *Here lies Leo Flower. He protected the Pope and did other stuff, too.* What a legacy to pass on. Pass on to whom? He knew he would trade it all in for a chance to take his own kid to Central Park.

But it was too late. There was no way he could ever have that dream. Each birthday, his dreams faded... they died year by year. Of them all, there was one he tried to hold- the one with a wife and kids. But at 60 you don't go courting with the idea of starting a family. He remembered a guy in a bar telling him he was nuts- that it was always the right time for a wife and kids. But Leo got no answer when he asked how a young kid of ten or so would handle having no father. Leo said he would marry if he could be guaranteed living to ninety and being healthy all the way. A thirty year old could handle his father's death, but it wasn't fair to a youngster. Kids need fathers. The proof was in the jails.

Disgusted, he said aloud, "Why don't I get out of here?" He turned off the radio and put down the book, but before he got up he looked at the phone. Maybe I should call Jacqueline. Maybe she could come over. He laughed. The woman leads a life of commitments with no time to drop everything and hold my hand because I'm feeling sorry for myself. Why the hell am I feeling sorry for myself? If I ever had a reason not to feel lousy this is it... so why do I feel like shit?

He got up, grabbed his jacket and left the apartment, stopping at the first bar he came to on 7th Avenue. He ordered a drink and looked around. The place was almost empty- a few guys in the back and a bartender with a shaved head and three earrings- gold hoops. Leo downed the drink and gestured to the bartender.

"Same?"

"Yeah."

As he mixed the drink, he looked at Leo. "Are you okay? You don't look okay- are you?"

"I'm fine. A little pissed off, but fine."

"What're you pissed off about? You're wife goin' out with another guy?"

"You think I'm married?"

"Yeah. You look married to me."

Leo sipped the drink and smiled. "A guy with a tie and jacket and a haircut is married. Is that the way you see it?"

"No. It's not only the clothes. It's your age, your look. You look like you're married."

"Well, I'm not married. I have never been married and I am beginning to realize I'm too old to get married. So..." He took another sip. "I am not pissed off because my wife is screwin' my kid's scout master."

"Then what are you pissed off about?"

"How old are you?"

The bartender smiled. "You tryin' to pick me up?"

"Jesus Christ. I ask how old you are and you think I'm putting the make on you." He finished his drink. "What is it? I'm not married so I like young guys?"

"Mister, don't get offended. I thought maybe, you know, maybe you wanted a guy."

"I'm not offended, but I am pissed off because I am not married. I am pissed off because I have never been married and I have it in my head I would have had a better life if I had gotten married and..." He paused. "... Maybe I could have had a kid like you for a son."

The bartender laughed as he placed a new drink. "You're upset because you're not married, is that what you're tellin' me?" Leo nodded.

"Mister, you may not believe me, but in the year I've been working this bar, you are the first guy who's pissed because he's not married. You are unique... absolutely unique."

"Most guys complain, right?"

"Complain? Are you kidding? If Murder Incorporated worked out of here, they'd be rich. Almost every night some guy asks if I know someone who could knock off his old lady. It's like the movies."

"Are you married?" Leo asked.

"Why would I want to be married?"

"I don't know... the usual reasons... to be able to spend your time with a woman you love. To have kids. To share things."

"I got that now. I got two kids from the same girl. We've been living together for the last six years. Maybe we'll marry when I graduate NYU, but... well, we're talking about it."

Leo looked at the drink, lifted the glass and slugged it down. "Kid, you got it right. I am an old fart and if I were married I'd probably be in here trying to hire you to knock off my wife." He got up from the stool, put a twenty on the bar and started for the door. As the bartender picked up the money, he said, "Don't worry, pal, it'll be different next time."

Leo stopped short and turned. "Now, what does that mean?"

The bartender waved him back to the stool and asked, "One more... on me?"

Leo nodded. "What do you mean? It'll be better next time?"

Moving closer to Leo, he asked, "Do you believe in life after death?" Leo could tell from the stare it wasn't a flip question.

"Well, to be honest, I do, but I don't think it's an AARP playground with free TV and unlimited shuffleboard."

The bartender placed an elbow on the polished wood. "Look... I don't know exactly what goes on, but it isn't anything like the movies. When the body dies, it's gone. After that, it's all mental until a new body comes along."

"All mental?"

"That's right."

"You're going to have to explain that."

"Well, what I mean is that the body dies, but the soul doesn't. The soul lives on until it gets a new body and then with a new body, it has another life on earth." Then with real emphasis, he added, "but the new life with the new body involves a life that is payment for the previous life. The one that was lived with the old body."

Leo stared at him thinking the kid's stoned out of his mind. "What do you mean, payment?"

"Okay... let's say in this life, you are a real sadistic sonofabitch, a mother-fucker of the highest order. All your life you're bullyin' people, pickin' on people, making everyone around you miserable. Mister... nobody gets away with that shit. There's a balance. There's a payment to be made."

"To whom?" Leo asked.

"I don't know. To the cosmos, maybe... I don't know, but that's the way it is. When that bastard dies, the soul that was so revolting in this life gets a body that makes the new life totally dependent on other people. So the fucker who was always making people crazy gets a new body that is a trap for the soul... it needs people for everything... like a paralyzed guy. Be nasty in this life, you'll lay in your own shit in the next one."

Leo stated intently at him. "That's retribution."

"That's right, Mister. That's exactly what it is."

"But why would a soul do that? Why would you or me be a miserable bastard if we knew we were going to pay for it?"

"We don't know or we know and we forget or we get smartass and don't give a shit because we think we're bigger than everything. I don't know why, but what I do know is that we pay up. The scales always balance out."

"So I'll have a family in the next life."

"Oh yeah, you'll have plenty of kids." The bartender's eyes were shining and he smiled. "I can see it now... you'll have a wife and some kids of your own and you'll be runnin' a private school or summer camp with hundreds of little buggers around all the time. You'll be knee deep in kids."

"That's a pretty picture." Leo laughed.

"That's what's gonna be. The paralyzed guy in this life might be an Olympic runner in the next. That's his payback for livin' the tough life this time." He smiled at Leo. "Don't sweat it, Mister. Eventually, you'll get exactly what you want."

"I hope I'm smart enough to appreciate it when I have it. I see so many people with good lives who are unhappy... always bitching and moaning... right in the middle of a good thing."

"People are weird. They forget or they fall into one of the big seven." He straightened. "Pride's the winner. Lotsa people think they're really hot shit. Like barnyard roosters... very touchy, dissatisfied, always looking for special treatment, very busy making themselves miserable. If they would only realize the life they are livin' is the one they asked for. If they could remember that, then they would stop bitchin' and really appreciate what they got."

"You know," Leo said, "at first I thought you were talking about fate. That our lives are set and we just live them out, but then I realized I don't have to be doing what I'm doing. I could dump the whole thing right this second and start a new page... a new story."

"Right. Like in the movies when the white-haired bank president looks with envy at the carpenter who's come to fix something. The banker always loved woodworking, but was pushed into banking by who knows what. If only he'd remember that what he wants is what he asked for in the previous life. In the movies, the guy dumps the bank to become a very happy wood worker."

"Yeah," sneered Leo. "But in real life he stays a banker and hates everyday of it."

"That's right and that's why so many people are so messed up and pissed off. They're all tryin' hard to be what they don't want to be." He leaned toward Leo. "You know, it's funny. When people meet a guy who's really content-really happy with what's going on, they put him down. I hear it all the time. Some angry dude comes in bitchin' that his brother-in-law or someone else is happy as a pig in shit workin' a dumb job for peanuts. And this guy, the one who's complaining... he's makin' a ton of dough and can't sleep, got loads of gas, is constipated, gets daily indigestion, and to top it off... he says he hopes he can live long enough to retire... because then he can become a painter... somethin' he's always wanted to be." He took a sip of water and continued. "And all the time this guy is yakkin' away, he's doodlin' a really great picture of me or of a bottle or a glass. It's obvious he's got real talent, but he's just too goddamned stupid and afraid to do what he knows he's supposed to do. " He took a breath. "Its weird, man... really weird."

Leo smiled, straightened his shoulders and got off the stool. "You know something, when I came in, I felt like shit, but I don't now. Right now, I feel great and I know it's not the booze."

"That's wonderful, Mister. I hope you feel that way tomorrow."

"I hope so too." Leo turned and started for the door. Then he stopped, turned and asked, "By the way, what are you studying at NYU? What's in your future?"

"If my plans work out, Mister, in a year I'll be a high school guidance counselor." Leo was laughing as he walked out into the night.

CHAPTER 32

IN MOST JURISDICTIONS, SLIPPING a cop money to fix a traffic ticket is viewed as attempted bribery. If the cop takes the money, then it is bribery. Court records indicate dollar amounts for fixing tickets to be between five and fifty dollars. The same records show most cops unwilling to take any bribe- at least those in the five to fifty dollar ranges.

However, when dollar amounts are in the thousands, the word 'bribery' no longer applies. Then we hear of 'donations,' 'scholarships,' 'bequests,' and the like. When the dollars are in the hundreds of thousands, the language changes once again. Then we hear of 'philanthropy,' 'grants,' and 'investments.' Dollar amounts beyond that level bring us once again to plain and simple language.

That is why a major aircraft corporation was greatly admired for their 'good deed' as their CEO called it, which put a new 747 complete with crew and flying personnel at the immediate disposal of the Vatican. In no way was this act considered a 'bribe' because first, the money is beyond simple calculation, and second, who is being bribed... and most important, for what?

'Good deeds,' like the plane on which the pope flew across the Atlantic, were accepted with a smile and acknowledged with a personally signed 'Thank You.' Those letters were suitable for framing, since they never specifically mentioned what directly constituted the prominently mentioned, 'good deed.'

The Pope had spent some of the flight watching the old movie, "Going My Way" because it evoked memories of when he, a Cardinal at the time, and Barry Fitzgerald got drunk trying to determine the difference between stage and film acting. By their second bottle of whiskey, they agreed that stage acting and preaching were similar, since both had scripts from which deviations were foolhardy. They also agreed that film acting was boring and since mistakes could be cut, there was no pressure. Fitzgerald stated at one point, "... any slob could do it." The Cardinal agreed and added, that nevertheless, he had always wanted to be in a movie.

Without excessive arm-twisting, the Cardinal appeared in Fitzgerald's next film as a small town priest confronting coal mine strike violence. Many in the church believed the Cardinal's rise was due to that role. The film experience had deeply impressed him and when he was elected pope, he insisted on the strongest mass communications division the church had seen to date. He was the first American Pope in the history of the church and some said he had been named pope because of his strong following. He was extremely popular and brought the church a face of ebullient good cheer, a condition almost unknown to the churchmen of yore, which though pious and worthy, were removed from the people they sought to lead. This pope was a man of the people and was greatly admired for that quality. Like many church leaders, he spoke many languages and always managed to create a lasting impression of good will and strength wherever he went.

"When do we eat?" the pope asked the intercom which sat on the desk in his small office compartment.

"Whenever you desire, Your Eminence." A voice responded.

"Let's do it now. What did they provide?" The voice detailed the afternoon's menu and after selecting, the pope invited most on board to dine with him.

The big plane flew steadily as the wine and food were consumed. The meal over, the pope excused himself and went to his stateroom for a nap. He slept an hour. Sunlight streaming through a window woke him. Sitting up, he stretched and saw the coastline of North America from the small window. He wasn't sure whether he was looking at the United States or Canada since it all looked the same. He wondered if God saw it that way also? Was it all interchangeable... the land of Canada being no different from the United States? Since God didn't bother with political maps, there was only a planet- only one of many in a vast universe.

He longed for the world as it used to be, when the Church was young and transportation meant hardship. Those were the glory days of development when wealth was acquired, when hearts and minds were claimed, when life was simple. Now it was a balancing act with Presidents, prime ministers, and kings and queens... all of them, unfortunately, almost instantly available. He dreamed often he could tell these leaders how to behave, how to lead their peoples. But some were politicians interested only in keeping their office as long as they could. Others sank into the muck of malignant villainy. He never understood why they couldn't resist their base desires.

"Your Eminence," the intercom spoke, "we are preparing for landing, please see to your seat belt." Thankfully, he recalled they were not landing in New York City, but north of the City at an airport in Newburgh. It was a joint commercial-military field with a runway long enough to handle any plane with any problem. Personally, he was not concerned with his own safety, but he was concerned with the crowds his arrival generated. The fewer who knew when and where his plane would land, the safer it would be for everyone. Looking from the window, he could see what looked like a line of toy cars waiting to take him to New York City. Shortly, he would be in his St. Patrick's apartment trying to sleep off the time difference.

After breakfast the next day, the daily appointment sheet was given to him and he noted a morning meeting with Monsignor Healy. Unaware of the content, he was surprised when his aide, Cardinal Bonaventura, told him it concerned a private audience scheduled immediately after the Saturday concert. At eleven, the Monsignor was ushered into the office reserved for special visitors. A few moments later, the Pope entered and after mechanical greetings, sat at his desk.

"Monsignor, what is the purpose of the Saturday evening audience?"

"The meeting is to guarantee your personal safety."

"My personal safety... guaranteed? How can you arrange that?"

"It's a complicated story which I will relate if there is time."

"Go ahead... tell me."

Healy began with Leo calling to say there would be an attempt on the pope's life. He told of meeting with the terrorists and of the agreement that had been reached.

"Am I to understand," the pope asked, "that meeting these people will prevent an assassination attempt?"

"The meeting will guarantee no attempt here in New York City, and from what Lieutenant Flower said, I feel safe to say the meeting might also offset attempts in other places as well."

"Is this Lieutenant to be trusted?"

"Yes. The Police Command willingly and with no exception affirm his trustworthiness."

"I want to meet him."

"Surprised, Healy repeated, "You want to meet with him?"

"Yes, see if you can arrange it for this evening... around eight. Since we are talking about my life, I want him to explain everything to me so I will have answers to the questions I now have and for the others I will have by tonight."

"I will contact him immediately." Healy rose and started for the door, but was stopped and told to use the telephone on the desk. He produced a small book, located the number and dialed. Leo took the call at his desk.

"The pope wants to meet with me?"

"Yes." Healy said. "He wants you to explain it all first hand. Can you be here at eight?"

"No problem," Leo answered with mild astonishment. "Where am I to go?"

"Use the side entrance."

"I'll be there," Leo said, hanging up.

Turning to the pope, Healy said, "He'll be here at eight."

"Good. Please be certain you pass the word to the guards that I am expecting him. When he arrives have him brought directly to me."

"Of course. Would you want me to attend this meeting?"

"No. I want to speak with him alone, but keep yourself available."

"I will be here if needed." The pope nodded and Healy headed for the door.

Leo stared at the phone. The pope wanted to meet him... a matter of hours from now. He called Hoffheimer, filled him in and then, not knowing what else to do, went to Fred's for something to eat. Later, as the cab bounced down Second Avenue, Leo wondered if they were backing out. He decided they weren't, since they needed no consultation for that, a phone call would have done the job. Was there a change of plans? This turn of events bothered him. It was like being called to the principal's office when you hadn't done anything. Meeting the pope beforehand never occurred to him and he figured the eventual audience would be nothing more than a quick, 'Hello, how are you?' And then out. Maybe it had all gone to smoothly... it was too easy from the get-go. Damn. There always had to be some grief... some payment to be made.

He got home, made some coffee and as he drank it, tried to relax and get a handle on what was happening. After a forced sit-down for thirty minutes, he washed the cup, showered and dressed. The cab ride uptown took his mind off things somewhat as he tried to explain to the Pakistani driver the difference between 'to', 'too' and 'two.' Leo thought he had done well, but the cab pulled away with the driver scratching his head, muttering about the complete stupidity that was English.

Leo pressed the buzzer alongside the door and waited. Shortly, a young priest who looked like Notre Dame's entire backfield opened the door. "Yes sir?" he asked.

"I'm Lieutenant Flower. I have an appointment." The priest blocked the entrance as he studied a clipboard.

"Yes," he said. "Here you are." He hung the clipboard on a hook beside the door and told Leo to follow him. They walked to an elevator and when the door opened, the guard pressed three. "Someone will be there to meet you." He said, as the door closed.

When the door opened, Leo was met by a teammate of the downstairs priest and escorted to an office. It looked similar to Healy's but the wood pieces were less grand.

"Please make yourself comfortable, Sir. He will be with you shortly."

The door closed on Leo's softly uttered, "Thanks." Checking the room, Leo saw a desk and two chairs- one on either side. The chair behind the desk was dark wood, green leather and big.

The one on the visitor side, was smaller, but otherwise the same. But as Leo looked at the smaller chair more closely, he was certain the front legs were shorter than the rear. He sat in it and smiled. The front legs were shorter. Years before, he had read that all the guest chairs in Admiral Hyman Rickover's Pentagon office were cut similarly. Supposedly, Rickover never lost an argument in his office, since his opponents were so busy trying not to slip out of the chair, they couldn't develop proper refutation to anything.

Leo moved the chair toward the desk hoping he could wedge himself into it, and concentrate on what was being said, rather than continually trying to keep from sliding off. As he adjusted it, the door suddenly swung open and the pope strode in. No ceremonies, no knock, just bang... here I am. Leo jumped to his feet and stammered, "Good evening, Sir." And moved to grasp the Pope's left hand to kiss his ring, but instead, Leo was offered the right and the two men shook like old pals who had been apart for a time.

"Lieutenant, I am pleased you could come on such short notice."

"Sir, it is my deep honor to meet and speak with you. You have long been a hero to me. I have been a policeman for most of my life and I have seen the end products of man not recognizing his worthiness. How I wish all men were able to focus on the good in the world." Leo was shocked and amazed by what he said. It had just burst out. He had not planned to say anything.

The pope smiled. "If that were the case, Lieutenant, you would be out of a job."

Now Leo smiled. "You're right about that, but I think you wouldn't be too busy either."

"Oh," the pope said, "I think I'd find something to keep myself occupied." Saying that, he moved to the chair behind the desk and motioned Leo to sit. Firmly planting his toes against the desk front, Leo pushed back into the chair, making himself as secure as possible.

"I want to know all you can tell me about this meeting you have arranged."

"Certainly, and if at any point I am not clear, please stop me. I want you to understand what happened."

"Don't worry, I am not afraid to ask questions. In fact, most say I ask too many. Just tell your story. I'll stop you if necessary."

Leo began with the death of Ilene and John, his transfer to Dignitary Protection, then Hoffheimer's assignment and the plan to deter an assassination.

Laughing, the Pope asked, "So, Lieutenant, you mean you told the terrorists you could arrange a meeting with me and then you told the Church you could arrange a meeting with the terrorists while all the while you were bluffing everyone?"

"Well... I wouldn't say I was bluffing. It was more a matter of giving everyone a chance to talk. I figured if I let them say what they wanted to say... to express themselves, there would be no violence."

"You're a good judge of men, aren't you?"

"Well, when I first met these men, these terrorists, we had lunch. I watched them eat. They relished the food and it seemed to me they were enjoying life far too much to want to die. I thought they were ready to jump at a chance to avoid violence."

"Did you get similar feelings about those you met here?"

Leo hesitated, then said, "I've been involved with Monsignor Healy in another matter and I..." The pope interrupted, "What other matter?"

Leo told him about John's work for Healy and how that brought them together and he told him he had used make-believe terrorists to finally convince Healy the meeting was vital.

"Who were the people you had posing as terrorists?"

"I used a woman officer from my unit and a doorman from my building."

The pope laughed. "They must have been very convincing, since Healy agreed."

"I figured he wouldn't be a very good judge- and he wasn't. At first, he was very resistant, but he reluctantly came around."

Leo saw the pope's forehead wrinkle and his eyes narrow. "Lieutenant, am I getting the feeling you don't like Monsignor Healy?"

Leo was surprised. He didn't like Healy at all, but thought he kept it buried. Either he didn't do a good job of hiding his feelings or the man he was talking with was exceptionally perceptive.

"Why don't you like him?"

"It isn't something I like to talk about. In fact, I've never talked about it."

"Is it so problematic?"

"I don't really know, but I guess it is, since I've always avoided it."

"Will you tell me?"

"I feel like this should be in a confessional."

"You're imaginative... so am I. Go ahead..."

Leo was torn. He wanted talk, but was desperate to keep his secret. He said nothing, but suddenly blurted out, "I was brought up in an orphanage, a Church orphanage here in the City. Monsignor Healy worked there when he was a young priest."

"So?"

"Here is the problem part, because I don't know if I'm dreaming or if I really remember the events. I don't know what to say."

"You're trying to say you think you were sexually molested at the orphanage and you think Monsignor Healy is the guilty party, right?"

Leo was stunned. Hearing those words spoken aloud was shocking enough, but hearing them spoken so openly was more so. "How do you know that?" Leo whispered.

"You aren't the first to bring this very unfortunate matter to my attention. Like you, I try to bury unpleasantness. I was going to do nothing about the matter, figuring that time would take care of everything. None of us are young men."

"But I'm not certain. I just can't remember... or I don't want to remember."

In almost a different voice, the Pope said, "My son, it can be true or not be true. Let's say it is true... it happened. So what? How did it matter in your life? What does it matter now?"

"I don't know if it mattered. Maybe my life would have turned out the same, but I don't know that. For many years, I've been thinking about why I never married. Maybe I'm kidding myself, but I think I wanted to marry and have kids... why didn't I? What stopped me?"

The questions hung in the air as the two men looked at each other. "I think it's all connected... that I haven't married.... my terrible relationships with women. I think everything... my entire life is somehow related to this episode from years ago, but I don't know. I just don't know."

"How old are you?"

"Almost sixty-one."

"Marriage does not make sense for you any more. You've achieved a stable life without it."

"So what do I do?"

"What do you do? You don't do anything. You live until you don't. Take the opportunities as they come- follow your heart."

"But what about Healy, I mean... Monsignor Healy. You said there had been additional reports?"

"Don't worry about that. I'll take care of Monsignor Healy. We've always taken care of men like him. The Church is good at that. Leave it to me."

Leo looked at his shoes. "We've come a long way from our original subject, haven't we?"

"Real conversation does that."

Leo didn't know what to say or what to do. He squirmed and then the pope said, "Lieutenant, you are a resourceful man. Putting all this together proves that. I'm not going to worry about you. Your life will work out very well." He paused, "Is there anything else?"

Leo breathed deeply. "I have what you might call a guest list... people I want to bring to the meeting when the terrorists do their video. I want to clear the list with you."

"Do you know all the people?"

"Yes, they're all known to me. There is no danger."

"Then I will leave it to your discretion. Cardinal Bonaventura will be instructed to contact you tomorrow. Work out the details with him."

"What about Monsignor Healy?"

"I will deal with the matter."

Leo nodded. The pope stood. "Good. Now I want to have a snack. I will see you after the concert... at our meeting." He extended his hand to Leo who struggled to his feet. Grasping Leo's hand in both of his, the pope smiled, let go, turned and left the room.

Leo flopped back into the chair realizing he was soaked, drenched in sweat. It had been quite a meeting- quite an ordeal. There was a slight knock and the door opened. The priest asked Leo if he wanted anything or did he want to leave. Leo said he wanted to leave and he was quickly escorted to the side entrance. A few minutes after he left the pope, he was in the street looking for a taxi.

CHAPTER 33

"WHERE TO, MAC?" LEO sat motionless, silent. When the cab swooped to a stop, he had entered, ready to go, but realized he didn't know where to go.

"Hey, Buddy, if you want to just sit there, let me know, but I'd much rather go someplace, wouldn't you?"

"Drive into the Park. Just drive around. I'll let you know where we're going."

"Okay, pal, you got it." The driver threw the meter and started off. "You let me know, okay? I'll be here in the front."

Leo didn't know where to go, but he did know he couldn't be alone. He considered the bar from last night, and then rejected it. It might be crowded. He couldn't drop in on Jacqueline. There was no one from work. Where? Then it hit him- Abe. If John were alive he would have gone there immediately. With him gone, there was only Abe.

Leo called out. "Go to the Regency... 61st and Park." The ride took a few minutes and Leo felt happy as he paid the driver and bounded into the lobby. Grabbing the house phone, he told the operator to ring Abe.

"Mr. Rosenberg's residence. Who is calling?" An unfamiliar voice asked. Leo was instantly depressed. He so wanted Abe to be home. Then he realized it must be the hotel staff taking the call. "Tell him Lieutenant Flower is here and wants to see him."

"Yes Sir, one moment please."

Abe's voice broke in. "Leo, how great to hear from you. You downstairs? Come on up." After a pause, he said, "Thanks Charley and will you see that Lieutenant Flower is escorted upstairs?"

The voice answered, "Immediately, Sir."

Leo replaced the phone. A minute later a bellhop materialized, "Lieutenant Flower?" Leo nodded. "Follow me, please."

As the elevator went up to the penthouse, Leo wondered what he would say to Abe and what he would have done if Abe had been out or if there was no Abe at all. Everyone needs someone to listen to him. Not to judge or offer advice, but just listen. The more I talk about everything, he thought, the better I'll be. Having no one to listen to you is terrible. It explains the loudmouths trying to get the bartender's attention; the people muttering aloud in the streets; the guy who brings a cannon to work and wipes out his co-workers because they had no time for him.

He had no one. No relatives, no real friends, no one. How did I let this happen? He asked himself. Why did I let this happen? The elevator door opened and there was Abe waiting in the hallway, smiling at him. "Hey, Leo, it's a great idea... dropping by like this. Come- come on in." Abe led the way inside and then to a den-like room Leo had not seen before. Lots of brown and green leather furniture, a TV and a big sound system, wooden cabinets and books everywhere,

Leo noticed there was an open book on the arm of a large chair and a side table with a half-filled glass of wine and a lighted cigar in an ashtray. Opening a cabinet, Abe removed a glass and poured wine from an open bottle. "Here, have some of this... its good stuff." Leo took the glass and drank most of it in one gulp.

"Son of a bitch... if you're thirsty, I'll get a pitcher of iced tea... slug wine like that and you can't even taste it."

"I know, Abe, I know... I just had a rough session and I needed something in a hurry." The expression on Abe's face changed as he recognized Leo's mood. "What's wrong? Now that I take a good look at you, I see things are not usual. What happened?"

Leo put down the glass and flopped into a chair. "I just came from a meeting with the pope and it didn't turn out the way I expected."

"You met the pope... tonight?"

"Yeah... how about that? He wanted to know about the concert and the audiences and then we got into some private stuff I never talked about... to anyone."

"Well, my boy, if you're gonna tell a deep secret to anyone, the pope seems like the right guy. I don't think he'll call tomorrow to tell you he wants a couple of grand or he'll go public."

"It isn't that... like it was a real secret. It's that I don't truly know if what I think happened really happened."

"Leo, that's a bit mystifyin'... Could you fill me in?"

Leo stared at him trying to decide what to do. Then he asked himself, why else would he have come to talk to Abe if not to tell him. "Abe, before tonight I would have never said a word, but that's obviously why I'm here. I've got to tell someone and you're elected." Leo sipped some of the wine. "Hey... this is good wine."

"Goddamn right it is... before you drank it like it was cow piss... but let's not get into wine talk."

"Right." Leo took a deep breath and looked at the floor. "I know I mentioned Ilene and John, the couple who raised me after the orphanage." Abe nodded. "After they were killed, I got a call from a Monsignor connected to St. Patrick's and he wanted to know if I had anything of John's that belonged to the Church. One thing leads to another and he comes to see me. When I heard him on the phone, I thought he sounded familiar, but when I see him, bells go off. I was already on edge because of his voice but when I see him... bingo! He was at the orphanage when I was a kid." Leo drank more wine.

"Ya recognized him, right?"

"I thought I did. He wasn't the same 'cause we're talking about fifty years, but something was there- maybe the voice, the posture... something rings a bell. Anyway, a week goes by and then it hits me, he was the young priest who ran the place. As soon as I place him, I start to sweat."

"Something happened between you and him, huh?"

"Oh yeah, but not just me. Lots of other kids were involved. It all swoops in at once and I realize he molested me and probably had a thing with every kid in the joint." Abe sipped some wine and looked at Leo. "So... now what?"

"Well, tonight as I'm talking to the pope he catches on I carry bad feelings for this monsignor and he wants to know why. Before I can tell him... he tells me. He knows all about this guy."

"Leo... you think the CIA is tops in intelligence... Let me tell ya... the Church is the best. I think they invented spyin' and also...gettin' even. If I was you, I'd forget the whole thing."

"The pope said the same thing. He tells me to forget about the monsignor-that the church takes care of its own problems."

"So what's botherin' you?"

"I don't know, but I can't help thinking that maybe that situation had a strong bearing on my life. That I've always been running away from it. Like maybe, I never really forgot about it and I'm ashamed... and... I don't know... maybe..." He took more wine and a few deep breaths. "Look, I guess I've always wanted to have a family and maybe this thing got in the way and I've been screwed up because of it."

"So, you're sayin' that even though you never really thought about it, it was there all the time... and... now, now you're askin' if somethin' you didn't consciously think about had the power to influence your entire life?"

Leo didn't answer immediately, but realized that was the key question. If he never thought about it, could it still have controlled his life? Finally, he said, "Abe that is the real and only question. I wish I had an answer, Abe. I wish I did."

"Hey... Leo...Don't chicken out. Tell me what you think."

"Well, the pope said... assume it's true and it did influence my life and now... I'm left with the aftermath and that's that!"

"Okay, but you can look at it the other way 'round and say it ain't true, then you and you alone made all the choices that brought you to this point. You did what you did 'cause you wanted to and you did it with no help from nothin' and nobody."

"So where am I?"

"Where are you?" Abe took the cigar from his mouth and dumped the ash. "You are right where you were before you realized anything about anything. Nothing's changed."

"But I feel different."

"Okay, so you feel different. So tell me how feelin' different is gonna make a difference." Leo considered what Abe said. "It won't make any difference. I'll get up tomorrow and do my thing just like always."

"Are you puttin' me on?"

"No... I'm sure. The pope said I was too old to really make changes. I think he's right. I feel like the fire house dog... a one trick act."

"Now... just you wait a minute. I ain't gonna say the pope is not a bright guy with a good head, but when it comes to marriage and family talk, I don't know if he's the right guy to be givin' advice."

"You don't think I'm too old to get married?"

"Jesus, Leo I don't know what's the right age. All I know is if you can't make it alone and some nice lady wants to marry you and you want to be with her, then you do it. If it makes you happy and her happy... what's the problem?"

"But who'd want to marry an old guy like me?"

"Hey... sonofabitch... wait a minute with that old guy shit... that kind of talk makes me feel just great." A moment later, he smiled. " But Leo, kiddin' aside, it ain't a matter of who... it's a matter of whether or not."

"So you really think a guy my age could marry?"

"I don't see why not. Shit, I'm almost 81 and I would do it tomorrow if I wanted. I got nothin' to fear and nothin' to lose... and neither do you."

Leo studied Abe's face and saw the toughness and the independence... that if he wanted something, he'd go after it and get it, and that it wasn't the set of his chin or shape of his face or anything like that... it was simply... he's the guy who sets a course and his ship sails. Leo watched a cloud of blue smoke as it drifted upwards. He sensed a feeling of satisfaction flooding over him, similar to how he felt years before when he had brought a tough case to a successful end.

"Goddamn it... you're right. What happened... happened. Tomorrow's what's important, not yesterday."

"Yeah, but that could be all talk. Are you gonna wake up tonight in a sweat because some guy played with you when you was a kid?" Abe sipped some wine. "If you're gonna say it, you got to mean it or else it's just bullshit."

"I know that."

Abe hunched forward. "Leo," he said softly, "you got to understand somethin' about people, about men... hell, women too... Lots of people had weird experiences when they were kids. It's nothin'... it's thinkin' about it that gets you nuts... but it's really nothin'. People can make anything into a problem. Hell, I bet there are guys who can turn a handshake into a dance with the devil. The thing to understand is that some sonofabitch took advantage of you and you can shake it off, just like you shook off shootin' that guy a while back."

Leo nodded. "I can see you're right."

Abe leaned back. "You know, I'm glad you came to talk to me about this. I enjoy bein' able to listen." He puffed the cigar. "I'm alone too much and I miss the old days when there was always someone around for a little schmoozin'."

"I know what you mean. I have the same feelings."

"I think it's too easy to be alone these days. People got TV's, computers... me... I go to books. People get trapped into bein' alone, but it ain't right. People need each other, we need to be social."

"I know that, believe me. I went out to a bar last night... first time in a long time. I used to do that often, but now I'm like you... a good book... good music and I'm out of it."

"Do you go to movies much?"

"No and I used to love to go. I'm really a fan, but... now...1 find the stories stupid and there's too much gun play."

Abe laughed. "We're a lot alike. We could be roommates... this place is big enough."

"Oh, I don't know. I've always had my own place. I guess I like it that way, but... I don't know. Sometimes I hate being alone... but then again... I wonder if we really do like to have other people around." Abe shrugged his answer.

Leo stood took a step and then stopped short. "Damn, I almost forgot."

"Forgot what?"

"The concert for the pope. I managed to get everyone, you, Vincent, Angel, Marty, Carlos... everyone's invited to an audience with the pope when it's over."

"Hey, that's great. Vincent will absolutely swoon. Meeting the pope... wow!"

Abe stood and put a hand on Leo's shoulder. "You look better now."

Leo realized he did feel better. He felt good and he felt right. "You've helped, Abe, and I really appreciate you took the time. If it wasn't for you, I don't know what I would've done."

As they walked to the front hallway, a sense of peace and friendship filled them both. They were relaxed and satisfied. Not for a long time had either man connected so well with another person.

"I'll see you at the concert, if not before."

Abe smiled. "You couldn't keep me away. I'll be there with bells on."

CHAPTER 34

LEO STOOD IN FRONT of the cathedral wondering about the men who built it. Was it easier for them because it was a church? Was there an inducement aside from wages that helped them as they stacked the massive stones? Would they have worked so diligently if it were a department store? Does a psychic reward outshine a tangible one?

One look gave the answer. When the union picked people for this job, they got men who probably would have worked for nothing or paid the union for the privilege. But now, things are different, now the guys want a boat, a house, and a camp in the country. Middle class people worry more about their neighbor's regard than salvation. But... like they say, what goes around comes around. Back then; if you wanted solid workers, you got them as they came off the boat. It's like that again. The new immigrants are going to rebuild what the old immigrants built.

Walking up the steps to the cathedral's front doors, he figured if he ever had a house built, he'd bring priests to the site and tell the workmen it was a building for the Church. Stuff made for the Church always seemed a little better than stuff made for atheists.

Reaching the top step, he turned to look into the street. There were people, cars, buses- and everything was moving. There was so much visible energy. Watching the crowds of moving people, he realized he would never leave the City. The natural world moved ahead too slowly, here, you could see people age. He recalled the old days of stakeouts where he saw people leave for work and then return. They were fresh in the morning, filled with energy, with straight backs and chins high in the air. That was changed when they got home. In the evening they looked beaten down... and beaten up. They had all grown older.

Trees in the country don't age as you watch them. There, it's life in slow motion. He looked at the buildings across the street and realized bricks ands concrete were like trees- they didn't age as you watched them. No, it's only the people- only in the City can you see people get old by the day.

He was so intent on his thoughts, he didn't notice the limo until it stopped. Then, he instantly recognized the car and driver and his heart stopped when the door was opened and Jacqueline stepped into the sunlight. She was so beautiful. She was wearing a maroon suit trimmed in black and looked formal and dramatically mysterious.

She walked to him like she had walked those steps thousands of times, an inner voice setting the pace. If acting in films had done anything for her, it had above all else, given her a sense of glamour, which manifested in radiant self-confidence. Directors had shown her how to walk- had taught her how to use her body to send the message her character had to convey. There is nothing like pretending to be who you are not to get a poised and thoughtful presentation of who you are.

Even those who did not recognize her, slowed to watch her mount the steps. On screen, her presence was so forceful; audiences watched her and no one else. It was the same on the street. People had to look. His breath caught as he watched her glide to him. Right foot, left foot, toes straight ahead, shoulders back, head up, alert, a twist of her head to move her hair in that incredibly feminine way, one arm holding a bag, the other in time with her swaying. She moved slowly, but it wasn't a false, deliberately tantalizing slowness, meant to tease or tempt. It was motion blessed with natural and graceful coordination. Watching her, he realized she made him feel like he owned the world. Could he feel this good about himself without her? Would he always need someone else to determine his worth?

She stopped a step below him. "You look so handsome."

"Watching you filled my head with thoughts that have no business being thought in front of a church- a cathedral no less."

"Oh, Leo, you do know exactly what to say. How come you are so smart?" He laughed. "Smart? No- lucky!"

"Leo, luck has nothing to do with it. Don't be so quick to sell yourself short."

I know my worth with everything but women, he thought. Why is that? I'm a competent, decent person, but when it comes to women, I always put myself down. Damn! "You have no idea how good you are for my ego. I wish you were around years ago."

"I was," she said.

"I know you were, but you weren't around me- and that's the point."

"I'm here now," she said softly.

He reached for her hand and gently pulled her to his side. Facing the street, they looked like a tourist couple posing for a picture. As they watched the street, a cab pulled up. Carlos got out, then Angel and Vincent. They wore suits except for Angel who wore his dark brown robe. Seeing Leo, they walked to where he and Jacqueline stood.

Extending his hand to Leo and bowing slightly to Jacqueline, Vincent said, "Good to see you again, Leo... and seeing you... Madame Rousault... makes my life brighter."

"It's good to see you also, Vincent," said Leo, as he nodded to Carlos and Angel who nodded back, but they were more deeply involved staring at Jacqueline. It was an electric moment and Leo got slightly agitated when he realized they shared his lascivious thoughts, but Jacqueline altered everything when she asked them, "Do you recognize me?"

Carlos squinted, while Angel's eyes widened. "I know you. I saw you yesterday on TV in a movie. You was in a bar with a whole bunch of Foreign Legion guys."

"I have often been in bars with the Foreign Legion. I think I was in more than ten of those desert movies."

"You're the first movie star I ever met, but you ain't gonna be the last. I'm gonna meet everybody after today... after singin' for this pope guy."

There was a voice from outside their little circle. "Goddamn right this is the beginnin'. You are gonna be bigger than Sinatra." They turned to see Marty who looked like Nathan Detroit straight out of *Guys and Dolls*. He wore a black and white hounds tooth jacket, a black shirt with a gray silk tie. Vincent's eyes popped. "Jesus, Marty, you look like you're going to the track. Isn't that jacket a little bold?"

"Don't be ridiculous. I figured everybody'll be wearing black or close to it, but I don't want to look like I'm gonna be buried." He held out an arm. "This is some jacket... cost a bundle." Looking from one to the other, his eyes settled on Jacqueline. "Lady, it's easy to see you got some class, wadda you think?"

"I think it is a beautiful jacket. It suits you and if it makes you feel good, then it is fine."

Marty beamed. "Leo, you got one smart lady there. She knows what's up."

Another voice asked, "Okay, what's goin' on. You look like a half-time huddle."

Abe shouldered his way into the group and waited for an answer. "We were admiring Marty's jacket. What do you think of it?" Leo asked.

Abe stared. "Marty, you look like a 1950 bookie goin' to Lindy's for cheesecake."

Marty laughed as his eyes flicked around the little circle, but then the smile faded and he stared at Abe. "The trouble with you is not only ain't you got no sense of fashion, you ain't got no sense of humor either."

"Believe me, I know fashion and I know humor, neither of which applies to you."

"Oh yeah... well, let me tell you somethin'..."

"Hold it! Hold it." Vincent broke in. "You guys are going to start in and this is no place for a- I can yell louder than you can- thing..."

Abe took a breath. "You're right... this is not the place." He raised his arm and swept it in an arc. They turned to see the steps filling with priests and nuns. As he stared, Leo felt a tap on his shoulder.

"Lieutenant Flower, I am Cardinal Bonaventura. Are these people with you?" Leo nodded and introduced everyone. The Cardinal shook hands and then announced it was time to enter and take seats. As they turned to do so, a pair of limousines screeched to a stop at the curb. The doors of the first flew open and six large men emerged. They moved to the second car as its doors opened. Inspector Magalana stepped out, scanned the street, turned back and nodded. A moment later, Prince Punteyaya got out wearing a robe covered in spangles, sequins, and gemstones. As he stood glinting in the sun, McGinty, Lor and Singh got out of the car.

"Are those three men the ones?" Bonaventura asked Leo

"Yes sir, they are." The Cardinal nodded to a priest at his side who with a cadre of other Priests, walked down the steps to surround everyone who had come out of Punteyaya's car. Leo excused himself and followed the group of priests.

"Lieutenant Flower, we have arrived!" called out the Prince. "How nice you have arranged for this group to look after us."

"I didn't arrange for them."

"Then who did?" asked McGinty. Leo turned and pointed to Bonaventura who was a few steps away. As he came closer, Leo introduced him to the Prince, who said, "Cardinal, these are the special guests for tonight's concert."

In response the Cardinal smiled, but he was staring at McGinty. "Mr. McGinty, we have several different camcorders available. Do you have a preference?"

"No, as long as I know how to use it."

"Fine. One of my associates will provide you with it when we are inside. Now..." he gestured to all..."let us enter."

They walked the steps into the cathedral following the Cardinal, who led them to the front. Gesturing to Vincent and Angel, he said, "Father William will escort you to a room where you can prepare." Vincent nodded and the two were directed away from the group. Then the Cardinal stepped forward and pointed at seats while calling out names. It reminded Leo of elementary school as they slid into their assigned places.

Once seated, Leo looked behind and saw Hoffheimer with Magalana to his right and Roberto and Melendez to his left. Fred and Irene sat alongside Magalana. How did they get here, he wondered. Catching Hoffheimer's eye, he gestured in their direction and smiling, Hoffheimer pointed at himself. Bonaventura noticed Leo looking behind. "Lieutenant, your Captain and I have been in touch. You haven't been as alone as you may have thought." Leo nodded slowly, realizing little, if anything, had been left to chance.

Continuing to scan the crowd, Leo recognized most of the Department's hierarchy alongside the Mayor and his entourage. The remaining seats were filled with nuns and priests eagerly awaiting a glimpse of the Holy Father. As he glanced right and then left, Jacqueline poked him. "Stand up." She said. Before he could ask 'why' he saw the pope entering from the right side of the sanctuary. Watching him, Leo saw he didn't stroll. His energetic walk displayed a dynamic force very different from the contemplative frailness of so many predecessors. Seeing him, the audience rose and applauded.

A broad smile formed on his face and he waved one arm like a boxer introduced to the hometown crowd. Stopping in front of his seat, he then raised both arms and signaled for quiet. Scanning the crowd, he caught Leo's eye, and nodded. Leo beamed. As the pope continued looking at the audience, his smile slowly faded.

"We are here for a special purpose. One that will become more and more important as we intercept our future." He spoke in a relaxed, but forceful voice. "Today, there will be no sermon and there is nothing to read. Instead, we will listen to melodies from our glorious past. Through these sounds and rhythms we will feel our connection to the Lord. As we listen, we should focus on the reasons why we have managed to carve out a history of two thousand years. The Church is not an accident. It is not a casual organization designed to amuse or please its adherents. The Church is a vibrant living force and we are fortunate to be a part of it." Stopping, his stern bearing was displaced by a warm smile.

"Seeing you waiting so expectantly reminds me of the days I spent, many years ago, in the music class of Sister Mary Alice. She would tell us to sit up straight, pay attention and get ready to feel the Lord's spirit flow through us." He laughed. "She knew exactly what to say and all I can do is repeat her words- so sit up straight, pay attention and let the Lord's spirit flow."

He waved again and sat. A moment later, a chair, a music stand, and a small platform were brought out and then, a moment after that, Vincent came out with his guitar. After Vincent sat, Angel appeared. He walked to the platform, turned to face the audience and after a moment, nodded. In response to his signal, the lighting was altered. The overheads were dimmed and small spotlights were directed onto him.

Remaining lights were focused behind him leaving the front of the sanctuary in semi-darkness. This lighting managed to create a halo around Angel that rendered him ghost-like and floating.

Though he was sitting almost directly in front of Angel, Leo couldn't make out his face. The cowl and the back lighting obscured it. Also, the robe's length obscured the platform so Angel really seemed to be floating. Leo's thinking was interrupted when Vincent played a simple chord introduction. A moment later, Angel sang. Leo hoped for a recognizable tune, something he could use as a standard, but Angel provided none. He hummed and sang syllables that had no meaning. Nevertheless, Leo was caught up with his voice. The sound of it was like a blending of reeds. At one point, he sounded like an oboe, then a clarinet, then like other instruments. As Leo listened, he realized some of Angel's sounds were not comparable to any instrument at all- some of Angel's sounds were not like any instrument Leo had ever heard.

The songs and chants were short and there were obvious beginnings and endings, but the music stayed simple and easy to follow. Also, there was nothing surprising or challenging in Vincent's arrangements. Leo had been waiting for some departure, a change of premise, a trademark- something that Angel would do to make the music his own, but Angel avoided doing that. He sang and the audience followed his lead.

Leo was at peace. He reached out, took Jacqueline's hand and felt himself floating. It was as if they were on a raft atop a warm, tropic ocean. Suddenly, the music stopped and there was silence. Leo opened his eyes and saw Vincent standing. "There will be a 15 minute rest and then we will continue." Then he and Angel walked off to the right. Leo was a trifle upset at the brevity, since he had hoped for a longer first part.

"My God." Jacqueline said, "Leo, look at your watch." Not quite understanding what she meant, he did, and was astonished to see almost an hour had passed. It had seemed no more than fifteen or twenty minutes. At first, he didn't believe it and wanted to check with someone else, but stopped when he saw others checking their wristwatches. How could that be?

"Isn't it amazing?" She asked.

"I can't believe it. I've been in situations where I thought time was standing still, but never anything like this."

"Do you believe in mass hypnosis?"

"I would have said 'no' forty-five minutes ago, but I don't know what to say now." All around them similar conversations started.

The pope leaned to his left. "Well, Bonaventura, what do you think of that?"

The Cardinal sat as if frozen, still staring at the spot where Angel had stood. "If I had not experienced it, your Holiness, I would not have believed it possible,"

"I sensed it the first time I heard him. I was in an automobile and arrived at my destination in what I though was too short a time. I was amazed to learn the ride had actually taken longer than was usual. It was a remarkable moment."

"I feel inordinately relaxed." Exclaimed Prince Punteyaya.

The pope looked over at him and smiled. "I'm sure everyone shares your feeling" The Prince leaned forward catching Leo's eye. "Lieutenant Flower, were you aware of this strange effect?"

"Not at all. The first time I heard him, conditions were different, but I would have remembered something like this." Leo looked at Abe and Marty. They shrugged a response.

"Carlos." Leo asked, "does this always happen?" Does time seem to fade away?"

"Man, you got no idea. I have been late for work a lot because he starts singin' and I start listenin' and before I know it, I'm off someplace else in my head."

"Is that why you've been late so much?" Marty asked,

"That's right, man. You always think I'm with some bimbo, but lotsa times I'm late 'cause he's singin' and I drift off to a beautiful beach."

"Are you alone on the beach?" Jacqueline asked.

"Oh, no... I ain't never alone. His singin' really turns me on." Jacqueline laughed.

They stopped talking when the pope stood and turned to face the audience. "This is a good example of the power that is in music. Let music open your soul and let the Lord's strength flow into you." He raised his arms, offered a silent blessing to the audience and then sat and waited for Vincent and Angel.

They came back to the little stage a moment later. Angel mounted the small platform, Vincent played an introductory passage and they were back into it. In a minute, it seemed, so was everyone else. Leo glanced at his watch, closed his eyes and let his spirit be buoyed by the music.

In the first part, Vincent had provided nothing more than a rhythmic background. Now, he played a melody line that Angel matched in unison, then matched it harmonically and then shifted back to unison. Leo couldn't sense a separation between the melodies, as one seemed to lead to another. After that piece, they drifted into a musical conversation. Vincent played a passage, Angel answered it, then Vincent played another statement and Angel responded. Leo's eyes closed and he smiled as he listened.

Sensing movement, he opened his eyes to see the pope rising from his seat. Vincent and Angel were gone. The lights were still focused on where they had been, but that space was empty. As the pope stepped forward and turned to face the audience, Leo glanced to his right and left to see many in the audience shaking their heads and blinking.

"There you have it," the pope said. "There you have the power of music. The Lord himself entered us and took us away. We were in his arms." He was silent for a moment, then said, "Please remain in your seats- try to recall what you felt- don't lose this moment."

A moment later, Cardinal Bonaventura leaned over to Leo. "Lieutenant, we will let the general audience commence and then we will have the private meeting."

"Fine," said Leo. Then leaning over to McGinty, he asked, "Getting your money's worth, pal?"

"Very interesting, to say the least."

"We will have the private meeting after the pope meets with this group."

"I wonder if I can film some of this stuff?"

Bonaventura didn't miss a trick. Almost before McGinty finished his question, one of the fullback priests handed him a video camera. He took it and pointed it first at Lor, then Singh and then he panned the audience and sanctuary. As Leo watched, McGinty rose from his seat and carefully walked and shot the space between his seat and the pope's. He spoke into the camera's microphone as he did so, explaining, Leo guessed, how easy it would have been to put a gun in the pope's ear and pull the trigger.

Then some of the burly priests picked up the pope's throne-like seat and turned it to face the audience. When they finished, the pope returned to it. Almost immediately, a line formed and one after the other, people came forward to kneel and receive his blessing.

As each member of the audience approached the foot of the throne, the pope offered his hand to some, while others kissed his ring. Very few spoke, most silently smiled, happy to be near a personage heretofore seen only at an electronic distance.

People acted similarly when they recognized Jacqueline. It was clear they wanted to talk, but unsure of what to say, they merely stared. Leo felt the notion of celebrity was directly tied to the culture that offers the title. In a different culture, the pope would be just another man and Jacqueline merely another woman.

Leo's thinking was interrupted when Cardinal Bonaventura told him the public audiences were complete and the pope was ready for McGinty. Leo left Jacqueline and located the three men, who shortly after, were escorted by a phalanx of guards and allowed to make their video. Before they were led away, McGinty approached Leo. "Lieutenant, our job is over." He gestured to the videotape he held. "You did everyone a service by arranging this meeting. A great many people are thankful it happened." He extended his hand and Leo shook it. "Take care of yourself, Lieutenant, we may do business again." Leo nodded as the three men and their guards left the sanctuary.

That's how it gets done, Leo thought. Everyone is polite; everyone smiles like we're the best of friends. That's the politics of it. As he thought about McGinty, he noticed Boneventura coming toward him. "Lieutenant, His Holiness wants to meet with you and your party."

"That's great. I'll tell them. By the way, I didn't see Monsignor Healy, was he here?"

"No, he was not... and at this moment, I would guess he is experiencing the joy of his new assignment."

"His new assignment?"

Leo thought he saw a wisp of smile at the corner of Bonaventura's mouth. "Yes, after years of devoted service in New York City, he has been given an opportunity in a less urban area. He is now the director of a home for retired priests and nuns."

"Where is it? Westchester?"

"Oh, no, a little more rural than that." Leo felt a punch line coming. "I know the Church has homes everywhere. A priest I knew once mentioned a place near Buffalo." Leo said.

"Yes, I know that place, but we have many locations. Monsignor Healy happens to be at one in Fort Vermillion, in Central Alberta... Canada... a location that serves the Northern Territories."

Leo swallowed. "The Monsignor... he didn't select that place on his own, did he?"

"Oh, no. His Holiness offered it to him personally. It is a great honor."

"Right," said Leo. "A very great honor indeed."

"Now," said the Cardinal, "let us meet His Holiness."

One after the other, they moved to the throne. The pope remained seated while Marty, Angel, Carlos, and Vincent talked with him. Then Abe, Jacqueline, and Leo stepped closer. Both Leo and Jacqueline kissed the ring while Abe heartily shook hands.

"Quite a concert, wasn't it Lieutenant?"

"Yes, Sir. I've never experienced a musical event like that."

"Did you..." Jacqueline asked the pope, "... ever experience anything similar?"

The pope nodded. "Once, years ago. I was studying for an examination and drifted into what I thought was a light sleep. Now I realize I was transported as most of us were today. The music I heard then was not unlike Angel's singing."

"You said 'most of us'... don't you think everyone had similar reactions?"

"Oh, no. Some are impervious. Their self-absorption is so complete; they are often unaware of things happening around them. They are like stone walls."

"I knew a guy like that," said Abe. "He was able to hold a conversation no matter what was goin' on. I can remember, one time, we are in a car and the cops are shootin' at us and we're shootin' at them, and Oscar, this guy, was talkin' about how important it was to learn the proper way to handle a sand wedge. He's drivin' about ninety, dodgin' bullets, and calmly goin' on about golf. It was a mad scene, but Oscar is talkin' like we was sippin' cocktails at some club."

"You were being pursued by the police?" the pope asked.

Abe smiled. "As you know, everyone has a past... some are just... a little more colorful than some others."

"Well put, well put!" Exclaimed the pope. "Now, tell me who you are."

"The name is Rosenberg. Abe Rosenberg."

"Probably not one of my flock, right?"

"Yeah... you could say that."

In the following moment of silence, Bonaventura leaned in to the pope. "Your Holiness, it is time for the private meeting."

"Thank you, Bonaventura. Please bring those I asked to see." Then he turned to the small group in front of him. "It has pleased me greatly to spend these moments with you and I hope we may meet again." He smiled and nodded. "I must thank those connected with Mr. Angel for bringing him and I certainly thank him for a most enriching and rewarding musical moment."

He stood and moved off through a doorway to the right of the main altar. With others, Leo turned to leave, but Bonaventura approached. "Lieutenant, a moment please." Leo stopped while the others walked on. "Lieutenant, His Holiness wants to see you and Mr. Angel."

Catching up with the others, Leo told them about the meeting and then he and Angel followed Bonaventura back to the altar area. As they walked, Angel said, "You don't need to call me Mr. Angel, I ain't no mister. I'm just Angel."

"As you wish," said Bonaventura, who directed them to the door the pope had used. He knocked twice, opened it and gestured for them to enter. When they did, he closed the door behind them. The pope was seated on a small sofa that faced two chairs. When Leo and Angel approached, he told them to sit. Then, shifting his gaze from one to the other, he stared at them. "Both of you are alone in the world... that is true, isn't it?"

Leo looked at Angel, not wanting to speak for him, but saw he was looking at objects on a table next to the sofa. "Yes, I'm alone," said Leo, "I've always been alone except for two people."

"You never found the right companion for yourself?"

"As I said the other day, I never did. I don't know how to connect."

"The woman you are now with... she is married to someone else, correct?"

Leo felt guilty and inadequate. "Yes, sir. I have great feelings for her, but I don't believe we can ever become a couple."

"That's too bad. You are relaxed in her presence." He picked up a sheet of paper and looked at it. "I see you were adopted by a man of the Church."

"That's true, but I was never formally adopted. They looked after me and became my surrogate parents. In my mind though, I considered them real parents."

"You lost them recently."

"Yes. They were murdered by a robber." Leo hesitated, and then burst out. "How could anyone kill an old man... a priest... and his old sister? It's beyond me. Two people without a penny, killed for nothing."

"So you are alone?"

"Yes, with them gone, I have no one."

"Has the killer been caught?"

"No. There are hundreds of killings like that every year... no clues, no real evidence. These crimes are impossible to solve."

"Do you have friends?"

"I know many people... men I've worked with, but close friends... no. But, Mr. Rosenberg, the gentlemen you met outside, we've become close recently."

"You miss having a father, don't you?"

Leo's eyes filled with tears so all he could was nod. The pope closed his eyes. A moment later, he turned to Angel. "And you... you are alone also?"

Angel had stopped his gazing around the room and had intently stared at Leo as he spoke. Now he stared at the Pope. "Yeah, but I live with a guy, Carlos... and Vincent is teaching me things and Marty and Abe look after me, but I'm alone. I ain't got nobody."

"How old are you?"

"I don't know. Fourteen, fifteen. I don't know. Nobody knows."

"How have you lived?"

"I took what I needed."

"From whom did you take?"

"I took from people who had what I wanted." He paused. "I done lotsa bad things... lotsa very bad things"

"Have you ever tried to understand why you have been given such a special gift?" Angel's eyes narrowed. "What gift? What do you mean?"

"Your singing. That's clearly a gift from God. Don't you wonder why you have it?"

"Sure I do, but I figured it's like payment for what happened to me."

"For what happened to you...?"

"Well, like I said, I've done plenty of bad things and one night... well... some guy did a bad thing to me. Ever since that night, I don't do bad things no more and I sing. It all happened at once. The bad things I did. The bad thing done to me and the singin'... it's like a package."

The pope stared with heavy eyes. "Are you saying you believe your singing is a payment from the Lord that balances the scales? Something good for something bad?"

"Yeah. Exactly. Vincent once explained to me what sinnin' was and as soon as he made it clear, I knew I had sinned real bad."

"We are all sinners," said the pope.

"Yeah, maybe so." Angel turned to Leo. "Have you sinned? Have you done bad things?"

Leo was caught by surprise for he had been thinking of what John would have said if he knew he was talking with the pope. "What?" Leo asked. "Did you ask if I have sinned?"

"Yeah. You're a cop and you got a fancy lady. The pope man here said we all sin. Is that so? Have you?"

"Of course I have. His Holiness is right. Everyone has done things they shouldn't have."

"Okay," said Angel, looking somewhat relieved. "Then I ain't gonna feel bad. I don't do bad stuff anymore... it's the past." He stopped. Then a moment later, he said, "I'm sorry about them old people gettin' killed." Leo nodded. There was silence.

"I brought you two together to settle something in my mind," said the Pope, as he leaned forward. "I thought both of you being alone might be able to help each other. Now, I see that is not possible." He stood and walked away from the sofa. Then he turned back to face them. "Lieutenant, you are searching and so is Angel, but you seek different ends. Things are best left as they are." He walked to the door and stopped. Leo and Angel stood and walked to where he was standing. Angel shook his hand and then Leo kissed his ring.

"Do you pray, Lieutenant?"

Softly, Leo answered, "No."

Smiling warmly, he said, "You might try- it can't hurt." Leo managed a wan smile as he, following Angel, exited the room

CHAPTER 35

AS LEO FOLLOWED ANGEL into the main sanctuary, he wondered why the Pope told him to pray and also, why he wanted to see the two of them together. He had said we were searching, but couldn't help each other because we were seeking different things. What do I want? He asked himself.

The pope had brought out I was alone, without a woman, with no real friends, and that I was seeking a father, and that Angel was in the same situation. But that's not true. When it all started Angel had no one, but now he does. Vincent is the father, Carlos is the older brother, and Abe and Marty are the uncles. He has a family.

But what is a family? Everyone knows the television cliché, but that holds no water. I've seen street kids phone their families for help and come up empty. I've seen families with hate as their binding rather than greeting card love. So what is it?

Then he realized what Angel has is not only people to look after him- but people he can care about, people **he** can look after. If Angel cares for Carlos or Vincent or anyone else, then he has family. I've been looking at it from the wrong way round, Leo thought. I've been looking for people to care for me, to love me. From the very beginning... the people who did not adopt me, I condemned and rejected them. The women over the years... it's always been me. I've been stuck on me and I wanted others to be just as stuck. A robot slave could have given me all the attention I craved, but a machine can't be family.

He thought about Jacqueline and realized he was a safe lover for her. She knows I would never turn up at the Embassy making demands. She's a married woman having a diversion. For women like her, there must be an endless supply of guys like me, all stupidly and totally self-involved. They change women like they change their shirts, endlessly seeking the magic.

Little do they realize that the women are changing them faster than the shirts that go in and out of the laundry. She was wise picking a guy like me. I'm so involved with myself; I could never make a problem for her. So what do I do now? Start over?

"Yeah." He said aloud. "That's exactly what I do. Start over."

"Hey man... what'd you say?" Angel asked.

"I think I made up my mind to start thinking more about others and less about me." Angel stopped and looked at Leo. "Yeah, man. I know what you mean. I never used to think about nobody. I didn't give a fuck about anybody or what I did to them." He paused. "It's different now. Vincent cares about me, Carlos cares about me... and I care about them. They mean a lot to me."

Leo smiled. "I guess we're both learning new ways." He stared at Angel for a moment. "I don't really know you, but I'm going to try and be your friend. You remember that. If you need me, I'll try to help." Angel stared up at Leo and then closed his eyes, but before he shut them, Leo was sure they had filled with tears.

The two walked in silence through the stark emptiness of the main sanctuary to the exit. A shaft of light cut into the darkness as Angel pulled open one of the doors and stepped out. Leo followed and saw them waiting. Hoffheimer, Melendez, Roberto, Magalana and the Prince, Nearby, Abe stood with Jacqueline, Marty, Carlos and Vincent. When Leo and Angel came down the steps, the two groups moved closer.

Jacqueline moved to Leo. "What did he want?"

"Best as I can figure, he wanted to pair me with Angel, since he knew we were both alone. I guess he thought we could be instant family."

"Really," she said, putting her hand to her collar.

"That's right... probably thought Angel needed a father and I needed a son."

"What did you tell him?"

"I didn't tell him anything. He told us. He said we we're after different things. But I think Angel's okay... seems he has a family."

She put a hand to his cheek. "And you? Who will look after you?"

"You," he smiled. "That's your job."

"And mine." Abe said, moving closer. "I'll take you to the zoo on Sunday."

"Very funny."

"I'm such a joker," laughed Abe, "... but forget Sunday- tonight is more important. Everyone's coming back to my place for a party. Okay?"

"Perfect," said Leo, taking Jacqueline's hand. "I'm ready for a fun evening."

"So let's do it." Abe motioned to the others and they entered the waiting cars.

When they arrived at the Regency, the staff was informed and within twenty minutes, an instant party was in the works. There was food, wine, and music. They ate and danced. Then to everyone's surprise and delight, Roberto sang a love song to Melendez. His voice was rich and masculine, perfect for the stage. All the while he sang, she stared at him, alternately biting her lip and trying to smile. At the end of the song, he was on one knee in front of her. With glistening eyes, they stared at each other, oblivious of the crowd. When he finished and stood, Melendez threw herself at him and they kissed. It was a magical moment.

A short while later, Abe, Jacqueline, and Leo were on the terrace. "Leo, you should be very proud of yourself. With all the celebration focused on Angel, we're forgetting your part in everything. Without your handiwork, there would have been no performance." Leo smiled as Abe patted him on the back.

"You know," he continued, "what you accomplished was magnificent. I never thought anyone could have brought the pope face to face with some bastards who wanted to knock him off. You had all of them in the same room smilin' at each other. The more I think about it, the more amazin' it gets."

Laughing, Leo said, "When you put it that way, it's amazing to me as well."

"It's strange, but you never seemed to get excited about any of it," said Jacqueline.

He looked at her. "Believe me, I tried to get excited, but it's all sort of abstract. I felt like a union boss who makes outrageous demands and gets management to agree to them with no fuss. It was all too easy, I guess."

As they talked, one of the uniformed hotel staff delivered a message to Abe. "You have a call," he said to Jacqueline. "George will take you to the telephone." Leo watched Jacqueline move inside to take the call.

"Hey, Leo, you really like her, don't you?"

"Abe, it's like heaven on Earth. I mean... for God's sake, she's a movie star and part of high society. I'm an old cop with no past and not much future. If you were filling out dance cards, would you put us together?"

"Leo, as much as I enjoy disorder, I don't think I would."

"So, it's sheer dumb luck that gives me a chance to be around her and I'm not complaining." Moments later, Jacqueline threaded her way back to where they were standing. "Leo, I'm sorry, that was the Embassy. A meeting of importance has developed and I must get back. I'm so sorry."

"Hey, you don't have to apologize. Come... I'll walk you out."

Turning to Abe, she said, "You'll have to excuse me. I have to leave."

"The fact you were here is good enough for me."

"You're so sweet."

"Heh, heh, heh... that's what all the girls say."

As Leo escorted her to the front door, she said, "Leo, there's no need to come downstairs with me, my driver is waiting and I'll have no problem."

"I wanted to be with you tonight,"

"I know. I will call and we will set a time for during the week, okay?"

"Fine. I'll be waiting for your call."

She leaned toward him and touched her cheek to his. Her closeness and perfume ignited his passion. In a husky voice, he whispered, "God, tonight of all nights." Saying nothing, she took his hand and touched it to her lips. A moment later, the elevator arrived and she was gone. Leo stood looking at the closed door, then turned and went back to the party.

Abe had come in from the terrace and was now on a sofa listening to Prince Punteyaya. As Leo sat, the Prince turned to him, "Lieutenant, I am relating to Mr. Rosenberg the astounding importance of today's events. He was as surprised as you to the significance of the meeting between McGinty and the pope. It may seem trivial to the grand scale of world politics, but as I have said, the powers supporting McGinty will favor my nation. Money will flow like oil."

"It's good to know someone will benefit."

"Mr. Rosenberg, you have no idea."

"I'll tell ya somethin' Prince, it all reminds me of the old days when the big shot gang guys wanted to show off. Ya see, all of 'em had plenty of dough and they loved to spend, so if this gang had new cars, another gang got custom cars. If the West Side guys had a nightclub, the East Side guys opened two. They were always tryin' to be King of the Hill."

"That's how it is in Africa at this moment. Leaders in many countries hold their people in contempt and are only concerned with how other leaders perceive them. There is a constant battle to outdo all others. When McGinty's video makes its way through the continent, it may spark a new competition."

"I hope," Leo broke in, "... it leads to a revolution in terrorism and maybe, when they see it, they'll decide to try and outdo each other using non-violent methods."

"You could be right," said the Prince. "It would be humorous, would it not, if you are contacted by other groups which want you to arrange similar impossible meetings."

"Yeah..." said Abe. "They'll need big balls to outdo today's meetin' with the pope. That wasn't small potatoes."

The Prince smiled. "I'm not sure of the exact meaning of that idiom, but

I recognize the intent and I heartily agree." Then turning to Leo, the Prince thanked him once again. The remainder of the evening progressed smoothly as everyone ate, drank, and envied Melendez and Roberto, who unaware of the stares, had eyes only for each other.

By nine-thirty, everyone had gone. Leo made it back to his place around ten and after a shower, sat on the bed wondering about the next day. What he was going to do tomorrow? How do you follow today? He fell asleep with the question unanswered.

CHAPTER 36

LEO COULD BARELY REMEMBER the last time he called in sick. It was years before and he gone to a Yankee game. Today, he was tempted to stay in bed for the entire day, but knew it would not be easy. The apartment was big enough to come home to and easy to leave, but it wasn't the right size for playing hooky. Staring at the ceiling, he wondered about the 'work at home' people who had a place like his. Living in it and working in it was the same as being in a warmly designed solitary confinement cell.

He shifted his eyes to the clock and saw it was 7:45, so going back to sleep was out of the question- he had slept enough. If he had a decent book a quarter finished, that would have made the difference, but there was none. Sitting up, he looked at the wall of books across the room and the pile by the sofa. There must be one worth reading again. He laughed at himself because he would have stayed to finish a book, but was too guilty to bring himself to start one.

"I must be nuts," he said aloud. Here I am a grown man and I have to make up a stupid excuse to allow myself to stay home. Now angry with himself, he got up, showered, shaved, dressed and was in the street looking for a cab 30 minutes later. When he walked in to Fred's and Irene saw him, she rushed over.

"Oh, Leo," she gushed. "I wish there was a way I could thank you for yesterday. To think I would meet the pope, kiss his ring and speak to him. I know priests who will never get as close as I was and I owe it to you. Thank you. Thank you." She threw her arms around him and sobbed.

Leo was dumbstruck. The rarity and importance to others had not fully registered. Only now, did it stack up. It was the pope- the one and only. Most Catholics go through life never even being in the same city, so yesterday's crowd got a chance that may never come again. All of them, the police brass, and the mayor, even the young priests of St. Patrick's got a shot that wasn't typical.

"Yeah, I guess it was a special day," he said to her.

"Leo, what's wrong with you. Special day? Of course it was." She was looking at him as if he had two heads. "I met the pope. My God, you... you had a private audience."

"Two," he said.

"Two?" She said with great surprise. "What's with you? Don't you understand what that means?"

He hesitated. "I guess I do, but it really wasn't as special for me as for you."

She stared at him. "Leo, take it from me, you need a change." Then she shrugged. "Leo, if meetin' the pope twice doesn't get up there with the A-list stuff, then what does?" That was a good question, he thought, a very good question.

"I wish I knew, I really do."

Backing away a little, she continued to stare. "Well, why don't you sit over there and let Fred make you breakfast."

Fred's enthusiasm over meeting the pope matched Irene's and he proved it by making Leo Eggs Benedict, but even that didn't break through the fog. As Leo was leaving, Fred said a few days off might do the trick as it was common to have a let down after a big deal. Leo thanked them both and headed for the building. He checked in, went to his office, turned on the computer and gazed at the screen. A little while later, he opened the blinds and stared out the small window.

About thirty minutes after that, the intercom buzzed. Hoffheimer wanted to see him. Pulling himself out of the chair, he headed downstairs. As he came into the office, Melendez shot him a great smile. Leo smiled back while noticing Rose and Gottlieb were not at their desks.

"They're out." She said, as she looked at him, her head tilted to one side. "Leo. Are you all right?"

"I guess so... I'm depressed, kind of in the dumps." Shrugging, he muttered, "I don't know."

She stared at him like a mother when she knows her kid is sick even though the kid says he's fine. "Go see the Captain. You'll get over it." He walked to the door, knocked and entered when he heard the magic word.

Hoffheimer was seated, but got up and came around the desk with his hand extended. They shook as he said, "Leo, what happened yesterday was phenomenal. That meeting is all the talk across the street. Last night they were only buzzing, but it's really starting now. By this afternoon, every country on the planet will have a report detailing the expert diffusing of a potentially dangerous situation. There is nothing but praise from every quarter and I truly congratulate you. What you did, probably no one else in the Department could have managed." Leo smiled in response.

"When I gave you that assignment, I never believed we could achieve such good fortune. My hope was that something different could be accomplished since you'd bring a new perspective. I never dreamed of what came to pass. Frankly, I'm still amazed."

"Everyone is saying the same thing. I wish it would stack up for me that way too."

Hoffheimer's eyebrows went up. "That's interesting, but I don't understand your reaction. Aren't you impressed with what transpired?"

Leo let out a breath. "I guess I am. It's just that I saw it all as work... it never seemed special. I know it was, but I don't feel it was."

Hoffheimer walked to the sofa and beckoned him. "Sit down... let's talk a bit." When he was settled, Hoffheimer asked, "Leo, when was the last time you took a vacation?"

"I never took a vacation- least not like I think you mean. Maybe I took a couple days off, but that was it."

"What are you trying to prove?"

"I'm not trying to prove anything, Captain... I just don't have any place to go... and ..."

Hoffheimer interrupted. "What do you mean, 'you have no place to go'. You can get to anywhere in the world from here in a matter of hours."

"I don't mean it that way. I mean I have no reason to go anywhere and I don't like to travel alone, so I just stay. It's easier for me to stay at my desk... to just keep slugging it out."

"Jesus Christ, Leo, life is not an endurance contest. There are other things to do besides-just slugging it out, as you put it."

"Captain, try to understand. I've been alone all my life and I don't know how to live differently. Working is what keeps it all making sense."

"Do you call this... what do I say... this ennui... this depression, an example of life making sense?"

"Sensible or not, that's what it's been and in all likelihood, that's the way it's going to stay." Hoffheimer stared at him for some moments. "I'm sorry to hear that. You deserve more. You deserve better." Leo nodded.

"Tell me... what would you do if I ordered you to take a week or two off?"

"Ha! I don't know," Leo laughed nervously. "There isn't anywhere I want to go. I guess I'd hang around... spend a lot of time in the movies."

"Well, a lot of people can't do that."

"Hell, Captain, don't get me wrong. I'm not complaining. I just feel down in the dumps. It'll pass... it always does."

"Is it Madame Rousault... is that the problem?"

"She's certainly part of it. You know, she's married and has a life that can only include me on its fringe."

"That must be rough."

"Captain, I've been through moments like this before. Whatever the cause, after a while the depression fades and I'm back to my old smiling self."

"I certainly hope it will fade, nonetheless, it's sad to see you go through it." He got up and walked to the window and then slowly crossed back to his desk. His manner changed after he was seated. He was Captain once again. "Okay, this is what I want you to do. I want you to take this week off and come in next Monday. By then I'll have a new assignment in mind that we can discuss and fine tune. Can you handle that?"

Leo knew he could agree to that, probably because it was an order and that's what he needed. It would doubtless be easier if Hoffheimer also ordered him to enjoy himself. He always could carry out orders. "That's okay, Captain. By next Monday, I'll be fine." He got up and headed for the door. With his hand on the knob, he said, "Captain, I want to thank you for trying to understand. I really appreciate it."

He closed the door and smiled at Melendez as he walked out. It took only moments to turn off his computer, throw some papers in the trash, straighten his desktop, and leave the building. The sun was shining as he reached the street so he decided to walk downtown. He peered into every shop window that had something to look at. Food stores, dress shops, shoemakers, plumbing supply houses, bars, restaurants- one after another. The people inside- doing today what they did yesterday- an endless parade of days, all fundamentally alike, all being spent to reach some magical goal- day in and day out- for what? What is the goal? Why do we do it?

Leisurely walking and day dreaming in New York exacts a price that Leo paid when he stepped onto a large turd that had been left mid-sidewalk by an animal probably as big as a station wagon. He felt the instant embarrassment delivered to those who are lax. Even with the leash law and the clean-up directives, there were hundreds of owners who never bothered to clean up after their animals. Spying a newspaper in a nearby trashcan, he used it to clean his shoe. As he was wiping away the crap, he thought about the animal that dropped it and decided wild animals have it easier than the pets locked up in tiny apartments. He thought about the great rampaging herds on the open African Plain and knew they were better for their freedom no matter the danger. He wondered about a world where the human herd was similarly wild.

What would be my role in that herd, he asked himself. In those groups, the older males offered protection and if necessary, became food for the predators. They were sacrificed so the young could survive. What could be more perfect than me being a cop- a single, expendable older male? There were many guys on the force who never married. The remainder was split between the married and the divorced. There were too many divorces. Being a protector and possible sacrifice is no job for a guy who wants to raise a family. It must be awful for a woman with kids to see her husband go out to face the crazies. And now, with the lady cops, it cuts both ways... now there are guys at home with kids while the wife is out on the street with a gun. That, he thought, must really be tough.

He made a right on 34th Street and headed west. There was no rush, so he forced himself to back off his usual pace and walk slowly. If I retired, he thought, I could do this everyday. I could walk anywhere, appear aimless, but all the while I'd be searching for King Solomon's Lost Treasure. He laughed aloud knowing he was not the type for that sort of retirement. At the corner of Third he stopped to figure what he was going to do. Heading back to his apartment, or to an early movie had no appeal. In the middle of the next block he saw a red neon sign... it said 'Billiards' and had a flashing arrow pointing down. That made sense. If this place was like the ones he used to go to, it would be dark, air conditioned, and have at least a couple of players good enough to watch.

He walked down the long flight of steps to the entrance, walked in and was struck by the similarity to the picture in his mind's eye. But being in the basement, there was no air conditioning. Instead there was the steady hum of de-humidifiers battling the dampness. Looking around, he saw there were several tables with action and people surrounding one. He walked over and took a seat on a high backed stool attached to the wall like in a shoeshine parlor. There were two guys playing, each about thirty and each had that yellowish, emaciated look that is the obvious trademark of anyone who spends most of their waking time underground.

Rather than the usual eight or nine ball, these guys were playing straight pool- and that is the game to watch. The ball and the pocket for each shot had to be specified beforehand, so very little luck was involved. To win, you had to play aggressively and defensively simultaneously. You had to make shots, but not leave a decent opening for your opponent. That required a good deal of finesse.

Leo watched and was happy an hour passed before he checked his watch. He was one of ten men watching the game. There were no women in the place. This could be a retirement. He could spend his days in the poolroom and his nights in a local tavern. He figured it would take about six months before he ate his gun. The poolroom wasn't the answer- he needed something to do.

CHAPTER 37

HE GOT A KICK out of being a cliché. On Tuesday, as he was shaving, the thrust of calling someone an old fire horse came through clearly. A picture formed in his mind that looked like a cartoon. There was a peaceful countryside, an old swayback nag munching grass in a field and beyond a hill, a village with its firehouse bell ringing like mad. With the sound, the horse grabs a piece of fence, and using it as a crutch, starts limping to the gate, ready for action. Though Leo saw his reflection smiling back, he knew it was no joke. Getting out of the game would be too costly.

He spent the morning wandering the village talking shop with all the ex cops he came across. They were working as bank guards, bodyguards, security guards and bartenders. The only one who seemed to enjoy what he was doing was a guy named Carver who used to work homicide from Manhattan South. He was working as a private investigator and loving every minute. Carver told him he could work for himself or join a major agency and as a private cop, the action doesn't stop. When Leo asked why it was better than staying on the force, he had no answer. He told Leo most of his cases involved the same kind of dumb bozos committing the same kind of dumb crime. That afternoon, Leo went to the movies.

On Wednesday, he called Abe and asked if he could come over. That night, at a table in the Regency's dining room, Abe lit a short, fat cigar and said, "You look like something's buggin' you. What's goin' on?"

"I don't know, but I feel like crap. The Captain insisted I take a week off and here I am in the middle of it, and I don't know what to do with myself. Everybody's patting me on the back for the job with the pope and I couldn't care less."

"Sounds to me like you need to be under a strain... Like you need the pressure."

"Yeah, maybe you're right. I spent some time talking to ex cops and most of them are out of their minds. So quitting is out and doing nothing is out. I feel like I'm spinning in place."

"Take it from me, Leo, a guy like you needs to be on the job, you need to be obligated. Make it through this week and go back to work. Two weeks from now, you'll be up to your ass in a new case and loving every minute." Visible doubt registered on Leo's face.

"Listen to me, wise guy, one time, me and Georgie are waitin' for a landlord to make up his mind about a fire and I was goin' cuckoo while he was on the pot. So I decided I got to get away and Georgie says, 'go to the picture show.' So I go, but not like to the regular double feature. I dreamed up an all day- all night event. I started at eight in the morning and went from one theater to another 'till about midnight. I think I must've seen about eight or nine movies- one after the other. After a while, I didn't know if I was in the street watchin' real life or in the theater watchin' the screen. I got so dizzy, it took me two days to get my head straight. By the time I was myself, the guy made up his mind, and I was back at it feelin' great."

Instantly, he knew Abe was right. I am a cop, he said to himself, and I'll stay a cop unless... unless what- unless there's good reason not to. With that settled in his mind, he said, "Okay, let's eat."

They ordered large steaks with trimmings and plowed through all of it as if they were escapees from some Diet Island. Over coffee, Leo mentioned that Jacqueline hadn't called and her silence was driving him batty. Abe said it was like being on death row waiting for the governor to call to get you off the hook. "Leo, watchin' the phone waitin' for it to ring will really get you nuts. She'll call or she won't and there's nothin' you can do."

He always knew varied perspectives were best when confronting any situation, but never fully realized how pointless was talking to yourself. Nine times out of ten all you get is one very biased view. Abe had made it clear – either she will call or she won't.

After dinner they went up to Abe's and watched a cop show on television that was so stupid, they almost laughed themselves into indigestion. Leo left feeling two hundred percent better than when he had arrived.

The next day he went to the movies, but didn't make it an Abe marathon. He saw one film at noon, another at four and the third at six. When he got out of the last one and stood under the marquee looking at the lights and people amidst the incessant racket of the street, he understood how easy it could be to mistake reality for just another loud, life-like film.

That evening, after a late dinner, he started a book about spies forsaking government work for corporate espionage and was starting to enjoy the book when the phone rang. As he moved to answer it, he saw it was after eleven. Immediately, he thought it was Jacqueline and his heart beat faster.

A voice he didn't recognize asked if Leo Flower could come to the phone. "This is Lieutenant Flower. Who is this?"

"This is Doctor Fred Davidoff. I'm calling from Lenox Hill Hospital. You might be able to help."

"Me? What's the problem? How can I help?"

"We have a patient who needs blood and we were hoping you might be a type match."

"The Department keeps full blood type records. Weren't you notified about that?"

"This is not a police case, Lieutenant Flower."

"It isn't?"

"No. The patient is Mr. Abraham Rosenberg and we've been searching for blood donors."

"Abe is sick.... oh shit... what happened?"

"I have no time for that. We need a donor, maybe two. If you want to know the details come to the hospital. Right now you can help by telling me your blood type. I've gone through a long list and there are only a few more to go."

"Sorry, Doc. I'm AB negative."

"You are? Fantastic. Are you healthy? Were you ever turned down as a donor?"

"Take it easy, Doc. I'm your man and I'm on my way. Where do I go?"

"Come to the emergency room."

"Fifteen minutes." Leo hung up and grabbed his jacket. For a moment, he was tempted to call a patrol car, but figured since it was late; getting a cab would be easy. He got one at the corner of Seventh. When he showed his badge and told the driver it was an emergency and that he should go through every red light he figured was safe, the guy grinned. "Shit man. This is almost as good as 'Follow that car!' I've been hacking for fifteen years and never got a shot at it."

"Well, this is your big chance. I want to be in Lenox Hill's ER fast... but not as a patient."

"Don't sweat it... just hold on." As the driver sped uptown passing every red light they came to, Leo envisioned disaster for Abe. When you're over eighty and need blood, it's bad. Wondering what happened, anger swelled in him. Was he shot? Mugged by some scumbag? He'd know soon. When the cab screeched to a stop at the ER entrance, Leo handed the driver a twenty and thanked him.

"I should thank you, that was great. Not one red light and not one cop- aside from you." He hesitated, and then added, "By the way, I hope everything's okay." Leo waved and went through the double doors to find Dr. Davidoff. As he looked around, he saw Marty and Carlos. Seeing him, they rushed over.

"Leo, they called you also, huh?"

"Yeah, Marty. What happened?"

"From what I got out of the people here, he was in his place, fell and whacked his head on something. He was knocked out and bleedin' for about three hours before one of the hotel people found him." His voice dropped. "Leo... he ain't doin' so well,"

From behind a counter, a nurse asked, "Excuse me, and are you Lieutenant Flower?" Leo nodded. "Follow me." She moved out at a fast pace, down a short hallway to a small room with two beds. Abe was in one. A man on the telephone was sitting on the other.

"Dr. Davidoff. This is Lieutenant Flower."

While the doctor finished his call, Leo looked at Abe. There was a thick bandage on the right side of his head and it was almost the same color as his face. Marty was right, Leo thought. Abe doesn't look so good.

"Lieutenant Flower," Dr. Davidoff said, simultaneously hanging up and waving him over. "Take off your jacket and roll up your sleeve. Here, sit on the bed." As Leo was doing that, the doctor asked, "Are you sure you're AB negative?"

"Absolutely, everyone in the department knows their blood type."

"Fine. I'm going to take some for a few tests." He gently prepared Leo and then slid a needle into his arm and drew the blood. Taking the vial from the needle, he handed it to the nurse. "You know what I want to know, right?"

The nurse took the vial from his hand and started for the door. "Five minutes!" she called over her shoulder.

Leo looked over at Abe and then turning slightly asked the doctor what happened.

"We're not absolutely sure, but best as we can figure, Mr. Rosenberg probably had a stroke, fell, hit his head... or... he just fell and hit his head. There's no way to tell now. When he regains consciousness, we'll know. The hotel people found him in a large pool of blood and called EMS. When they got there, they reported a head wound and significant blood loss. They brought him here."

"How did you get my name?"

"In a case like this, we try to locate friends and relatives. The EMS guys got his address book from the hotel staff and I've called every one in it to see if they're his blood type. You were the only positive hit."

"The only one?"

"Yeah... and since only 40 percent of the population is in the AB negative category, he's very lucky you're his friend." With a flourish, the nurse bounced back into the room. She looked first at Leo and then the Doctor. "He's perfect."

"Great." He said, and turned to Leo, "Take off your shirt and relax on the bed, we'll do it the old fashioned way."

Leo stripped the shoulder holster and then his shirt, putting all of it under his jacket at the foot of the bed. A moment later, the doctor approached with a tangle of tubes and needles that looked like it came from a Frankenstein movie. Less than five minutes later, Leo was hooked up and blood was flowing. Whenever Leo recalls that moment, he shivers.

"Hey," said the Doctor. "That's very interesting."

Leo looked up from the pillow. "What's interesting?"

"Are you related to Mr. Rosenberg?"

"No. Why?"

"Look." The doctor pointed to a patch on the inside of Abe's arm. "You have one in exactly the same place."

Leo looked over and saw that Abe had a brownish blotch on his arm just like the one Leo had. "What is that, Doc?"

"They're called 'cafe-au-lait' spots and they're pretty rare."

"Is that why you asked if we were related?"

"Yeah... and also the blood."

"That... and the blood." Leo repeated hesitantly. "So, what does that mean?"

The doctor put a hand under his chin. "Well, a cafe-au-lait spot occurs in... let me remember... about ten percent of the entire white population. Put that together with the AB negative, which occurs in only about forty percent, and you have a good chance of some kind of blood relationship." He moved to adjust a valve. "Are you sure you're not related? Mr. Rosenberg looks old enough to be an uncle or..."

"I don't have any uncles," Leo said. "I was raised in an orphanage."

The doctor's eyes widened and he asked, "You mean... you mean you never knew your parents?"

"No." The two men stared at each other. Then, surprised at the firmness and steadiness of his voice, Leo asked, "What are the odds?"

Walking closer to the bed, the doctor said, "Well, we have three factors, don't we? We have the cafe-au-lait spot, we have its location, and we have the blood. That's strong stuff, Lieutenant. Each element supports the other. I'd put good money on it."

Leo was amazed. "You've got to be kidding."

"Why? Is the thought so awful?"

"Awful? Are you serious? Doc, I'm almost an old man and the thought of discovering a relation... my father yet... it's impossible. It would be incredible if I were ten, but now... I don't think anyone would believe it. I don't think I can believe it..." His voice trailed off. "Even though I'd like to."

"Now, wait a minute, before you leap to any conclusions, you've got to understand something. There is absolutely no way to guarantee paternity here. Paternity by blood group is at best only sixty percent accurate."

"So that leaves a forty percent chance of inaccuracy."

"Right. But... don't forget the cafe-au-lait spot. As I said, only ten percent of the white population has one and you two have it in exactly the same place... now... that could be a coincidence... but... I'd bet against it... so... you put it all together and you have a very, very good shot at a blood relationship."

"Son of a bitch," Leo exclaimed. "Son of a bitch." Looking over at Abe, he saw the grayish pallor was gone. There was color in his face. My blood, Leo thought. That's my blood making his cheeks glow. It's unbelievable.

He turned to the doctor. "Now look, Doc, whatever happens here, I want you to do me a big favor." The Doctor stared at him. "I don't want any of this mentioned to Abe... to Mr. Rosenberg and I don't want any talk about DNA matching. Right now, we're friends... we like each other... our lives are connected. I don't know what we'd gain by opening this up."

He nodded. "Anything you say. I won't bring it up, but... He'll eventually find out you gave blood."

"That's okay. I think he'd do the same if the tables were turned."

"Okay. All of this stays with the three of us." At that moment, the two men turned to look at the nurse at the foot of Abe's bed. She was staring at Leo, her eyes the size of coffee saucers. "But Lieutenant, he may be your father. How can you keep that from him?"

Leo sought words to make it clear. "Nurse, you have to understand our relationship. If he knew he was my father, nothing would change. Right now, we probably have a better connection than most. We're good friends... what more do we need?"

"You really think it would serve no purpose?"

"Yes, I do, and what's more, it might create complications."

The nurse inhaled and then let out a deep breath as she looked at Leo and then at Abe. "Okay. I'll not say a word. If he ever finds out, it won't be from me."

Leo relaxed, leaned back and stared at the ceiling thinking about the craziness of it all. Do I really have a father? Could it be true? Confused and delighted, he watched the nurse and Doctor monitor the instruments and then, it was over. Disconnecting everything took only moments. Happily, Leo sat up and a wave of dizziness hit him.

The doctor grabbed his arm. "Hey, hey... take it easy, stay there... you gave a lot of blood and you're not fourteen."

Leo sighed and let his head hit the pillow. He was tired and this was quite a shock. "Okay, okay, no arguments."

His next recollection was the nurse waking him. As he opened his eyes, he looked at the other bed and saw it was empty. "Oh, no!" He cried.

The nurse followed his eyes and then put a hand on his shoulder. "No, Lieutenant. He's fine." The doctor had him moved to an upstairs room. He's expected to wake soon. In fact, he may have already."

"What time is it?"

"About two-thirty."

"Is it okay if I go?"

"Sure, but don't exert yourself. Go home and get some sleep. Come back tomorrow." He nodded and moved his feet to the floor. Stiffly he got up, put on his shirt, holster and jacket and after thanking the nurse, walked out to the waiting area. To his surprise, Marty and Carlos were still there. When they saw him, they got up.

"We was waitin' for you. You okay?" Carlos asked. Leo nodded and they smiled.

"Where's Angel?" Leo asked Carlos. "He won't come here. He said he got a real problem with hospitals, but he told me he's goin' to pray for Abe."

Leaning closer, Marty touched Leo's arm. "The Doc told us you gave him blood and it made all the difference. That was good, Leo. He also said Abe might have had a stroke and there could be problems."

"Marty, all we can do is hope for the best. Did they say when we could see him?"

"Yeah, they said that we can see him tomorrow. Jesus... I sure hope he's all right."

"Yeah, I like that old man too much to lose him now."

"You know, Leo, that's funny. Me and Carlos were sayin' the same thing. With all that's goin' on, the guy we all count on is Abe. He means a lot to all of us."

As they waited outside the entrance for a cab, Marty told Leo that Vincent would join them the next morning and that Leo shouldn't be angry with Angel for not showing up. "Yeah," Carlos said. "When I told Angel we was comin' here, the kid freaked. He got a real thing about hospitals. I got no idea what's got him so bugged, but he won't be here- that's for sure."

"It's not important. He can visit Abe when he's home."

"Yeah, that's what I figured."

A few minutes later, they grabbed a cab which Leo kept after he dropped them at Carlos'. Continuing downtown, he thought about everything the Doctor said, and particularly, about the odds being in his favor. The idea of it all excited him, but he realized it didn't mater if it were true or not. What mattered most, he said to himself, was that he was no longer alone. "I have someone," he said aloud. "Finally, I'm no longer alone."

CHAPTER 38

THE NEXT MORNING, BEFORE he left for the hospital, Leo managed to reach the ER doctor and was saddened when he learned that Abe might have trouble with one leg. The doc said he had suffered a slight stroke, but was lucky since the damage seemed mild. Not really knowing what to expect, Leo headed uptown.

"Only two at a time and no longer than ten minutes. You guys got that?" They nodded at the nurse and Marty and Carlos immediately went to Abe's room. Leo remained with Vincent in the sparse waiting room.

"You know Leo, it's strange about Angel, but he really is out of it about hospitals. I wish I knew why."

"Yeah, they told me last night. But it's no big deal, the kid can visit Abe when he's out of here." Vincent nodded. "How's it going with the two of you?" Leo asked.

"Leo, you can't imagine. We had to find a rehearsal hall on Staten Island so we could get away from the *paparazzi*. When we used a New York place they were all over us, one of them even followed me into the John and bugged me about pictures while I'm trying to take a crap. Those people are really nuts."

"It's what they do, Vincent. They do it for money, but also for the recognition they get from their own. To me, those guys are like movie stunt men. They do all sorts of crazy, impossible things and no one except the insiders know who they are. I look at a picture and I couldn't care less who took it or what they had to go through to get it, but other photographers know so it really matters to them."

"Well, that makes sense, but they're still a great pain in the ass."

They were silent until Vincent asked, "Leo, how long have you known Abe?"

"Not long, not even a year. A while back I was looking into some police business and I stopped into Marty's and there was Abe. Because of some stuff in my personal life, I don't think we hit it off right away, but that passed quickly and we got to know each other. More and more I find him to be one hell of a guy. He always surprising me with who he knows, what he knows and what he's into."

"I know what you mean. Meeting him for the first time can be kind of a shock. Everybody has built in views of old folks and Abe isn't like anybody's idea. He is one tough and smart cookie... and he knows so much. There aren't many people in the city able to tell a good instrument from junk, but he can. I don't know how many times he turned me onto a beauty that had floated into Marty's."

"Marty doesn't have the same knack?"

"Oh no. Marty would look and see what you'd see. Like a violin isn't crackled, nothing's falling off, it hasn't been painted purple... you know what I mean, but when it comes to judging tone or quality, well... Marty would say, 'Hey, it's a violin, right?' Abe is a whole other story. When he'd tell me there was a good instrument available, there was."

Their attention was diverted to an opening elevator door from which Marty and Carlos emerged. The nurse sitting across from them stood up and pointed at Leo and Vincent. "Okay, you two can go up. Don't tire him out with dirty jokes. He needs to gain strength, so no screwing around, got that?" Afraid to say anything that might upset the nurse, Leo and Vincent nodded.

As they walked to the elevator, Marty came up to them. "Hey, he's fine. If he didn't have that bandage on his head, you wouldn't know anything happened."

That piece of news made it easy for Leo and Vincent to relax as they went upstairs. When they got to the room, they tiptoed in and saw Abe sitting up and looking okay. When Abe saw them, he shouted, "Sonofabitch, look who's here!"

As he walked to the side of the bed, Leo tried to remember the last time he'd been on a hospital visit. The only ones he recalled were when the Department turned out to comfort a shot up cop and his family.

There was a bandage about the size of a dollar bill on Abe's head, but he had color in his cheeks and he had shaved or been shaved and his hair was combed. What Marty said was true, without the bandage, you would not know he was sick and judging from the expression on his face, Leo figured Abe would really have loved a cigar and a drink.

"What happened, Abe? Do you remember?"

"Vincent, it was weird. I remember walking into the den to get something and suddenly I smell burning rubber. My first thought is that I left a lit cigar somewhere in the joint and it was all gonna go up in smoke. I guess I was gonna check the other rooms 'cause I remember turning to leave and then I got dizzy and that's it. Next thing I remember is a Doc staring at me asking me how many fingers he's holding up."

"Abe, you were lucky the hotel people checked on you."

"You're damn right, Leo... and before I forget, I want to thank you for the blood. They told me you were right there, bingo... in a flash. And what is more, the nurse told me that 'cause I got blood from you and got it fast, it made a big difference."

"Abe, it was the least I could do."

"Yeah, yeah, yeah," he said, his eyes glistening.

A Nurse came into the room to tell them visiting time would be up in a few minutes. Before she left, Abe half hollered he wanted a lean corned beef on rye for lunch. The look she gave him was priceless. It was a combination of 'so would I and hell will freeze over before either one of us gets it.' Knowing their time was short, Leo asked, "Abe tell the truth. How are you?"

"I really feel okay, Leo."

"The Doc told me you might have a bum leg."

"I know. We went through all that. He wants me to move to Florida and sit on my ass 'til my lights go out. I told him to stuff it. I figure I got ten years or more to play with... and if I don't... I don't." He took a deep breath. "One thing is for sure, though, I ain't gonna spend what time I do have waitin' for the end. I'm gonna keep doin' what I please. And... if I need a wheel chair, I'll get me a Ferrari wheel chair. I'm not gonna let a bum leg keep me from anything."

As he and Vincent looked at Abe, Leo knew that eyes never see what is really there in front of them. My eyes see an old man with a bandaged head sitting up in a hospital bed. What they don't see is a hardy old guy filled with life that would tell you he was a tough son-of-a-bitch, if you happened to ask.

The nurse came back to tell them visiting was over and if they wanted, they could come back that afternoon or evening. They turned and started for the door, but Abe stopped them.

"Vincent, give me a minute with Leo, okay?" Vincent nodded and went into the corridor as Leo walked back to the bed.

"Leo, come... sit down."

"What is it?"

Abe slid his hand across the sheet and took hold of Leo's. "I want to thank you for what you did. A lot of guys would have got real busy when the Doc made clear what he wanted, but you came through. I will never forget what you did. There haven't been too many people who put themselves out for me. That was a heavy favor."

Still holding his hand, Leo said, "Abe, I haven't had many chances in my life to do a favor for someone who meant something to me."

"Well, I certainly appreciate that. Havin' a friend like you is very special." Leo smiled and squeezed Abe's hand. As he stood and started for the door, he said he'd be back to visit that afternoon. Abe told him not to bother since the Doc wanted him to get started with the physical therapy that afternoon.

"Okay... I'll see you tonight."

"Wonderful... and Leo... bring that sandwich... okay?"

CHAPTER 39

DURING THE NEXT FEW days, Leo spent evenings with Abe and waited for Jacqueline's call. Even with the sadness her silence created, he appreciated being back at work. He thought his job a blessing after the tortuous week off. When he had returned to the unit, Hoffheimer told him to start working out a private cryptographic system for Dignitary Protection. He said he wanted it simple to use and unbreakable as possible. To Leo, it sounded like Hoffheimer was asking for a cup of coffee and a four hundred foot pyramid built before dinner.

Leo tried to educate him about codes, but Hoffheimer was adamant. "I don't want you to develop the code of codes. We need one we can learn and use with efficiency and speed while it remains difficult for our average opponent to crack. Okay?" So Leo now had a new assignment.

When he wasn't up to his neck thinking about cryptography, Leo was filled with thoughts about Jacqueline and the possibility that Abe was his father. The paternal pieces fit even though it still seemed impossible. He envisioned his mind as a pendulum that swung between labeled extremes- one reading, 'It can't be,' while the other said, 'Yes it can.'

Years of training had forced him to carefully consider all collected evidence, and he got a kick that at the top of his proof pile, even ahead of the doctor's view, was the strong argument advanced by the waitress in Goldberg's who said he looked Jewish and could be related to Abe.

At both the office and at home, he pondered the situation and wondered what to do. If Abe was not his father, then at least, he was a very good friend. That was reason enough to stay close. But when the medical material was stirred in, the need for closeness became even more demanding. So Leo was a constant visitor at the hospital and helped in every way he could.

Two weeks after the fall, Abe returned to his apartment. Prior to going up for a visit, Leo went to Goldberg's to get some food. When he walked in, the waitress grabbed him. "Is he okay? I heard he couldn't walk. He ain't goin' to kick, is he?"

Leo assured her Abe was fine and that yes, he did have a game leg, but all Leo wanted right now was to pick up two of Abe's special combinations. When she heard Abe wanted a special combo sandwich, she let out a whoop and stood by to watch the carvers prepare it. Leo left with the good wishes of the entire crew. It was similar with the hotel staff.

The last picture of Abe for some of the staff had him unconscious and sheet-white, so they presumed he was finished, but now, with him back in action, they were happy. The feelings these people had for him deeply impressed Leo and he knew it wasn't the result of the money Abe threw around. People asked about him as a friend. He meant more to all of them than a twenty dollar bill.

Upstairs, they sat in front of the television eating the sandwiches, drinking tea, and talking about Angel's success and how strange it had been. Eventually, their talk took a different tack. As Abe lighted a cigar, he asked, "Did you hear from Jacqueline yet?" Leo was a bit surprised at the question.

"No, I haven't. There is a total cut off from her end. I can't get in touch with her."

"My boy, I don't think she's gonna call."

"Why do you say that?"

Abe knocked some ash from the cigar- one of the short fat ones. "Leo, my boy... let's take a good look at this whole thing... okay?" Leo leaned forward. "First," Abe said, using the cigar as a baton, "First, she's an ex-movie star, but if she was asked tomorrow to make another movie anywhere in the world, she'd probably agree, and then she wouldn't be an ex-movie star any more. Then she'd be a regulation movie star. Second, she is now the wife of the French Ambassador to the United Nations and that puts her in the center of high society all over the world. Add to that, plenty of dough, a personal staff, a personal driver and hell... you know."

Leo nodded. He knew only too well. From day one he had been asking himself what was going on, but he learned as a kid, when good fortune falls in your lap, you don't stand up.

"Third," Abe said, but Leo cut him off.

"You don't have to say any more. Ever since this started, I've been asking myself, 'why?'"

"The 'why' is easy... she thinks you saved her life." He waved his hand as Leo started to say something. "Yeah, yeah, I know, you don't think you did. What you think doesn't mean a thing. She felt she had a debt. Now, I'll bet, she feels the debt's been paid. End of story."

"Is it that simple?"

Abe's face lit up with a broad smile. "Hey, Mister Don Juan, I got some questions for you. I want you to think about how may times you left a dame's place and your exit line was, 'I'll call you'.... How many times? One time, two times, more than twice? In other words, my boy, how many women are right now still sittin' by the phone waitin' for you to call?"

Puzzled, Leo said, "I don't follow."

Abe laughed. "Oh, I think you do." He leaned into the chair cushion and puffed the cigar. Then very slowly, he asked, "How many dates have you ended with a slick walk-out that had you promising to call the next day or the next week?"

Leo smiled, almost laughing. Now he understood where Abe was going and he instantly realized he was right.

"That's right. That's right. You know what I mean. Just like you casually dumped all those girls or women, Miss Jacqueline has just as casually dumped you. Now you're sittin' by the phone waitin' for a call that ain't gonna come."

Nodding slowly, Leo said, "You're right, Abe... I know that... but I love her."

"So maybe you do. So what's the big deal? There gotta be zillions out there moaning over the one that got away. Happens every day." Leo sighed and pushed back into the soft cushion.

"Okay! That problem is over, right?" Then, more softly, Abe added, "Leo, it'll take some time, but believe me, the sun will rise." Leo closed his eyes and nodded.

"Okay, now let's talk about problem number two. The physical therapist thinks I'm never gonna get full control over this leg, and since I can't handle crutches, a wheel chair is gonna become part of my story."

"Is that the problem... that you'll need a wheel chair?" Abe nodded.

"What's so terrible about that? We'll order one of those motorized units."

"I already did."

"So what's the problem?"

"It's that I can't live alone anymore. The Doc, the therapist, they're all over me about that. If I need help in the middle of the night, I can't rely on a hotel staffer gettin' up here as soon as I call. That means I'm gonna need someone here in the apartment with me and that means I gotta get a live-in person."

"So?"

"Hey, I don't want a stranger all over the place."

"All over the place? Are you kidding? This apartment has room for ten people and if they were here right now, we wouldn't know it. This place is enormous."

"I know. I know. It's just I don't think I'd be comfortable with a stranger running around."

"Well, you might set it up so they'd be here only at night, since the hotel staff is at full strength during the day, getting to you then wouldn't be a problem."

Abe nodded. "Yeah... that's a good idea."

Looking at Abe, Leo sensed the strength and the love of life that poured out of the man. As he stared, he felt a rush of tenderness and concern sweep over him that made clear this is what he had been waiting for. This was the important moment. He was filled with feelings of affection and caring that went beyond what he felt for Jacqueline or what he had felt for John and Ilene... He took a deep breath. If he had been outside he would have seen a rainbow. It was a magical moment that melted away tons of oppressive weight. He felt so wonderful, he almost cried, and he knew this was the right moment. Very slowly, he said, "Abe, wait, I've got a better idea."

"What's that, my boy?"

"How'd it be if I moved in here... and I was the person who would help you in the middle of the night?"

Abe stared at him. "You? You'd move in here? You'd leave your own place?"

"Sure... why not? I've always lived alone and I'm sick of it. You've always lived alone and now you can't anymore. I'd say we were made for each other."

"Leo, you'd do that for me? You'd give up your life and move in here with me?"

"Abe, I wouldn't be giving up anything. I'd just be starting a new page."

They sat staring at each other until in a soft voice, Abe asked, "Are you really serious, Leo? It would mean changing everything. It would mean your life would no longer be what it was."

"I'm ready for that, Abe. I think I've been ready all my life."

Nodding and smiling broadly, Abe sat back, took a drag on his cigar and looked at Leo for a long moment.

Then, still smiling, he said, "Leo... Leo my boy, you know something... you better hang on, we are going to have one hell of a time."